NED HOPE

C000117601

A
Proper
Contentment

NED HOPKINS

Ned was born in Edinburgh but has spent much of his life in London. He worked in the BBC's News Information department before going on to train as a teacher specialising in Drama. For many years he divided his time between administering vocational qualifications for a national awarding body and working with non-commercial theatre companies in the London area. He now concentrates on writing plays and novels and contributes reviews and occasional articles to *Sardines* theatre magazine. Ned's numerous works for the theatre include *Darling Hypocrite*, the musical *Cliché*, an adaptation of Henry James's *The Portrait of a Lady*, the award-winning *Earnest Endeavours* and *A Lot of it About* for Organised Chaos (in 2013) at the Lowry Studio, Salford.

Reviews of his debut novel

Play On

published in 2018

'a fascinating study of family life… beautifully written'
(Bookworm)

**'Hopkins' prose is a pleasure to read – it's sparkling and witty…
a decided page turner.'**
(Kindle customer)

'Beautifully crafted novel… Loved it!'
(Amazon reader)

**'…I really cared about all of… (the characters)…and wanted to go
on finding out about their lives.'**
(Larger Than Life Stagewear)

ISBNs:
Paperback: 978-1-80227-143-0
eBook: 978-1-80227-144-7

Cover picture by John Oakenfull

Author's Note
Although many of the incidents in the book reflect those in the lives of a real family, all names and many locations have been changed. The supporting characters are fictitious.

For

John
and in memory of my parents
Norman and Marjorie,
and my aunt Winifred

Contents

BOOK ONE

Family Matters

1918 - 1957

1

Odd One Out

1918–1932
Bessie

Fingers of dawn struggled through the gap in the curtains. Downstairs the grandmother clock chimed the half-hour. Half-awake, Bessie sat up and excitedly rubbed her eyes. Christmas morning!

Now eleven, she could recall the carefree years of her early childhood and compare them with the nervous mood of the past four years. About a fortnight ago, everywhere had begun to sparkle with decorated firs and good intentions, lending an atmosphere of strained jollity to their Cheshire village. The fear of war had been replaced by barely suppressed hysteria as everyone, still numb from the slaughter of relatives and friends, struggled to adjust to peace. People were determined to make the most of the holiday and celebrate both the religious festival and memories of their loved ones no longer around to share them.

The names on the base of the stone memorial planned for the square would include that of Stanley, her favourite cousin, who had always brought her bonbons on her birthday but been shot only days before the Armistice. Bessie was old enough to be aware that 1919, now only a week away, also looked bleak and uncertain. Only the other day, she'd overheard the postman telling Polly how his brother-in-law had died in the trenches, not from wounds, but a vicious 'flu that was spreading across Europe. Hostilities may have ceased, but the legacy of four years' distress and privation lingered on, with new worries on the horizon.

At least the festivities provided respite and an excuse for people to spoil themselves, even if food shortages and a lack of seasonal luxuries encouraged improvisation. To give her parents their due, they'd always tried to make Christmas as enjoyable as the prevailing mood allowed.

Weighing up two plump pillowcases decorated in red and green ribbon sitting temptingly on the ottoman at the end of the bed, she wondered: had Santa managed to obtain tangerines and walnuts this year? Strictly speaking, she was too old to believe in the cheery old man with a long white beard, but the colour and excitement of the season permitted a temporary, necessary indulgence in its myths and traditions.

By rights, she should wait for everyone to get up, but the temptation to peek inside her pillowcase was too strong. Checking that her elder sister, Flo, was still asleep beside her, Bessie turned her attention to the large label on the nearest enticing bundle.

Happy Christmas, Bessie!
PTO

Larger than Flo's, her pillowcase looked unusually heavy with a firm lumpiness. Trying hard to maintain her exhilaration and suppress any niggling doubts now forming in her mind, she dragged it up and over the eiderdown.

Tearing off the ribbons, chunks of shiny coal from her father's yard tumbled out onto the counterpane.

The back of the label read:

Polly's got the day off.
When you're dressed, please sweep out the grates
and light the fires ready for breakfast.

She burst into tears.

Flo, awakened by the sobs, saw the coal and giggled.

'I suppose you were in on this too?' Bessie wailed.

'Sorry.'

'How could… how could you all be so beastly!'

'It only a prank, Bess.'

'I expected to pull my weight today as usual, but…'

'Don't worry, Polly will pop in later to prepare lunch before returning to her family for the rest of the holiday.' They always allowed Polly, the maid, to stay with her family over religious festivals. 'After all, it's her Christmas too. But the grates must be ready for breakfast.'

Mesmerized by the coal blinking facetiously up at her, Bessie was at a loss for further words.

'Look.' Flo produced another half-full pillowcase hiding below her side of the bed. 'Here are your real presents. Mother said you can have them as soon as you're up and the fire in the dining room's lit. When I'm dressed, I'll come down and help make a start.'

Normally Bessie would have pursued the matter, but Flo was four years older and it was best not to antagonise her.

Not today.

She heard doors opening and other voices on the landing.

'Brush the coal dust off the sheet before anyone sees!' Flo said.

Too late. The rest of the family were already drifting in.

'*We wish you a merry Christmas!*' they sang high-spiritedly and, on seeing Bessie despondently lugging the pillowcase off the bed, broke into gales of laughter.

Only Roy hugged her. 'Sorry, sis,' he said.

Which was all very well, but, being a boy, he'd never be asked to lay a fire, while Flo would already have cherry-picked the tasks she liked doing best.

His sympathy made her well up yet again.

* * *

Flo was the first to be born, immediately becoming the centre of Arthur and Ellie's indulgence as they waited for the son and heir who must surely follow. But nature can be contrary. Four long years passed, and the next baby turned out to be another girl.

As soon as she was old enough to work it out for herself, Bessie saw what a disappointment she'd been. When Roy appeared fifteen months later, her parents' attention was swiftly deflected to him – with interest. Despite this, Bessie bonded with her brother and they became inseparable, growing up to share many of the same interests and friends. Bessie might not have been the sex her parents wanted, but she possessed enough masculine characteristics to be game for anything competitive or daring. As children, whenever the pair got into trouble, there was always someone with whom to share both the blame – and penalty. He remained steadfastly in her corner.

If Bessie sometimes felt marginalised, she was sufficiently well-adjusted to see the advantages of her position in the scheme of things. It helped her handle the vicissitudes of family life with a degree of dispassion. People didn't expect as much from her as they did from the other two. Observing quietly from the shadows as the spotlight swerved from Roy to Flo and back to Roy allowed her to be more objective.

Even so, some things were easier to deal with than others. A continuing annoyance was having to wear her sister's old cast-offs. 'Flo's pretty and dainty; she looks good in these fancy frocks,' she'd complain. 'I look silly in them.'

'Yes, dear,' her mother would reply. 'But there's still plenty of wear in them.' The implication being *no one will be looking at you.* All the same, open-featured and sturdily built, Bessie was served better by dark fabrics and uncluttered lines.

Never a strong woman, Ellie grew more and more fatigued as she struggled to cope with a large house and family of five. Along with housework were other constant demands on her energy such as Flo's airs and graces and her husband's exhausting dynamism. Bessie's calm, cheery nature brought steadiness to the daily round which, as her younger daughter grew older, she came to rely on more and more.

Much as she sometimes resented being taken for granted, Bessie tackled most of the chores thrown at her with good grace. She needed to be kept busy. One of the compensations of spending a lot of time in the kitchen was being privy to the fascinating tales Polly and her mother told of their contrasting childhoods. More useful were the snippets of gossip she gleaned about what was in store for them all.

It was during one such cosy domestic hour as she was darning a pile of socks, while her mother buffed the silver tea service, that she plucked up courage to ask, 'Flo's big birthday's coming up. Have you any idea what she'll do next?'

'Well, I shouldn't be telling you this…' Ellie began.

'Go on,' Bessie urged.

'…but your father intends to train her up to help him in the business. He'd hoped when you were old enough to manage without me that I'd be able to assist him. But, as you know, I've never recovered from Roy's…' She prissily avoided spelling out the words *breech birth* from which her body would never fully recover. 'It means anything but light work is out of the question.'

'And what about Roy when he's older?'

'He has plans for him, too.'

'What sort of plans?'

'As the only son, it's only natural that one day, when your father retires, Roy will take over with Flo. He's devoted his adult life to building the business up. We're relying on them to keep it going to make sure we've got an income in our old age.'

Strange, Bessie thought, when his own father and mother had probably never had such expectations of him. 'I've often wondered how he got started?'

'Long before we met, when he was fifteen,' Ellie said, 'he experimented with all sorts of projects. Starting very small, saving hard; turning farthings into pennies – then tenners. Eventually, he was able to purchase an interest in our current coal business. Now, we own it outright.'

'And what's he got in mind for me?'

'Oh, we'll worry about you when the time comes.'

Arthur and Ellie were complete opposites. The eldest of ten children, what he lacked in refinement he made up for with ambition. He'd won her affections at a party, early in his journey from penniless but precocious teenager to successful entrepreneur. She, attractive but diffident and delicate, was from a more genteel background. Having lost her father early on, she'd been grateful to be rescued from a household dominated by her mother and two sisters by the spirited Arthur. Since Roy's birth, he'd become even more protective of her.

The children shared their father's love of horses: not only the athletic, racing thoroughbreds with their potential for helping increase – and sometimes alarmingly decrease – his income, but also the team of easy-going shires which, groomed to perfection, were entered for horse shows they invariably won. The wall behind his desk was crowded with photographs of the handsome beasts sporting incongruous rosettes, impressing visiting clients and helping consolidate his image as a successful, self-made man.

The house was furnished to reflect Arthur's social aspirations – with mixed results. Often, after he'd attended an auction, a pantechnicon drew up outside the house to deliver an eighteenth-century black-and-gilt lacquered cabinet, a Jacobean carved table or a heavily mounted watercolour of a Utopian landscape. If the bargains never quite managed to make friends with their less grandiose, store-bought roommates, they at least provided interesting conversation pieces.

For as long as Arthur handled their income wisely, the Taylors lived affluently. His Achilles heel was a penchant for gambling. When he miscalculated, his luck often bounced back. Occasionally, with disastrous consequences, it didn't. Then everyone suffered.

Although they'd never be close friends, as Bessie moved into her teens, the age gap between the sisters mattered less and they found ways of muddling along together. It's not easy sleeping in the same bed as someone else if you're continually at loggerheads.

Why they were obliged to share a room was never made entirely clear. 'Ever since she was born,' Ellie once told her as if it were a special secret, 'Flo's been terrified and needed company at night.' As she became a woman, the arrangement provided Flo with a confidante on whom she could offload her problems. The advantages were not all one-sided. In due course, the sisters' nocturnal discussions would educate Bessie on the pleasures and iniquities of the dog-eat-dog world beyond the home.

She envied Flo's ability to turn her hand to anything from fine sewing to French conversation. 'Could charm a vulture off a battlefield, that one,' Arthur would say.

It's difficult to keep secrets in a family. When Flo discovered Arthur's plans for her, she beseeched him to let her go to Paris and learn the millinery trade. It was not to be. As so often happened when there was a battle of wills in the Taylor household, Flo's obstinacy, as Arthur no doubt foresaw, failed her at the last fence.

It said much for her that she accepted her lot with good grace and was soon enjoying, if not always the day-to-day running of the office, certainly its chief perk: lively afternoons with Arthur at the racecourse, a time-honoured forum for the interaction of local businessmen.

'Many a deal is struck over lunch or in the bar after a race,' she explained to Bessie. It went without saying that it helped the boss having a chic, unattached woman in tow.

'You've not met my assistant, Florence, have you?'

Clients weren't to know she was his daughter. Not right away. Even at the start of her new job, as a worldly seventeen-year-old – looking and behaving as if she was twenty-two – Flo's presence in company could create a flirtatious frisson. She quickly learnt to make subtle use of her feminine skills – not only to the firm's advantage.

Flo usually succeeded in anything she cared to turn her hand to. Bessie saw how her savviness was an asset to the firm. 'It's only a pity,' Bessie told Roy,' 'that the charm she uses manipulating other men doesn't help her achieve greater influence over her own father's extravagance.'

* * *

From the one-room village school, where she'd trudged the younger children to and fro' and assisted the teacher with their lessons each day, Bessie moved on to the girls' High School. For the past few years, she'd been happier there than ever before in her life, holding her own in Maths and French and excelling on the games field. She also developed dramatic skills and provided brio, if a lack of poetry, to her role as Bassanio in *The Merchant of Venice*.

Her greatest frustration was having her school timetable interrupted every Friday by her parents' insistence she stay at home to carry out domestic work.

'It means missing netball practice and conversational French,' she'd object.

'That's too bad,' came the riposte. 'Who else can help do the shopping and housework ready for the weekend?'

Even the Headmistress's complaints went unheeded.

Having watched Flo sacrifice her personal career aspirations to save her father the cost of an extra pair of hands in the business, as Bessie's carefree schooldays days drew to a close, her concern deepened as to what would happen to her.

Rarely looking for trouble until it hit her and, having over the past year thrown herself with ever greater abandon into school life, she'd turned a deaf ear to cautionary voices. As the member of the family always regarded as an afterthought, she'd dared to hope her parents had forgotten about her and clung to a wild dream of staying at school long enough to sit her final exams. Successful grades in the recently introduced School Certificate would give her a head start in seeking a respectable occupation before, maybe, marriage and motherhood beckoned. Perhaps a traineeship at a post office such as the one where her friend Enid worked or, failing that, a job in a pharmacy or as a sales assistant at one of the smart stores in Deansgate. Anything to make best use of her strong personal and numeracy skills.

Then, one evening as the end of the summer term drew near, Arthur arrived home earlier than usual and immediately closeted himself with Ellie in the morning room, forbidding anyone to disturb them.

The omens weren't good.

For over an hour, the muffled dynamics of Arthur's assertive baritone and her mother's frail soprano modulated from contrite solo (*him*) to hysterical aria (*her*) before concluding in a minor key duet. Flo, Bessie and Roy, sitting it out in the dining room, only caught the odd phrase, but, from the ominous tone of the muffled conversation penetrating the heavy door, guessed something calamitous had befallen them.

The cause was never in doubt. Its outcome uncertain.

When their parents emerged, Ellie was still wiping her eyes. 'I've lost a lot of money,' Arthur told them. 'From now on, we're going to have to draw our horns in.' He offered no apology and showed little sign of penitence. Admitting weakness was not his style.

The full impact of how serious the situation was only arrived when he announced: 'This afternoon, I put the house up for sale. As soon as it can be arranged, we'll be moving somewhere smaller, which will be cheaper and easier to run.'

What followed completely shattered her hopes.

Lacking the tact to take her aside and discuss the matter with her, as was customary when important decisions with far-reaching consequences were made, it wasn't until supper the next evening Arthur made his grim announcement. An unusually downcast Polly having removed the remains of the casserole and dirty plates, he turned to Bessie and informed her, 'I've written to your school.'

She saw the strained look in her father's eye. Her stomach tightened. 'About what?'

'Thanks to my spot of bad luck, I've... well... it's been necessary to let them know you won't be going back in September.'

Bessie felt sick. Her knife and fork clattered onto her plate.

'Careful, we can't afford to replace that service, and you've spilt gravy all over your new blouse,' Ellie said, unhelpfully.

Roy and Flo, probably warned in advance, found the good grace to act appalled.

'But I was to have sat my preliminary School Certificate exams next year and was hoping I might be allowed to do a secretarial and bookkeeping course.'

'Sorry, lass. I don't know what put ideas like that into your head. As well as moving house, other strict economies will need to be made.' Arthur lowered his voice. 'Your mother has given Polly two weeks' notice.'

Another gasp went round the table. That explained why she'd not been her usual self all day. Polly was everyone's friend as much as a servant, and her loss would be hard on all of them.

'So…'

Bessie having, by now, guessed what was coming, said, 'And I'm to take over her duties?'

'Well…'

'And skivvy full time for you?'

'I wouldn't put it quite so bluntly, but…'

'How *would* you put it then?'

'That's no way to speak to your father!' Ellie intervened again.

'I'm afraid that's about the size of it.'

Her own feelings were dispensable, as usual. Her life, in fact. How could she foolishly have imagined she might succeed where the favourite daughter had failed?

As her father left the room to search for his tobacco, Bessie again caught her mother's eye. 'It'll be alright, luv, you'll see.' It was as if, in his brief absence, Ellie could afford to be sympathetic.

'I'll do my bit and try to be tidier,' Flo volunteered.

'It's just not fair,' Roy said.

'No one's asking you, lad,' Arthur said as he re-entered, pouch in hand. 'There's no way your mother can supervise a household of five single-handed.'

Single-handed? Never in her life had Bessie seen her mother do anything more demanding than a little sewing or light dusting. Occasionally, if pressed, she might make porridge or heat up a can of soup.

'Besides,' Arthur went on, 'with you at grammar school, the cost of two lots of fees is now completely out of the question. I don't know how I'm going to continue with one.'

Muggins would be expected to do almost everything, she thought. She supposed she'd survive, having so far lobbed most of the balls served her back over the net with a determined grin. Nothing, though, could suppress her rage at the thought of losing any chance of bettering herself. Even picking up basic office skills *sitting by Nellie* – or rather Flo – where they might at least have the odd laugh together would be preferable to an existence trapped every day at home with her well-meaning but helpless mother.

As if reading her thoughts, Arthur said, 'What do you want with qualifications, anyway? This is a fine opportunity for you to acquire everything you need to make a man happy – when the time comes,' he added quickly.

Bessie winced, her eye noting the ornate condiment set in front of her and momentarily tempted to hurl the pepper pot at him. As soon as the meal was over, she'd disappear upstairs and have a good cry, but for the moment, she gritted her teeth and attempted to finish her apple tart. She was unwilling to give her father the satisfaction of seeing how keenly she felt their proposed treatment of her.

Though he could be a despot, she normally got on well with him. They were both strong-minded and shared an interest in sports of all kinds, as well as a lively sense of humour, even if, sometimes, she would like to have strangled him. This was the pillowcase-of-coal ruse all over again, writ large. Not, in this case, for just a morning – but eternity.

If the thought of having to leave behind all her schoolfriends and sporting activities initially felt like a joke in very bad taste, as her remaining week at school, then the day and finally hour came for her to clear her desk, the full realisation of her dreary life to come finally sank in. Her future was determined until either her father won a colossal windfall or a prudent marriage levered her out of it.

If the first was pure fantasy, the second was unlikely to happen any time soon.

* * *

The Taylors moved from the country to a smaller house nearer the town.

The new home being easier to look after than their previous sprawling mansion, Bessie got her new life under control surprisingly quickly. She learned how to oil the domestic machinery and keep the family dance on its toes: shopping, cooking, washing, mangling, ironing and ensuring everywhere was kept immaculate and everyone well fed.

As soon as he could, Arthur gave her an allowance of a few shillings a week. By managing her money very carefully, including what she might legitimately save from the weekly household expenses, there was just enough for buying clothes, occasional trips to meet friends for tea and the cinema, and other recreative activities.

As well as making the beds upstairs, she was also responsible for those in the garden: one of the areas of her remit she never looked upon as drudgery. With her green fingers, eye for colour and flair for bedding, the seasonal changes always brought fresh and often rewarding challenges. Above all, time in the garden provided a chance to enjoy the fresh air and briefly escape her more mundane tasks. Plants don't always behave exactly as you would wish, but when they finally mature, lighting up the garden in receding heights, shapes and hues, it was gratifying in a way leaving a room clean and tidy, only to find it looking as if a herd of elephants had trampled over it two hours later, could never be. Pushing a mower or aerating the earth with fork and spade released Bessie's mind and let it soar. Alone in the fresh air, with some cheerful birds or an impertinent squirrel or two for company, she might come to terms with the latest family debacle and dream optimistically of a more stimulating future.

Where did she read *flowers bring a room to life?* In spring she sowed and planted, throughout the summer months harvesting the blooms of colourful annuals and ongoing perennials. Rarely was the cut glass bowl on the dining table – a bowling trophy of her father's – or the vase in the bay window bereft of a cheerful arrangement. Out of season, it sometimes meant spending precious coppers on a bunch of robust chrysanthemums, or looting wilder species from nearby common land to augment an artistic selection of evergreens, but it gave her satisfaction.

Naturally sociable, the Taylors encouraged friends to visit for light, informal suppers at weekends followed by lively discussions, games of whist, canasta and bridge or lusty singsongs around the piano. By now, Bessie dealt with most of the household's catering arrangements – a sphere of operation where she could exercise a degree of control and imagination. As nominal head of the household, she considerately ensured Ellie's thoughts were always obtained in the compilation of weekly menus and related grocery lists.

When the repetition got her down, for variety Bessie set herself a weekly cleaning project, lessening the need for too much work, as tradition normally required, in the spring. As one, then two, years passed, she sometimes recalled her father's point about honing her domestic skills in readiness for one day making a good home of her own. She didn't wish to dwindle into a sad old maid, though meeting a man who met her demanding criteria wouldn't be easy.

As she left her teens behind, she finally revolted.

Rarely showing her frustration and anger at her virtual imprisonment, one day, after being put upon once too often, Bessie exploded. 'I've done everything you asked me to for over three years. I insist on being allowed to work outside the home and get the chance to interact with other people.'

Arthur found her a job as a clerk at a nearby post office where she was happy and quickly made several lifelong friends. The proviso was the necessity of making up the time lost doing domestic chores by catching up in her evenings and at weekends. Much as she enjoyed working away from home, having what amounted to two jobs inevitably took its toll.

One day, she collapsed and was forced to leave the post office. Even then, she couldn't be spared for a much-needed annual holiday with Flo and Roy to renew her energy. Enviously waving them off on holiday with friends to the Norfolk Broads, she resigned herself to staying behind to keep Ellie company.

Fortunately, with her ability to get along with people, Bessie's extrovert and self-reliant personality ensured she would never become a victim. The only one of the family to regularly attend the nearby church, her membership not only kept her moral compass in working order, but the social life, when she could snatch some precious spare time, provided an escape from the claustrophobic atmosphere of home.

Several wise and understanding older friends, who were drawn to both her outgoing personality and flair at the card table and tennis nets – sometimes spiced with an impish gamesmanship – took her under their wing.

They were her salvation.

2

Husband Material

1933 – 1943
Bessie

'How do you contact the Loch Ness Monster?'

'Drop him a line.'

The joke had been doing the rounds since the sighting of Nessie some weeks earlier, generating a stream of similar quips and amused speculation wherever people gathered. Conjecture about Nessie at least made a change from downbeat news of the industrial slump and sinister rumours of Germany's unstoppable Social Democrats.

One May evening, Hugh Owen burst into the tennis club house, a convenient five minutes' walk from his home. Members were slaking their thirst after a competitive hour or so on the courts and jovially debating the veracity of the sightings.

'Anyone have enough energy left to take me on before the sun goes down?' he said.

Through the open doorway of the kitchenette, Bessie, at that moment helping Hugh's sister Connie prepare light refreshments, caught the young man's look of desperation. 'You've managed to tear yourself away from your books, then?' she called.

'Been up in my room ever since I got home from work. Thought I needed some fresh air and exercise.'

Connie, with whom she'd become friendly since her family's latest move, had told her how 'just before leaving school, Mother and Father advised him to apply for an apprenticeship in cotton.'

'That would have seemed a safe bet a few years ago.'

'Exactly. They weren't to know then the extent to which the depression would cripple the industry.'

'What happened?'

'Thanks to the help of a close family friend, at the ripe old age of twenty-four, he's now with a good electrical engineering company. Actually, it's something that's always fascinated him. The industry's really taking off. It's one he already feels more suited to. The downside is having to follow his arduous days in the factory with spending every evening and part of each weekend studying. He needs to support his training with professional qualifications if he's to move beyond the shop floor.'

Bessie appreciated the problems created by the economic climate. Arthur's business was suffering too. It was fortunate that, by now, Flo and Roy had acquired greater influence over Arthur's weakness for taking needless risks. Even so, they could no longer afford Bessie's weekly allowance. She was at least permitted to once again help out part time in a shop run by some friends to keep her clothed and bring additional cash into the home, while Flo and Roy were starting to help out more at weekends.

Their new address, a modern, red brick, semi-detached house, was situated at the end of a long road in leafy Chorlton-cum-Hardy adjacent to a spacious park. If it wasn't as grand as the homes of her childhood, the neighbourhood enjoyed good social amenities such as the thriving tennis club.

Connie and Hugh lived with their parents in a large Victorian lodge diagonally opposite the Taylors' and close to the park gates. Although both families became acquainted soon after the move, due to his tight work-study-work schedule, Hugh was still only known to Bessie as Connie's brother, whom she acknowledged with a cheery exchange of pleasantries. She had yet to get to know him.

That was about to change.

Thinking how unselfconsciously dashing he looked that evening, despite his scruffy whites and tousled hair, Bessie took pity on him.

'Will I do?' she asked.

'Really?' he said brightly, having heard of Bessie's vaunted sporting abilities. 'You looked busy.'

'Never too busy for a game.'

'Thanks,' he said smiling.

'Come on then!' She picked up her racquet and gently pushed him outside.

She soon saw that the young man lacked her unforced ease with the game, but, for reasons still in her subconscious, subtly allowed him to win.

* * *

In the weeks and matches that followed, Bessie came to see Hugh as a man she both liked and trusted. They discovered much in common and were entertained by the same things. Not being overly sentimental, she tried not to think too much about what was happening to her. Yet their mutual compatibility and growing attachment blossomed naturally over more matches, coffees, teas and, sometimes, a glass or two of something stronger on a Saturday evening when there was time to explore each other's interests and values.

In due course, *like* became *affectionately disposed towards*.

Then something deeper.

It was only as time went on that Bessie began wondering if the strength of her feelings, genuine as they were, lacked a greater need for physical intimacy. Shouldn't she be experiencing, well… more urges? Whilst he'd quickly become a dear friend, neither of them had, until then, shown much interest in each other's bodies. She enjoyed the occasional hand-holding and companionable security of Hugh's arms around her shoulders, but, having observed and felt disgust at the heavy petting that went on in quiet corners

27

of the tennis pavilion late on Saturday nights, she still prided herself on being above the messy antics of the *racy set* as she called them.

Hugh never overtly attempted to take things further. She assumed he was sexually inexperienced like herself, though, as time passed, she sometimes sensed he wanted something more than, at this point, she was willing to give. They both knew it would be some years before they could afford to get married and they couldn't take any risks, even if they'd really wanted to.

Roy was also starting to date. One young woman, Georgie, around Bessie's age, became an ally. She was a likeable, worldly young woman, and Bessie envied her independence as a trainee buyer in Ladies Fashions at Kendal Milne. Also her smart clothes and lively chatter of life in the city. Bessie's sales experience in the local shop had strengthened her self-confidence. It was the type of work she could be trained to do herself, if not necessarily in Fashion. In the meantime, she decided to make the best of things and enjoy what time she could spare spending it with her fella.

Flo, of course, was rarely without a beau, often going out with more than one man at a time. Judging by the state of her clothes when she arrived home, with their pungent whiff of what Bessie came to identify as a man's smell, she didn't exercise much restraint. She presumed the men – Flo never dated *boys* – knew how to protect her sister. Although most of them were in a better position than Hugh to support a wife, the moment they became serious and the dreaded word *marriage* was mentioned as opposed to *engagement* – the terms of which seemed negotiable – they were dropped.

Before they went to sleep one night, Flo quizzed Bessie.

'You and that Owen lad make a good pair.'

'Yes.'

'Are you both… serious?'

'I think so, although it's hard to make plans until the end of Hugh's apprenticeship is in sight. Why?'

'Just looking out for you. I'd hate to think of you putting the best years of your life on hold for a man – and missing out on anything,' she added meaningfully. 'But, presumably, you're not.'

'What d'you mean, Flo?' Bessie knew exactly what she meant but found it hard answering the question for herself, let alone anyone else.

'Even an unofficial engagement loosens… constraints.'

'Constraints?'

'Just as long as he looks after you,' Flo side-stepped. A vulgar phrase, Bessie thought. It made her feel superior for keeping her own emotions under tighter control than presumably her sister did. She meant to carry on doing so, too. Not wishing to prolong the discussion, she turned her back on her sister and went to sleep.

One evening, not long before Bessie started seeing Hugh, an ex-boyfriend of Flo's had taken her to the cinema and, on the way home in his sports car, put his hand on her knee. She knew it was a sign he wished to move the conversation in a direction she dreaded, and as politely as she could, pushed it away.

Maybe it was simply a line to test her reaction, but when he said, 'You're not like your sister, then – she's quite a goer,' Bessie's body language quickly told him what she thought of the remark. 'Oh, but I didn't mean…Well, I'm glad you're not like that, Bessie. It's what most girls want.'

Unsurprisingly, she'd hit back with, 'but I'm not most girls,' whilst privately appreciating his frankness.

Who were *most girls* anyway? Or *most people,* come to that? Wasn't it possible to be a member of the gang and a team player without compromising your principles? So far, she'd usually been accepted by people she liked on her own terms and hoped any child of hers would have the strength of character to be their own person too, never feeling they must behave as everyone else did to fit in and be liked. It said a lot for both Flo's ex, and herself, that they remained on good terms. Indeed, far longer than Flo and he ever did.

Some months later, a ring appeared on her hand.

At least it shut people up.

* * *

In the years that followed, Bessie and Hugh travelled from being a pair of idealistic youngsters to a sober, pragmatic double act. She waited patiently as the years passed and he was qualified to land the kind of job he'd been aiming for. The only snag – it was with a firm two hundred miles away, in an industrial area in Edinburgh.

'My prospects look promising,' he assured her. 'Do you mind terribly moving so far away?'

Did she mind? Did Rapunzel mind being released from her tower? Well, perhaps that trajectory had become rather complicated, but with Hugh by her side, she believed things would work out.

They were married on Easter Saturday.

With little cash to spare, Arthur nonetheless managed to fund a quiet but tasteful wedding at Manchester Cathedral. Bessie was now a few months off thirty-one. In his smart suit, Hugh, only ten months her junior, looked older, although he sometimes behaved younger than she did. Not that he was childish in any way, but there would always be a naively boyish air about him.

The ceremony was followed by lunch with family and close friends at the Grosvenor Hotel. Terrified lest the speeches wouldn't be finished before the cab arrived to speed them to their First Class seats on the 3.30 pm train to Scotland and brief honeymoon at the Caledonian Hotel, she ate only a couple of mouthfuls.

The long wait was over.

One evening in the weeks leading up to the wedding, a well-meaning friend gently handed Bessie a booklet entitled *What to Expect from Marriage*, obliging her to face up to the full implications of her role as a wife beyond the purely domestic. Hugh and she might be soulmates, but their physical compatibility had not yet been seriously tested. If ever she'd agonised about the degree of physical commitment involved in marriage, she trusted, given how companionable they'd always been, that when the time came, the necessary responses would kick in as, she imagined, happened with most newly-weds.

Conjugality might even turn out to be quite pleasant, after all. She innocently imagined it to be rather like sleeping with her brother. Not exactly, of course, for although she cared a great deal for Roy, she couldn't imagine ever being *that* close to him – but she knew what she meant, or thought she did. It was all about mutual care and affection, wasn't it? That was what she understood, and took it for granted Hugh did too.

Indeed, when they finally found themselves in their hotel bedroom late on their wedding night and, overcome by tiredness from the long day, flopped separately into the single beds the hotel unwittingly allocated them, it was tactfully agreed to postpone consummation until the following morning. Her matter-of-fact attitude to sex allowed Bessie to put the anti-climax she then felt down to the five-year delay. Had time blunted desire? At least her view of Hugh as a more handsome, attentive replacement for her brother wasn't far off the mark.

She chose to set aside the curiosity and strange pangs she'd felt at Roy's growing closeness to his best mate, Billy.

For two days, the couple behaved as typical sightseers until the moment came to transfer their cases from the luxurious hotel into humble but comfortable digs on the north side of the city, close to Newhaven, and get to know their friendly new landlady, Mrs Cameron.

The following Tuesday, Hugh began his new job while Bessie searched for somewhere permanent for them to live. After a few weeks, they collected the keys to 130 Forth View Road: a sturdy, mid-nineteenth century, grey-stone terraced house in a pleasant, leafy nearby street which sloped down to the estuary. Next came the all-important visit to *Patrick Thompson's* furniture department to spend their wedding money.

Once they'd moved in, everyone from neighbours to tradespeople went out of their way to be welcoming. It was a relatively egalitarian dormitory of the city where folk from all walks of life happily co-existed, the community spirit heightened by shared anxiety over the worrying international situation.

Bessie, however, had more immediate matters on her mind.

Late one evening, she caught Hugh deep in a slim paperback. On asking what he was reading, his face went bright red and he quickly put it back in his briefcase. His initially clumsy nocturnal choreography improved as the weeks went by. There was too much trust and affection between them for it not to. Still, although Bessie came to look forward to their loving closeness in bed – at least when Hugh remembered to have a bath beforehand – she was never to get from intimacy the thrills that the novels of Jan Tempest promised. Sex would always make her feel grubby, and, once Hugh rolled off her and began snoring, she'd slip out of bed to wash and change into a clean nightie. Still, they desperately wanted to start a family and were soon tackling connubiality with the conscientiousness of two kids let loose on an advanced set of *Meccano*.

It was particularly unkind, therefore, that one, two and then three precious years sped by with no success. Bessie got it into her head she was letting Hugh down. Her feelings of guilt only led to anxiety, which didn't help at all. A poor helpmeet she'd turned out to be. Not that he ever gave her any reason to think she'd disappointed him. Physical exhaustion after a long, tough day in an industry committed to providing electrical goods for the war effort put a damper on procreative pursuits too. Thinking positively, she kept reminding herself how much luckier she was, now with her own home and a husband earning a regular salary, than many women with partners in military service, often in faraway places, who must dread opening the newspaper each morning.

She could appreciate Flo and Roy's battle, simultaneously managing the business and the onset of Ellie's dementia.

Bessie and Hugh forced themselves to face up to the unthinkable.

'Maybe, I can't conceive?' she said one evening over their kippers.

'It doesn't matter,' he said kindly.

Except it did. Had she waited all these years to create her own family only to be thwarted by nature in this way?

Sometimes in life, when unhappy events occur, some good emerges. Hugh's father died only eighteen months after they were married. A year later, her much-loved mother-in-law became terminally ill and the lodge on the corner of the park was sold. After dividing the proceeds with Connie, there was enough money left to invest in specialist medical advice. Following an unpleasant examination, Bessie embarked on a gruelling course of treatment, followed by an operation.

She faced up to the project with gritted teeth and prayed for a positive outcome.

Finally, early one morning in the autumn of 1943, as she was turning over Hugh's fried bread with a spatula, she was hit by a sudden spasm of nausea, forcing her to dash to the small lavatory off the scullery.

When it happened again the following morning, Hugh forgave her his burnt breakfast.

That night and thereafter, she slept easier.

So did he.

3

Waiting

1944
Bessie

'It won't arrive for ages. Maybe in the morning.'

'Then why's my body on Red Alert?'

'Nervous things, bodies, at a time like this. An actress was in your bed the other week. She said it was like stage fright.'

'For herself or the baby?'

'Both, I expect.'

'I'd be a bit frightened at the thought of meeting me face to face.'

The nurse smiled and adjusted the top sheet. 'Still, it must be feeling a bit jittery, waiting in the wings.'

'Are you into that sort of thing, then: amateur dramatics?' Bessie asked.

'No, but I love seeing shows and… films, of course. Anything with Katherine Hepburn.'

'Me too, when I can persuade my husband to come with me. I once played Bassanio at school.'

'And…?'

'That was scary too, but…'

'What?'

'I don't know, I just want whoever-it-is to be here… and safe.' A thought struck her. 'Imagine if it turned out to be twins!'

'Well…'

Suppressing her worst fears, Bessie tried to make light of it. 'Two for the trouble of one, though, eh?'

'I don't want to raise your hopes…'

'No?'

'…but that would have been discounted months ago.'

'I was joking. Still, you hear stories of people getting last-minute surprises.'

'Whoever-it-is will come when they're ready. Trust me, you've some hours to go yet.'

The phrase *it's my job, I know* hung silently in the air. The nurse hadn't given the baby a sex. Her unborn child wasn't an *it* but a *someone*. They'd already decided on Sam or Jean, and whichever they were was growing impatient. Doctors couldn't get the timing right every time, she thought, seriously hoping that on this occasion they had. She didn't want to hang around in the nursing home any longer than was needed.

Sighing inwardly, she finger-wagged herself. Most women at delivery point must be over-anxious. The girl was right. Relax and be patient!

The nurse adjusted a hospital corner and looked at her watch. 'Room 3 should be ready for her anaesthetic. Better go and check. Pull the cord by the bed head if you require anything.' And, with a reassuring grin, she left her alone.

Bessie lay back and looked across the bleak room through the tall window to the elegant roof tops of the New Town buildings beyond where the summer evening was drawing serenely to a close.

Strange how the first part of her life was book-ended by two world wars.

Mercifully, even at the height of the blitz, Edinburgh missed out on the vindictive air raids suffered by Clydeside and parts of Manchester, although neither of their families had been affected. Recollecting the trauma of that time, she mused how fortunate it was that, so far, things in Scotland had been easier. Even so, hastily retreating from the West Coast three years earlier, Hitler's men had spitefully emptied their remaining landmines over Leith, destroying several tenements including a smart hairdressing salon she'd patronised.

Marguerite Coiffeuse was now relocated in a small disused cobblers' shop off Leith Walk. Freda, the owner, continued performing stylistic miracles with a swivel chair salvaged from the wreckage and a hurriedly appropriated assortment of scissors and elderly tongs, in a pungent atmosphere of fried hair and setting lotion.

Bessie empathised with Freda. Her own home might not have yet been caught by German bombers, but only eighteen months after settling into Forth View Road, they'd watched, aghast, as their carpets and other newly-bought furnishings had been ruined when an accidental conflagration, caused by a workman repairing the rooftop with a blowtorch, set the first floor of the house ablaze. Mrs Cameron's spare room was once again commissioned to shelter them as they waited for the house to be repaired and the insurance claims processed.

Nowhere was devastated like London. Now, apparently, there were sneaky doodlebugs to contend with. She prayed they wouldn't come up as far as Scotland. She didn't want to die. Certainly not before she'd got to know her baby properly. Shuddering, she wondered how her friend Elspeth was coping down in Bromley. Or should that be *up*? She thought of England as *down*. Northern folk did. *Down South* they said. Yet for a train journey, it was always *up to London*. It was confusing.

Elspeth, whom Bessie had met on holiday in Beaumaris with some of her bridge friends not long before marrying Hugh, was, through no lack of effort on her part, still single. By chance brought up in Edinburgh, she was a few years younger than Bessie, though far more worldly. When war broke out, she'd moved to London to train as a physiotherapist, but despite the distance, it hadn't prevented the women meeting up when Elspeth visited her family in Morningside.

She'd recently written about a terrifying night out with an off-duty American Lieutenant:

'On hearing a faint buzzing noise in the air as we strolled across the park, he hurled me to the ground throwing himself protectively on top. Fortunately, the bomb caught a nearby

greenhouse, but staggering to my feet and running away from the debris, I lost a shoe and gained a… well, let's just say it brought us closer in every way!'

Maybe Elspeth wouldn't be unattached much longer and, after the war, they would turn into airmail pen-pals?

She missed Elspeth. But Bessie had become accustomed to maintaining good friendships by correspondence. The important ones were rarely damaged by distance. If anything, the relief at knowing people you cared about were safe and keeping busy during this difficult time made them all the more precious. Like most married women, Bessie supported the war effort and, until she became heavily pregnant, enjoyed her time as a volunteer in the naval canteen. She knew all about Americans.

Elspeth, having finished her training and now attached to a hospital, was using her newly acquired skills to help both injured servicemen and civilians physically affected by the hostilities. Such initiatives reduced the number of nursing recruits available for private medical care. Bessie appreciated that each nurse in the home she was in was doing the work of two. It explained why there were insufficient staff to watch over her until strictly necessary, though it didn't stop her feeling anxious they might forget about her.

The Belview was supposedly reliable and good value. Hugh kept saying, *'It better be, the fees they're charging!'* There were rumblings about a free health service for everyone once the war was over, but there was enough on politicians' minds right now. Though, like a lot of people in the medical profession, her own saintly Dr Macdonald, who'd guided her through her recent problems, saw nationalisation as a possible threat to his income and had still to be persuaded of its wisdom.

On one side of her room, through the thick walls, Bessie could make out the piercing howl of a new life desperate for air.

Another impatient twinge. It would be her turn soon.

Could the sounds from next door have reached her own baby? She'd been calling her bump *baby* since it had first made its presence felt months ago on a tram trundling over North Bridge. Technically it was still a foetus until it was out and about. Such a cold word, *foetus*, she thought. In a few hours, Sam – or Jean – whom she felt she already knew and had certainly chatted to whenever they kicked her, sometimes with expletives she'd picked up from Roy years ago and didn't normally approve of, would be released into a scary world. In a few hours' time, they'd be stridently asserting the right to be their own person.

Another twinge.

It would be so easy to panic, especially when, as now, the building was silent, the only sounds of life coming through the partly open window: an occasional slowing down or speeding up of a car engine as it turned in or out of Queensferry Street to the sporadic accompaniment of clattering heels on the pavement.

Should she check the bell perhaps? Unhelpfully, given her size, it wasn't positioned for ease of accessibility. How had all the other pregnant women who'd waited in this room coped, she wondered – was she so unusually elephantine? Mercifully, the moment passed. The baby must have decided on a last snooze before summoning strength for the final push.

She relaxed.

God, those dreary walls could do with a lick of distemper, she thought, sinking back into her pillows and shutting her eyes to banish the expanses of dirty beige around her.

Now she could hear the distant shriek of a seagull seeking its way back to the Forth, reminding her of the sights and sounds from her bedroom at home. To the right of their house, the remaining dwellings in their terrace swept down and around the corner to where the trams rattled past the shops: westerly towards Granton or to the east under the railway bridge with its huge posters of the Bisto twins and upcoming shows at the King's Theatre. Running right along the front, the sea wall held back the moody expanse of water beyond, often bobbing with busy boats and the occasional ferry.

Boats held the romance of possibility. Who's on them? Where are they going? On a good day, they could gaze across to Fife, its shoreline glowing in the sunshine, with tiny lights winking across when darkness fell.

Whatever the weather, she liked nothing more than to wrap up and make her way down to the shingle, gingerly avoiding any flotsam and jetsam, looking left and letting her mind reach out around the corner to historic

Cramond and North Queensferry. Alternatively, she'd swivel her eyes in the opposite direction towards the bustling Port of Leith. Strolling along the seafront, she might pass Newhaven fishwives in shawls, long, striped skirts and grubby aprons, heaving baskets brimming with the day's shiny catch.

She let the swish-and-bump of the waves wash over her mind and the wind caress her face until the chill kicked in and bit her cheeks; then she'd return home revitalised, prepared to face any worrying news the day might bring.

Another twinge brought her mind back to where she was.

Then another.

She looked at her watch. *8.35 pm.* The light was beginning to fade, the walls closing in on her. A more insistent pain attacked her abdomen.

It was *strictly necessary* time.

Straining every muscle in her upper body to heave herself up, she reached for the cord.

* * *

When it finally happened, the delivery was straightforward. But Bessie had forgotten the stomach ulcer she'd developed which required a controlled diet.

They were grateful for the generosity of kind neighbours, several of whom kept bantams in their back gardens, while, in the summer, others cultivated lettuces and cucumbers in frames and tomatoes in greenhouses. There was usually a good supply of apples, pears, raspberries and root vegetables in season too. Everything both during and after the war was shared or exchanged, whilst a friendly greengrocer supplied whatever produce he could find at the official market – and quite a lot that wasn't, thanks to underground networking. Living by the sea, fresh fish was often available too. Rarely did people go short.

For Bessie, avoiding alcohol, tea and coffee was not a problem, nor, given the harsh limitations of rationing, the need to limit her fat intake. Enjoying a seemingly healthy diet before and after Sam was born, she never gave any thought as to whether or not her condition and its medication might affect the milk she was producing.

Bessie only began to worry about him, an otherwise engaging child, when, after a few months, red itchy rashes and blisters began to appear on his skin and, as Sam grew older, lingered and irritated him more and more. The specialists bandied about terms like *allergy* and *atopic* but were unable to reassure her that her own, possibly corrupted, bodily fluids were not the cause.

Severe infantile eczema was diagnosed and various lotions and creams prescribed. It became a nightly ritual for her to sit Sam on her lap in the antique nursing chair that had belonged to Hugh's family and wrap cool, lotion-soaked bandages around his arms and legs.

The domestic fatalities continued, and in the miserable winter of 1947, Ellie died.

Bessie took Sam with her to attend the funeral and meet his grandfather in Manchester. His skin was worse, possibly aggravated by the tiring journey. The first night, they had to change his bed sheets twice. The unhappy trip, which turned out to be the last time she ever saw her father, convinced her Sam's condition required professional attention. Indeed, the consultant considered it severe enough for him to be placed in the children's ward of the Edinburgh Infirmary under the care of a Sister who was respected for her success in managing juvenile skin diseases.

'How long will he need to be here?' Bessie asked her.

'As long as it takes, I'm afraid.'

Back home, Hugh put his arm around his wife's shoulder. She flinched. However well-meaning he was, no man could fully appreciate the special bond between a woman and her child, however much he cared about both of them. To be fair, women didn't always appreciate how helpless men felt around infants, becoming more use once they could join in playing with them, especially if it involved trains and cars. She squeezed his hand. It was a battle she must deal with in her own way, while making sure he didn't feel left out.

Once they had, with reluctance, handed Sam over to the Sister's care, they were shocked to be told: 'We dare not let you see him until his treatment is complete. It would distress him as much as yourselves.' Her head understood but her heart struggled to accept it. 'It's for his own good.'

Bessie could see Hugh saw it as his role to be the cerebral, objective one but knew he struggled to summon the strength to deal with their ordeal as much as she did.

'He could be away for six months or more. He'll miss his third birthday,' she said.

'We'll get through it and make it up to him when he's better. He'll understand.'

'Will he. How?'

But Hugh could only look sadly across the room and out through the window.

4

Alone

1947
Sam

Something was wrong.

A large, dimly lit room. Footsteps echoing beyond.

Not his room.

Not his bed.

In a cot.

Sam knew that because he'd slept in one before he was old enough to have a bed of his own.

But where was he?

His wrists were tied to the sides with thick pink bandages, white gauze concealing his arms and legs which itched during the night. Often in the day, too. The only relief came when he scratched the irritating patches. That made them sore and sometimes blood appeared and his mother got upset.

Where was his mother? When she heard him moving and moaning, she always appeared with a six-sided green bottle of cool, sweet-smelling lotion, bathing the red patches to ease the itching and let him get to sleep.

He tried moving his right arm, but the bandages prevented him reaching as far as his left arm and leg. It was the same with the other arm. He couldn't touch any part of himself.

Through the bars of the cot, he could just about make out several more, all exactly the same, with other children in them. Most of them asleep except for one who was quietly snivelling and another making gurgling noises.

Where was he?

Unable to move much and feeling alone in this strange place, he felt afraid. Why didn't she come?

He began to whimper, then to cry. 'I want my mummy!'

He screamed.

Someone in a dark blue dress with a small white hat on her head appeared by the side of his cot. Looking down at him kindly, she soothed his brow with a damp cloth.

'There, there now, hush... hush,' she said.

But it wasn't her he needed.

What was happening to him? He had to know his mother wasn't far away. She'd know what to do.

The minutes passed.

His mother still didn't come.

He screamed again.

And again.

* * *

After the first shock of finding himself completely on his own, Sam gave himself up to the way things now were.

He was never able to talk about his seven months in the Infirmary. His memory of the time he spent there hid itself beyond conscious reach. Yet, buried somewhere in his mind, traumatic triggers would always be inexplicably activated when least expected, releasing angry flashes of panic and a sense of helplessness.

He learnt to love deeply but would never completely trust anyone.

5

Estrangement

1948
Bessie

Arthur died while Sam was in the Infirmary.

Of course, it wouldn't register with the child, but, as his third birthday came and went without celebration, it saddened Bessie and Hugh to know that, apart from Arthur, whom he'd fleetingly met, he would never know any of his grandparents.

Coming to terms with being orphaned, Sam's incarceration in hospital affected Bessie deeply. After a few weeks, she could cope without seeing him no longer.

'I'm bringing him home,' she told Hugh.

'The Infirmary would have let us know if he was ready.'

'He must be after all this time.'

'It's only been a few weeks.'

'I don't care.'

'But…'

Ignoring his protestations, she caught the tram to the hospital and marched into the Sister's office. 'I'm sorry, I can't carry on like this. I must see my lad. And I'd really like to take him home with me, too.'

The Sister, accustomed to mothers undergoing similar stress, put on her understanding face. 'Please take a seat, Mrs Owen. I fully appreciate all you're going through. Sam's making progress, but we warned you this would be a long, drawn-out treatment. Also, seeing you could set him back. Certainly, he's not in a state yet where you could manage him without professional help.'

But Bessie was unconvinced. She was in a dark place. After a long discussion, during which she became uncharacteristically emotional, the Sister took her along to the ward.

Sam looked at her strangely. When she bent down to touch him, he began to cry. It pierced her to the core. Was it because he recognised her – or because he didn't and imagined she was a stranger? Or, was he angry with her for deserting him?

Her small son's reaction hardened her resolve. 'Please,' she told the Sister, 'will you prepare him for leaving. I'll take a taxi home.'

'You appreciate you're discharging Sam against our best advice,' the Sister warned her, before lifting the bemused child, still covered in bandages, out of his cot.

'If you find you are not coping, you must bring him straight back.'

Hugh and Bessie realised their mistake almost immediately. Sam wouldn't settle at home. All evening and all night he tore at his bandages on his hands, arms and knees. Blood suppurated through them. They could see he was still tormented by the irritation. She did everything she'd been advised to help him: changed his dressings, applied the ointment as directed, but nothing helped him get to sleep for very long. He went on tossing, turning, crying.

The next morning, tired and bleary-eyed, Hugh said, 'I'm afraid we've no option but to take him back.'

Bessie wept.

Hugh rang the hospital.

Coming home on the tram alone was even harder the second time.

* * *

At suppertime one evening shortly afterwards, Bessie was clearing away the remains of the macaroni on which she'd squandered their meagre weekly cheese ration when the phone rang. Telling Hugh to help himself to the bowl of stewed plums, she dashed into the hallway and picked up the receiver.

The faint crackle on the line denoted a long-distance call. Manchester, she thought. But who?

'It's me,' Flo said.

Her heart sank. 'Hello. Is everything all right?'

There was an ominous silence. Of course not. Why else would they be ringing?

'I hope it isn't an awkward moment?'

'We're in the middle of our evening meal, but otherwise...'

'I'm sorry, but Roy wants a word with you.' Then why get you to ring and break the ice, Bessie thought. Flo sighed. 'You don't know how lucky you are being away from it all in Edinburgh.'

Lucky for what? And why did this sound more like the preamble of a rebuke rather than an indication of envy? Not even a courteous enquiry about Sam languishing in hospital? No, unmaternal Flo would be far too absorbed in her own problems for it to have occurred to her.

'I can understand there must be a lot to do, especially with Mother and Father going one after the other,' Bessie said.

'Yes. It was bad enough dealing with Mother's dementia during the war,' Flo went on, 'continually mopping up all her little puddles and messes, trying to keep the house looking and smelling presentable while juggling our arrangements to take our turn at the office and keep the business ticking over. Father wasn't much use by then, and Roy still hasn't fully recovered from his combat fatigue...'

Also, Bessie thought, although it couldn't be mentioned within his hearing, the death of Billy, shot down over Holland in 1942. Roy had been badly affected by that, too, it seemed. 'We'd have gone under if he hadn't been invalided out of the army and come home to help.'

Bessie knew how rough the past few years had been for them, but forward planning had never been one of their stronger points. A something-will-turn-up mentality always stifled any motivation to move their lives forward.

'If only you'd been able to persuade Hugh to look for a job closer to home.'

Bessie gritted her teeth, refusing to rise to the bait. Home might now be Edinburgh, but she was forced to admit, if only to herself, the downside of living so far away from both their families. Quite apart from the time spent travelling, the expense of regular trips to Manchester to assist Connie and visit her own parents had eaten up much-needed spare cash. Journeys on heat-starved trains chugging through blacked-out landscapes in winter, or hugger-mugger with hot and sweaty uniformed men and women during the warmer months, hadn't been any fun, either.

She was fully aware how, when Roy went into the army, Flo had managed alone and recognised the difficulty she must have experienced trying to recruit outside help for their mother at a time when most able-bodied people were engaged in the war effort. While a part of her felt guilty she'd been unable to offer her family more support during that period, it was only a small part. It didn't take into account the strain of juggling her own priorities and attempts to keep faith with everyone.

It was a sad fact to come to terms with that Flo and Roy would never adjust to her leaving home or resist any opportunity to reproach her for doing so. As far as they were concerned, she'd been unforgivably disloyal going off and leaving them to cope with both the business – from which she'd never received any financial benefit other than, once upon a time, a roof over her head and some pocket money – and two helpless, elderly people.

Dealing with the build-up to and aftermath of the bereavements had necessarily been disruptive to both families' lives, aggravated by the deprivations of the period. Few people had not suffered in some way or other, their own families coming out of it more fortunate than many. Connie had looked after her and Hugh's parents in their final years while maintaining a much-needed job and income. She was an intelligent and capable woman, and they'd been delighted at her recent elevation from teaching Domestic Science in a girls' school to an appointment as Senior Lecturer at the college where she'd once trained. Hannah, who looked after the Institutional Management department at the same college, was now an important part of her life and would remain so for the rest of it.

And it was Connie who'd dealt with the depressing organisation of Mr and Mrs Owen's funerals, the related paperwork and the sale of the family home, on top of her tiring job. She had as much right to feel sore over the burden she'd carried virtually alone but, being the person she was, remained good-natured throughout that difficult patch and thereafter.

Bessie tensely clutched the phone as Flo moaned on a little longer, before saying, 'I think it's best that Roy speaks to you.' There was a short pause with some muffled whispering in the background. She could picture her sister by the small table with the barley sugar legs at the bottom of the stairs, then handing over the receiver of the awkward candlestick telephone to Roy.

'Hello Sis,' Roy said, his voice always warmer than Flo's. 'I'm afraid this isn't easy for me.'

Now we're getting to it, she thought.

'We saw the solicitor yesterday. As you know, Dad left a third of the house and business to each of us. He could be an old so-an-so at times, but he knew what was right and proper.' Roy made it sound as if Arthur had always behaved above and beyond the call of duty, although, admittedly, he'd been generous when times were good, and Bessie would always be grateful to him for giving her a good send-off when she got married. 'But then, he drafted his will quite a while back when you were still around.'

Ouch. Was Roy suggesting she'd automatically forfeited the goodwill built up over the fifteen years she'd looked after them all? It wasn't the fact that her brother and sister felt obliged to ask for her share of their father's money in order to survive. She understood that. What hurt was their lack of graciousness in doing so. An unwillingness to acknowledge everything she had once done for them. Always good at protecting her dignity, she chose not to reveal how disappointed their attitude made her feel, so she simply said, 'Go on.'

'Then you can guess why we're ringing,' Roy said, awkwardly clearing his throat at the end of the line as if assuming he could skip additional explanation.

'I think so. You want my share of our parents' money?'

'It wouldn't be for ever,' he said.

She went silent, unconvinced. Once it would never have occurred to her to doubt him.

'Are you still there?'

'I was just thinking.'

'Well?'

'I'd only ask…' she began.

'Yes?'

'…that if ever you sort yourselves out and sell up, you might bear in mind Hugh and I only rent this house. Anything you could spare by then to help us put down a deposit on our own place would be much appreciated.' There was little chance of that happening, but why should she let them off scot-free?

'Holding on to the house, however, isn't the main problem.'

'The business?'

'We're struggling to keep going. Profit margins were always slim, but even though people still need coal, it's not in demand as once it was. In the current climate, we have to be competitive to stay in the game. The nationalisation of the industry might be good for the miners, but it's already impacting on us middlemen, and competition from minefields elsewhere is great. We're having to charge more to pay their wages, and the bigger boys are pushing us out. They can provide a better service than we can afford. The shire horses went some while back, but now even the lorries we invested in to replace them are getting out of date and eating up money in repair bills. We could do with another driver, too. It's crippling us. There's barely enough coming in to pay our salaries and make essential improvements. We believed Father had investments but only discovered yesterday that they don't pay out or amount to as much as we'd hoped. If we could borrow your money, it would help get us back on our feet.'

Bessie hadn't an avaricious bone in her body, but with the whole country bankrupt, Hugh and she were feeling the pinch too. She couldn't help reflecting that after a year during which they'd experienced nothing but worry on the home front and continued austerity outside it, there was barely enough in their own kitty for even a few days' break at North Berwick, only twenty-six miles away, to help recharge their batteries.

In better times, the loss of four parents within a few years might have provided a much-needed boost to their finances. Unfortunately, the property market was suffering from the prevailing post-war economic uncertainty too. Once the Owens' home had been sold and the funeral and solicitor's expenses dealt with, there was only enough from Hugh's own legacy to pay for Bessie's medical expenses and the other costs incurred before and after Sam's arrival. At least her brother and sister had their own home. Not that she couldn't see the difficult position Flo and Roy were in, nor begrudged them a livelihood. She simply wanted them to know they couldn't continue to walk all over her as they'd done in the past.

She had a fair idea what some of Arthur's Boulle furniture and precious ornaments might fetch, too. Recalling how they'd always mocked their father's pretentiousness, she couldn't imagine why they'd want to hold on to museum pieces that might be sold to advantage and replaced with cheaper items more appropriate to life in a suburban villa. There was a smartly framed period landscape sketch she'd always admired, which might have sold well. Had they bothered having any of these items valued or was the antiques market suffering in the prevailing climate too?

'Are you still there?'

'Yes…' she said.

I mean, you've both got everything you need, haven't you?'

'Well…'

'And, I promise, we really will make it up to you just as soon as things pick up.'

Not unless she kept nagging them. And possibly involved solicitors. But she would never do that, as they would have guessed. She simply said, 'I'll have to trust you, then, won't I?'

'Thank you, Bess,' Roy said, adding, 'And how are you both doing?'

'We're coping,' she said.

'And my beautiful godson?' Roy threw this in as, what sounded like, a polite afterthought.

'He'll be in the Infirmary for quite a while.'

'Sorry to hear about that,' he said, as if she'd been complaining about the prevalence of greenfly on this year's roses. 'Well, I'd better get off the line. The cost of these trunk calls is prohibitive.'

'We're very much aware.'

'Bye.'

Gently replacing the receiver, Bessie went to make coffee. After the tense conversation, the macaroni cheese was still reluctantly digesting in her stomach and her portion of plums looked up sadly from the bowl as if aware it wasn't wanted. Her appetite might have gone, but she badly needed some caffeine, her duodenal ulcer now a thing of the past. Flo's attitude hadn't surprised her. For all her feminine glamour and mirthful chatter, she knew how calculating and emotionally unreliable her sister could be, but she expected better of Roy. What had really happened to her good pal? Flo referred to his issues as *combat fatigue*, but Roy had never been involved in direct action during the hostilities. Any mayhem he'd observed in the army and, above all, Billy's death had affected him far more than she had thought. The sad thing was, she would never know the truth.

Poor Billy, who had always been the life and soul of the party. She could see the two young men now, walking side by side up the road to the club: Roy, six foot two and broad-shouldered, his brown, slicked-back hair and generous features set off by immaculately kept clothes, and Billy with his reddish wavy hair, green eyes and schoolboy chuckle. The lads had been inseparable. Before Billy's death, Roy was an extrovert who took life in his stride. Now, whenever they met up, he appeared introspective, withdrawing from her whenever she tried to rekindle their old intimacy. It was as if he couldn't handle the fact that Hugh had replaced him in her life.

Once when she had been staying with them, Bessie tried talking to Flo about the changes in her brother. But her sister wasn't comfortable delving into other people's personal issues, especially those close to her. Roy spent a few nights with them during their early days in Forth View Road but had been surly and disparaging about the nest she'd made. His spitefulness had hurt her. Physical exhaustion she could understand, but psychological injury was too complex for her. She only knew that, while ointments could soothe Sam's discomfort, there was no equivalent for a chronically damaged spirit.

Of late, there had been indications Roy was settling into some kind of new normal, but she guessed he still wasn't ready for the stresses and strains of the now fraught and competitive business world. If her money helped relieve that, it would probably be worth her sacrifice, but from now on, it would be down to Flo to help him rediscover his enthusiasm for life. No longer able to reach him, Bessie would never cease hoping for a rapprochement but feared their relationship could never be the same again.

Her having walked out of her parents' home with nothing but a couple of cases and her wedding outfit would always rankle. Now, with both parents gone, the pair didn't even have the decency to offer her so much as a small piece of their mother's jewellery or one of their father's hideous ornaments as a keepsake. That wasn't like the old Roy, who had shared his last half-sucked gobstopper with her and lent her his tennis racquet when hers was broken.

Was it too late for the pair to still find other people to care about? Someone in whom Roy, in particular, could confide and who could counteract the self-serving aspects of Flo's personality?

Even another Billy?

But at that point, a shutter came down. There were some aspects of human nature even Bessie's probing mind was, at this point, ill-equipped to investigate. Knowing the limitations of her brother and sister's horizons, she doubted they were ever likely to change. The irony was that Flo, seven years Roy's senior, was the one person in the family with whom he'd never connected. Now, if only by default and financial need, it appeared they were destined to be stuck with one another.

Hell is other people was a quotation doing the rounds.

Despite Roy's glib assurances, she predicted that, even if things worked out for them, having convinced themselves of their moral right to her inheritance, they would eventually justify it as an entitlement. She was left counting her blessings. With a generous-natured husband, kindly sister-in-law and a son who, she prayed, would soon be restored to them, there was at least the satisfaction of knowing how much more fortunate she was than them.

The phone call, orchestrated no doubt by Flo, confirmed she was irrevocably cast out. From now on, she'd have to live with the knowledge they had metaphorically, and probably actually, changed the locks.

6

Little Gentleman

1948 – 1951
Sam

Sam held Bessie's hand as they walked down the road to the shops.

Mr Campbell was coming towards them up the pavement. Bessie slowed down to greet him. A strange old gentleman with an unkempt beard and thick horn-rimmed spectacles who lived some doors along the road from them, he always seemed surrounded by an aroma: mothballs mixed with something more intimate – as if he hadn't washed for a few days.

When he bent down to ask Sam, 'And how are you, wee fellow?' not in the tones he had used to greet his mother but in that high-pitched voice grown-ups often adopted when speaking to pet cats, Sam wanted to say: 'Why can't you talk properly and not look like I might hiss at you?' But instead, he just lowered his head and remained silent.

'Oh dear, is he always this shy?' Mr Campbell asked Bessie in a tone of exaggerated disappointment.

'Not usually. Are you?' she said looking sharply at him. 'I think he's just a little in awe of you.'

When they moved on, she wanted to know why he'd been rude.

'I didn't mean to, but he smells and his beard is scary,' Sam said.

'Santa Claus has a beard. He's not scary.'

There was no answer to that, except 'But I've never actually seen him except in *Binns* and that didn't count, because everyone knows he's not the *real* Father Christmas and only a man dressed up and pretending to be.' How people smelt was important to Sam and either drew him to them or pushed him away. Tobacco and outdoorsy smells were friendly – and the *Soir de Paris* his mother wore on special occasions. He'd told his parents the *Binns* Santa smelt of scent too.

'Probably an out-of-work actor,' his father had muttered dismissively to Bessie. A remark Sam hadn't pursued.

Today, though, he sensed he'd overstepped a line and there would be a reckoning.

Sure enough, the next afternoon after lunch, Bessie invited him to sit close to her 'for one of my *serious talks*'. He'd learned to recognise the firm tone of voice she adopted on such occasions and how it was likely to lead to a lesson on improving his manners.

As they were settling down after tea, Bessie said, 'I'd like to play a little game with you.'

'A new game?'

'Yes. But there's a reason for it.'

Oh, that sort of game. The lesson kind, he thought. 'What reason?'

'You'll be starting at Laverockbank very shortly.'

'What's that, Mummy?'

'It's a school for boys and girls of your age. It will help you to read and write and do sums before you go on to the bigger school.

'Will there be other children there?'

'Quite a lot. And it's important you know how to greet them and get on with them. Although you and Hamish up the road get along, I know you still find it... well, a little awkward meeting new people.'

'You think I'm afraid of them?'

'Are you?'

'Well...'

'We all have times when we're frightened of people. It's important we learn not to be. Or at least not to show it. Soon, you'll be spending every morning away from here and meeting lots of children and other grown-ups. They might be more frightening than Mr Campbell, so…'

Her drawn-out *so* suggested something tiresome was coming for which participation wouldn't be voluntary.

'Now, I want you to go over to that table and come up to me as if you've never met me before,' Bessie said. 'Come towards me… good… put out your hand. That's it. And, when I take it like this, grasp it very firmly. Even tighter. Now say "Hello, how nice to meet you."'

Sam could do the first bit, but speaking felt awkward.

'Hello,' he mumbled, 'how… um…'

'What was that?'

'How nice to m…' he said a bit louder, then stopped. 'I can't. It's you. I know you. It feels silly.'

'Unfortunately, people often make up their mind about you when they first meet you. If you smile, speak up and shake their hand firmly, they'll want to get to know you better and… it helps break the ice.'

'Ice?' Sam was confused. He remembered when the evenings had been long and dark and it was very cold outside. Next morning, the footpath was slippery with frozen water. 'But it's not been like that for a long time.'

'*Breaking the ice* is an expression we use. It means freeing things up. When you meet people for the first time, good manners help both people feel more comfortable with each other and get to know each other more easily. Right?'

'I… think so.'

'Now, this time, I'd like you to go outside the room, close the door and, when I tap on this little table, enter…'

'Enter?'

'Come back in and walk nicely up to me again and do what you did before.'

Sam tried.

'Don't run… Too slow… That's just about right. Oh dear, wrong hand. Try again.'

And again.

'Now, look me in the eyes… And again. This time, smile. Open your eyes wider. That's it! No, take a bit longer. Don't forget, shoulders back… you're getting the hang of it. Now, do all those things together.'

Next, Bessie pretended to be different people, pulling faces which reduced the tension and making him laugh so much he had to start all over again.

He began enjoying himself.

'Well done!' she said at length.

Making his mother happy made him happy.

Every week or so after that, Bessie put Sam through his paces again 'just to keep you up to scratch' and his social skills started to come more naturally. Each time he met someone new, his good manners were less and less forced. And eventually became automatic.

Ever after, whenever Sam was required to walk into a room full of strangers, he found he could suppress his innate shyness and act with a confidence he didn't always feel.

* * *

'Come in and sit down,' Miss Taggart commanded.

They'd trudged up the three flights of stairs to the small kindergarten. It consisted of two large rooms on the top floor of a late Victorian tenement.

The woman met them with a welcoming smile. With her neat brown hair parted in the middle, eyes twinkling behind rimless spectacles and maroon tweed suit over a blouse and beads, she reminded him of Aunt Connie: straight-forward and no-nonsense. He watched her take in his shy demeanour and lazy left eye, now almost masked by new National Health glasses. Lack of visual coordination meant he could rarely kick or hit a ball straight and it hindered his ability to catch things, but she wasn't to know that. Nor how, within a few years, chronic asthmatic symptoms would also wreck any enjoyment he might have gained from sporting activities, the terror of compulsory cross-country runs on bitter January days being a hell to come.

When it came to doing anything he found uncomfortable, Sam soon realised that no one understood quite how he felt. Grown-ups kept saying things like 'pull yourself together', 'make an effort' or 'you can't let the side down' which, when he tried to oblige, hampered his breathing and distressed him.

Years after, he wondered whether his stay in hospital, with all the empty time he'd had to observe people's body language, had heightened his facility for construing other people's behaviour. Thus, when Miss Taggart gently offered her hand and his newly acquired skills kicked in, he perceived, from the slight stiffening of her body and barely concealed look of concern, she'd noticed the rough skin on his.

The necessary formalities completed, she stood up to indicate the interview was over.

'We'll see you on the twenty-first then, Sam?'

'He's looking forward to it,' Bessie said giving him a gentle nudge.

'How many other boys and girls will there be?' he said.

'Sixteen, I think.'

His eyes widened. 'Goodness, that's a lot!'

'A nice, round number. Divides easily by four,' Miss Taggart added, then turned to Bessie. 'Doesn't he speak beautifully!' she said.

Sam groaned inside. It was a compliment people had started to pay him. One he increasingly came to regard as a mixed blessing, along with 'isn't he a little gentleman?' to the point where such remarks either felt loaded with expectations he was unable to fulfil or intended as a criticism. An accusation even. At home, too, his somewhat prim voice stood out in contrast to his family's warm Mancunian cadences. Maybe that was why, as he grew older, he came to welcome any opportunity to hide his real persona and mimic the accents and rhythms of voices around him.

At the weekend, Hugh took him to the Botanic Gardens and neighbouring Inverleith Park. There they would watch, intrigued, as older children sailed toy yachts across the pond to the accompaniment of distant cheers from the spectators of matches in the playing fields beyond. Trips out and about with Bessie on other days usually involved a tram to Frederick

Street followed by window shopping along Princes Street, with, if he was lucky, a stop at Mackie's or Crawford's tea rooms. For him, a lemonade and a bun; for her, a pot of tea and, afterwards, a Player's Navy Cut.

One afternoon, Bessie took him to a special shop. Inside was warm and calm. Bright lights focussed on a pale wall with a table covered in a soft, off-white material in front of it. A kindly man gave him a toy to play with asked if he could take pictures of him in various positions. He was asked to sit very still while a camera was trained on him, and he enjoyed his twenty minutes sitting on the table, the centre of attention.

The pictures arrived in the post a few days later.

'Why do you like that one 'specially, Mummy?' he asked as Bessie kept returning to inspect a certain print.

'Because it shows the tops of your knees with no scabs left on your legs. I'm so proud of you!'

The next day, they visited a shop nearer home to buy a white and gold frame for the photo, which became a permanent fixture wherever they lived, perched on top of a mahogany bookcase in the living room, a growing source of embarrassment when new friends came to visit.

Activities at Laverockbank began at 9.15 with a hymn and a prayer in the front room high up above the street, followed by movement to music. The children then lined up at the door and moved into the brighter classroom at the rear to grapple with the rudiments of what grown-ups referred to as *the three Rs*. On cold days, a gas fire brought extra cheer and warmth to the rooms. At some point between lessons, each child was given a small bottle of creamy milk and a straw: their daily third-of-a pint doled out from a large crate the milkman had lugged up several flights of stairs for them. 'Now drink every drop,' Miss Taggart insisted. 'It's a gift from the government and will help you grow healthy and strong.'

Here Sam learnt a picture of a large rosy apple represented the symbol *A* and *John did not eat his food and mother was vexed*. A counting frame of coloured beads helped fix in his head the numbers one to nine and then up to twenty, though he would always prefer using his hands for counting and never stopped *carrying ten*.

Miss MacTaggart showed the children the proper way to tie their shoelaces, but, contrarily, Sam favoured the *double-bow* method. 'A divergent thinker, I'm afraid,' he heard Miss Taggart tell Bessie when she collected him one lunchtime. He didn't understand what she meant, and, from the expression on Bessie's face, neither did she, but, before the matter could be discussed further, the conversation had moved on to the delicate matter of next term's fees.

At Sunday school in the small hall attached to the nearby Victorian church, Sam became fascinated by a host of angels in a picture on the wall, convinced the one in the second row with the lop-sided wing and cheeky grin was Mrs McKenzie from across the road, who'd often given him a toffee when they met. Watching as four men carried her coffin down the treacherous stone steps from her front door and slide it into a shiny black limousine was his first intimation of mortality.

'I'm afraid she's died,' Bessie said.

'Why?'

'Because she was a very old lady. It was her time.'

After that, there were no more toffees.

One day, he arrived home as Bessie was making custard with dried milk and vanilla essence to accompany a suet pudding for lunch, confounding her by coming out with: 'Miss Taggart says that, if I'm a very good boy, when I get to Heaven, I'll be able to eat ice cream every day.'

Bessie looked nonplussed.

* * *

At the end of Sam's first term at Laverockbank, Bessie said, 'I've got tickets for us all to see Jack and the Beanstalk.'

'That's a story.'

'Right, Sam. And a pantomime.'

'What's a pantomime?'

'It's a story with songs and dancing. Each year a different well-known tale. We'll be going with Aunt Connie to a matinee after Christmas.'

'What's a matinee?'

Bessie explained, adding 'and we'll be sitting in a box.'

'A *box*?'

'Yes.'

Sam's eyes widened, visualising Bessie, Hugh, Aunt Connie and himself all squeezed into a large tea chest like the one he kept his toys in beneath the kitchen table, perched on a ledge somewhere he couldn't comprehend as the story unfolded before their eyes. It sounded rather scary. He hoped the Giant wouldn't get too near them and gobble them up.

The afternoon arrived. Spellbound, Sam couldn't keep his eyes off the stage.

His return to earth as the lights went up at the interval was barely eased by the tub of ice cream his father pressed into his hand. Once finished, he fidgeted until the entr'acte began and the fantasy resumed.

At five-thirty, the curtain came down for the last time. The other members of the family, who'd been yawning or looking at their watches for the past half hour, hastily put on their scarves and coats and chivvied him to do likewise.

'It's not really over, is it?' he said, still miles away, gazing down at the now silent orchestra pit where the players were packing up their instruments.

'Afraid so,' Aunt Connie said, gently prising his hands from the plush edge of the box. Aren't you ready for your tea?'

Sam's imagination having been stimulated as never before, he found it hard tearing himself away from the warmth of the auditorium.

'Hurry up, lad,' Hugh said.

'You don't want to be left behind, do you?' Bessie added.

'Don't I?' he thought.

He wanted the story, the fun, the vibrant colours, the twinkling sequins of the costumes and the picture-book settings to return one last time. To hear again the song everyone had been taught, the tune of which was still going around in his head, along with a multitude of images: merry dancing around the maypole, the Spirit of the Beanery and her helpers spinning on tiptoe in the dream ballet as the scene dissolved from the Giant's Kitchen into the Enchanted Garden. A world which, until this afternoon, he'd only seen in picture books. Today it had come alive right before his eyes.

Could he ever become a part of it?

His favourite part had been when Jack heard the Giant shouting *'Fe, Fi, Fo, Fum, I smell the blood of a young Scotsman'* and he scrambled for safety into the huge pie on the outsize table, a minute later breaking through the crust to vanquish his arch-enemy with a huge sword, shielded by a soup tureen lid. Retrospectively, he never felt too sorry for the Giant, knowing he wasn't really dead and would reappear as a guest at Jack's wedding to Princess Daisy.

Bessie held out her hand. Reluctantly taking it, he followed her along the little passageway which led from the boxes down into the foyer, dodging the legs of other children and adults as they jostled out into the cold night to join the queue at the bus stop.

In the weeks that followed, whenever he was alone on trams, walking to school or trying to drop off to sleep, he'd enter Jack's world. Now he was sailing on the revolving stage in shiny silver armour; now in Giant Blunderbuss's house with everything twice the size it was in real life; now the amiable butt of jokes delivered by Jack's mother, who looked like a man in a frock and, for no apparent reason, became the Giant's charlady.

In his head, he was soon transforming their living room into a theatre and organising his own version of the story. Aunt Connie's pianist skills would, of course, be roped in to provide the music.

* * *

In due course, Sam moved on from the cosiness of Laverockbank to another, larger school in a big house. Here there were several classrooms and a hall doubling as a gymnasium, all surrounded by a play area and garden for playing ball games. While he enjoyed making new friends and grew fond of his pretty form teacher, Miss Nicholson, he also found himself becoming more aware of his shortcomings. Especially an allergy to numbers. Adding-up and taking-away he could do, but *times-ing*, as he called it, and dividing confused him. Miss Nicholson stuck gold stars at the end of good work at the end of each week. He won a few for Writing and Drawing but mainly got red crosses for Sums.

One day, his friends were excitedly discussing Walt Disney's film of *Cinderella,* which was scheduled to be shown at a local film house the following week. Most of the boys' mothers were taking them. It was Sam's favourite story. He begged Bessie to take him.

'If you get a gold star for Sums this week, then we'll go.'

Asking him to empty the Forth with a thimble would have been easier.

He never got to see *Cinderella.*

Bessie was disappointed, too. 'I'm sorry, I know you've done your best, but you need to learn that I always keep my word, even when it seems unfair.' It wasn't always easy living with someone with such inflexible integrity, and it only occurred to him a long time afterwards that Bessie might not always have been able to afford every treat she wanted to give him.

So far, his experience of acting consisted only of a non-speaking role as a shepherd in the recent nativity play, but at least it had introduced him to the thrill of dressing-up and singing to a packed audience. To make up for missing *Cinderella,* he was excited to learn that he'd next be playing the horse in a dramatisation of an A.A. Milne verse for the school's spring concert.

All he was required to do was go up to Christopher Robin and invite him to go with him to the village to buy some hay. It was only two lines, delivered in what he hoped was a gruff, horsey voice, but, once again, any fear he initially felt at speaking in front of rows and rows of people was more than compensated by the strange exhilaration of playing someone or, as on this occasion, some creature, other than himself.

* * *

Increasingly, his father's job required him to stay away from home. Bessie explained he was visiting his company's London headquarters. One week, when Sam was on half-term, she accompanied him there while Sam stayed with her good friend Marje in her spacious apartment overlooking Dundas Street, filled with exotic ornaments that her husband had brought back from Siam.

Marje was an artist. It was a pity she hadn't any children of her own as she was a natural teacher and, like Connie, had the knack of treating young people as if they were adults. Sam loved colour and was enchanted when she showed him how to mix tints together, transforming them into other colours and variations: reds and white into pinks and yellows and blues into different shades of green. Marje also taught him to play rummy and introduced him to a new powdered coffee called *Nescafé*, measuring just enough for each cup with the tiny metal spoon in the lid of the tin and topping it up with hot, frothy milk.

When the time came for Bessie to pick him up and take him home, Sam could tell she was very excited about something. No sooner had she stepped inside and given him a hug than Marje asked if she'd had a successful trip.

'It's lovely,' Bessie said, somewhat mysteriously, failing to elaborate on what *it* was. 'We only agreed on it yesterday. I must get this laddie home, but I'll ring you later with all the details once I've explained it all to him.'

Which intrigued him even more.

As usual, when she had something important to tell him, Bessie waited until they were both alone and settled. Hugh having stayed on in London, she made his favourite supper: *mock crab* with scrambled eggs, cheese and tinned tomatoes. As he watched her spoon the steamy pink and yellow mixture onto slices of margarine-covered toast, he waited eagerly to know what was happening.

'I expect you've been wondering what's up?' Bessie said, hungrily biting into her own toast.

'Something important?'

'And very exciting.'

'We're going on holiday?'

'Even better.'

What could be nicer than spending another fortnight in Elie on the Fife coast, where they'd spent part of the previous September? 'What?'

'We're moving.'

'What do you mean, Mummy?'

'We're leaving this house and going to live in London.'

'London?'

'Well, not in the centre of London, but on the outskirts in a lovely house with a big garden with loganberry bushes and things.'

'What's a loganberry?'

'A cross between a raspberry and a blackberry,' she explained, quickly adding, as she saw Sam's mouth framing another question, 'it's a mixture of two fruits.'

Sam was intrigued. He looked forward to seeing his new home and tasting his first loganberry.

'Daddy and you will have your own sheds: somewhere for you to invite your friends to play.'

'And I won't have to go to school and do any more sums?'

Bessie laughed. 'Sadly not! You'll be going to a new school about five miles away. It's one of the best in London. In due course, if you're clever and do well enough, you might even be able to go to another one, for older boys, in London itself.'

'Why do we have to leave here?'

'Because Daddy's company needs a new Deputy Manager for its London office.'

'Whereabouts in London? he said, trying to sound better informed about the vast metropolis than he was.

'Not very far from Westminster Abbey.'

'So that's why he came back last time with a book with pictures of London for me?' Bessie nodded. After supper, he went to find it and looked up the Abbey. Bessie explained that Nelson's Column was only a few bus stops away, too. He'd heard stories about Nelson and liked pictures of old ships with sails. Peter Pan had duelled with Captain Hook on one when they'd seen the play at the Lyceum with Margaret Lockwood. Maybe he'd be able to visit Nelson in his strange hat and feed the pigeons that kept him company.

On a late May morning, he said goodbye to his teacher and classmates, then visited his friend Hamish up the road for the last time. He couldn't believe he'd never see him again. *Forever* doesn't mean much to a boy of six. Hamish gave him a jigsaw puzzle of Edinburgh Castle to remember him by.

While he was out, the last few pieces of furniture were removed from the house and stored in a huge van. Bessie told him they'd be spending their first two nights in England in his father's lodgings so as to give the van time to arrive and be emptied.

Sam watched Bessie lock the front door of the only home he'd ever known. Uncle Archie, a friend of his parents, was waiting by his car on the pavement to take them to spend their last evening in Scotland with his own family.

At 10.30 pm, after more heartfelt goodbyes, they drove to Waverly station to catch the sleeper to London.

Climbing into his narrow bunk in their train compartment, he felt safe with Bessie, who, at that moment, was climbing a little ladder before tucking herself into her own bunk above him. He trusted her implicitly. He couldn't imagine the many changes the next few days would bring. It was the excitement of the moment that mattered, and he was confident she would make sure everything worked out right.

Sam snuggled down as the train eased itself out of Waverley, gently gathering speed as it slipped out of the city and embarked on the first lap of the four-hundred-mile journey ahead. The gentle chugging smoothed away the excitement of the day behind and thoughts of the strange new one ahead, lulling him to sleep.

* * *

'King's Cross!' a voice called.

It was strange awakening with different bedclothes around him. Where was he?

It all came back to him. The train had stopped. They'd arrived. In a different country: England!

'Wakey-wakey,' Bessie said, peeking over her bunk and down at Sam and wrapping her travelling gown around her.

He could hear an echoing sound beyond the walls of the carriage, men moving up and down the corridor, the clatter of breakfast trays and knocking on doors. Every minute or so, a voice would call 'come in' followed by a bright 'thank you' and the contented chinking of tea cups.

Now it was their turn.

Knock-knock.

'Come in.'

The attendant entered and placed their tray on a ledge. 'We've arrived, folks! It's 8.30 and you have until 9.15. Then we'll need to ask you to be on your way.'

Sam drew up a few inches of the window blind and peered out of the grimy window.

The station was bustling with life. Whistles blew. Announcements boomed over the public address system. Platform vendors touted for trade, and men in uniforms pushed trolleys piled with luggage or issued directions, while people of all ages scurried knowingly hither and thither clutching valises, newspapers and umbrellas en route for jobs in the city.

'Put that blind down, luv, I need to get dressed!' Bessie said.

Half an hour later they were out on the platform, hailing a porter and blending into the bustling sea of people.

'There's Daddy!' Bessie yelled, waving furiously at the welcoming face behind the platform railings as they followed the porter to the barrier with their cases on his trolley.

'I've a taxi waiting,' Hugh said, tipping the porter then hugging them joyfully. 'Next stop, Victoria!'

In the taxi, Hugh asked the driver to take them 'the scenic route'. Pushing his nose against the window, Sam excitedly watched as many of the places he'd seen in his picture book sped by: first Piccadilly Circus, Trafalgar Square where he waved to the admiral, The Mall, St James' Park and Buckingham Palace, with the gold and crimson Royal standard waving.

Finally, the taxi turned a corner and pulled up alongside another station forecourt.

There was breakfast in a steamy station café.

And yet another train to yet another unfamiliar place.

A new world.

A new life.

Bessie winked at Sam.

Sam blinked excitedly back.

7

Down South

1951 – 1953
Bessie & Hugh

Ninety-eight Howard Road was the last even-numbered house at the top of a hill. A six-minute stroll down to a parade of useful shops – nine trudging back with heavy shopping.

Until the arrival of the railway in the mid-1850s, Beckenham was little more than a hamlet. A large park with a lake, the home of a variety of wildlife, had been created early in the century out of an estate where a manor house had stood. It was one of the many lungs of open land in South London designated as conservation and recreation areas, some of which, during the summer months, hosted fairs and flower shows. Expanses of green broke up the network of leafy avenues of dignified Victorian Gothic or red brick period houses, alternating with drives and crescents of mock-Tudor and other less pretentious villas typical of the housing boom of the 1920s and 30s. Despite the developments of that time, the area had so far clung on to its old-world charm.

You never said 'I'm going into town.' It was always 'down to the village'.

If, as she settled in, Bessie was sometimes exasperated with the surprisingly limited lives of a few of her new neighbours for whom London, barely ten miles away, could have been Timbuktu, she quickly adapted to her new world, finding her modern home easier to manage than the one she'd left. Her sunny, spacious new kitchen, with two windows overlooking the back garden, was always pleasant to work in. It comfortably accommodated the friendly enamel table upon which she'd rolled out many miles of pastry. Either side of it sat the bentwood chairs they'd bought not long after their honeymoon and which always reminded her affectionately of her early married years. She had looked forward to cosy evenings involving informal, stove-to-table meals when there were just two of them. She no longer dreaded the long evenings when Hugh was late home, for Sam was now good company and becoming quite domesticated.

Of course, she missed being able to walk out of her front gate and turn towards the sea, but to compensate, she had responsibility for her new well-established garden now meeting her creative needs in a way the confined outdoor spaces of Forth View Road, with its salty air, had failed to do.

Guarded by an ash tree, a smart wooden gate opened onto a path of crazy paving sandwiched between handkerchief lawns bordered with evergreens leading to the brown-stained front door. The rear windows gazed across a tiered shrubbery broken up by pathways, a rockery, a vegetable patch – including the loganberry bush – and a couple of rose arches. A flat rectangular lawn, large enough to sit out on and adequate for playing simple ball games, dominated the lower level, while on a terrace to the left and separated by an arbour of rhododendrons, sat the large sheds Bessie had enthused about to Sam.

The English summer encouraged informality. Whereas in the crisper weather of East Scotland, schoolboys had been buttoned up, at Sam's new school they wore open-necked, short-sleeved Aertex shirts and, on hot days, swam naked in an inflatable sport pool at the edge of the playing field.

Middle-class Scottish women still adhered to constraining pre-war etiquette. Once when Connie was visiting, they were invited for morning coffee by a neighbour. Arriving without a hat and gloves, Connie was reprimanded for ignoring the rules.

'But it's only three houses away!' she said indignantly.

'Maybe,' her hostess retorted, 'but you're not in Manchester now. We do things properly here.'

No such foolishness was likely to trip her up in Beckenham. If Edinburgh considered the North West socially unstructured, they'd have been shocked by how seemingly laid-back South London was. Not that it couldn't be precious in its own way. Fortunately, Bessie believed in complying with the prevailing local customs and quickly adjusted to the more nuanced ways of her new home. After all, it wasn't as if she was trapped. The bustling city was only a twenty-minute ride away from the nearest station.

After a few months, however, it became apparent her son wasn't settling into his new environment as quickly as she was. 'We wanted to give Sam a good start at Stanwich, but something prevents him concentrating,' she told Connie. 'I think he's intimidated by the casualness of life here. His classmates are more world-wise than the children he's been used to. He's starting to feel self-conscious about his hands, not to mention his specs.' Despite the months in hospital, the skin condition kept returning, when 'the other boys refuse to hold hands with me.'

She discussed his lazy left eye with Hugh. They agreed to seek advice from a Harley Street specialist to find out if it was operable.

The Owens couldn't have picked a happier time to relocate. London was fully alive that summer for the first time since the crowning of George VI in 1937. For five glorious months, the Festival of Britain put austerity on hold, filling the streets with renewed energy as tourists from all over the UK and exotic representatives from the Commonwealth poured into the capital to visit the futuristic exhibitions and celebrate a new era.

On a sunny but stifling afternoon, Bessie and Sam took the bus from Victoria to Oxford Street, cutting across Cavendish Square to Harley Street.

After inspecting Sam's eye and asking Bessie a lot of questions, the specialist advised against an operation. He suggested they waited to see whether time and routinely updated spectacles would help it right itself. If it was still a problem beyond adolescence, he could always consider surgery then. At least, Bessie thought, they'd be saved the worry of that for a long while. Sam's spectacles gradually became a part of him.

His looks gave little indication of how he might develop. He'd inherited his mother's tendency to plumpness – tactfully referred to as *buxom* in her case and *well-covered* in his. Bessie admitted to herself that, but for his mop of tousled mousey hair and inquisitive green eyes, Sam might be considered a plain child. Mercifully, he'd inherited her roguish sense of humour and an ability to laugh at himself.

Wishing to dispel the heavy earnestness of the hour spent in the specialist's stuffy consulting room, Bessie decided the rest of the afternoon should be given over to fun. Grabbing Sam's hand, they made their way along Wigmore Street past Debenham & Freebody and back to join the throng of sight-seers and shoppers on Oxford Street. The exhibition itself was focussed on the South Bank, but theatres, stores and restaurants across the Thames had all taken advantage of the celebration of technology, with a visual emphasis on futuristic designs and gimmickry. They were soon staring in wonder at Selfridges' extravagant Festival-themed windows and those of other department stores.

Sam began complaining about his tired feet. Both thirsty and peckish too, Bessie guessed they couldn't be far from Marble Arch and the Cumberland Hotel where she'd once stayed with Connie on a weekend break. After some more exploring, they were soon freshening up in the Cumberland's gleaming toilets, after which they flopped into comfy armchairs in the tea lounge and flagged down a friendly waitress.

The girl returned within minutes with a pot of tea, an icy tumbler of fizzy lemonade, a plate of sandwiches and a couple of fancy Kunzel cakes on a tray. She set it down on the little table between them. Sam beamed.

Replete, they sat back and gazed in awe at the kaleidoscope of colour and movement around them: an ever-changing tableau of neatly dressed waitresses in their crisp brown and white uniforms weaving in and out of the tables, whilst handsomely groomed people of different nationalities came and went, chatting in their own tongues.

Even chic British women in their New Look suits or floral dresses and Miriam Lewis millinery couldn't compete with the dazzling robes and headdresses of visitors from exotic climes. The British men in their sober suits simply faded into the background. Bessie made a mental note to treat Hugh to some less staid casual shirts when she got the chance. They'd have to be tasteful, mark you. Hectic Caribbean fronds mightn't go down well, even at Birchington-on-Sea. She chuckled to herself. She'd have to compromise, as usual, with something stripey.

'What are you laughing at, Mummy?'

'Now, we don't want that last egg sandwich going to waste, do we?'

* * *

By autumn, the Owens had slipped into a comfortable routine. Sam moved up to the main part of the school, coming home and regaling Bessie with all he'd learnt about Julius Caesar, Boadicea, Grey Owl and the beavers and, his favourite part of the school day, the adventures of *Mumfi the Elephant*, which Miss Morrison, with a mischievous twinkle in her eye, read to the class before they prepared to go home each afternoon. Bessie understood he was finally making one or two friends and appeared more settled.

It was in June the bouts of sickness and nagging abdominal pain began.

And, as the weeks progressed, Bessie's symptoms grew worse.

She saw a doctor, Dora Perkins, a cousin of Elspeth's, and was sent to the South London Hospital for Women for an x-ray.

A few days later, a phone call advised her to return as soon as possible. 'Not only is your appendix grumbling, Mrs Owen,' the consultant said, 'but it's situated on the wrong side of your abdomen. We must get you back here and remove it.' Elspeth stepped into the breach and helped Bessie host Sam's eighth birthday party, while she battled to hide her discomfort with a feigned smile. A small bag was packed in readiness.

Only after settling into the ward did they think to tell her that the key members of the surgical team were still away on their summer break. 'As your appendix isn't getting any worse right now, we'll keep you here on bed rest and carry out additional tests,' the young doctor said. 'You'll be at the front of the queue as soon as we're ready to operate.'

It never happened.

The following week, shingle-like blisters enveloped Bessie's brain, singeing nerve endings and destroying part of the sight in one eye. 'I'm afraid your wife has caught encephalitis,' they informed Hugh.

For several months, her life hung in the balance.

* * *

October and November went by. Hugh juggled work, hospital visits and domestic commitments, dropping in to see Bessie whenever he could, using the journey home to collect himself and put on a good face for Sam.

Connie travelled down from Manchester to look after them on alternate weekends. By November, Bessie was making sufficient progress for Sam to visit her in hospital with Hugh and, on this occasion, Connie. Pale and weak as she was, with a hastily applied slash of bright red lipstick applied in their honour, Bessie managed to haul herself up into a semi-sitting position and smile brightly.

Sam bent down to be hugged.

'And what have you been up to?'

'Aunt Connie has been playing the piano for me,' he said.

'How lovely!'

'I explained to him that I learnt to play on that instrument,' Connie said, 'but how, not wishing to upset the neighbours in the flat beneath, I passed it on to you in the hopes Sam might want to learn one day.'

'He's starting lessons next year, aren't you?' Bessie said, not adding, 'if we can afford them.'

Sam nodded enthusiastically.

'My hands are getting careless from lack of practice. I'm glad of the chance to play.'

Bessie turned to Sam. 'What are your favourite pieces, luv?'

'The music from that show we saw last year,' Sam said, adding with barely a pause for breath, 'the one with the dancing cowboys.'

'*Oklahoma!*?'

He nodded. It was the first grown-up musical he'd ever seen, still on tour, which had visited a large theatre several stops away from them. 'Aunt Connie bought the sheet music specially for me.'

'You told me how much he'd loved it,' Connie said, pleased her purchase was a success.

Bessie was wondering when she'd be well enough to walk down a corridor again, let alone visit the theatre or cinema, when Sam spontaneously broke into a shrill rendition of *I'm Just a Girl Who Cain't Say No*.

Hugh grabbed his arm. 'Hush, lad! People are trying to rest.'

'Don't stop him,' a young woman at the next bed interrupted. 'It takes me back to my wedding anniversary.'

'My twenty-first birthday treat!' called out another, younger patient. Sensing Sam's awkwardness at the fuss he'd caused, Bessie smiled and asked, 'And what else has Aunt Connie been playing?'

'Ivor Novello and Billy…'

'…Mayerl,' Connie prompted. 'I throw in a few favourite Schubert and Tchaikovsky pieces for good measure, although you especially enjoyed *The Haunted Ballroom*, didn't you Sam?' Sam nodded but needed to go to the toilet. As Hugh lead him away, Connie leaned over to Bessie and added quietly, 'Sam's reaction was interesting. The waltz is in a minor key and tricky to play. I really don't do it justice anymore, but… I must tell you…' here she lowered her voice, '…when I faltered during an awkward key change, out of the corner of my eye, I caught him in mid-jeté behind the sofa!'

They roared with laughter.

'He loves dancing to music,' Bessie said. 'Any chance he gets. Even during Concert Hour – and it's not easy trying to boogie to Beethoven! I'm never quite sure whether it's an indication of an emerging love of music and dance or whether he's simply working off his childish energy.'

'Possibly both?'

Connie went on to tell her sister-in-law how she'd also introduced Sam to a few basic cookery techniques and his successful first attempt at making jam tarts. 'I think there's a budding cook there, too.' Bessie smiled. 'Can't imagine where he gets it from.'

She constantly worried about her menfolk. How were they keeping up their spirits when Connie was unable to be with them? And she had a recurring nightmare of Hugh struggling to explain to Sam she might never come home again. Whilst she stubbornly refused to accept that might happen, Bessie couldn't completely ignore the concerned looks passing between the doctors and nurses during their daily rounds. She took heart in the knowledge that despite, or possibly because of, being a sensitive child, Sam could surprise them with insightful flashes of maturity.

'I've told Sam that you're no quitter but willing your body to heal so as to rejoin us as soon you can,' Hugh reassured her. But what was really going on inside their heads?

The weeks ticked by and still Bessie hadn't been given a discharge date.

Sam immersed himself in his school work. 'We're learning all about silk worms and we were given one each to draw. I accidentally squashed mine with my elbow and got told off,' he reported. Though it didn't stop him acquiring his first – and last – *Excellent* monthly report. Bessie always credited his moment of glory with giving her the motivation to pull herself back from the brink. When, on later occasions, he disappointed her with unsatisfactory school grades, she'd chide him, if only half-jokingly, with 'the only time you were top of the class was when I was in hospital.' Then she saw how much it stung him and regretted it.

* * *

As each month passed, Hugh found it harder to cope.

He fell into debt.

He'd moved them to London with the expectation of becoming manager of his firm's London office and taking over from his current boss. The extra income would at least have covered Sam's school fees, but the tiresome man, understandably hell-bent on hanging on to his job and accumulating the best pension he could, cussedly refused to budge.

With no savings, the family was totally reliant on Hugh's salary. Never having been a borrower, he was obliged to negotiate a temporary bank loan to make ends meet. 'Sam's school fees are the main problem,' he told Connie. 'And then there's that ghastly woman's wages.'

The woman in question was Miss Hammond, whom he'd hastily engaged as a housekeeper and to look after Sam and himself when they got home in the evening. A fifty-something, *nai*cely-spoken gentlewoman down on her luck, on meeting Sam, Edna Hammond had shown little of the experience with children she'd been at pains to recall at her interview. 'As you know,' he moaned to Connie, Sam's normally a well-behaved child, but he runs rings around her.'

Always neat and tidy, with an endless wardrobe of home-knitted twin-sets in shades of coffee and beige, personal presentation was Edna's strongest suit. Sadly, even the rudiments of domesticity were a trial to her. 'The simple meals she produces swim in fat, and even rustling up a plate of tinned spaghetti on toast is an effort. Her cleaning skills are perfunctory too. We'd forgive her if she was warm and engaging, but she affects an irritating air of superiority, carrying out her other duties too with a pained expression. "I was never obliged to perform menial tasks when I was companion to Lady Cunningham," she informed me yesterday, as if I'd asked her to clear out the drains.'

Having discovered Miss Hammond's inadequacies too late, he now repented, though hardly at leisure, as he had none. Each day created a fresh challenge to put on a good front when he increasingly despaired of their lives ever getting back to the way they were. It didn't help that his job, negotiating the sale of large electrical equipment to regional electricity boards and other industrial organisations around Greater London, often involved long journeys. Unless he was accompanying a colleague in a car, he was reliant on public transport, which meant he was sometimes late home.

'Bessie's hospital stay may be funded by the NHS,' he confided in Connie, 'but there'll be Dr Perkins's fees to find on top of everything else once she gets home. God knows why she's still insisting on going privately, but Bessie has a lot of faith in the woman. Of course, she's good at her job and very reliable.'

'I was impressed the one time I met her,' Connie said. 'And though I support the NHS, I can see Bessie is going to depend on more personalised support when she leaves hospital.'

Which she did – three weeks before Christmas. She should have remained under medical supervision, but it was the view of her physician that, given her strong personality, she might recuperate more quickly at home.

* * *

Two days after she got home, the smog descended.

For seven days and nights, a sulphurous soup swirled for miles around London, turning every street and byway into a clammy, twilit world and making it impossible to look further than next door's garden. The putrid air insinuated itself through gaps in the doors and window frames of the villas in Howard Road, grubbily misting up glass and discolouring drapes, bedspreads and any painted surface in its path with a fine layer of grime.

Healthy people like Hugh and Sam coped and survived, but many vulnerable and elderly people weren't so lucky. Hardly the *welcome home* Bessie had looked forward to, nor a promising start to a lengthy convalescence. Still very frail, she nestled beneath the blankets, regularly sipping water or *Lucozade*, listening to the radio and dozily fretting away the time until Sam and Hugh were safely indoors again.

London sighed with relief as the grey-green haze finally lifted, replacing the depressing autumn with a chilly but manageable winter. Christmas beckoned and then Coronation Year, with its promise of pageantry, celebration and, like the Festival of Britain, the opportunity for everyone to take pride in their national identity and the expectation of renewed prosperity.

An indication of easier times ahead appeared with the cheering announcement that sweets were to be derationed in February.

Bessie quickly assessed the difficulties that had beset them all due to her illness, with a guilty awareness of how even partial recuperation would take some months. Also, given their financial plight, she knew economies had to be made.

How could she help?

For a start, Miss Hammond, to whom she'd taken an immediate dislike, had to go. She could see that, for the time being, Hugh and Sam needed extra help. Nevertheless, weak as she was, she decided they could make a start by reducing the woman's hours and whittle them down slowly, by which time Sam would be able to take over more chores. Building on Connie's work and his natural instinct for anything domestic, she continued to groom him in elementary home management, including how to make a pot of tea and take it up to her on a neatly arranged tray complete with embroidered cloth, crockery and biscuits. Each afternoon when he arrived home from school, he'd bring it up to her, and, sipping together in silence, they'd listen to *Mrs Dale's Diary* and chat for a while. Only when he'd washed up, changed his clothes and begun his homework was Miss Hammond re-scheduled to appear and prepare an evening meal – but now according to Bessie's testing specifications.

As Bessie had calculated, the new regime broke her spirit. Within weeks, the good spinster had given notice and, or so she said, found a better position. Her absence brought respite in many ways, though Hugh constantly feared Bessie might over-tax herself. In fact, it was the making of her. Despite the doctor's strict orders that she should keep to her bed for much of the day, always her own person, Bessie found sufficient energy to spend long enough downstairs to supervise supper and ensure Hugh and Sam were properly fed. Over the following months, her strength gradually returned, if not to its old level at least enough to make her feel she was fully in charge once more. She still arose late but gradually extended her fully-dressed hours, resting every afternoon and returning to bed after the *Nine O'clock News*.

Her first job on a Monday morning was to draw up a list of dairy requirements for Sam to stuff into an empty milk bottle on the front doorstep before leaving for school. Most other local tradespeople delivered to homes as well. From the telephone on her bedside table, she liaised with the grocer, greengrocer, butcher and, when necessary, the coal merchant. By now she'd got to know the local tradespeople and enjoyed her growing interaction with them and the outside world.

In his capacity as assistant housekeeper, Sam moved on from setting trays and washing up to the more exacting etiquette of formal table-laying and preparing vegetables. In due course came dusting, whisking the Ewbank and Hoover over the carpets and polishing the silver and brass. It was, therefore, no surprise when he arrived home in his Cub's uniform with a Housekeeping badge, which she helped him sew on his green jumper himself.

If there was an element of *déjà vu* in all this, Bessie made sure Sam's domestic tasks didn't interfere with his schoolwork and other interests, trusting her maternal instinct to make him feel he was making a useful contribution to home life and helping her get back to normal.

Always creative with her housekeeping allowance, Bessie eventually found she could afford some help again. This time, a local woman to come two mornings a week and assist with the weekly wash and deeper cleaning. Her personnel skills were more thorough than her husband's, and Rosie Flagg proved a good choice. A chirpy woman in her mid-thirties, with two daughters around Sam's age, Rosie's husband had been invalided out of the war and was unable to earn a living. Her unforced brightness brought cheer as well as cleanliness to the house. Rosie became indispensable, although her chores were always completed more efficiently during term time when Sam – who'd found a new ally and lover of musicals – wasn't around to intrude into her vacuuming time with discussions on the merits of the current Hollywood fantasy at The Regal, when he was always in danger of breaking into impressions of Jane Powell or Ann Miller.

It was perhaps unsurprising that, along with most people, especially children who were bombarded at school and in magazines with information about British historic triumphs, pomp, ceremony and the Royal Family, Sam became obsessed by the main event of the current year.

'He can't wait to get home and rush off to play Coronations with the Penwarden girls at eighty-seven,' Bessie reported to Connie. 'I fear he's the instigator. They allow him to boss them about and do exactly what he suggests. Poor Deirdre and Benita are coerced into taking it in turns to doll up. They wear one of my old bedroom curtains for a train, with a paper crown, two wooden cooking spoons and a tennis ball for orb and sceptres, and process around the garden as Queen and Lady-in-Waiting, while His Nibs follows on behind, singing the national anthem and generally stage managing. It's driving me mad! I can't wait for June 2nd to be over and done with.

Sam's obsession with dressing up and playing families worried Hugh. 'Isn't it a bit inappropriate?" he asked Bessie. 'Can't he find some proper friends in the road? Preferably boys his own age?'

'There aren't any nearby,' she reminded him. 'At least he's mixing with other children and enjoying himself. We have to face it: that's the way he is.' She wasn't quite sure what she meant by that, but Hugh nodded knowingly.

Connie would always put in a good word for her nephew. 'You may be right, Bessie. Not all boys need to be always scoring goals and getting their knees dirty.'

But Bessie was anxious about Sam on other counts, too. One of the things that particularly bothered her was the tiring five-mile journey he made twice a day to and from school by bus, train and on foot. During his first year at the school, the mothers of the pupils living in the same area had agreed on a rota, taking it in turns to chaperone the boys as far as their own railway stations. Increasingly, as he grew older and was involved in out-of-school activities, Sam travelled under his own steam and was sometimes waylaid by bullies.

From the tearful tales he regaled her with when he arrived home, she was gathered that he was never going to be very popular with many of his contemporaries. That didn't augur well for the future. She could see how, while adults found Sam's quaint Scottish civility endearing, his contemporaries might find it irritating.

8

Moving Up

1955-1956
Bessie

A shiny blue Vauxhall Wyvern sat on the drive.

Mr Grayson had finally vacated his office in Victoria Street and handed it over to Hugh. The car transformed their lives. A good driver, Hugh was never happier than sitting behind the wheel. Which was just as well, given it was primarily intended for work. Nonetheless, the Owens thought of the vehicle almost as 'one of the family', coming to rely on it for weekend jaunts into the countryside, holidays at the coast and, above all, at least as far as Sam was concerned, trips to the nearest theatre.

Now his own boss, it was Hugh's responsibility to woo, nurture and later thank his top clients in a style that encouraged repeat business. Camaraderie oiled the wheels of commerce. With rationing, finally, a thing of the past, a healthier economy was emerging. Corporate entertaining boosted the profits of manufacturing companies such as his own with a knock-on effect for London's hotels, restaurants, nightclubs and sporting arenas.

His private secretary maintained a diary crowded with appointments including after-work socialising, which frequently involved smart industry-related dinners and balls at Grosvenor House, the best seats at Drury Lane and much *haute cuisine*.

By now, Bessie's energy level had improved sufficiently for her to join Hugh in town some evenings to help him entertain his customers, especially diverting their wives when the moment came for the men to talk shop. It wasn't unusual, if a couple was affable and outgoing as they were, for them to become personal friends.

Socialising with people of all types and ages came easily to Bessie. Naturally gregarious and having learnt from her father how business could be successfully mixed with pleasure, she handled her role with enthusiasm. It was unusual for her not to discover points of mutual interest with people. She bonded easily with both men, who recognised the good sport in her, and women who, like herself, were usually middle-class housewives returning to humdrum domestic duties the moment the glad rags went back on the rail.

Having a growing family, Rosie was grateful for the extra pocket money she earned keeping Sam company on the long evenings Bessie and Hugh were out. Less happily for everyone concerned, during the summer months when his parents were obliged to attend conferences at well-known coastal resorts, Sam was farmed out for the odd week to stay with the families of boys from Stanwich whose mothers Bessie had befriended. She was only too aware that, while the adults had become good friends, the boys only tolerated each other. Those weeks were always an endurance test for them both. Much as Bessie kept telling herself it was good for Sam to be freed from her apron strings once in a while, that such short breaks encouraged him to stand on his own feet, it wasn't always easy telling herself she must put Hugh's interests first.

Like all other parents, Bessie and Hugh knew Sam's transition from childhood to adolescence would change the parent-son dynamic. She wanted to retain their strong bond while recognising his right to be true to himself but wished he was better equipped to defend himself against the slings and arrows of adult life.

By shelling out on a course of boxing lessons, she hoped the self-preservation techniques he might acquire from them would be useful when he was set upon by other boys. Alas. 'You're wasting your money,' the coach advised her as she collected him at the end of his first session.

'I don't like fighting,' Sam explained on the way home. 'I think I'm a pacifist.'

It also bothered her that the image she and Hugh created outside the home as an affluent couple was something of a façade. While work-related costs came out of Hugh's generous expenses allowance, everything else had to be paid for with his salary. Living on a peppercorn rent in a house owned by the firm with the use of a car was part of that, his income for all other outgoings being adjusted accordingly. A major expense, such as an annual holiday, could still wreak havoc with the household accounts. Bessie wasn't ashamed of her home, but while she kept it comfortable and spotlessly clean, she often wondered whether first-time visitors with a mistaken idea of their lifestyle were taken aback by the threadbare patches in the carpets and faded curtains.

Much as Bessie enjoyed socialising, it upset her to be handed 'expenses' for a new cocktail dress knowing Sam badly needed a new pair of walking shoes. She felt uncomfortable driving off a few days later, glammed-up in a chauffeur-driven car, for a few hour's hobnobbing in Park Lane, having that morning handed in his down-at-heel lace-ups for one last fix at the cobbler's.

They were living parallel lives. For each life a different standard.

More and more, she found her loyalties divided. She watched Hugh embracing his new job with relish and a sense of entitlement, with growing concern. He seemed to be losing patience with the simpler lifestyle they maintained at home. Not that she was unhappy. He was doing what he loved and did best, which was the main thing, but the disparity between *work* and *play* could cause tensions when one became the other and vice-versa.

Hugh was now only tolerating rather than enjoying the company of less sophisticated friends. On evenings when he wasn't socialising with clients or colleagues, he'd be attending self-improvement classes in Public Speaking or preparing himself for his Advanced Motorist exam. He'd recently been nominated to become a Mason, which took up another night. Often, an hour's chat before bed was Bessie's only time with him, having spent the rest of the day by herself and, when he wasn't at school, with Sam.

Their triangular setup with herself at the apex, caught between her soulmate and breadwinner and their son, wasn't always comfortable. Her two best friends deserved her attention equally: the man she'd waited so long to marry and respected for his integrity and conscientiousness, and the progressively more non-conformist, somewhat effeminate son whose arrival had involved so much worry and hassle.

She never seriously worried about the strength of her marriage, having no reason to suspect Hugh of infidelity. How could she? He was always too busy. Collaborating regularly with him as she did, she'd surely have noticed if anything was amiss. Weeks at a time went by and she wouldn't see him much before ten o'clock when he would appear with a cast-iron alibi.

His mistress was his work.

Thrown together so much with Sam for company, the two of them spent many evenings enjoying wide-ranging discussions on current events. It gave Bessie the opportunity to air her firm views on everything from Princess Margaret's affair with Group Captain Peter Townsend – where, admittedly, she tried to see both sides – to the hanging of Ruth Ellis, for what she considered a *crime passionnel* and not cold-blooded murder. She also entertained him with stories of her eccentric family which, not having brothers or sisters himself, intrigued him.

When the three of them were together, she increasingly acted as an intermediary between father and son. Thus, if Sam wanted to go on a school outing, the cost of which could only be within his father's gift, she'd prepare the ground and prompt him to take it from there. Likewise, with matters she was unwilling or felt ill-equipped to discuss.

Late one afternoon with the fire crackling in the grate, they were chatting about local matters when, unthinkingly, she mentioned the arrival of a neighbour's new baby, forgetting Sam was now ten and, though young in some ways for his age, was at the point in his development when he might ask awkward questions.

'Mum?'

'Yes?'

'I've never really understood.'

'About what?'

'Babies. I mean, why is it only married women are meant to have them?'

Unusually at a loss for words, after thinking about it, Bessie said lamely, 'Because marriage is a sacrament.'

'Sorry, I don't under….'

'Men and women get married when they love each other very much,' she hurried on, 'and want God to recognise it. It very often leads to having a family.'

She could see Sam found words like *sacrament* and *love* somewhat abstract.

'Yes, I know that bit, but *how* does that happen?'

'They want to be very close to each other, and…'

'Yes?'

'The man passes his seeds to the woman to fertilise her egg.'

'Egg?' He looked puzzled. 'Like a hen's?'

'Sort of, but that's a slightly different kind of egg.'

If Sam looked confused about eggs, *seeds* completely flawed him. 'I always think of seeds as tiny dry things in paper envelopes with pictures of candytuft and sweet alyssum,' he said with a frown.

'N… no. Not quite like that either.'

'So, what does the man's seed look like… where does he get it and how does he pass them to her?'

'Ah,' Bessie said. She was now well beyond her comfort zone.

'And, you still haven't explained about unmarried people. Aunt Connie has a friend whose daughter had a baby and *she* didn't get married until after she'd had it.'

'No, and I didn't approve of that at all. As you know.'

'Didn't they want God to recognise them, then?'

'Well, it's… difficult.' Bessie, who usually felt safer discussing theological rather than biological issues, felt the ground opening up beneath her. 'Sorry, I've told you as much as I can. You'll have a better idea how these things work when your body changes. In the meantime, you'd better ask your father anything else.'

'But you know he's not easy to talk to about things like that,' Sam persisted. 'He always says, "Ask your mother."'

'I'm sure he'll tell you when you're ready.'

'I'm not a casserole,' he said somewhat disgruntled.

Bessie knew she was taking the coward's way out and was tempted to justify herself with 'but that bit's *his* job'. Instead, she got up, murmured, 'Gosh, is that the time? I really must find my chip pan,' and disappeared into the kitchen, leaving Sam looking confused.

Bessie instructed Hugh to take Sam on one side about the issue. 'It's not going to go away,' she said. But he kept procrastinating, telling her he was waiting for the right moment.

By chance, the issue arose quite unexpectedly some weeks later when he was lunching with his colleague, Bob, in The Albert.

Later that evening, when Sam was in bed, he recounted the conversation. '"And how are your lads?" I asked him.

'"Charlie's not long started at prep school," Bob said, "but Dan had his eleventh birthday last week and is asserting his independence. There have been a few words recently."

'"Going biking with his friends and not saying where he's going or where he's been?" I asked.

'"Things like that. He's fixated on a couple of girls in the choir. First stirrings in that department."

'"Tricky age, isn't it?" I said, and told him Sam was starting to ask awkward questions we weren't sure how to deal with. He agreed and explained how he'd dealt with the matter.'

'How?'

'Stumbled across a copy of a book called *Grow Up & Live*, apparently.'

'Ah. I remember noting the review a while back and thinking it might be useful one day,' Bessie said. 'The author's a doctor and a bit controversial but writes clearly and sympathetically about adolescent problems. What did he do then?'

'Left it casually lying around where it soon vanished for a few days. Problem solved!'

'And so…?' Bessie wanted to know.

'On my way home, I popped into a *WH Smiths* and…' Hugh produced a blue Pelican paperback in a brown paper bag from his briefcase, '… Ta-ra!'

She gave him an enigmatic smile.

The perfect cop-out.

* * *

On their nights alone, Bessie helped Sam with his homework before supper, after which they'd listen to *Educating Archie* or, their favourite, Vic Oliver's *Variety Playhouse*.

When Hugh eventually arrived home, he wanted Bessie to himself to unload his work worries as, earlier, Sam had with his ups and downs at school. He respected his wife's opinions and suggestions for dealing with awkward situations. While she got on well with his secretary, members of his team and many of his business associates, being apart from his office life lent her objectivity to any dilemma.

Such problems often concerned the rival ambitions of other regional managers. One, in particular, would score points with the firm's directors by passing off as his own, negotiations that Hugh had slaved over independently for weeks and brought to a successful conclusion. The man would slyly arrange to accompany him to the clincher meeting and, the minute the deal was concluded, slip out of the room mumbling 'must see a man about a dog' to make the all-important call to Head Office. Such underhand behaviour was alien to Hugh, who was too open and honest for his own good. Certainly Bessie, who'd spent many years coping with the exploitative natures of her family, thought so. When Hugh clenched his fists and said, 'I'd like to beat the living daylights out of him,' she'd agree wholeheartedly while massaging his ego and assuring him his moment of glory would come.

On the nights he arrived home in time for supper, Hugh poured Bessie a sherry and a stiff gin and tonic for himself: Sam's unspoken cue to go and play in another room. He always knew when to take a backseat and hand her over to his father. Being a law-abiding, well-behaved child probably contributed to his having such a hard time at school. She'd been a mischief-maker herself as a girl and, in certain moods, could still reveal a devil-may-care streak. A gene she had neglected to pass on to her son.

Scenes would occur when Sam was tired or tense. He had much of Hugh's ability to focus intensely on things that mattered to him, which made him elated when they went well but depressed when they didn't. But while Sam tended to get his anger noisily out of his system as quickly as possible – often to the surprise of anyone in his line of fire – Hugh tended to suppress his feelings, allowing them to simmer, sour and erupt when least expected.

One particular Saturday lunchtime, Sam arrived home from school weary after a long morning aggravated by a train cancellation. As soon as he'd washed his hands and sat down to lunch hoping for something appetising, a grilled pork chop was placed in front of him. Thin slices of roasted pork with plenty of crackling, crispy-topped stuffing and roast potatoes was one thing, but as soon as he tried piercing the tough, pale meat on its implacable bone, Bessie could see he had no appetite for it. He grimaced and, after making a reasonable attempt to eat some boiled potatoes and cabbage drowned in gravy, pushed the rest to one side, put down his knife and fork and sat back.

'No pudding for you, then,' Hugh said.

Sam folded his arms. 'I'm sorry, but I don't like it.'

'Meat is very expensive. Many less fortunate lads would be grateful for the good food your mother provides.'

Bessie winced at this ruse to drag her into the argument. Left to herself, she'd probably have discussed the matter calmly with Sam. He wasn't usually a fussy eater and only refused food if he really couldn't force it down. 'Hugh, couldn't you manage Sam's chop so it won't be wasted?'

But Hugh wasn't letting the matter drop that easily. Bessie knew it had been a difficult week for him. To crown it, earlier that morning an essential component of the lawn mower had gone missing and it no longer worked properly. He'd complained about the need to fork out for a new one just as the deposit on their summer holiday in Bognor was due. Unfortunately, he wasn't blessed with her patience. Faced with what he'd regard as Sam's mulishness, she guessed he would want to show him who was boss.

'You've got to learn to eat what you're given. We're both enjoying it. So can you,' he growled.

His tone obviously upset Sam.

The atmosphere grew heavier by the minute, as did the despised chop which became more leaden and less appetising the cooler it got.

When Sam was born, they'd agreed always to support any disciplinary action the other took. It wasn't always easy for Bessie, who could read both of them. If only one of them could find a way of graciously backing down: Sam by compromising and eating a couple more mouthfuls, Hugh by limiting his annoyance to mere sulking. She feared that wasn't going to happen.

High Noon.

She was more accustomed to Sam's often short-lived anxiety attacks. He was rarely volatile for long when he was with her, but his father's impatience could invoke a stubborn streak. As usual, when it became a contest of wills between the two males and she was caught in the middle, she found herself silently sympathising with Sam while knowing she must back Hugh.

'I *insist* you eat it,' Hugh said, slamming down his knife and fork and wiping his mouth with a napkin.

'I *won't!*'

'Then it's going into the fridge to be brought out every mealtime until it's gone.' He indicated the plate. 'Bessie!'

She dutifully picked it up, watching Sam growing distraught as his intransigence continued to fuel Hugh's wrath. When she arose to replenish the gravy boat in the kitchen, Sam, now close to tears, followed her while Hugh, his face red and fierce, jumped to his feet.

Flashpoint. 'Go to your room!'

'*No!*'

That was it. Hugh completely lost it, moved around the table and clipped Sam over the head.

'I *hate* you!' Sam yelled, rushing out of the room, up the stairs and into his bedroom, slamming the door behind him.

Bessie saw that, while Hugh regarded an occasional show of strength to be his parental duty, for Sam it was an extension of the coercive behaviour he endured from his tormenters at school. The difference was that there he had the moral high ground when he attempted to hit back. At home, when his father triumphed, even if he was simply sticking up for himself, it was regarded as insubordination.

There was always the same immediate winner. But, although Hugh would never admit it, two ultimate losers.

It was at times like this Bessie wished they could have provided Sam with a younger sister who might have taken his side or at least comforted him when he retired to his room to lick his wounds. Two to one was rarely fair.

She hated watching Hugh hurt Sam both emotionally and physically. He didn't deserve it. Admittedly, violence in the home arose from momentary anger and was never premeditated, yet Bessie saw how Hugh's occasional moments of fury both terrified and alienated their son. He'd win the battle but lose the war. More crucially, some of his son's respect for him.

Such occurrences created an unpleasant atmosphere that lingered for hours, whoever had, or had not, been to blame. Even when Sam was strictly in the right, he could never see when he was winning and undermined his case by losing self-control. She grew exhausted trying to keep the peace. It was like being back umpiring slanging matches between Flo, Roy and their father back in Chorlton.

She was also aware that Hugh was sometimes uncomfortable with the strong bond between Sam and herself. It was a pity. Neither had any need to feel threatened. In Hugh's case, his insecurity only created unnecessary friction when both of them fought for her attention.

* * *

As Sam attended school on Saturday mornings, he was allowed Wednesday afternoons off. Whenever there was a good film to see, even on stifling July afternoons, Bessie and Sam flopped excitedly into The Regal's tip-up seats.

Once in the darkness, they'd sit with mounting anticipation through the obligatory newsreels, trailers and supporting Edgar Lustgarten thriller until the British Board of Censors' black-and-white certificate appeared and, with a roar, the brash overture struck up and the latest Hollywood extravaganza exploded in vivid technicolour onto an increasingly widening screen.

While Bessie herself always enjoyed most forms of entertainment, she found it fascinating to turn and watch Sam swept up by the cleverly choreographed production numbers. His ability to leave the cinema humming tunes and quoting dialogue he'd heard for the first time that afternoon intrigued but baffled her. Where had it come from, this fascination with the performers and performing? Not from either side of the family, apart from Connie, who relished a wide range of cultural activities. Her own people always saw such entertainment as an occasional escapist diversion. Sam was becoming chronically infected by it and taking it, she feared, too seriously.

Interestingly, his obsession with films and shows spilled over to an interest in everyday clothes – both his own and hers. He delighted in any opportunity not so much to dress up for the sake of it but so as to become someone else. Was he unhappy with who he was? On the other hand, whenever he asked if he could borrow an old frock, she soon learnt it wasn't because he enjoyed wearing women's clothes *per se*, which might have been worrying, but whether he was playing the Swineherd or the Princess, getting the costume right was what really mattered.

This fixation with clothes applied to what she wore, too, especially for her role as the London Manager's wife. Once when they were out casually window shopping for a new evening dress for her, he spotted a stunning copy of a Dior with its pinched waist and full organza skirt.

'You'd look lovely in that!' he said.

'Princess Margaret might, you mean,' she retorted. 'With my figure, I need something straighter and looser.' She watched his face fall but saw from his thoughtful expression that he could see she knew best what suited her.

Each spring holiday from then on, Bessie waved Sam off at either St Pancras or Euston to stay with Connie, ensuring he was in a compartment with at least one sensible-looking woman. Returning home after a week of plays, films and visits to museums and old buildings, he'd return bubbling over with what he'd seen and learnt. Bessie was impressed by the extent to which the trips always enhanced his knowledge of social history, literature and art.

From now on, whenever Sam visited Manchester, she notified Flo and Roy and he would always spend the Saturday or Sunday with them. She argued to herself that, as his godfather, Sam had a duty to stay in touch with his uncle, and vice versa. He became her ambassador. To give them their due, he always appeared to have been looked after well and suitably spoilt, always returning with pocket money Roy had pressed into his hand as they said goodbye at the bus stop. One time, they had even taken him for a jolly afternoon at the fairground. He admitted that only the stories Bessie had regularly recounted about her younger days put him on his guard and prevented him from being totally charmed by them. If the passing years did little to dimmish the dull ache of disappointment inside her that things between the three of them would never be as they once were, maintaining contact with them in this way eased the burden. She could never reproach herself for not doing 'the right thing'.

* * *

As an only child, it was more or less inevitable Sam would be self-resourceful. He was never happier than when surrounded by card, poster paints and paper scraps of people in period dress: anything that could be strengthened by card, then attached to wires to become dramatis personae for the Pollocks toy theatre he'd inherited from a friend. The readymade *penny plain, tuppence coloured* sets that came with it had been immediately discarded. He preferred to create his own and spent hours writing and producing original stories, illuminating the stage with bicycle lamps.

Sometimes, he'd invite a friend for the afternoon, recruiting them to participate in a concert or improvised play, for which Bessie and a long-suffering neighbour would provide the press-ganged audience. She never ceased to wonder why, when he was often the underdog in the classroom, his friends at home willingly allowed him to draw them into his world of make-believe.

Occasionally, like Hugh, Bessie opened her heart to Connie. 'If only he'd use his powers of persuasion to win over more of the boys who make fun of him at school. Are they jealous of his take on life, or is it because they simply don't understand him?'

'If you want my opinion...?' She steeled herself for her sister-in-law's carefully considered comments as, having spent her professional life in education, her views were usually sound. '...I think he's probably going to find life difficult until he grows up. Other young people are happiest following the herd. They're too busy trying to be accepted by their group and suspicious of anyone who doesn't meet their received norms, unable to appreciate everyone is unique in their own way. It's not that Sam doesn't want to be liked, but he relates to the world on his own terms, whatever the cost.'

'It's the terms I worry about,' Bessie said. 'I had to give him one of my little talks the other day. "Sam," I said, "these little shows you put on for us. I'm not sure it gives the right impression, you wearing my old cocktail dress clutching a photo of Howard Keel and singing *My Secret Love*."'

'But, as you know, he doesn't see it that way,' said Connie, who had her own angle on gender issues. 'For him, it's simply a song with a good tune he enjoys performing.'

'Maybe. But I can't imagine what Mrs Penwarden thought. I could see it wasn't going down too well.'

'That's what he told me. He said he was pretending to be Doris Day and was disappointed when she'd looked somewhat embarrassed.'

'What did you say next?'

'Something along the lines of, "Next time, how about, well... pretending to be Howard Keel holding a picture of Doris Day?" He's a great fan of hers and took my point. Although Doris can be quite tomboyish.'

Bessie looked confused.

9

Pulling the Strings

1957
Hugh & Sam

Hugh was concerned.

On a personal level, he was disappointed Sam showed little interest in the things that mattered a lot to himself. The car, for instance, which his son seemed to appreciate solely as a means of transportation. Nor could he understand why he always left the living room whenever Bessie and he settled down on Saturday afternoon to listen to the sports programmes. Most boys were fascinated by soccer, cricket and tennis. He got irritated when Sam put on silly voices and struck poses, telling him to 'stop being so affected.'

With a parent's natural aspirations for the boy's future and, in what he believed were his best interests, he saw it as his role to influence Sam's aspirational choices until he was old enough to take full responsibility for them himself. But when exactly was *old enough*? Sam's personality, often disappointingly immature for his age, could also reveal flashes of sophistication and precocity when least expected.

He couldn't understand how such an inquisitive lad only muddled along at school. It was as if his brain bypassed anything he couldn't usefully apply to an area of his life he cared about. Sam excelled in *soft* subjects. He was good at Reading, Composition and Painting and had poems published in the school magazine. Once, he even won the school's annual Nature Study prize. Unfortunately, they would be of limited use to him as he moved onwards when acceptable grades in another language and, above all, a proficiency in Maths would be expected.

A lot of Hugh's hard-earned salary was invested in Sam's education. Bessie and he wished, as far as possible, to equip him for life in a world seemingly hell-bent on self-destruction. Everyone trusted the worst wouldn't happen for a long time, if ever, yet there was a new fatalism in the air. The so-called nuclear 'deterrent' raised the spectre of terrors far, far worse than anything the Nazis had achieved. Sam would require ways to stay sane in the precarious years ahead. Good qualifications might not protect him from international violence but could at least provide tools for reasoning with and help make the most of the time he was given.

Left to themselves, Hugh and Sam, despite their different personalities, got along well enough, especially when they were on holiday when they'd enjoy strolls together along the beach or gather blackberries in the country lanes. Relaxed and carefree, they'd get to know each other better, discuss the world at large and often discover more in common than they'd assumed.

Both were voracious readers. Hugh had always loved books: for their own sake and to lubricate conversation in both social and semi-business situations. Apart from a little tennis and swimming, since his youth he'd never had much time for recreative pursuits, but there were often quiet moments during the evening and at the weekend when he could pick up a paperback. He'd taken full advantage of the growing range of Penguins to acquire an eclectic library.

He was pleased to note how, in bed, either with a torch long after his official *lights out* time, or when he woke up early in the morning, Sam generally had his nose in a book. After moving on from Enid Blyton, unaccounted gaps began to appear in the book case and he'd catch him curled up in an armchair lost in his copy of *Pygmalion* or *A Murder Is Announced*. If the first provided an opportunity to discuss Shaw's take on early-twentieth-century socialism, the second enabled them to share observations of plot devices in detective fiction. When a gap appeared in the slot where *Grow Up and Live*

100

had been strategically positioned, it was Bessie who found the errant book under Sam's bed and wisely ignored the discovery.

Like his sister, in his own way, Hugh enjoyed seeing the pleasure Bessie and Sam derived from their trips to the theatre but, while he admired the artistry involved, could never envisage it as a career choice for anyone. Thus, as Sam's obsession with all things theatrical grew unabated, he fretted about whether it was putting unhelpful ideas in his head and holding back other aspects of his development.

The Owens' one connection with that ephemeral world arose when, by chance, they met a couple of actors on holiday at Bognor who subsequently became good friends.

Desmond and Joan told them how they'd begun married life in a studio flat above a pharmacy in a grubby little street off Tottenham Court Road, surviving on handouts from their parents – when unable to get roles or secure temporary work as demonstrators in Selfridges' basement. Things changed as Des graduated to being the go-to actor for bumbling solicitors and curates in TV plays and tours of popular thrillers. A spate of character roles in serialised Victorian novels had finally made him a household name. While the upward incline of their fortunes, and yet more help from his father, allowed them to progress to their own small semi in Surbiton, they still mined comedy from tales of leaner times, often on the dole, in claustrophobic conditions, frustrated by having to bring up their first son on a diet of cheap carbs and hope.

Hugh was shocked to discover quite how precarious theatrical life was. Even now, and despite having good agents, Des and Joan rarely knew where the next job was coming from. A lucrative tour or film role often meant one of them being away from home for weeks on end. They aimed to take work opportunities ensuring there was always someone at home to look after their, by now, two boys. When they were both working, a large percentage of their wages went on childminders, which, as they were the first to admit, wasn't ideal.

Whilst coming across as a respectable, home-loving couple with similar family standards and concerns to themselves, however companionable and entertaining Des and Joan were, their professional world was difficult for Hugh to relate to. Their chatter reflected the Sunday papers' fascination for impropriety, even amongst the most respected stars – not to mention the prevalence of sexual perversion which, though strictly illegal, seemed endemic and, for the most part, cheerfully indulged within some circles. He knew Bessie accepted people she instinctively liked and ignored aspects of their lives she didn't want to think about. While he didn't consider himself narrow-minded, he struggled to come to terms with behaviour from so-called *artistes* who disregarded normal codes of behaviour. Nevertheless, there was nothing, how could he put it, dubious, about Des – apart from his being somewhat larger than life. Was there?

At any rate, it wasn't the sort of higgledy-piggledy life he envisaged for Sam, who was at his happiest when he felt secure. Admittedly, the lad was still young, but he'd need to change a great deal over the coming years to survive in such an unstable, cut-throat environment.

Hugh couldn't see that happening.

* * *

By now, Sam was the leading light of his school's Puppet Club. He arrived home one day, his eyes shining, and announced: 'Hancock's father has invited us to put on a show for local children one lunchtime during the Christmas holiday.'

'That's exciting,' Bessie said delightedly. 'Isn't he the man that works at the V&A where you visited their marionette collection once?'

'Yes. Apparently, they have a vast lecture theatre, and they're going to arrange for our stage and everything to be taken there.'

Hugh's reaction was more measured. 'Don't get too excited about it. You know how you get worked up.'

The Club had been started some years previously by one of the teachers who was a speech trainer. She used marionettes as psychotherapy for boys with speaking difficulties. Her work had attracted the interest of another teacher who saw its performance potential as a way of fostering the creative and dramatic gifts of other pupils, too. Run mainly in lunch hours, the Club provided long-term projects for those with handcraft skills and/or an aptitude for acting. Only their voices were heard, the puppets being manipulated by other boys on a bridge above the stage. Given the enthusiasm the shows generated amongst members, one skill usually encouraged another.

Such was the high standard of the work produced that the school's puppetry work had gained national recognition.

A new play was selected every year and each boy tasked with making a specific puppet character. This year's play was a version of *Snow White*. Measuring, sawing, chiselling pieces of wood and assembling the puppet's body with interlocking screw-eyes to enable movement was not Sam's strongest suit. Nevertheless, he always managed to make an acceptable doll, moulding the necessary papier mâché head and giving it painted clay-moulded features and false hair. Costuming the diminutive performers fell to the boys' mothers. Bessie was fazed by the thought of tackling the detailed needlework required and usually delegated the task to Connie.

The performances were first given to the school and on subsequent afternoons to parents and friends on a well-built miniature stage erected in the school hall with handsome backcloths designed by the Art teacher. The boys on the bridge above gave each puppet life using a wooden cross-shaped control to which the ends of the strings attached to its arms, legs, back and head were connected.

Having done his duty on the practical side, Sam came into his own once rehearsals began, providing the voices of – for this year's presentation – the Witch whom Wicked Stepmother visited for advice on how to poison Snow White, and the brave Prince whose kiss finally returned her to life.

Unfortunately, the date chosen for the performance, early in January, was not a good one for Hugh. 'I'm sorry, son, but I've an important business engagement in Slough that day. You know we always try to support you whenever we can.'

Sam was disappointed, but hopefully his mother would make it. Then, when the all-important morning dawned, she awoke with a migraine and had to take one of her special pills and stay home in bed to fight it off.

Sam tried to be philosophical. He was getting used to doing things on his own. Fortunately, as soon as he arrived at the Museum on Cromwell Road, he was caught up with his responsibilities and the heady, if nerve-wracking, anticipation of putting on a show.

If Hugh had been ignorant, or chosen to ignore the significance of the occasion, he was chastened later that day when his *Evening Standard* fell open at a photograph of happy East End kids meeting the puppets after the performance, headlined:

MAKING FRIENDS WITH SEVEN DWARFS.

* * *

A week or two later, he made an appointment to see Mr Randolph, Sam's Headmaster. They had met before, of course, but not for some time.

Hugh arrived at the sturdy, polished study door slightly apprehensive and feeling he was a schoolboy again. 'It's an important year for the boy,' he began, accepting a cup of tea from a pretty young woman in a smart blue twinset who smiled at him reassuringly. He reciprocated.

'An absolute gem, Moira,' the Headmaster said, catching Hugh's eye knowingly as she left the room. He drew his chair into his desk and seized a pair of spectacles to run his eyes over the first two pages of the file on his blotter. 'I don't know what I'd do without her.' Having established a degree of intimacy as men of the world to put his visitor at his ease, he changed his tone. 'Now, you're absolutely right to be concerned about Sam. All years are important, of course, but especially this, as he approaches his teens and moves on to higher things… which he'll be doing in…' he flicked back through the pages, '…eight months' time.'

'His poor grades are a matter of concern for his mother and me,' Hugh said, carefully setting down his cup on the edge of the desk.

'And his chances of getting into the school you've got his name down for?'

'Yes.'

'Well, we've always known Sam has an aversion to numbers, and any language but his own – as you know – is not is his strongest suit. Still, there are some months to go. He could surprise us yet.'

If the head was privately concerned about Sam's progress, he sounded upbeat. 'He's doing well in English and Art, however, so, no problems there...'

'We've gathered.'

'...but yes, he struggles with... some other subjects.' Hugh made as if to speak but Mr Randolph forestalled him with a slight gesture. 'He's not a dunce by any means. Just can't concentrate on anything he doesn't see a use for.' He picked up a sheet of paper from the file. 'His form mistress says: *Sam's a dreamer with a low boredom threshold. Too many rules – mathematical and grammatical – daunt him and constrain his imagination. Sometimes, he's in simply too much of a hurry.* Here, Mr Randolph peered over the top of his glasses. 'So, a lively brain, but we have to accept his goals aren't the same as ours, and...'

'Yes?'

'I'm not trying to exempt us from any lack of responsibility, but I really don't think it's due to any lack of effort on our part. His teachers are some of the finest in the country and have helped get many boys into leading public schools, but...'

Here it comes, Hugh thought.

'I honestly think it would be the same wherever he was.'

'They broke the mould, etcetera?'

'Precisely. He probably doesn't think too much about what will happen to him next. It's often the case at his age. A week is a lifetime, let alone nine months. Long term, I'm sure he'll find his level. Nonetheless, I appreciate your anxiety about how he will meet the challenges in sight.'

Hugh raised his eyebrows and sighed. 'What do you suggest we do to encourage him to focus more: external coaching?'

'It's worth a try.' The Headmaster gave Hugh a long, penetrating look, as if weighing up whether he could handle what was coming next before adopting a softer, more confiding tone. 'Look,' he said, 'it's my job to be frank with parents…'

'I appreciate that…'

'…and as you see, I always try to emphasise the positive aspects of their boy's abilities, based on both my own observation and feedback from their teachers. I assess each one as a whole, not merely as an exam-passing machine – however important that is. All parents worry about their son's academic progress but can underestimate their other talents: things which might stand them in good stead if traditional routes fail.'

With growing apprehension, Hugh sensed where the conversation might be heading.

'You're paying us good money to prepare Sam for the next stage in his education. We'll have failed you if we can't help him achieve the goals you've set for him. Sometimes, however, it can be worth approaching the problem sideways.'

Hugh raised a puzzled eyebrow.

'Another skill may provide the key...'

'Key?'

'…to unlock the door. Which leads me to some comments Mr Hancock, a parent who works at the V&A, passed on to me.'

The name rang a bell with Hugh. 'Ah yes, Sam was involved in a puppet show there a few weeks ago,' he said, making it sound as if he didn't attach a great deal of importance to the event. After all, how could voicing puppets have any bearing on acquiring the ability to resolve algebraic equations?

'Apparently, he acquitted himself extremely well,' the Headmaster continued. 'Mr Hancock was impressed. In his position, he knows a lot about the theatre and has useful connections. Sam also participated in a national marionette exhibition at a large hotel in Holborn some months back.'

'So, I believe,' Hugh said, 'but...'

'The man seems to think he has talent. And not only in acting, either.'

Hugh looked puzzled.

'Ah.' He paused. 'Surely, you were aware Sam ran the show almost single-handed?'

Hugh wasn't going to admit his ignorance. 'Well... he loves anything like that.'

'Not only did he provide some of the puppet's voices, showing confidence using a microphone for the first time, but acted as stage manager, organising everyone, coordinating props and scene changes. Juggling skills like that, at his age, is quite impressive.'

'You think so?'

'Indeed. So...'

'Yes?'

'Maybe you'll have to accept that's his forte.'

'The *stage*?'

The Headmaster ignored the note of shock in Hugh's voice – as if he'd suggested Sam trained for deep-sea diving. 'If his talent continues to develop, it may well indicate he's cut out for something in that area. He's still comparatively young I know, but...'

Hugh thought how he had become an apprentice to a textile firm when he was fifteen, only two and a half years older than Sam was now. Though decided not to mention it.

Mr Randolph continued. 'I wonder whether, rather than trying to send him to another *conventional* school, he might not be happier, and even flourish better academically, at a good stage school where he'd be amongst young people cut from the same cloth? The Italia Conti, for instance, has an excellent reputation.' Hugh winced. Mr Randolph noted his reaction and hurried on. 'Admittedly, it's a precarious vocation, but the skills he'd acquire could also be used in an alternative, more... grounded career than performing.'

'Such as?'

'By adding on teaching qualifications, for instance. And since commercial television hit our screens, it has opened up various technical and creative opportunities for young people. The BBC needs to look to its laurels. My godson, for instance, is training to be a studio manager with Associated Rediffusion.'

Hugh wasn't interested in other people's children. Besides, although Bessie and he were planning on renting a set once Sam had safely won a place at his next school, he assumed television was simply an extension of the stage.

At that moment, Moira knocked and popped her head around the door to tactfully remind Mr Randolph of his next appointment. Without appearing to be hastening Hugh's departure, Mr Randolph skilfully drew the interview to a close.

He thanked the Headmaster, left and made his way to the station. Thinking over their discussion, he was reminded how, on one of Sam's visits to Manchester, Connie had arranged for the two of them to attend rehearsals for and transmission of a Children's Hour play at the BBC's studios in Piccadilly. He'd come back bubbling over, not only from the excitement of meeting Herbert Smith, the director, and his cast and getting autographs but with a surprising grasp of the technology involved. Maybe he should have mentioned that to the Headmaster. He had certainly been encouraged, if unsurprised, to learn of Sam's potential as an organiser. After all, it was a family trait, if an avenue he was unconvinced they should seriously explore.

The idea of his son attending a stage school with a throng of precocious brats when one colleague's son was already doing well in the Sea Cadets and had a sound career in the Navy ahead of him, while another boy they knew had recently won a scholarship to St Paul's? No way! He clung to the hope that Sam, like most of the offspring of friends and clients, was bound for a good public school and, in due course, university.

Having his boy setting out on a path that might only lead to an insecure, even heart-breaking career was something he couldn't countenance. The priority was to get him through his Common Entrance. Only if he failed should they consider other options. In the meantime, they must help redirect his attention to his classwork.

* * *

Back home, Hugh discussed the interview with Bessie. As always, she was delighted to hear any praise heaped on Sam.

'He'll be delighted to know he impressed people at the V&A.'

Hugh looked at her warily. 'You mustn't tell him!'

'Why ever not?'

'He doesn't need any more encouragement.' He then told her about Mr Randolph's stage school suggestion. 'But I think it's in his best interests to stick to our plans, don't you?'

She was aware the question was rhetorical. Knowing how the lives of her brother, sister and herself had been managed by her own father, Bessie didn't care what Sam did with his life as long as he was happy. Her father had set out to use his children to maintain his own career, with no thought of their right to decide on how they wanted to spend their lives. She also knew how Hugh had been encouraged to pursue an apprenticeship in the fated cotton industry and only found his true vocation in his twenties. If he'd begun in electrical engineering earlier, she might have been married at twenty-five.

Why was her husband being so inflexible? Should history be allowed to repeat itself? Was it due to Hugh's fear of how a son at a stage school might look to his business associates? While she'd also prefer Sam's life to go down a more conventional route, Bessie was in two minds as to what was best for him.

'I'm sorry, but unless he gets gripped with something else overnight,' she said, 'which I very much doubt, it would break his heart not being allowed to do what he loves.'

She saw Hugh putting on his I-must-tread-more-carefully look. 'We'd really never stop him, of course. Ultimately any major decision must be his choice, but, until he gets settled in another school, I'd like us to well... not exactly discourage these activities...' he said.

'But not *en*courage them?'

'Exactly. Help him concentrate more on the things that really matter.'

A Proper Contentment

Bessie nodded, half-heartedly, sighing inwardly and wondering how on earth she was going to keep her side of the bargain. She felt uncomfortable that her loyalties were being compromised yet again.

* * *

One afternoon some weeks later, Sam came home depressed. He'd failed to win the school reading competition.

'I only came second.'

'That's still pretty good.'

'But I've let my house down.'

'Not you.'

Sam blinked back a threatening tear.

Bessie's resolve crashed. Sam rarely got much praise over more important issues. It was important he felt better about himself.

'Actually...'

'What?'

Bessie cautiously relayed Hugh's conversation with the Headmaster. When she'd finished, looking as awkward as she felt, she heard herself saying: 'But you mustn't tell your father I told you.'

'Why ever not?'

'He was delighted, of course, but....'

'But?'

'Well...'

'Doesn't want me to get swollen-headed?'

'Something like that. So, let's keep it a secret, shall we?'

'Why?'

'Please. Just between just the two of us. For the time being?'

'I suppose,' Sam muttered as he slouched off to unpack his homework.

He looked confused.

And hurt.

110

* * *

In the spring, Hugh was having lunch with an older colleague when the conversation got round to education.

'With all your commitments, how are you and your wife going to cope when your son goes on to his next school?'

'It's beginning to worry us. Increasingly, Bessie and I are required to be away at night. He'll be thirteen when he leaves Stanwich. Not old enough to be left on his own for long periods. It's not always easy finding places where he can stay for a night or even, from time to time, spend up to a week. We're already beginning to exhaust the goodwill of friends and neighbours who are kind enough to put him up.'

'Had you considered boarding school?'

'It had crossed our minds. But it would have to be the right sort of place. He's a sensitive, artistic lad.'

'I could send away for a prospectus of my alma mater, Debenbridge. I had a great time there. It's on the edge of a historic market town and surrounded by beautiful countryside. Your boy is very interested in drama, isn't he?'

'Why?'

'As well as sport, it has a good reputation for music and putting on plays.'

Hugh's interest intensified. A decent boarding school with plenty of artistic outlets might be the answer to their worries.

A few days later, a glossy brochure arrived. Bessie and Hugh discussed the matter with Sam, showing him the photographs of the spacious, leafy grounds, the three Victorian houses and the school hall with its imposing stage.

On a perfect June day some weeks later, Hugh drove Sam the ninety miles to Debenbridge to meet the Headmaster and look around. Provided he could pass the all-important Common Entrance exam, they hoped to be able to offer him a place.

Won over by the thought of spending his spare time acting, Sam was pleased his parents were no longer so anxious about him. He got through the exams and gave himself up to the long summer holidays ahead.

He'd worry about going away to school when the time came.

BOOK TWO

Separate Lives
1960 - 1995

10

Idol Days

1960
Sam

'Soon be over,' Davison whispered to him.

'Yeah. Don't worry, Huntley doesn't beat the hell out of you, like Banfield,' whispered another boy, a hardened criminal more accustomed to the wrath of a tougher prefect. Sam noted cynically that today's allies were two of the boys who usually enjoyed tormenting him but closed ranks now they were in trouble together. Even so, he was grateful for any comradeship going.

Reprisal for serious offences was delivered by masters. Senior prefects for misdemeanours. To his way of thinking, the disparity between six hits from a length of bamboo on a trousered backside for a crime such as theft and six heavy swipes on a thin pyjama-ed one for merely leaving your locker untidy or, as in this case, a light-hearted practical joke, was indefensible.

At Debenbridge that was the way things were.

'It'll make a man of him,' he'd overheard a neighbour telling Bessie the day he set off for his four years away from home.

What was a man supposed to be like? He merely wanted to be a person. His own person.

It was the last Sunday evening of term. Busily getting ready for bed, the other boys in the dormitory averted their gaze as he summoned his courage to face the inevitable.

The poignancy of the situation lay in the fact that Clive Huntley, the more charming of gifted twins Clive and Paul Huntley, and also House Captain, was his idol. He and Sam had discovered a shared passion for books and all things theatrical, and being two years ahead of him, he was encouraging Sam to widen his horizons, introducing him to writers and artistic concepts he would not otherwise have had an opportunity to engage with until he was older. Both brothers were natural teachers, and intrigued by Sam's persistent creative itch, Clive was mentoring Sam's first serious attempts at playwriting.

An incident that had occurred the previous day was, however, to sorely test their relationship. After breakfast on the Saturday, Sam returned to his dormitory to make his bed and prepare for the rest of the school day. It was the last weekend prior to the Easter holidays.

An anarchical hint of spring spiced the air.

It was the pre-school half-hour assigned for such chores, and some of the boys were in a prankish mood. Several had already stripped neighbouring beds down to the mattresses. Pillows, sheets and blankets were strewn all over the dormitory floor. Instead of quickly pulling the ruffled bedding together, they would now need to be remade from scratch. The bed next to Sam belonged to his pal, Davison. Racing him up to the dormitory, Sam stripped his own before Davison could beat him to it. Normally goodie-goodies, there was no malice involved. It was simply end-of-term high jinks.

On overhearing the rowdiness in the corridor, Clive Huntley stormed into the room at the height of the devastation, lost his temper and told Sam and the two other culprits to report to him the following night.

They knew all too well what that meant.

A swinging.

It was now thirty-six hours later. Sam shut the book he'd been unable to concentrate on, looked at his watch, retied the cord on his dressing gown, stood up and made his way along the corridor.

* * *

Later in his life, Sam preferred to gloss over his uneven secondary schooldays. Not only because of his regularly disappointing academic grades but the many other failures and indignities that blighted his early teenage years. Yet, despite the many tough times he'd endured over the previous two-and-a-half years, until now, this particular term had been the most satisfying of his stretch at Debenbridge.

It had all begun promisingly enough. Coming from a good preparatory school, he'd been slotted into a third-year A class. The rot set in when, somewhat out of his depth and having done badly in his end-of-year exams, he was dropped into the parallel B form. Making insufficient progress there too, he was now in the same class repeating the year with another set of boys with an average age six months younger than him – suffering the humiliation of watching his immediate contemporaries graduate to the Fifth Form, with all the privileges that went with their new status. He envied Davison now allowed to sport a stylish Maurice Chevalier boater decorated with ribbon in school colours during summer months, instead of the habitual *schoolboy* cap.

Sam always recalled, with mixed feelings, the dreary lessons delivered by a team of largely self-satisfied, second-rate masters. Also, the demeaning bullying, the agonising cross-country runs on frosty days and wasted hours standing on windy touch-lines dutifully cheering on housemates. Just as abhorrent were the draconian Thursday afternoon drills with the Combined Cadet Force and Field Days along the Suffolk coast when, driven by incoherent barking from uniformed masters, he battled for breath with gunfire and explosions detonating all around him as he stumbled through the tall grass to catch up with his platoon.

'Move it, Owen, or you're a dead man!'

There were plusses. The best thing about Debenbridge for Sam was, as he'd hoped, the opportunity provided for him to graduate to full-blown acting. By the end of his second term, he was playing a dizzy ingenue in a blonde wig wearing a succession of pretty dresses. Admiring his handiwork beforehand, the Senior English master, powder puff in hand, remarked, 'Strange, how the plainest boys make the prettiest girls!'

The teacher who most frequently directed him – known as Bullseye for his accuracy with a piece of chalk when he caught a boy not paying attention – targeted Hugh and Bessie the next Speech Day. He ran by them the idea that, if Sam's talent continued to develop, he'd be willing to prepare him for a scholarship to RADA. He'd succeeded with two other boys a year or so earlier. The next day, there was the inevitable family pow-wow. "If you're honest," Hugh said, 'don't you think you're unsuited to an actor's life? Suppose it didn't work out. What would you do then? We really feel it would be in your best interests to work towards a university place."

There were respites in the sickbay too, recovering from regular bouts of throat and chest infections, to give him occasional oases of calm, indulged by a succession of sympathetic matrons. During the Asian flu epidemic, he devoured the complete series of Arthur Ransome's *Swallows and Amazons*, and in later confinements progressed to Neville Shute and Daphne du Maurier. Convalescence also provided time to devour and commit to memory the contents of the latest copies of *Plays and Players* and *Theatre World* his mother posted him. He still hadn't mastered how to parse a Latin sentence properly but could tell you who was starring in the new play at Wyndham's.

The boys weren't exactly prisoners. Provided they always looked presentable in their school uniforms – worn even at weekends – they were free to explore beyond the school gates in their spare time and go into town to buy tuck, have haircuts, borrow books at the local library and stroll along the bank of the Deben. When the weather was good, an exeat might allow them to go further afield. The charm of the surrounding countryside always elevated Sam's spirits, despite the bitter East wind which blew off the river at nights and through the open-topped windows of the unheated dormitories.

There were occasional treats, too: concerts in the vast Ipswich Gaumont to watch Basil Cameron conduct the Royal Philharmonic; Shakespeare and Shaw at the Rep – on the way back begging the coach driver to stop off for pokes of tongue-scorching fries at a side street chippy.

Sam first established a friendly rapport with Clive and his brother Paul when, within days of starting at the school, he joined the Play Reading Society. Soon all of them were appearing together in school productions. It was hard to maintain the unwritten behavioural protocols between juniors and seniors in this beehive community when he was wearing a long dress and being wooed in front of parents and fellow pupils as inamorata to one six-former in the winter – and cast as a stentorian aunt to another in the spring.

As at most public schools – even very minor ones such as Debenbridge – selected fourteen and fifteen-year-olds were assigned as fags to prefects. Their duties included the maintenance of study fires in winter, keeping the rooms neat and tidy and running errands. When, at the beginning of the current school year, Sam was allocated to Paul as a fag, he also found himself constantly in Clive's company. Between the rallies of puns and literary jokes batting to and forth between the brothers' desks, Sam absorbed much anecdotal but valuable information on poets, composers, novelists and playwrights. That and the informal instruction he received from them on the craft of writing verse would serve him well in the years to come.

Like Sam, Clive avidly followed the progress of current Broadway hits heading for the West End. There was little likelihood of either boy seeing them in the near future, but at least they could listen to the LP of *My Fair Lady* on a borrowed record player and exchange gossip on the upcoming *The Sound of Music*. Along with the Huntleys' encouragement of his literary pursuits was the inspired teaching of Dave Jasper, the young music master, whose choral rehearsals and music appreciation classes covered everything from Bach to Irving Berlin. Clive would later collaborate with Dave on an original musical play – Sam appearing as a chorus member in yet another of his mother's cast-off summer frocks.

Sam identified with Clive to the extent that, on nights when sleep eluded him, he fantasised he was keeping him warm and safe in bed, his feelings for the older boy, if not completely unsullied by lust, springing from genuine affection and admiration.

By now he was able to distinguish between his platonic feelings for Clive and what he took from the mutual fumbling he indulged in with willing contemporaries on long Sunday afternoons in empty changing rooms or among the dense bushes bordering the school playing fields. He knew that, even if his feeling were reciprocated – which he doubted – given Clive's integrity and seniority, any intimacy between them was destined to be confined to shared artistic interests.

An only child, before coming to Debenbridge, Sam's opportunities to compare his own developing body with that of other boys had been confined to titillating sex games with his good friend and neighbour, Steve. They were the same age but, in the year before Sam went away to school, Steve's body had suddenly matured. As they were close friends who'd always enjoyed an open and uninhibited friendship, what with Sam's becoming increasingly sexually curious and Steve at the stage where his by now fully functioning equipment was demanding attention, on wet afternoons, the devil happily found work for idle hands. These episodes had provided enticing intimations of the delights in store for Sam himself and confirmed his growing fascination with the male form. Whilst some of his other good friends were girls and he was fond of them, he was indifferent to the thought of seeing them naked.

Steve, on the other hand, had always been interested in chasing girls and, whilst he indulged Sam's theatrical interests, was sporty, being – as Bessie called him – as a 'regular lad'. Sam appreciated Steve's masculinity, which rubbed off on him and somehow made their occasional intimate moments acceptable. Recently, though, when Sam returned home for the holidays, whilst they remained on good terms, he could tell that Steve had moved on. With his smart jackets and bronze hair neatly slicked back into a fashionable DA, he was now fully committed to the opposite sex. As the years went on, the two boys would drift even further apart.

Their friendship had, however, taught Sam to appreciate how the physical and emotional aspects of sex, whilst most satisfying when linked by a warm friendship, could also be enjoyed separately. With Clive, he was happy to settle for the wholesome and higher-minded aspects of their friendship, even if it couldn't stop him daydreaming.

* * *

Sam's initial excitement this fatal weekend was heightened by the knowledge he'd be soon be returning home for Easter with — if the rumours were correct — the news his well-received performance that week, as Lady Bracknell in *The Importance of Being Earnest*, had once again won him the coveted school Drama prize. It must have felt like an unintentional snub to Clive, who'd ably played the gorgon's nephew, Algernon.

Maybe it would encourage his parents to reconsider his future.

Then came their unexpected confrontation over the bed-stripping, which destroyed his peace of mind but also revealed a side to his character. Even if he couldn't defend himself with his hands, he would go to any lengths to challenge an injustice verbally.

That first day, already fretting about the indignity and discomfort to come while attempting to make some sense of what had happened, Sam tried to see Clive and reason with him, but the older boy was always out of the study, apparently busy with more important matters.

The evening arrived and Sam's partners in crime, slotted to be punished ahead of Sam, duly queued to pay the price of their foolishness. By the time the last one returned to the dormitory, melodramatically rubbing his behind with a big smile of relief on his face to inform him it was now his turn, Sam had vanished.

Down in Mr Bradshaw's office, he was making a last-minute plea for clemency to his housemaster. 'I shall be sixteen in a few months' time,' he began, 'and while I know it was childish behaviour, such a harsh punishment for momentary high spirits is unjust. An apology, or possibly being told to sweep and clean the dormitory would surely have been enough.'

Mr Bradshaw wanted to know the full details of the crime. When he finished talking, Sam guessed, from the way the man frowned and pursed his lips, that he secretly agreed with him. 'Look, let me have a word with Clive and get back to you,' he offered. 'Go to bed, get a good night's rest and come and see me after chapel tomorrow.'

The next morning, he prayed not for his sins, which he considered a very grey area, but for a satisfactory resolution to the issue.

'I've had a chat with Clive,' Mr Bradshaw said when they next met. 'I can understand, with the excitement of the play and the holiday approaching, you were both on a high yesterday morning. It's been a tiring few weeks for him, too, but he has other responsibilities to contend with and couldn't let off steam as you did. He admits he snapped and possibly overreacted.'

Sam dared to hope he was off the hook.

'Unfortunately,' Sam's heart sank, 'the other two boys have already grinned and borne their punishment without any argument.'

'And it wouldn't be right to let me off?'

'Well… While I agree the decision was heavy-handed,' Mr Bradshaw tried not to smile at his accidental choice of words, 'it would be equally unfair to let you off when your friends have suffered. And it would rebound on you, wouldn't it?'

'I take your point,' Sam said with a sigh.

'So, I suggest you grin and bear it tonight. By the time you get back next term, it'll all have been forgotten.'

Tonight. It was only ten hours away, yet sounded like a week. After the thrill of successfully representing his house in the play, he'd spoilt it by simply sticking up for himself – as his parents always told him he should. Not only that, but he'd found himself in a fraught situation with the one person in the school he truly cared for.

* * *

He waited while Paul and the other six-former the twins shared the study with vacated their desks and left the room.

Clive's mood was as sombre as his own. They looked at each regretfully. The hurt and stress Sam was feeling evaporated into pity.

'I don't like having to do this, you know,' Clive said.

'It's spoilt a really good week.'

'For me, too. Sorry. You were fantastic as Lady B.'

'Thanks.'

Sam tried to read what was going on behind his sad expression. They both knew the charade must be played out before they could attempt to pick up their normal relationship.

'Well… better get it out of the way.' His lips briefly thawed into a half-apologetic smile. Sam hadn't expected any sudden change of heart, but at least the look might be interpreted as 'this will hurt me more than you.'

'Put your dressing gown over there.' Clive indicated a low-backed chair strategically placed six feet away.

Sam bent over, clung on to the back for support and gritted his teeth. He could hear something being picked up, presumably the plimsoll, and moved into position.

There was a three-second pause followed by six half-hearted thwacks.

'Right. Get up.'

He did so, slowly. Clive may have been as gentle as it's possible to be when repeatedly striking someone's rear with a size ten rubber-soled shoe; all the same, after the first three hits, Sam's behind had become too numb to fully register the remaining blows. It stung badly. In fact, his whole body was complaining. He'd have to lie on top of his mattress for a while before summoning the strength to roll over, pull the sheets over him and try to get some sleep.

As he put his dressing gown on, Clive opened the door and stood back. Passing him on the way out, Sam couldn't bear to look at his idol. Involuntarily turning to close the door, he glimpsed the older boy in profile, staring dejectedly into the fireplace.

For the time being, something between them had changed, although, as it turned out, the incident wouldn't damage things for long. The following term, they picked up where they'd left off, and, later in the year, Clive wrote a song set to music by Dave Jasper for Sam to perform at a school entertainment.

He had learnt a valuable lesson. The people you admire the most aren't always perfect, and if, like Mr Bradshaw, they also have charge over you, however much you may like them, they may choose to exercise their power pragmatically.

Pragmatism wasn't the same as fairness.

11

Women Together

1965
Bessie

The two women finished their jacket potatoes with prawns Marie Rose and half-heartedly scanned the dessert menu. Elspeth had completed her meal. A substantial portion of potato remained on Bessie's plate. They were sitting in Grant's café, having pottered around Croydon market for fruit, visited a nearby stationers for birthday cards and perused the up-coming fashions a couple of floors down. They usually enjoyed their outings, but Bessie knew she wasn't her usual cheerful self and saw Elspeth giving her thoughtful glances.

As they tried to catch the waitress's attention, Elspeth said, 'Oh, heck, let's skip sweet and coffee. I'll take you back to Shirley Hills and we'll have one in comfort there. There's a tray of coffee buns I made first thing with just such an eventuality in mind.' Bessie gave an acquiescent smile. 'Besides, I need your advice on my patio border. I'm thinking white begonia, gaillardia and something blue-ish. Veronica, perhaps? But I'm open to suggestions, and you always have such a good eye. I'll get you home in time to make Hugh's supper.'

'He's at his Lodge tonight.' Bessie sounded tired. 'With Sam away at college, it's just me and Dusty – when she's not out hunting.' She knew her loss of appetite was a symptom of the general weariness that was dragging her down. One of Elspeth's buns might just provide the sugar rush she badly needed.

'Welcome to my world!'

'You're fed up, too?'

'Gibby's in the Big Apple, and Colin's spending the week in Cornwall with a friend. We're both practically widows! Why not stay on and we can keep each other company?'

'Dusty has to be fed at some point.'

'Excuses, excuses. I'll get you back in good time.'

The cat had been left food, and there was always a bowl of water on hand. A few more hours wouldn't hurt.

'Time for a girly heart-to-heart,' Elspeth said.

'You read me like a Georgette Heyer.'

'You're far more cool, dear.'

Bessie laughed at her friend's use of the vernacular, especially as applied to herself. 'That would be lovely!'

The pair had renewed their friendship when the Owens came to live in South London. Could it really be fifteen years? They were in touch several times a week. It was Elspeth who'd unsparingly given of her time to drive her around to look at various properties all those years ago and helped her decide on Howard Road. More recently too, when they'd moved into a detached house, all picture windows and mod cons with hot air central heating, and handier for Hugh's office which had re-located to a new high-rise building in Croydon. One way or another, Elspeth had been a source of companionship, support and advice for most of her married life. When Marje, Bessie's confidante in Edinburgh, had tragically succumbed to cancer, Elspeth became particularly important.

At the end of the war, Brad, the Lieutenant who'd gallantly protected her the night of the doodlebug, broke her heart by returning to his fiancée in Cincinnati. But Elspeth's distress had swiftly evaporated when, at a VE Day dance not long after, she'd jitterbugged into the arms of Gibby, an off-duty naval Captain. 'A rank higher than my previous beau,' as she'd been quick to point out.

Gibby was only ever called Gilbert 'when he needs his wrist slapping' as she told everyone tongue-in-cheek. In fact, he wasn't the sort of man you argued with, and she'd been contentedly dancing to the magnetic Yorkshireman's tune ever since.

Soon after their honeymoon in 1945, he was recalled to the ongoing hostilities in Asia. When their son had arrived nine months later, she was left to bring him up on her own until the Navy let Gibby go, after which he'd reverted to his pre-war career in finance.

Well-educated, with the air and ability of someone who takes upward mobility as a given, Gibby had dexterously climbed the corporate ladder until, now, he was responsible for the personnel function of a large international oil company. Like Hugh, his job often took him away from home, but, in his case, he shuttled back and forth between Moorgate and Manhattan rather than within the Home Counties. His salary now enabled them to live in a large five-bedroomed detached house in a discreet fir-bordered road a mile or so away from the Owens, surrounded by people in a similar income bracket.

Like Bessie, Elspeth was a good mixer and, with her socially compassionate nature, would have been happier living far less ostentatiously. She was certainly no snob. As well as being within easy reach of each other, the pair also had only sons to share an interest in, both loved gardening, sport and fiction, and saw eye to eye on most issues of the day. Elspeth had a disarming way of making light of the disparity between their lifestyles, and Bessie was never intimidated by it.

It helped that Hugh and Gibby got along well and respected each other, too. Hugh was sufficiently senior in his own small firm to understand the pressures of Gibby's job and had never forgotten his kindness when he'd offered to lend him money during the difficult months of Bessie's illness. He'd not accepted it, of course, but the gesture had cemented the bond between them all.

Once settled in the car, Elspeth said, 'So, I can guess what the matter is.'

'Am I that transparent?'

'Only because I suspect we're both in the same boat. Go on.'

'Well...'

'Remember, it's me you're talking to.'

Bessie finally dived in. 'All the time Sam was living at home, family life went on more or less as usual. When Hugh was busy in the evenings, I often went up into town and joined Sam for a meal and a show, or we'd go to a film at the local fleapit. On the nights he wasn't otherwise engaged, we'd curl up in our respective chairs with *Compact* and *Z Cars* happily enough. There was always plenty to talk about, too. But time marches on. Now, Hugh often eats out, and there's no Sam to cook or wash and iron for. Not even an untidy bedroom to sort out every other day.'

'Sounds blissful.'

'You'd think so, but...'

'You miss it?'

'Funnily enough, yes. I've...'

'Lost your *raison d'être*?'

Bessie nodded. 'I'm now redundant.'

'At least you know they're both busy and happy.'

'Indeed. Sam's into everything at college. Hugh and I were concerned teacher training might be another blind alley after his year clerking with the BBC. But the course plays to many of his strengths. He's even getting good grades for PE because he does well on the theory side. Came home lecturing me about the development of human life from conception to birth. What he doesn't know about fallopian tubes is nobody's business.'

'Spare my blushes!'

'Indeed. As if we hadn't put all that behind us ages ago.'

'I mean, how does that help teach kids their seven times table?'

'Goodness knows. At least his lectures on the female anatomy make an occasional break from the dramas-about-dramas he's involved in. Did I tell you there are more girls than boys at the place? So...'

'Ah.' It was an enigmatic sound rather than an exclamation. Elspeth, whose sister worked in a West End theatrical agency and regularly entertained her with gossip about her louche friends, had her own theories as to where Sam's love life might be heading. She very much doubted it involved putting his newly acquired knowledge of female biology to practical use. She knew that if Bessie had a fault, despite her protestations of how curious she was about how other people lived their lives, it was that she was sometimes in denial about aspects of human behaviour she had little or no experience of.

Capable of thinking creatively and, with her contagious laugh, seeing the funny side of many situations, when confronted with behaviour that taxed her view of the world, you could catch a glimpse of Bessie's strait-laced corset. People in the wider world might live unconventional lives, but she couldn't always connect them to anyone she knew. She had, for instance, always accepted Connie's special relationship with her close friend and colleague, Hannah. But only because she'd shared a bed with her own sister and never thought twice about such an arrangement.

'College seems to be the making of him,' Bessie went on. 'He's really taken to it. Lots of good grades for his coursework. And he got a good report for his first teaching practice, too.'

'You must both feel very relieved.'

'He seems to be sorting himself out. And Hugh finally feels vindicated for having poured so much hard-earned money into his education.'

'I'm glad it's paying off.'

'Everything crossed!'

'I always said he was a late-developer. Colin's the same. Not the brightest of bunnies, but...'

'He inherited both your and Gibby's charm, though.'

'As Sam did yours – and Hugh's.'

'Well...'

'Let's hope they can bank it!'

'Though... I know this sounds strange...'

'Go on.'

'...Sam's newfound confidence is part of my problem.'

'I can see how you must miss him when you've always been so close.'

'It's not only that.'

'Sorry, I'm not with you.'

'I've… I'm now the odd one out again.'

'*You?*'

'I feel particularly uncomfortable at holiday times when Connie comes to stay and there are four of us. It used to make a nice even number. But Hugh still has a younger-brother inferiority complex and Connie has always been, dare I say it, quicker on the uptake. She never struggled as he did to make his mark. Sailed through school, went to college, loved teaching, became a lecturer and was then promoted to vice principal of the college where she'd once been a student. Since then, she's been a big fish in a small pond. He's had to do things the hard way. Now he's made a success of his career, he likes to show her how knowledgeable he is – even about things in her own territory! Spouts forth, only to be corrected by her when she thinks he's getting above himself or disagrees. Then Sam chips in with his pennyworth from his college studies on educational theory, psychology or whatever, and…'

'They don't give you any air space?'

'No. And look at me somewhat pityingly as if I couldn't possibly understand. I'm back again with my father, brother and sister in the old days when they'd start talking shop whilst happily tucking into whatever I'd spent hours to put before them, and trying to shout each other down. If I ever dared to offer an opinion, they stopped and looked at me long-sufferingly. I was chief cook and bottle-washer; I couldn't possibly be expected to understand the cut-and-thrust complexities of wheeler-dealing. It's the same now – only the subject matter has altered. Connie and Sam are wrapped up with college matters, while Hugh likes to try and compare them with his own world or, worse, his tough years as an apprentice. He forgets it was a quarter of a century ago. Times have changed considerably.'

'I'm sure they don't mean to freeze you out.'

'Nevertheless, here I am in my mid-fifties, back where I started.'

'I find it hard to believe you'd let anyone patronise you for long. I'm sure you get your own back, don't you? Just because you never got the chance to go to college doesn't mean you don't have a good head on your shoulders.

Whenever you and I and get involved in a serious discussion, I'm impressed at how logically you present your case. You're always practical, full of common sense, and cut through any flimflam.'

'Thanks for that. I don't know what I'd do without you to help me believe in myself. They don't really mean to be unkind, but I can't help feeling snubbed believing they think I can't appreciate where they're coming from. Quite often they're right. After all, they've enjoyed educational advantages which I missed out on. But I don't even score points for showing an interest.'

At that moment, they approached a roundabout. The conversation suddenly went on hold as a careless driver attempted to cut in and overtake them. Elspeth uncharacteristically swore under her breath as she blasted her horn and revved up the Rover to show them who was boss. When they were safely on their way again, she said, 'I've got an idea. I'll elaborate when we get home…'

One-and-a-half cups of freshly-ground coffee and a coffee bun later, Elspeth momentarily left the conservatory, leaving Bessie to take in the magnificent sweep of spring flowers in the spacious, well-maintained garden, returning a few minutes later with a box file in her hands.

'Sorry I took so long. I'd put all this stuff in a safe place and forgotten exactly where.'

'Don't worry, I've been admiring your Tazettas.'

'So, that's what those white narcissi are called?'

'Only showing off. It was on the bag of bulbs I bought, but most of mine only produced green spears. Yours are like something in Kew.'

'There you go, belittling yourself again,' Elspeth said, having now sat down and opened the box. She produced a thin booklet from the file and handed it to Bessie. 'It's the luck of the draw. My phlox were a disaster last year and look at what a show yours were! Now, take this pamphlet home with you and be sure to read it.'

Bessie dived into her handbag for her reading glasses and began studying it. '*The British Women's Forum?*'

'As you know, I've been a member for a couple of years now.'

Bessie knew all about Elspeth's membership of what she referred to as the 'Forum'. But although she courteously remembered to ask her about it every so often and received a brief summary of its activities, until now she hadn't paid too much attention to the detail. Possibly this had something to do with a fracas with the Church Flowers committee some years back. One argument over the suitability of myrtle as opposed to leatherleaf fern as a filler in an altar arrangement had turned especially nasty and jaded her appetite for ever belonging to a group dominated by women again.

'It's done wonders for my self-esteem,' Elspeth went on. 'I'm expecting to be on the committee next year. After years as a housewife, when my most exciting activity beyond the garden was organising the white elephant stall for the church fair, I finally feel I'm making a contribution.'

'Towards?'

'Matters of national importance, the community… *me*!'

'And you're sure there's not a woman among them for whom the unshakeable principles of *recession* and *accent* in floral décor are the eleventh and twelfth commandments?'

'No! We're a national organisation that aims to ensure women like us play a part in society. There's nothing parochial about us, except that we all live within a couple of miles of each other.'

'How do you do it?'

'By raising awareness of local and national issues and involving ourselves in decision-making. Above all, we campaign to eradicate discrimination. Especially against our own sex.'

'Sort of modern-day suffragettes?'

'In a way, although we don't chain ourselves to the Downing Street railings anymore. Well, I haven't done so far, anyway,' Elspeth added with a grin, 'but it's early days. People like Helen Gurley Brown…'

'*Sex and the Single Girl*?'

'Yes. That and Betty Friedan's *The Feminine Mystique* have helped usher in a more liberated climate. They were both new to me, but I can lend you my copies, if you like. They thumb the nose at men who've had it all their own way for far too long.'

'Well…' Bessie said, uneasily aware of her own uncompromising stance on sex before marriage.

'Us… mature… women don't have to be *swinging*, if that's the word, to recognise the upside to the renewed struggle for equal rights. I don't know about you, but if I had a daughter, I'd like her to have the same freedoms as a man. It's a matter of choice. Why should we continue to allow men to dictate to us what we can and can't do when they go ahead and behave exactly as they please? The stench of 'fifties bigotry still lingers in the air.'

'You read that in *Cosmopolitan* in the hairdressers,' Bessie teased.

'More probably something that new girl – Joan Bakewell? – said on TV.'

'As you know, I'm still a bit old-fashioned myself about some things,' Bessie confessed.

'Like the pill?' Elspeth.

'Another can of worms.'

'We've had a few lively discussions about that, as well.'

'I bet. As you and I have, too.'

Bessie recalled Sam telling her how one of his new friends, Wendi, had confided in him how she'd missed her period and feared the worst, thanks to a fling with a boy she'd met at a holiday camp. Sam said he'd tried to comfort her but wondered why a sophisticated girl like her had allowed such a thing to happen.

'Surely you took precautions?'

'Yes,' she'd wailed, 'but there were only three in the packet.'

Bessie, while sorry for the girl's predicament, still felt sexual mores were relaxing too quickly for her liking.

While she mightn't approve of *free love* herself, she knew Elspeth, if unlikely to have any wish to experiment with a more relaxed moral code, firmly believed women should be allowed the opportunity to enjoy sex outside marriage without fear or shame. In the case of Wendi, rigorous exercising, hot baths and plenty of gin had spirited the problem away. Countless other women who had unprotected sex were not so lucky, causing themselves a multitude of problems. At this point, Bessie was still conflicted as to how this matter should be handled, tending to be critical rather than compassionate about such *mistakes*.

As if reading her thoughts, Elspeth said, 'It so happens one of the issues the Forum is due to discuss shortly is the thorny matter of Abortion Law reform.'

'I'm not sure how far I can go along with that,' Bessie said, thinking how, if Sam hadn't finally come along, she would have persuaded Hugh to adopt a child someone else was unable to care for.

'Fine, and you've every right to your own point of view,' Elspeth said. 'That's what I find so interesting about our discussions. I often start off by thinking I know exactly where I stand on an issue, then, when I've done my homework and heard different points of view, I discover myself, if not always switching sides, at least modifying my standpoint. It provides an opportunity to educate myself.'

Bessie's interest was piqued. Now her world had shrunk and she was feeling marginalised again, the idea of discussing topical issues of universal concern with other women and acquiring an informed opinion about them was appealing.

'Tell me more about how you operate.'

'We're affiliated to the national body but have our own constitution and take it in turns to meet at each other's houses. The agendas comprise topics put forward by members or raised by the regional branches. Each October there's a conference – last year it was in Buxton – where we meet up with members from other groups and vote for resolutions we believe should be taken forward. Sometimes to the highest level of government.

'How?'

'By lobbying our MPs.' Elspeth paused. 'Look, why not come along to the next meeting and meet everyone? Actually, I'm hosting here on Thursday the 22nd. We're a jolly crowd.'

* * *

And, as Bessie discovered, they were.

The group comprised ten women ranging in age from early forties to late sixties, apart from one enthusiastic thirty-year-old.

It was refreshing getting to know everyone. Elspeth was right: the discussions could become quite controversial, but the current Chair was both firm and tactful and generally managed to keep any controversy from over-heating. During the tea break, Elspeth's famous homemade sultana scones and lemon drizzle cake mollified even the most vociferous members, who, when not arguing, turned out to be good company, several having a great sense of humour as well as things in common with herself.

Not being a driver, Bessie had splashed out on a cab to get to the meeting. She was delighted to find that one of the members, Fran, who she recognised from trips to *Sainsbury's*, lived about half a mile away from her and could provide a lift home. 'I'll pick you up next time – if you decide to come again,' Fran said as her parting shot after dropping her off at her front gate. 'I hope you do.'

Bessie had already made up her mind.

Thereafter, belonging to the Forum gave her a degree of mental stimulation she hadn't experienced before: a new lease of life with a circle of lively new friends, some of whom she soon began socialising with outside meetings. A couple of the women were more right-wing than herself, several identified themselves as Liberal or politically independent, while another member was fiercely socialist. This made for a bracing but balanced mixture of views. It was gratifying when, by means of friendly persuasion, they were finally able to agree on a matter of importance. When not, they respected each other's opinions.

She discovered she had a voice. One that was listened to, if not always agreed with, and learnt to accept the group's decisions with good grace.

On the abortion issue, Bessie's own struggle to have a baby had made her very much aware of how precious life was. She remembered walking down Leith Walk towards Tanya's hairdressing salon one afternoon in 1943 and, on spotting an unattended double pram containing West Indian triplets outside a newsagent, for a fleeting moment thinking, 'Surely, they wouldn't miss just one?' Admittedly her mental and emotional state was due to overwrought hormones, but her desperate need to become a mother had always coloured her thinking on such matters. The thought of destroying a foetus was repugnant to her.

When, however, one of her new associates recounted her sister's distressing experience giving birth to a severely handicapped thalidomide baby, its short life causing unimaginable suffering to both infant and parents, it made Bessie stop and think more carefully about how even legitimate babies were not always born with the chance of a decent life.

By the time abortion was finally legalised two years later – at least by registered practitioners regulated through the NHS – Bessie's views were aligned with those of the rest of the group. She felt a considerable glow of pride when the role the Forum and other women's pressure groups had played in achieving the new legislation was publicly acknowledged. She was finally beginning to feel she was becoming involved in the world around her and contributing her own penn'orth of effort.

It was also thanks to the Forum that, when Sam was on vacation and especially when his aunt was around, she could now hold her ground in family arguments on controversial issues in an informed way, and even surprised herself – and Hugh – how lucid she was becoming. A well-meaning man, Hugh found it harder to move with the times and there were aspects of contemporary society he couldn't adjust to. 'I blame the Beatles,' he'd say, shaking his head uncomprehendingly, apropos of popular culture in general.

One afternoon when Bessie and Sam were discussing mutual friends, Hugh entered the room and overheard Sam use the word *pregnant.* 'I'd never have used a word like that in front of *my* mother,' he said disgustedly as he slammed the door behind him. They'd looked at each other and chuckled.

Bessie was delighted with the men's surprise when she reported back on an afternoon spent with Elspeth and some of her new friends at the Houses of Parliament.

'You mean, you really met Harold Wilson, Mum?'

She smiled. 'To begin with, he kept us waiting, which was annoying, but when he finally turned up, he was effusively apologetic. "Ladies, I'm so sorry," he said, "my last meeting dragged on far longer than scheduled." Within minutes he'd accepted our deputation, was chatting away and had us eating out of his hands. Charm personified! He may not be a Conservative,' she concluded, 'but he's certainly a ladies' man.'

There was silence before Sam laughed out loud. 'Well done!' Hugh merely grunted.

It probably escaped Bessie's attention – not that it would have signified, anyway – that not long before abortion was legalised, the *Sexual Offences Act* was also voted through.

It was hardly an issue of specific interest to the Forum – except as an item of legislation which furthered people's rights to live the way they wanted – but another member of the family had certainly taken note.

12

Classic Situation

1969
Sam

'Consider Hecuba's position. Her home has been destroyed, her husband and sons violently executed and her position taken away. Yet, she retains her integrity while asking how she should deal with her grief. If you were directing *The Trojan Women*, what advice would you give the actor playing her?'

The tutor looked inquiringly around the table. Sam, currently mesmerised by the tanned, muscular arms of the man in the pale blue polo shirt sitting next to him, was about to let the question pass when one of them shot up.

'Joss?'

'Ask the actress to get inside her head?'

'Precisely. Rule number one. Anything else?'

'Imagine how she feels being stripped of her identity and made a slave?' another man asked.

'Absolutely.'

Next, a woman in a T-shirt with a Van Gogh sunflower straddling her voluptuous chest waved for attention. 'Kirsty?'

'Her agony at the thought of her beautiful daughter now a tyrant's concubine, too?'

'Yes.'

'And her confusion when Cassandra passes off the relationship as being a genuine match?' piped up a fourth person.

'Indeed. There's always something intriguing about Cassandra, isn't there?'

Is there, why? Sam wanted to know, finally homing in on the discussion. For some reason, he always found Cassandra rather irritating, even if her wisdom was never appreciated by her contemporaries. He'd probably be considered chauvinist for saying so, but, as with real people, you were either drawn to mythological characters or not. Baddies like Clytemnestra were far more fun.

At that moment, the sun emerged from behind a cloud and, streaming through the open window, caught the fine hairs on the back of Joss's arms. Delicate wisps of pale bronze and gold gleamed as he stretched out to pick up a biro.

Sam was forming a question in his head when a bright-eyed Glaswegian woman beat him to it. 'If it was me, I'd be more worried about ma wee lassie than maself.'

'Valid point. So, you see, we've already got the ball rolling before we've even started analysing the text.'

'Shouldn't *that* be Rule Number One?' Sam finally piped up. 'Surely the text is always the starting point for both actor and director?'

'Good thinking. You could say the two go hand in hand.'

Well, one could hardly discuss a character *before* investigating the dialogue, unless you'd already seen a production of the play or read about it, Sam thought. But the room wasn't air-conditioned, and, despite the mild breeze wafting in and tickling those enticing hairs, it was too hot to be argumentative.

If truth be known, he still quite fancied the tutor as well: a tall, slim and compelling academic type but, alas, not much sense of fun and prone to be pedantic. He'd chatted him up in the bar last year, but, confined by tutor-student protocol, they'd both sensed the futility of developing their mild attraction and, instead, settled for a lively discussion on the production values of the National Theatre's recent all-male *As You Like It* – which had at least provided an opportunity for some flirtatious asides. Besides, at that point, Sam hadn't been quite ready to fully explore his sexual inclinations.

In the intervening months, Sam's stage experience had been augmented by principal roles in two large-scale musicals, during which he'd also made a couple of well-adjusted gay friends, whose domestic partnership appeared to be unreservedly accepted – at least in operatic society circles. Their friendship was providing him with the opportunity to open up about his confused feelings, the sympathetic guidance they offered allowing his remaining lingering inhibitions, in principle if not practice, to finally thaw. All that was needed was the opportunity to meet someone with the key to finally release him from himself.

Here in the semi-rural East Midlands, the balmy August weather and being surrounded by a surfeit of attractive, intelligent males reminded him how late he was leaving it to 'get a life', as his old college friend Tansy had recently urged him.

He'd first spotted Joss the previous evening when everyone was assembling in the hall for an introductory chat from the course director and, unaware of Sam's presence, he had settled on a chair in the row in front. Sam guessed he was a few years older than himself: medium height with good skin and a stocky but trim body topped by a clean, open face. It wasn't that he was especially handsome; it was his compact, smiley ordinariness which appealed. Catching little of what Joss was saying to the person sitting next to him, he was, nonetheless, struck by the man's friendly but unselfconscious demeanour. It contrasted favourably with some other course members who, in carrying voices, were busily impressing each other as if auditioning for the RSC.

Afterwards, he'd been too caught up renewing his acquaintance with people he knew, and too inhibited, to introduce himself. They had, however, exchanged awkward grins when queuing at the bar. Awkward for Sam, anyway, who was always disconcerted by attractive men in better physical shape than himself.

That morning, Joss was the last to arrive in class. After excusing himself, he'd quietly sidled into the spare seat next to Sam – who had immediately found the close proximity of the man disturbing.

It was the group's first session. For the next eight mornings, the bunch of ten men and women of mixed ages would be investigating the challenges to actors and directors of selected dramatic texts dealing with *Myth, Ritual & Magic*. Along the corridor, another group was exploring relevant aspects of Genet's plays, and a third, Shakespeare's use of transformation. In the afternoon, they'd all change into looser clothing for improvisational work with other tutors.

Spotting, some eighteen months earlier, an advertisement in *The Stage* for an annual summer school on the theme *Fact & Fantasy*, Sam had signed up and, having enjoyed it, done so with the same organisation again this year. Situated a mile away from an old market town, the school took place on the campus of a residential training college which, during the long summer vacations, provided a venue for various adult education courses. He'd felt in his element the previous year, spending quality time with like-minded people, and made some good acquaintances. It reminded him of the happy three years he'd spent on a similar site not so long ago while training to be a teacher in Manchester where he was now living and working.

The summer school attracted not only educational specialists in drama but an assortment of keen theatre-goers, amateur actors and directors. The tuition was of a high standard. Sam, ambitious to move forward in the adult education and non-commercial sectors, was grabbing any opportunity to extend his knowledge and skills.

'Why,' the tutor said, 'do you think Hecuba loathes Helen so much?'

'She sees her as being totally disloyal, doesn't she?' It was Kirsty again. 'I mean, Helen has already destroyed a nation and is about to undermine what's left of the woman's dignity.'

'No one can stand her, can they?' Sam heard himself say.

'Except the men,' Joss replied.

A titter went around the room.

Sam looked at Joss.

Joss looked at Sam. And winked.

'Now, I'm going to put you in pairs,' the tutor said, quickly going around the table and delegating partners. Sam's heart skipped a beat realising he would be teamed up with Joss. 'I'd like you to find some time on your own later to discuss the relationship between the two women, and, when we reassemble tomorrow, I'll get you to feed back. We'll compile a list,' here he indicated a flipchart in the corner, 'as a starting point for character development. Then we'll put the text to one side, push back the tables and chairs and create our own confrontations between them. Ok?'

Putting away their biros and notebooks, people shuffled towards the door, all talking to the person they were paired with.

'Howdy pardner,' Joss said touching the brim of an imaginary Stetson.

'Hi,' Sam responded, a little awkwardly.

Everyone was now congregating in the hallway leading to the cafeteria. Joss and Sam headed in the same direction and joined the queue.

'You probably gathered, I'm Sam,' he said, unnecessarily sticking out his hand. Bessie's social training ran deep.

'And I'm...'

'Joss.'

'Yes.'

Sam liked the warm, firm grip of Joss's hand. His bashfulness began to evaporate. As sometimes happened, he then risked spoiling things by coming out with a foolish follow-up. Without thinking, he heard himself say, 'Bags me be Helen.'

'Hadn't got you down as the *femme fatale* type,' Joss said.

Sam sighed inwardly with relief. 'Chance and all that.'

Joss roared. 'Never know your luck!'

Glancing at him, Sam caught the mischievous glint in the other man's eye but, instead of holding his look, clumsily turned away. If their flip exchange had successfully tested the water, he was unprepared for the frisson it triggered. Had the two of them managed to cross fifty miles in two minutes, or...? Go slow, Sammy, he told himself.

'Next!' the serving lady called across the counter. 'Chicken pie or Toad-in-the-hole?'

This time, he dared not look back at Joss.

After passing on the hot food and lingering with their trays in front of the prepared salads, they made their selection and moved towards a small table for two in the corner.

'To be truthful...' Joss said, 'I'm a bit out of my comfort zone here.'

'Euripides is daunting until you appreciate where he's coming from.'

'Don't misunderstand me, I've always been crazy about the theatre, but the Greek classics are certainly a challenge. Actually, it was the reason I chose that option. I'm quite well-versed in Shakespeare, if you'll pardon the pun, and Genet's a bit too...'

'Poetically erotic?' Sam volunteered.

'Quite,' Joss said with another knowing smile.

'We'll be going on to *The Bacchae* later in the week. Very bloodthirsty.'

'What larks, eh?'

Wishing to push the conversation on, Sam said, 'So, what do you do, work-wise?'

'Well...'

'Sorry, you don't have to answer that.'

'No, it's just boring. I'm an accountant.'

Sam felt a groan forming in his throat until Joss added, 'I'd always envisaged myself doing something arts-related, but... parental pressure and all that.'

'Not you too?'

'You're an accountant as well?'

'No. I meant, parental pressure.'

'That's interesting,' Joss said. 'No, I'm being rather unfair. My family are always very supportive, but as I was coming to the end of my time at uni, I realised that as I didn't want to teach and hadn't done well enough to go for a doctorate, a mediocre English degree wasn't going to be the open sesame to anything I'd vaguely considered doing. Dad said, "You've always been good with figures. Why not go for that and...?"'

Sam finished his sentence for him '…you can always follow your artistic bent in your spare time?'

'How did you guess?'

'Long story.'

'It meant more study, of course. I got an office job for a couple of years until I was better qualified and then set up on my own. When you get into the nitty-gritty of people's businesses, it can be absorbing. More importantly, it pays the bills.'

'Were you a late developer then, theatrically speaking?'

Joss nodded. 'It was only when someone invited me to take a walk-on with a local drama group. I really caught the acting bug. Until then I'd simply been an enthusiastic audience member. Always imagined being on stage would be scary.'

'You obviously enjoyed it?'

'And found I was quite good at it, too.' Here he gave Sam a sham self-deprecating look. 'Other people seemed to think so, anyway, which gave me confidence. It was healthy to be with a group of other people on my nights off. Bookkeeping can be lonely. Now I've more free time but recognise I've a lot of catching-up to do. The emphasis here is as much on the practical as the academic side of drama, which will be helpful if I go on to direct. That really appeals to me: taking what seems obscure on the page and giving it dramatic life. I'm learning a lot already.'

'You certainly seem on the ball.'

'Thanks.'

Sam was beginning to feel comfortable with Joss. The dining room was emptying fast and everyone else had either paired off too or got into groups of their own. They were left undisturbed in their bubble. The need to keep talking appeared to be mutual. The conversation flowed effortlessly on.

'So, what was the last thing you were involved in?' Sam said.

'*The Threepenny Opera.*'

'Not everyone's cuppa, Brecht. All those alienation devices.'

'Great, edgy songs, though. We had a very go-ahead director, ex-OUDS and all that. He turned our hall into a theatre-in-the-round. A sharp learning

145

curve for everyone! As I sing a bit too, I found myself playing the Balladeer. Even got some solo dance steps. I was petrified until I started singing and dancing, then … sort of took off.'

'The music fuels you.'

'Certainly does.'

'How did it go down?'

'Everyone raved. If they didn't like it, they were aware it was a bit highbrow and weren't going to admit it.' He paused as if deciding whether he should ask: 'Don't you find there's something a tad self-satisfied about amateur companies and the way their audiences uncritically pander to them?'

'Cringe-making comments like "how do you remember all those lines?"'

Joss laughed. 'Absolutely! Though you sound far more experienced than me?'

Sam took a deep breath. 'Oh, I don't know about that…' He didn't intend to scare the guy off by over-playing his hand.

'Tell me how you got started.'

'How long have you got?'

Joss gave an amiable shrug. 'Let's have coffee. We're not in a rush.'

A few minutes later, he returned from the counter with the drinks and a couple of eclairs. 'I'm not eating one on my own,' he said. I'll work it off in the movement session this afternoon.' Sam sighed, thinking of the pounds he needed to lose himself, while pleased someone was taking charge. 'Right, then,' Joss said, 'your brilliant theatrical career, now!'

'I was sent away to boarding school at thirteen.'

'Ugh!'

'And left at seventeen with three useless O Levels but four Drama prizes.'

'Gosh! What went right?'

Sam briefly summarised the rest of his teenage years and losing the battle with his parents to study for a theatrical career. He decided to play down how softly and oh-so-well-meaningly they'd fanned his insecurity.

'Even your mother?'

'As always, she tried playing good cop and lamely said, "You can act as a hobby."'

'Now I see what you meant earlier,' Joss said.

Sam glossed over the two unsuccessful two years he'd spent battling to obtain sufficient qualifications, aided by private tuition, to win a place at university and how, when he continually failed the required science and language subjects, the scales falling from their eyes, Hugh's patience had finally run out. 'I'm not sending any more good money running off after bad,' he'd told Sam. 'You'll be nineteen in a couple of weeks. You're on your own now, lad. I've got to start saving for my retirement. There'll always be a home for you here, but it's up to you, now, to get yourself a job and contribute towards your keep.'

'In the nick of time, a long-delayed response to an application for a clerical post with the BBC arrived. For over twelve months, I commuted into central London each day, brushing shoulders with iconic faces in the Broadcasting House cafeteria and rushing to and from the *Woman's Hour* offices hugging files of newspaper cuttings. Things were ratcheting up that year on the culture front. Cliff and Petula suddenly became passé. Overnight it was all The Stones and the Mersey Beat.'

'Remember it well,' Joss said. 'But what an opportunity!'

'For the first time in my life, I made some good friends. Once a week, in all weathers, we'd go swimming after work. Then supper afterwards at a small coffee house in Soho.'

'Not *Act One - Scene One*?' Joss said. Sam nodded. 'I loved that café. Great homemade burgers!'

'Bliss!'

'It's a men's shirt boutique now. Pity.'

Sam gave a moue, thinking how strange it was they were discovering so many small but significant things in common. 'It was a great place to work, but the job wasn't leading anywhere. When I discovered I could spend three years training as a teacher *and* specialise in Drama, I leapt at the chance. They were the happiest years of my life and the time I really began believing in myself.'

'A compromise that pleased your parents, too?'

'I think so, although they couldn't understand why I wanted to go into teaching. I'd always hated school. Last month I completed my second year at a primary school in Withington and am now teaching everything *except* Drama.'

'You must have had a reason.' Joss said.

'I feel most comfortable with younger children. I easily get bored concentrating on one thing all the time. With youngsters, you're constantly thinking creatively on your feet to keep their attention. I wanted to save the theatre for what I think of as my *other* life.'

'So now you have two lives?'

'Yes.'

'Daddy and Mummy knew best after all?'

'I may never know. I'd still have liked the chance to see whether I could have made it on the stage. In another life, perhaps.'

He felt was talking about himself so much. 'Now, how about you?'

'Acting?' Sam nodded.

'As I've indicated, it's great spending several evenings a week letting off steam after straining my eyes looking at figures all day.'

'I can imagine what fun the Kurt Weill must have been. I do musicals too these days but haven't yet had a big solo.'

Joss licked his finger and drew a one-up sign in the air.

Sam laughed. He desperately wanted to carry on chatting but, after glancing at his watch, said, 'Better get moving, it's ten to two. See you later?'

* * *

Over the next few days, Sam and Joss spent a lot of time together both alone and in the company of other people on the course. As everyone got to know each other, which was inevitable seeing as they were constantly discussing human dilemmas, it wasn't always easy to find a quiet corner to pick up where they'd last left off. Also, bonding requires discretion in a goldfish tank.

Whenever they were alone, the two delved deeper into their past lives. Joss filled Sam in on his own childhood in a village in Hertfordshire. The eldest child of four with three sisters, he'd never strayed far from home before going to college himself.

Stimulated by the occasional well-placed double entendre, a strong rapport was developing. Neither of them had so far opened up about their emotional lives, despite a tantalising undercurrent of tacit curiosity and sly looks. They found themselves thinking along similar lines, quoting from plays and books they both loved – and even completing each other's sentences.

On the third night of the course, Joss and a couple of women met up for coffee in Sam's room to discuss a scene they were preparing. When everyone had gone, Sam noticed Joss' cream-coloured sweater which he'd left behind on a chair. Picking it up, his first instinct was to take it to him along the corridor but, strangely aroused by its comforting softness, couldn't let it go.

He tried reading a book, but Joss's voice and impish smile kept intruding. He made himself some more coffee, but that kept him awake. He undressed and got into bed but was unable to sleep.

Joss refused to get out of his head.

Sam had been infatuated before, not only with Clive Huntley. He'd enjoyed surreptitious tendresses for a couple of other boys.

But this wasn't like any of those. This was different.

He reached for the sweater, burying his face in the lambswool and inhaling the heady aroma of soap powder mingled with the faint but alluring musk of Joss's body, and clung to it for several minutes, overcome by a mixture of frustration and desire.

It had taken him all his life to meet someone with whom he shared such a close mental affinity. Could he dare hope it might be reciprocated, or was that too much to wish for? Blinking back tears, he quickly withdrew his head from the wool, dabbing the slight damp patch that had formed on the sleeve with a towel, and placed it on the open window ledge to dry.

13

A Walk in the Wood

1969
Sam

After dinner on the fourth evening, Sam and Joss agreed to go for a stroll along the nearby country pathways.

An extended wood ran along the left-hand side of a small river beyond the college grounds which, after about a mile, led to the main road. You could either walk further on into the village or turn and saunter back along the pavement to the main gates.

They walked in companionable silence along the path between the trees to the accompaniment of trickling water, scurrying sounds of tiny creatures in the undergrowth and the odd flutter of a restless bird in the branches above.

By now he knew Joss lived in a flat in North London but not with whom, if indeed anyone, although his conversation was always peppered with the names of friends of both sexes, one of whom, Bren, had cropped up a number of times and twitched Sam's curiosity.

Eventually, he ventured, 'Are you happy in Islington?'

'Yes. It's a tiny two-bedroomed place off City Road, but we like it.'

Sam tensed slightly. '*We?*'

'Bren and me. We… live together.'

'Ah.'

151

'I should have explained. I was going to,' Joss said awkwardly, 'but kept putting it off.'

'I think I… assumed.'

'There's never the right moment is there? Not back there. You don't want everyone to know your business. Some people are still a bit strange about two men living together, even other so-called thesps. It's fine while you're still students, but there comes a point when…' Sam waited jumpily for the end of the sentence. It didn't arrive. He then said, 'He's considerably older than me.'

'Ah.'

'Forty-five to be precise.' He paused, then added, 'He was my English tutor at university.'

Sam tried not to sound too taken aback. 'I see.'

'I bumped into him one night at *The Cherry Orchard* during my last vacation. Afterwards, he invited me for a drink at his club on the pretext of finding out how college was working out.' One thing, or rather one glass of Chablis, led to another and we bared our souls as we'd never had the chance to before. We both confessed we'd always fancied each other and, before I knew what was happening, I'd been bundled into a cab and was on my way to Islington. After that, we met up whenever we could. As soon as I graduated, I moved in with him.

'How did your parents feel about… Bren?' There, he'd spoken the man's name aloud.

'I don't think they tumbled for a while. Mercifully, by the time they did, they'd got to know and become fond of him. Mum and Dad are very broadminded and pretty unshockable. And parents can turn a blind eye and deaf ear to things they don't want to know too much about, can't they?'

'Tell me about it.'

'Besides, at the time, my sisters' flower-powered love lives were causing them far more problems than mine. My leaving home simply gave them mental space to worry about them even more. They may like to kid themselves they're bohemian, but the idea of a fifteen-year-old spending half her time in a hippy commune when she should be practising her viola is far more of a problem than a sane son shacked up with an old queen.'

'Your sisters sound as if they might be fun?'

'Mercifully, they're settling down in careers now. The eldest is married, and the youngest has joined the army. My best mate is my middle sister, Katy. She's four years younger than I am and very artistic. A clothes designer with bags of talent – and gay friends of both sexes, too. So, very understanding. I often wonder whether she's hiding something from herself. There are a lot of references to "Petra" and a "Bonnie". Funnily enough, everyone, especially Mum and Dad, now come to me with their troubles rather than the other way around. I'm regarded as the sensible, grounded member of the family!'

'Was it a problem for you with Bren being your tutor? I presume this was before the Act?'

'For my last term, especially. He felt uncomfortable with the situation and gave up lecturing.'

Sam was impressed by the degree of their commitment.

'Until the law changed, we had to behave all butch and discreet. His first love had always been writing. I encouraged him to do a part-time course in Journalism. He's theatre editor of *Culture Vulture*, the arts magazine. There's not a lot of money in it, but my work pays quite well and we get by reasonably, although…' Here Joss paused.

'Yes?'

'I… I think I may be getting too old for him now.'

Sam looked at him uncomprehendingly.

'In *that* way. He prefers getting his oats from younger men.'

'How much younger?'

'Anything over twenty-five is a bit yawny to him. I'll be thirty in a couple of months. Make no mistake, he's no paedo. As he says, he likes 'em to have feathers on. Preferably, oriental ones. Our anniversary meal last year in a local Chinese restaurant turned out to be a great mistake!'

Sam smiled politely. 'You look far younger.'

'But not twenty anymore. And not Chinese. Don't misunderstand me. We're devoted to each other. He's my rock. We just give each other a lot of slack – if you know what I mean?'

Sam didn't. Not totally. He was in turmoil. He could see exactly what Joss meant. But here he was, having at long last possibly found a soulmate, being told the man was in a devoted although, what did they call it... *open?* relationship? Which meant he might be available for... what exactly?

Joss broke the silence. 'You're shocked, aren't you?'

'N...no....'

'Come on. I'm not stupid.'

'Honestly, I'm not,' Sam said, untruthfully.

'Surely you have someone special in your life?'

'Not at the moment,' he said cagily.

Pause.

'Here I've been jabbering away about myself, taking it for granted that we're both well... you *are*, aren't you? You must be. I've not been barking up the wrong tree, have I? If so, you deserve an Oscar.'

'I'll take that as a compliment.'

'Sorry, I... I didn't mean you're terribly outrageous.'

'Not *terribly* then.'

'I'd just assumed, with your great sense of humour, you were a kindred spirit.'

'I'll settle for that.'

'Good!' We clicked right away, didn't we?'

'Yes.'

'You're still a bit of a conundrum, though. I've been honest about myself and I've learnt a lot about you but nothing very... personal, either. Don't tell me you're having a terribly hush-hush affair with an Arabian prince or something?'

They walked over to a fallen log. Sam sat down and Joss joined him. His head was still buzzing. He still wasn't quite sure where he stood. Was he being auditioned as a potential add-on lover, or... what? Joss had been sending out signals but so far hadn't made a move. Although they lived many miles from each other, albeit within striking distance of his parents, he might not get the

opportunity to make such a good friend again and didn't want to lose him –
even if he must remain just a friend.

'Your turn then. Off you go,' Joss said. 'I promise it won't go any further
than Brer Fox slinking into the bushes over there.'

'Freud would have had a field day with me,' Sam said at last.

'Lucky old Siggy.'

There he went again, teasing. He took a deep breath and began. 'Call me
Oedipus…'

'Oedi or E-Y-D-I-E?'

Sam glared at him. 'Look, I'm trying to be serious.'

'Sorry, go on.'

Slung causally around Joss's shoulders, Sam spotted the cream sweater.

It finally clicked. Arms… wool… *need.*

He closed his eyes for a moment to make the connection, before saying,
'Something occurred when I was about twelve which, I've realised, affected
me more than I'd thought. My mother was sitting on a chair at the dining
table nursing her after-lunch coffee and wearing a favourite cardigan. There's
something very comforting about wool, isn't there?' he said, half to himself.

'I know what you mean.'

'Anyway, I approached her from behind and, as I'd done many times
before, spontaneously hugged her. I don't think there was a special reason.'

'Do you need one to cuddle someone you love?'

'I hadn't thought so till then. I just wanted to.'

'Before, she'd always relaxed, reached for my arms and squeezed them
affectionately. On this occasion, though, she… didn't.' Sam trembled slightly.
Narrating the incident had brought it poignantly back.

'Go on…"

'She tensed up, as if saying: "You're too old for that anymore. You must
become a man and stand on your own feet."'

Joss said nothing.

'I never tried again. I'd always been brought up to give her a peck on the
cheek before going to school and arriving home, and at bedtime. Those little

formalities continued, but from then on, much as I knew she cared for me deeply, I knew I could never really… hug her again.'

'You make me feel so lucky. My parents are both very tactile.'

Dare he tell Joss about his reactions to the sweater; risk revealing his feelings for him – or would that be disastrous? Just because Joss had told him all about himself didn't mean he was attracted to him, however well they seemed to be getting along. He couldn't risk dropping his guard only to see his arms stiffen as Bessie's had done. It would set him back immeasurably if, after all that had happened over the past few days, Joss rejected him with something along the lines of: 'Yes, we've a lot in common, and I like you a lot too – but not in *that* way.' He hoped he knew him well enough by now to trust he wasn't playing with him, either. Though, how well did he really know him? How much did you ever know anyone – especially a man you'd only recently met?

Sam knew he was a sexual novice. Whoever lumbered themselves with him was in for a lot of work. His experience of handling his own and anyone else's body hadn't moved on much since his days in the bushes with other fourth-formers. It was ridiculous, a man of almost twenty-five admitting that to himself, but there it was. As for the Bren problem, it didn't seem much of an issue for Joss. If anything developed between them, that was something he'd have to deal with a step at a time and try to put into perspective.

Confused and uncomfortable, he looked ahead through the trees to the sky where the last of the light was fading. Surrounded by reassuring tree trunks and mature August foliage, the premature twilight enfolded them in a world of their own.

'When did you first sense you were gay?' Joss said at last.

'I suppose you always know, don't you, but can't put a name to it?' Sam told Joss about Clive. I've always been attracted to men, although that never stopped me getting close to several women I grew fond of, either.

'How close?'

'Shared beds with them and… snogged. Not a lot else. None of them took me seriously as a suitor and soon dumped me for more macho guys. It's the ones I didn't try it on with who've remained special friends.' Changing tack, he said, 'I used to think the way I was… am, was partly due to being sent away to an all-male boarding school.'

'Situational homosexuality, I believe it's called. The jury's still out on that.'

'Did you, Joss?'

'No. They can't lay that one at my door. Though I imagine being surrounded by so much bubbling testosterone has its upside?'

'We were in dormitories of twelve. Early on, when we were all going through the same changes, discovering the new sensations our bodies were capable of and learning it was even more exciting to share them with someone else, yes. But as we grew older, we became more secretive and learnt it was taboo. Not that it stopped happening. It was currency amongst certain prefects to vie for the prettiest fourth former and get them to run errands for them in exchange for a tanner and some innocuous fun.

'A tanner?'

'Sixpence. Or a bar of *Fruit & Nut*. But I'm sure most of them grew out of all that.'

'You never did?'

'No. And as you pointed out, until two years ago, it was still illegal. I've always been a law-abider.'

'Boring! Then?'

'To cap it, I went through a religious phase.'

Joss groaned. 'And discovered it was sinful as well?'

'Yes.'

'Double whammy.'

'Not to mention the ongoing guilt of knowing I was programmed to meet a nice girl, get married and have two children, a car, a four-bedroomed house with a garden and a reliable job with a pension plan.'

'It was the way we were brought up. I managed to jettison that guilt quite quickly.'

'Maybe that's the difference between us. There's a small part of me, even now, that thinks that's what I want,' Sam said.

'Want, or believe is expected of you?'

'Both. I'd quite like to be a Dad. Wouldn't' you?"

Joss didn't answer right away, then said, 'Wouldn't it be amazing if, in our lifetime, male partnerships were legalised and we could adopt babies or get someone to have them for us?'

'Have our cake and eat it?'

'Just a thought. You didn't even have some fun at college?'

'One Sunday evening, I met a friend of a friend in a pub in Manchester. He drove me back to college and on the way back pulled into a lane. After some necking, he invited me away for a weekend.'

'Did you accept?'

'No. It was tempting. But… something held me back.'

'The tape under your pillow?'

'Probably.'

'And since then?'

'I've friends in amdrams who encourage me to go out and enjoy myself. Unfortunately. . .'

'What?'

'I… I've a body-image problem.'

'Don't we all. I'm always nervous about people seeing my appendectomy scar for the first time. It's a particularly long one. Why?'

'I'd feel embarrassed to…'

'*Why?*

But Sam wouldn't elaborate.

The light was now almost gone in the wood. They were beginning to notice the air growing cooler and their legs were telling them to move on. Joss got up and held out his hand. Sam took it and also stood.

Hand-in-hand they took a few paces towards the road which, as the street lights flickered on, gradually emerged in the distance. An owl hooted and something in the undergrowth rustled, twitched as if settling down for the night, then fell silent.

After several paces, the men instinctively paused in the shadows beneath a wych elm.

'You've got to stop all this,' Joss said.

'All what?'

'Analysing. You must take your life in your hands and enjoy it more.'

'Women… men… I feel so inadequate?'

'Why?'

'Undesirable, I suppose.' There, he'd done it. Made a complete idiot of himself.

'No, you're not. You're… beautiful.'

Sam turned to him, incredulous. With his clean-cut features and tidily parted mousey hair he guessed he was pleasant enough to look at – though his shaving mirror always told him he'd never shed a certain boyish, but unsexy, eagerness. Apart from that one time with the man in the car, something always prevented people considering him lover material. No one had told him he was attractive before. And certainly not beautiful. Could he trust Joss? In the silence of the August evening, he heard his heart thumping.

Desperately seeking confirmation, he nervously murmured, 'Am I?'

Joss took Sam in his arms.

When they released each other, Joss, as if not wanting to break the spell, lowered his hand, lightly pressed it into the small of Sam's back and massaged it reassuringly.

Together they continued strolling towards the road. Only on reaching it did they feel obliged to draw away from each other.

'When we get back…' Joss said.

'A drink in the bar to be sociable?'

'And then?'

Sam was terrified to respond.

Joss answered for him. 'Your room or mine?'

* * *

Throughout the hour they spent chatting to fellow course members, Sam wondered whether people could see he was only physically present. Going to bed with someone was, he knew, the most natural thing in the world. After all, wasn't this what he'd longed for ever since parting, with barely a handshake, from Clive Huntley eight years before? He felt both elated and apprehensive about what was to follow, like a child eager to unwrap an important birthday gift yet fearing the long-awaited experience might turn out to be an anti-climax – with himself doing the letting-down.

Louis Armstrong made way for Otis Redding before someone slipped yet another coin into the juke box and the intro to Aquarius from *Hair* insinuated itself into the hubbub.

Joss glanced at him and casually raised an eyebrow.

'Time for me to go and do my homework,' Sam said to their friends.

'Bugger the Bacchae,' Joss muttered.

They reached Sam's room first.

Another hug.

'I'll take a shower and be back with you in ten,' Joss said.

'Good idea, I'll do the same.'

Joss returned having washed and changed into a clean T-shirt. Sam was already in bed, decorously covered in a sheet. Slipping off his clothes, Joss bent over the bed and gently kissed him. 'Move up,' he said, pulling back a corner of the sheet and slipping in beside him.

He needn't have worried. Joss was a gentle lover and patient teacher. Not that he required much tuition: instinct took over. In any case, the following hour was mainly one of affectionate togetherness. 'Is this enough for you?' he asked timorously at one point, having read sufficient gay pulp fiction to know what might be expected of him.

'We can experiment another time. Tonight, I just want to be with you,' Joss said.

Eventually they flopped back exhausted on the pillows and drifted off to sleep.

Sam woke the next morning still snuggled up against Joss's back. 'Well, that was a first, in more ways than one,' he said.

'What d'you mean?'

'I've never slept with anyone in a single bed before.'

'Have to admit I'm one up on you there,' Joss said. 'But it worked, didn't it?'

The look on his face provided the answer.

When Joss left to return to his own room, Sam looked in his shaving mirror.

Was it his imagination, or was there a slight change?

* * *

The final day of the course arrived.

Sam was going to London for a couple of weeks to stay with his parents and catch up on some shows.

'Then we'll be travelling back to London together,' Joss said.

'I won't cramp your style?'

Joss punched him lightly. 'Have you booked for anything yet?'

'*Hair*. And the National's *double-bill* of Shaw's *Back to Methuselah*.'

'An interesting collector's item. Look out for a cute young actress who comes out of an egg. Felicity Kendal, I think her name is.'

'And there's *The Merchant of Venice* in Edwardian dress at Regent's Park. I'd like to see *Promises, Promises*, but it doesn't open until next month. Maybe at half term. And…'

'Stop! I'm getting giddy. Maybe we can try for seats for a matinee in the Park?'

'That would be nice. Perhaps the Saturday before I go home?'

'Consider it arranged. My treat. You must come to dinner with us, too.'

'You mean you're going to tell Bren?'

'I already have. I phone him every other evening. He's dying to meet you.'

'I'm not very young. Or Chinese.'

'D'you imagine I'd have considered introducing you to him if you were?' They both laughed. 'Of course, he doesn't know quite *everything* but knows me too well not to have a pretty good idea. I hope we can all become friends.'

'Would you like that?'

'If you would.'

'I can't bear the thought of never seeing you again.'

'That won't happen. As long as neither of us gets silly. It's tough on me, too. These past few days have been special. But my life is with Bren, and I have to release you to the delights of your flat in… Rusholme, over the bookmakers?'

Sam nodded. 'You must come and stay over. They do some good productions at The Library Theatre.

'I'll try and scrounge a couple of days when there's something on I want to see.'

Terrified of taking anything for granted, Sam said, 'I've a Z-bed for visitors.'

'I don't think that will be necessary, do you?'

His face lit up then fell again as he wondered how he'd cope with an on-off arrangement.

'Cheer up. But look, it wouldn't be fair if I asked you to save yourself for me. Nor must you. You don't know how amazing you are. I like to think I've helped launch you, and nothing would make me happier than to watch you sail off on your own and start having fun. Just don't rush into trying to meet Mr Right too soon. Be very careful who you get to know and suss them out before accepting an invitation for coffee – or offering one yourself. Now's your chance to make up for lost time and get some lovely experience behind you. Someone else, almost as fabulous as me, is bound to come along in due course. In the meantime, there's still lots for us both to look forward to.'

It was hard for Sam to be miserable for long when he was with Joss, who seemed to have inherited his parents' relaxed attitude to life. They'd married much younger than his own and had children before reaching their thirties. Joss's father was only a couple of years older than Bren and had recently started going to cricket matches at The Oval with him.

The train journey passed quickly in a feast of yet more theatrical reminiscing and some critical analysis of novels they'd both either enjoyed or loathed. Back in London, Sam felt a pang as Joss disappeared to the

Underground line which would carry him off to The Angel, while he stepped on the escalator for the platform in the opposite direction.

* * *

'There's a call for you,' Bessie called up to him.

It was the Monday morning. He was enjoying a lie-in.

'I think it's that new friend of yours.'

As good as his word, Joss was ringing to confirm the tickets for *The Merchant of Venice* and offer a couple of dates for dinner at Islington.

Bren and Joss's cosy flat made him feel immediately at home, its floor-to-ceiling bookcase crammed with novels, plays, travel and art books of all descriptions and the finest hi-fi sound system he had ever seen. Their collection of LPs included, along with many box-sets of operas and classical music, original cast recordings of every musical he'd ever heard of. And quite a number he hadn't.

Squashy sofas, a couple of well-used Victorian armchairs and a large coffee table left little room to manoeuvre in the living room, while the tiny second bedroom doubled as Bren's study and dining area and, with a sofa-bed in one corner, sleeping quarters for guests. The meal from the galley kitchen, which comfortably allowed only one person to work at a time, was delicious. As well as everything else, the men were both good cooks, which put into perspective Sam's own reliance on packets of *Vesta* spaghetti bolognaise.

Sam needn't have feared meeting Bren. His openness and easy wit disarmed him almost as soon as they shook hands. It was immediately apparent that Joss and he were two sides of the same coin. They reminded him somewhat of Ernest Shepard's drawings for Winnie-the-Pooh. If Joss was Tigger, wise Bren, shortish with dark eyes peering through large, brown-rimmed spectacles, bore a strong resemblance to Owl.

On their last afternoon together before his return to Manchester, Sam was, understandably subdued. It was a perfect mid-August afternoon. The theatre in Regent's Park was the ideal setting for a farewell meeting of like-minded friends. Yet the thought of parting with them both, especially Joss, was almost unbearable.

As they took their places after the second interval in readiness for the trial scene, Joss sensed Sam's mood. 'Portia wins, you know.'

They smiled at each other. Then Sam looked away. He didn't want him to see the moistness that had begun glazing his eyes.

14

The Invisible Enemy

1973
Bessie

The problem began when the men came to service the hot air heating system. It transpired they had left an essential valve to work itself loose.

That was Friday. Late on the Sunday afternoon, Bessie felt a strange headache coming on. It wasn't quite like one of her occasional migraines, but with her history of funny heads, she took one of her special pills just in case.

The medication had no effect.

Bizarrely, when she moved into the living room where she and Hugh were spending the rest of the day, the pressure behind her eyes and queasiness lifted. Nor did it return when she made brief trips to the kitchen for tea and snacks later.

She thought no more about it.

The next morning as she cleared away the breakfast dishes, she was hit by a heavy, nauseous feeling and returned to bed for what, she assumed, would be another hour or so.

By chance, Hugh, off work that day, as so often after breakfast when he had a quiet morning ahead, sat in his favourite Parker Knoll with *The Telegraph*, oblivious of the gas silently, odourlessly, seeping through the vents above the skirting board close to his chair.

Around eleven o'clock, a heavy thump aroused Bessie from her nap. 'Hugh,' she called, 'are you all right?' When he didn't answer, she put on her slippers and went downstairs. Noticing the cloakroom door was ajar, she knocked. 'Hugh… Hugh… are you in there?'

No response.

She tried pushing the door but it wouldn't budge. There was just enough space for her to crane her neck around it and see Hugh collapsed in a heap, his feet obstructing the door. A strong smell of vomit pervaded the air. She tried again: 'Hugh, Hugh, can you hear me?'

Again, no reply.

Bessie dashed to the phone table and dialled 999.

They always kept open a small glass panel at the top of the window. The fresh air must have slightly revived him for, as she returned, she heard a low moan. 'Are you all right, luv?' In response came a sound part groan, part 'no'. At least he was still conscious, she thought. She next heard him struggling to haul himself back off the floor and tried gently pushing the door again. This time, he'd been able to pull his legs in sufficiently for her to squeeze further into the room.

'Sorry, I don't know what's come over me,' he managed to splutter.

'Don't try to get up,' she added as he started pressing his hands on the floor to raise himself. 'Stay as you are, I've sent for an ambulance.' She fetched a cushion and gently placed it behind his head against the wall.

His face was cherry red.

After an anguished quarter of an hour, during which she kept him conscious with aimless prattle, the ambulance arrived and was parked in the driveway, the crew at the door with a stretcher. They rang the bell and, once inside, quickly assessed the situation. 'Open as many windows as possible,' their leader commanded, 'but for God's sake don't strike a match, flick a switch or use a cigarette lighter! And where's the gas switch? If it's not turned off immediately, we'll all succumb to the fumes.'

'On the wall – here,' Bessie said, pointing.

One of the crew turned the switch off while another, a woman, advised her to pack some overnight things, 'to be on the safe side – they often like to keep carbon monoxide cases in.' Bessie went upstairs to unearth the bags she always kept partly packed, normally in readiness for stop-overs in smart hotels rather than medical emergencies. She slipped into a pair of sensible shoes and collected their coats and scarves.

Once at A&E, Hugh was swiftly examined and made comfortable while a bed was prepared for him in Intensive Care.

After a couple of hours, during which time Bessie was also placed on a trolley and underwent various health checks, a doctor appeared in her cubicle to explain how Hugh's heart had been affected by the quantities of carbon monoxide that had quietly infiltrated his lungs, possibly resulting in a slight stroke. 'From what you've told us, he must have been sufficiently conscious to rush to the toilet and away from the full force of the gas. The nausea would have saved his life. We'll need to keep him here to carry out further checks.'

'He will get better, won't he?' Bessie said.

'Hopefully. Although we won't fully know the extent of any lasting damage to his heart or brain for a day or so. There's a strong possibility he won't be up-and-running for quite a while.'

'And myself?' Bessie asked, still feeling weak, slightly sick and headachy, but hoping it was mainly due to tension.

'You're likely to pick up more quickly, Mrs Owen. Staying upstairs prevented the gas reaching you to the same extent as your husband. We'd like you to stay here under observation too. With luck, we'll have you home again in a few days' time. It's a treacherous poison, I'm afraid. Neither of you should expect miracles. Now, about notifying your next of kin?'

Ever resourceful, Bessie kept emergency telephone numbers in her diary. The doctor asked the ward sister to telephone Sam's school and arrange for their neighbour, who kept a key, to be contacted and agree on arrangements for Dusty to be fed.

* * *

After a few days, Bessie was deemed sufficiently fit to return home, leaving Hugh in hospital for a further week. Matters seemed under control.

When Sam arrived home late on the Friday night, tired and spaced-out and looking as if he could do with a few days healing time himself, she began to worry about the effect the gassing was indirectly having on him, too.

Over the next forty-eight hours, Bessie tried getting Sam to open up. Concerning herself with his worries shifted some of those about Hugh and herself. She knew that he was not happy at the school he had moved to after leaving Withington a while back, but for someone who normally opened up to her easily about himself, he remained stubbornly quiet and deflected any attempt to be drawn on his own problems.

Something wasn't right.

15

Inner City Blues

1973 – 1974
Sam

When the head came into his classroom one afternoon to inform Sam that Bessie and Hugh were both in intensive care, he battled to juggle his wish to support them with his deepening work problems. The fact that he couldn't do much as he lived and worked two hundred miles away, only intensified his guilt. Who was keeping an eye on the house and looking after the cat, and, above all, what would he do if one or both of them remained invalided for any length of time?

For the last two-and-a-half years, Sam had held a post of special responsibility at a junior school in a problematic inner-city area of Manchester. He'd accepted the post as a step-up from his initial teaching job further afield at a school that largely drew children from what were archly referred to as *good* homes.

There, once he'd got the measure of the forty-odd children in his boisterous class and developed a rapport with them, the years passed enjoyably and often productively enough. By the third year, however, with no dead-men's-shoes in the offing, he'd felt he was getting into a rut and risked going for another rung up the professional ladder.

Sometimes, though, we don't know when our rut is the safest place to be. Sometimes, it's best to leave well alone.

Close to the boundaries of Moss Side and Hulme, Oakview School – a misnomer indeed – was a culture shock after Withington. At the interview, he'd somehow convinced the Head of his need for a challenge and had spent the past two years realising, too late, the extent to which he'd overestimated his capabilities.

As with many heavily populated urban districts, life for the inhabitants of the poorer parts of Manchester was often a never-ending struggle. Most of Sam's new pupils arrived each morning from one of the nearby back-to-back houses and tenements currently awaiting demolition as part of the city's slum-clearance programme – or the isolation of a new, impersonal tower block. His teaching practice, by now some years back, had limited his experience to kids from well-established and neighbourly council estates, the college having sheltered him from schools in fragmented communities with intakes of children of various nationalities and religious backgrounds such as this.

The diverse ethnicities mixed in with those from longer-established Mancunian families should have created a lively, cosmopolitan atmosphere. More often than not, however, the petty rivalry and tribal feuding of neighbouring families spilled over from the children's home lives into the classroom, kickstarting the morning with dispiriting quarrels which bubbled under the surface and throughout the day. Coming from a relatively small radius of homes, the inter-family relationships also intrigued him. Some of the children in the school were the aunts, uncles, nephews or nieces of those of a similar age to themselves. Those whose parents took their membership of a non-conformist church seriously would sometimes report back how Sam misinterpreted the scriptures according to their beliefs and, fuelled by newly acquired self-righteousness, berate him the next day in front of the class. He felt sorry for the handful of brighter children who struggled to keep their heads down, enduring the erratic climate around them in dignified silence until seriously incited – when they proved themselves more than capable of holding their own.

Tension amongst the better-adjusted children might be contained fairly quickly, but an irrational outburst from a single unstable or hyperactive child could ignite mayhem. Sam found himself conflicted, spending too much time and energy engaging the seriously backward and often disturbed children at the expense of the rest of the class, which, on a good day, was willing to meet him halfway and also deserved his attention.

He especially dreaded having to supervise a coachload of boys on their weekly trip to the local swimming pool, when any attempts to maintain discipline was almost always met with humiliating failure. Returning them to school a complete, undamaged group became his criterion of success.

Generally, Sam liked the children and was concerned for the educational development of the least fortunate, however wilful they might be. Many parents, even those of the most deprived children, were decent-minded people wanting the best for their offspring but trapped by their circumstances. It was only a minority who gave their children inconsistent guidance on matters of morality and acceptable behaviour and sometimes mistreated them, who caused the most problems. Given the conditions in which the families coped, often with a serious lack of income and privacy, it was hardly surprising the school's literacy level was eighteen months below the national average.

Under such circumstances, class discipline, and hence achievement, was totally dependent on the consistent firmness and personal magnetism of the teachers. Sam often felt guilty at missing the support of the more comfortably-off parents he'd known in Withington, who'd been more aspirational and better equipped to take a constructive interest in their offspring's development.

In some ways, Sam was a good teacher. Unfortunately, the specialist skills and, most importantly, the cool objectivity required in this particular environment were beyond him. One of the legacies of the victimisation he had endured at school was a self-defensive volatility that kicked in at the first sign of any kind of aggression. The situations here might be very different, but the often tense and, at times, coercive atmosphere was not dissimilar; it was a failing Sam kept under control for as long as things were reasonably normal. Normality, however, was rarely a feature of life at Oakview. Without warning, a single act of insubordination could cause his frustration to erupt and rouse the children, at the very moment they needed him to be icily calm.

He kept telling himself he'd signed up to impart knowledge, not be a social worker, even if his boss saw the role differently and required a broader set of skills. After making several attempts to change his job, it began to dawn on him that Oakview's notoriety, far from improving his prospects of further advancement, was holding him back from finding a niche where his creative teaching style would be better appreciated.

When, out of the blue, he found himself acting as Deputy Headmaster, covering for a colleague on maternity leave, the pressure cooker was poised to explode. His only safety valve was provided by the support he received from a teacher in the parallel class to his own, Jennie Bancroft, who helped keep him grounded and, whenever possible, cheerful.

Younger than Sam and not long out of college herself, Jennie was blessed with a calmer, more focussed presence in front of her class and fared better in the erratic climate of the school than he did. If it hadn't been for the times their classes joined forces and teamed up for story-times and games when, to the delight of the children, they became a relaxed double act, he wouldn't have lasted as long as he did. Both having a good sense of humour and sharing theatrical interests – Jennie was a competent actress – they got along very well.

Trouble traditionally comes in threes. First, Jennie suffered a bad attack of glandular fever which laid her low for several months when, more than ever, he could have done with her around to boost his morale. In addition to his already increased workload, Sam was now also required to monitor the roster of supply teachers who stood in for her. Then came his parents' gassing calamity. One of these issues he could have dealt with, two would have added additional hassle, but he'd have coped. Three drained any energy left over to cope with his taxing classroom problems.

Sam began behaving erratically and lost any remaining respect the children had for him.

Connie, who by now was retired and living only a few miles away, was the one person he might have turned to for help, but she was on a long post-retirement cruise around the world with Hannah. Besides, pride would have prevented him turning to her with his professional problems, understanding though she would have been – and later was. But by then the damage was done.

Things came to a head when Sam accidentally hurt a child who, resisting his attempts to get her to sit down, forcibly collided with the edge of a desk. Next day she was off school with a badly bruised thigh. Mortified, he tried to hide his distress but failed. This only weakened his class control more. To give them their due, his colleagues could see what had happened. The acting head, in consultation with the local school inspector, agreed he needed time off and released him for two weeks' sick leave. Later, on medical advice, it was extended to the end of the term.

His GP prescribed Librium to subdue his nerves, which only agitated him more. She then suggested he consulted a psychiatrist. But there was little point. He knew exactly what was wrong.

After a few days' rest, he felt well enough to make the journey back to South London to help oversee his parents' recovery and try to regain his sanity.

Once reassured that Hugh and Bessie were finally on the mend, he cashed in some of his savings and took a trip to Paris. There, long walks in the early spring sunshine along the banks of the Seine, visits to the Louvre and Versailles, an evening in the presence of the scintillating Zizi Jeanmaire at the *Casino de Paris* and romantic moonlit encounters around the steps of Sacré-Coeur helped him put his life back into perspective.

Returning to Rusholme, he deliberated: what should he do next? He was being paid until the end of term, but that wasn't far away. By now considerably refreshed, he knew he must make a decision: risk going back to the school or start all over again in another less stressful job. It didn't take long for him to make up his mind. After signing on at a job agency, it took only ten days for him to be offered a job in a local Council office which, amongst other things, oversaw the administration of local education.

It would take Sam a further year or so to get over his unhappy time at Moss Side and the feeling he had badly let down not only himself but the people who had shown faith in him. For a long time afterwards, he suffered occasional panic or anxiety attacks and developed a fear of heights and of trains and buses flying past him at high speed. While he found ways of managing these neuroses and accepted them as the legacy of a bad period in his life, they never completely went away and reoccurred whenever he felt deeply unhappy or insecure.

His new routine in a calm, comfortable office with three affable colleagues, his own desk, a coffee machine – and a tin of regularly topped-up biscuits for the four of them – provided a chance to collect his wits and recalibrate his future.

Jennie's own illness at this time incapacitated her to the extent that she, too, felt unequal to the task of going back to the classroom. Submitting her notice, at the end of the term she gave up her flat and returned home to live *pro tem* with her parents in Bramhall. She took a part-time secretarial course and brushed up on her self-taught shorthand and typing skills. A quick learner, having both poise and charm, Jennie soon obtained the post of PA to the Head of Marketing of a white goods company.

Despite the lingering effects of her glandular fever, she appeared to have few problems coping with her job. After Oakview, looking after only one 'unpredictable little boy' as she referred to her boss, a happily married man who doted on her, was easy. Finally feeling strong enough to leave her parents' home, she moved in with her friend Sue in a pleasant flat overlooking Seymour Park in Old Trafford.

Economic constraints imposed by the recession prevented companies from giving annual bonuses to staff. As a thank you for her good work, at the end of her first twelve months with *North West Electrics*, that autumn Jennie was offered a luxury break at a destination with A. N. Other of her choice.

On a romantic whim, she chose Vienna. Not just Vienna, but the Hotel Sacher, famous for its old-fashioned luxury and legendary calorie-clogged chocolate cake.

She invited Sam to go with her.

16

Viennese Whirl

1974
Sam

He lay back on the pillow, Jennie asleep beside him. Muffled sounds of city life beyond the smartly curtained window invaded his thoughts.

After their stop-over in Frankfurt to entertain family friends of Jennie's and, with their flight yesterday morning having been cancelled due to fog, they'd cut their losses and caught the train to Vienna. After a late arrival at the hotel, followed by a stroll around the Opera House and neighbouring streets to familiarise themselves with the local geography, they'd returned to their over-heated room and collapsed exhausted into bed. A day had been squandered. Better make up for lost time.

Nothing much happened beneath the goose-filled duvets that night. Nor would it the next. It rarely did with Jennie. Not that she wasn't affectionate – but only so far. Sam's highly-sexed colleague Tony would have considered their idea of romance very tame for a couple who'd been seeing quite a lot of each other over the past eighteen months.

Jennie ticked all Bessie's boxes as a suitable mate. She was pretty, wholesome but, above all, a girl who stuck to the rules. Sam enjoyed being with her and, occasionally, even getting very close to her. Snuggling up was the nicest thing about being in bed with someone, especially if you cared for

175

them, which, in Jennie's case, he did, even when it sent certain messages to parts of his body, making him wish she'd acquired more experience of men. Too often, after an encouraging start, she'd drift contentedly off to sleep, leaving him to sort himself out.

It was then he missed some of his other conquests. Sex was far less of a palaver with men.

His sexual emancipation hadn't paid dividends as quickly as he'd hoped. On the one hand, his relationship with Joss and Bren was working out well. For a while, of the two it was Bren who went out of his way to invite Sam to stay with them whenever he wanted to catch some of the latest West End shows, combined with a duty visit home. It wasn't that Joss was less welcoming, but whenever they were together, he seemed to be treading carefully. In due course, Sam had got his feelings for him properly in perspective; Joss was as good as his word and occasionally visited Rusholme. If the mental affinity between them remained as strong, if not stronger, than ever, the bed-sharing, whilst still enjoyable, had by now settled into a cosy convenience rather than an opportunity for high passion.

Despite having taken his new friend's advice and thrown himself with abandon into a colourful if belated love life, his escapades never seemed to progress into anything lasting. It wasn't as if Sam went out of his way to target men who were already spoken for, or those who were wriggling out of an existing relationship and wanting fun-without-involvement – or were merely emotionally shallow. They seemed to be drawn to him like a magnet. He jokingly told people he kept changing his aftershave to no avail.

One guy, Xavier, visited him regularly over a period of six months. Apparently, his marriage was breaking up, he was living alone and negotiating a separation. Sam finally caught him in high spirits *en famille* and arm-in-arm with his attractive spouse at a matinee at The Palace, after which there had been a tearful scene and they'd parted company. Having invested a lot in the relationship, he'd felt betrayed and belittled by the man's dishonesty and felt foolish at all the tell-tale alerts he'd let flutter under his radar: particularly the plethora of excuses as to why it was inconvenient to take him back to his 'temporary accommodation' and how, whenever they were together, around ten o'clock he began anxiously glancing at his watch. When blind with infatuation, Sam was sadly prone to take people's justifications at their face value.

Two other men with whom he still got on well hadn't been prepared to relinquish their easy-going *modus operandi* for an emotional straitjacket. At least they'd been honest.

Most significantly, one evening a couple of years back at the Edinburgh Festival, Sam fell heavily for an older man he met in the interval of a concert at the Usher Hall. Alistair wasn't in a relationship with any*one*, but the merchant shipping company for whom he worked as Chief Engineer demanded his fidelity on the high seas ten months of the year. Certainly, Alistair had gone on to provide Sam with free accommodation for subsequent Festivals and become another good pen-pal. All the same, it was yet another hopeless affair that had left him fretting as to where his attempts to find a meaningful relationship were taking him.

On the coach coming back from Scotland, Sam gave himself what his mother would have called a *serious talk*. Might he not, in the long term, be better off settling for a good friend, a companion who may not fulfil all his needs but would, at least, provide some permanency? He was thirty-one. He'd failed as a schoolteacher and now, to date, as a predominantly gay man.

It struck him that Jennie had always been there for him and never let him down during a difficult patch when she had health issues of her own. Adversity having brought them together, it continued to do so as they both managed the lingering, if diminishing, fallout of their bad experiences and fought to reinstate their old self-confidence. He was grateful for her good company and loyalty and came to look on her as a companion. A *girl*friend even – if not entirely in the accepted sense.

There was therefore no reason, after all this time, for him not to assume Jennie regarded him in the same light. Given he talked fairly openly about the other people in his life, some of whom she'd met, he'd convinced himself she understood his situation and regarded him simply as a good, loving friend. If another, more suitable male person came along who wanted more from her, then he would understand. And vice versa.

177

Maybe it was due to the stasis brought on by the harsh gear changes in his life that blinded him to the next messy situation he was creating for himself.

Once in Europe, Jennie revealed the extent to which she depended on him. He noted how close to tears she became at the airport when, the fog having almost wrecked their chances of getting to Vienna, he'd taken control of the situation and, with her suede-gloved hands seemingly sewn to his arm, arranged for them to catch a train to Frankfurt station and from there the Trans-Europe Express to Austria. The – albeit costly – luxury and scenic thrill of the ride at least provided some consolation for the lost flight.

He might have been wise if he'd reflected at more length on the extent to which, over the past year, she'd adopted many of his interests: buying the records and novels he enthused about, asking to be taken to many of the same shows and films and baking his favourite cakes when he visited her. Although it made him wish she would cultivate more interests of her own, he was either in denial that Jennie now saw their companionship in a more serious light than he'd suspected or was taking advantage of the companionable opportunities she gave him – such as their current break – while he sorted his life out. Perhaps a bit of both.

As they trailed around the state apartments of Schönbrunn, admiring the glittery eroticism of Klimt's paintings in the Belvedere and the handsome white Lipizzaner horses prancing elegantly at the Spanish Riding School, Jennie appeared to be managing her post-fever energy well enough. Their sightseeing was, however, somewhat hampered by tiring diversions due to the unwieldy building works for the U-Bahn train system, currently under construction. Consequently, when evening came, exhausted from so much time out in the chilly late-autumn air, she pleaded to be excused from going out yet again to an operetta or concert, preferring a leisurely meal and an early night.

* * *

Sunday arrived and their last dinner.

In the background, a sprightly quartet endeavoured to breathe life into its over-familiar Viennese repertoire.

Jennie, now fully recovered from the rigours of the day, her cheeks attractively flushed and looking at her best in a peony-and-cornflower patterned chiffon hostess gown, took the moment to unveil her Big Plan.

Delicately piercing her garlic mushrooms, she said, 'I've been meaning to say something but wasn't sure when would be a good moment.'

Sam sipped his Blaufränkisch. He was used to Jennie's subtle ways. Steady and grounded at work, in everyday life her moods could be more precipitous and catch him off guard. This time, it was the *good moment* that did it.

His defences slackened by the gracious ambience and prospect of good food and wine, he tucked in his napkin and braced himself for whatever was coming.

'Go on.'

'A few days ago,' she began, 'I was talking to my grandmother.'

'I like your grandmother.'

'I know, and she likes you, too. And...'

'Yes?'

'She mentioned her will.'

'Ah!'

'She was wondering, rather than leaving me whatever she was intending to when she goes, whether it might be helpful to give me some of it now.'

'I can see that could be handy. And you said?'

'I made all the right noises like: "You mustn't even think about such things – you're going to live to be a hundred," etcetera. She appreciated my tact, but emphasised it was a serious suggestion.' Here Jennie paused, took a sip from her glass and looked at Sam meaningfully.

Why was he starting to feel uneasy? The waiter materialised at a nearby serving station with their wiener schnitzels. Neither of them said anything while he set down their main course in front of them. It gave Sam some moments to consider an appropriate reaction. The matter hadn't been mentioned for nothing.

'*Guten appetit*' the waiter muttered, then melted away.

'I thought I'd ask your advice as to what I might do with it,' she said.

He thoughtfully prodded a piece of meat. 'I'm delighted for you,' he said guardedly, 'but while I appreciate your asking, surely accepting it and what you do with it is something only you can decide.'

'Really?' she said quickly, looking up at him again, this time more piercingly.

After carefully finishing his mouthful, he said, 'Did your Gran indicate the sort of sum she had in mind?'

'Five thousand pounds.'

'That's a lot.'

'Yes.'

'You don't think it's a bribe to turn you into Amy March so that, when she's no longer mobile, there'll always be someone handy to read her a chapter of *Pilgrim's Progress* and push her round the park?'

Jennie laughed. 'Naughty Sammy! You know how fond I am of her. She's very practical. And yes, it may be a sort of insurance policy to keep me on side too. But I think she...'

'What?'

'...genuinely thought I could do with it now.'

'*To?*'

'Put down a deposit. On a flat.'

There was no denying where this was heading.

'I get on very well with Sue, but she only sublets the place we're in, and besides, I want somewhere of my own.'

'Then go for it.'

'I intend to. The money went into my bank last week'

'And when are you going to start looking?'

'Me? I'm thinking of making an appointment with a *Nationwide* manager next Saturday morning, followed by another with an estate agent in the afternoon.' Then it came. 'And I... I was rather hoping you could accompany me?'

As the musicians triumphantly concluded the Gold & Silver Waltz, Sam pretended her last phrase had been drowned by the crescendo and smattering of applause that followed, deflecting his attention to the immediate problem of whether or not to squeeze room for one of the tempting desserts now wobbling past on a trolley. 'Your eyes are bigger than your stomach,' Bessie would tell him when he overate.

But Jennie's unwavering eye wasn't to be ignored. 'Well?'

Not wishing to sound over-enthusiastic, he said, 'I... could, I suppose.'

'I'll take that as a *yes* then.'

He gave a non-committal smile.

'If so, I was wondering...' Dreading the next line, Sam raised his eyebrows, '... about the problem of your own living arrangements?'

Jennie knew full well he was outgrowing the flat in Rusholme. His landlord had made things easier for him by warning his niece would be taking it over when she began at university the following year. Although there was no immediate rush, before long Sam would need to start looking for somewhere else to live. 'I'd be looking for a flatmate to help me with the mortgage,' she continued, 'so it naturally occurred to me: why don't we join forces? After all, we'd both have the benefit of a larger space, security – and independence.'

He placed his knife and fork together and sat back. Despite his initial fears, the glamorous atmosphere of the Sacher Hotel, the excellent meal, Jennie's winning smile and the chirpy Annen Polka on which the quartet had just embarked were conspiring to make him see the grain of practicality in her train of thought. Ignoring the reservations that also rumbled in his head, he heard himself saying, 'It's... well, worth considering, I suppose.' And might at least solve an immediate problem.

'Only considering?'

Two helpings of chocolate hazelnut pudding and ice cream later, the conversation, still subtly orchestrated by Jennie, grew even more seductive.

Sam's mind slowly changed tack. It occurred to him, if he managed things very carefully, moving in with her might possibly give him a more stable home life while allowing him some space when needed.

Jennie's carefully prepared speech continued to roll on like the nearby Danube. Irresponsibly refilling his glass, Sam soon became too befuddled to reach the off-switch of the red light flickering in his brain.

'And you never know, if after a while we found the arrangement was going well, we could perhaps make it... permanent?' she said.

He was conscious of the time-lapse between question and response.

'You mean...?' he said eventually.

'Why not?'

'Get...'

'Engaged, yes.'

'Or...?'

'Or? I don't think *or* is really my style, do you? Let's do the job properly.'

How, in five minutes, had they managed to move so quickly from her mulling over buying a flat to getting married? Flat-sharing was one thing, but, assuming it worked – and it was a fairly big *assume* at that – would he then be prepared to take their relationship a leap further? He chose his words carefully, 'So...'

'Yes?' Jennie gave him a quizzical look.

'Why don't we give it a go for six months, and then...'

Without giving him a chance to finish his sentence with a proviso such as '...we can make a final decision,' or even 'if it hasn't worked out, we must promise to stay friends,' to the amusement of the waiters and other customers, she turned and threw her arms around him.

'I knew you'd agree!' she said.

'*Six months*, mind!'

'Anything!'

By the time they got back to their room, Sam was too sleepy to do anything but let Jennie's vocalised fantasies about her ideal home, décor and furniture waft over him, relegating any further thought of the feasibility of the venture to when they were on the plane the next morning.

Reality might then illuminate logic.

Indeed, flying over Germany twelve hours later, Sam wondered whether, in addition to that half bottle of Blaufränkisch, there been some *special* mushrooms amongst those in their starters the previous evening? He'd been offered an opportunity to swap his unproductive free-wheeling lifestyle for one he'd been conditioned to believe would lead to proper contentment. Why then, despite all his sound reasoning, did he feel he was being pulled in a direction which, in his heart, he wasn't quite convinced he wanted to go?

* * *

In the end, the question was taken out of his hands. Any lingering chance of avoiding the path to respectability was blown to pieces two mornings later when, shovelling *All-Bran* down in readiness for a dash to the bus stop, he heard the telephone ring.

'You need to get the paper on your way to work,' Jennie said excitedly, ignoring any pleasantries.

'Do I – why?'

'The engagement!'

'Sorry, what are you on about?'

Her exhilaration now bubbling over, she squealed, 'It's… *in*!'

'In what?' Sam heard himself mutter as his mouth struggled to keep up with his brain.

'*The Daily Telegraph*, of course.'

Of course. 'Not *ours*?' he said disbelievingly, although his throat was already drying up.

'No, Richard Burton and Liz Taylor's.'

Sam had never been deluged by shattered ice, but this must be what it felt like. 'But I'd thought we'd agreed…'

'Daddy pointed out it would take another six months after that for us to plan the wedding and everything. That means it would be at least a year before we tied the knot. I can't wait that long, can you?'

He didn't reply.

'He knows this guy in Fleet Street, and he felt sure you'd think it was for the best and wouldn't mind if…'

More silence.

'You aren't cross, are you?'

Convulsed with alternating spasms of fury and fear, *cross* was way down his spectrum of emotions right then. 'But Jennie…' he managed to splutter at last.

'You really *are* pleased, though, aren't you darling?'

Oh God! 'What did your mother say?'

'That it was obvious it was what we both wanted, so why wait?'

It must have been the mushrooms.

And it was too late to argue. How could the information at this very moment being pored over by millions of people in homes, offices, buses and trains throughout the UK – and even other countries – possibly be retracted? No point getting upset and making a scene. All Sam wanted was to get off the phone as quickly as possible, get his head around what had happened and consider damage limitation. 'Thanks for letting me know,' he said, in a controlled but expressionless voice. 'Look, I'm in a rush. Big departmental meeting in an hour.' A fib, of course. He'd been looking forward to a relaxed working day, but that was no longer going to happen. 'I'll phone you as soon as I get home and we'll make some plans. Ok?'

'Love you,' she said.

He failed to return the endearment. 'Bye,' he said and hung up.

Getting off the bus at his stop on Oxford Street, Sam slipped into his usual newsagent and bought a copy of the offending newspaper. The man behind the counter gave him a querying smile. 'Usually a *Guardian* man, aren't you?' With an enigmatic look, Sam slammed down the money. 'Keep the change' he said as he dashed out and into the nearest coffee bar.

Sitting on a stool with his cappuccino, he flicked through the paper to the Births Marriages & Deaths columns. Sure enough, there under Forthcoming Marriages was:

**Mr S Owen and
Miss J Bancroft**
The engagement is announced
between Samuel, son of Mr and
Mrs James Owen of Beckenham,
Kent, and Jennifer, daughter of
Mr and Mrs Stanley Bancroft of
Bramhall, Cheshire.

On auto-pilot for the rest of that morning, he shuffled paperwork around his desk, responding to the banter of his colleagues with an occasional non-committal grin. The mundane office atmosphere provided a sense of normality, a screen behind which his inner turbulence could hide for as long as he kept silent. It almost worked. Only his mate Tony, who knew about Jennie, threw him the odd concerned look.

By lunchtime he'd come to a decision. He must accept that, short term, there was no escape. With his predisposition to rush into things, this time he'd not only dug himself a cavernous pit but jumped straight into the excrement lying at the bottom. He needed to slow down and let the charade play itself out.

Was there still a possibility they could make it work? Maybe this was God's way of giving him a chance to be like most other men. The thought of a little Sam or Jennie appearing someday was not totally disagreeable.

During the lunch hour, Sam felt obliged to telephone Bessie and Hugh. Regular breakfast time *Telegraph* readers, they'd already spotted the announcement. Surprised and confused as to why he hadn't warned them but not wishing to ring him at the office and having had a short time to consider the matter, they were now able to overlay their initial reaction with a modicum of forced delight. Connie, whom he phoned next, reacted similarly, congratulating him with some stiffness. He put it down to her mind being on the current upheaval of packing up her home of twenty-five years in readiness to move with Hannah into a new house in Wilmslow. They'd talk at more length later in the week. At least it had given him a chance to wish her well for the move and reminded him to organise a card.

Although they'd been a recognised couple all his life, it was only when Hannah's invalid mother had died the previous year, and they were now both in retirement, that they were finally able to consider cohabitation. Sam had always envied their lifestyle allowing them each other's company when they wanted it with nights off to do their own thing in between. Now he saw the benefits of their being able to support each other in their final, needier years together.

His next stop was his bank where he withdrew the hundred pounds previously earmarked towards the cost of a Hi-Fi music centre.

On the Saturday, Sam met Jennie for coffee in Deansgate. Together they searched for the jeweller which Tony, in whom he'd confided, had recommended. They next honoured their appointment with the building society, coming away with details of how to secure a mortgage and other tips for first-home buyers. After a quick lunch, they signed on with an estate agent, coming away clutching swatches of leaflets.

Travelling on the bus back to Jennie's flat to show Sue the ring, they perused the information they'd been given. No particular flat jumped out at them, but they at least now had an idea of what was available in their price range and preferred area. In the evening, they celebrated with a Chinese supper before a show at the Opera House.

The next day, Jennie drove Sam to Bramhall for one of Mrs Bancroft's special Sunday roasts.

'One word of warning,' Tony had said, 'you'll find you won't have much say in anything until the deed is finally done and dusted. I gave in and accepted it all rather than getting stressed out. Let the travelator carry you along. Remember, it's not your big day. It's theirs. After all, they're forking out a heck of a lot.'

With everything washed up and put away, the four of them sat down after lunch in the chintzy lounge of Silvan View. Comfortably replete, Sam gazed down the room and through the smart conservatory windows to velvety lawns trimmed and weeded within a millimetre of their life, and the late autumnal trees beyond.

So, this was what he could expect for thousands of weekends to come? Possibly not too terrifying a prospect. The Bancrofts were a united, hospitable family after all. He felt sure, when they eventually met, Bessie and Hugh would get along with them too.

His reverie was interrupted by the click of china on china as Mr Bancroft plonked down his coffee cup on the saucer, placed it on the sofa table beside him and briskly cleared his throat. 'You'll be glad to know, lad,' he announced, 'we've booked the wedding for Saturday, May 22nd, at St Michael's & All Angels.'

Sam's heart sank. 'Next year or the year after?' he said.

'*Next*, of course!' his host chuckled, drolly. 'No point in hanging around. We were very lucky. They're usually booked up eighteen months ahead. But fortunately, we know the vicar well,' he added, tapping his nose.

A given, he thought.

'We suggested a two-thirty start,' Mr Bancroft went on, as if it was a steeplechase event at Aintree. 'Gives people such as your parents, travelling long distances, good time to get there. Though they'd be more than welcome to stay overnight with us, wouldn't they, Mona?'

Mrs Bancroft nodded tactfully.

'That's very kind of you, Mr and Mrs Bancroft. I'll let them know,' Sam said, hoping the *very* hadn't come out as irritably as he felt.

'Stan and Mona, please. You're almost family now.'

'Thanks, *both* of you.' He couldn't yet bring himself to take advantage of the newly presumed intimacy between them.

'We hope you don't mind, but...' the man went on. Sam, who was beginning to mind a lot, bit his lip. '...I also took the opportunity of arranging for you both to go and have a preliminary chat with the Rev on Wednesday at five-thirty. Nice man, I'm sure you'll get on famously. They'll let you have a few hours off work, won't they?'

'*My* boss was only too delighted to give me the time,' Jennie chipped in, 'and came back from his lunch break with a bottle of champagne so everyone in the office could drink our health.' She turned to Sam. 'I meant to tell you.'

Wednesday was a rehearsal evening, dammit! He'd have to ask the Stage Manager to run through lines until he got there. Why couldn't the man have checked the provisional arrangements with him? They'd thought of everything. The whole thing was spiralling out of control. He recalled Tony's other cautionary words about the months of preparation that lay ahead for the Big Day. The endless arguing over guest lists, venues, menus and clothes, all driven by the bride's parents – his own barely consulted, he presumed.

The Bancrofts went on to inform him of the other arrangements they had thoughtfully anticipated. These included the number of seats allocated to the groom's party for the church service and reception. As he'd feared, it was significantly lower than that for the bride's contingent. Sam could see an argument brewing when he came to raise the matter with Bessie, who'd reel off the family friends whose weddings they had attended over the years and now would expect a return invitation. There was no way of massaging the figures to allow anyone of importance other than Connie, Hannah and his best man – Joss or possibly Tony? – to support him. Partly the problem of being an only child with few relations. Jennie, on the other hand, had an adored brother, grandmother and countless aunts, uncles and cousins.

Nodding robotically as each subsequent decision was announced, he half hoped a storm would blow up on his way home and he'd be struck by lightning. *Thunder in November.* Now that would be a good title for a play. He might even get run over, though at the usual pace of Manchester traffic, it would be just his luck to be rescued in the nick of time.

Stop dramatising! he commanded himself.

As he was pondering on how to diplomatically handle this minefield, Jennie, who'd been smiling silently throughout the conversation, said, 'Sorry, everyone, but all this excitement has knocked me for six. I'll go and have a little lie-down for a couple of hours. You don't mind, do you, Sam?'

After she'd left the room, Mrs Bancroft picked up her crochet needle and renewed work on the trolley cloth in her hands. As if reading Sam's thoughts, she said, 'You must forgive Jennie; it still doesn't take much to exhaust her. She's been under a lot of strain recently.'

He, of course, hadn't. 'Does her doctor have any idea when she might be completely over the long-term effects of the glandular fever?' he said.

'Normally it's only a few months at most, but she had it so very badly. I'm surprised she hasn't told you this herself, but at her last check-up, the consultant insisted on running some more tests and even hinted at the possibility of an underlying blood condition.'

'How serious is it?'

'He hopes she'll grow out of it. In time.'

How much time, he wondered? Eighteen months had passed already. It wasn't that he was unsympathetic, but why couldn't this discussion have taken place earlier and allowed him to prepare his reaction better?

'It's always a gamble with these things, isn't it?' Mrs Bancroft continued ominously. 'She has to take the pills he's prescribed and avoid too much stress. But you'll know, having recently been away with her.'

No. Sam had been aware Jennie got tired easily, but in Vienna she must have organised her medication very discretely. She'd never mentioned any additional health issues, and he'd never seen her take anything stronger than an aspirin.

'You need to be patient with her.'

Of course. Although it unkindly crossed his mind it wasn't Amy March he was marrying after all. It was Beth.

17

After the Show

1974
Sam

Much of Sam's spare time that week was taken up with rehearsals for *The Constant Wife*. It was the first full-length play he'd directed. The opening night would be on the Thursday.

He had a lot riding on the production.

During a recent appraisal of his life, he'd taken a hard look at how he spent his spare time and wondered whether he was making the best use of it. He still wanted to gain a higher profile in community theatre and make better use of his training and knowledge. After leaving college, there had been the spell with the large operatic society and, in between musicals, making guest appearances with other 'legitimate' companies. Rehearsing and performing several evenings a week provided a necessary antidote to demanding days in the classroom. And, while he didn't regret putting behind him the stressful environment that he'd encountered at Oakview, he now missed the educational process in a wider context.

Fun though it was, if he was being honest, his acting talent never developed as Bullseye had once predicted. Maybe the disappointment of being dissuaded from a stage career all those years ago was responsible for suppressing his original promise. Or perhaps his involvement in too many musicals was to blame. The genre encouraged you to present yourself in a more heightened way than in a straight play so as to project over – or sometimes against – an orchestra to the back of a large theatre. Sam moved well, could put over a number and was a reliable character actor, but it took a strong director to tone down his natural exuberance. What was once considered a burgeoning talent seemed to have been corrupted by a tendency to overact, a weakness drama school might have toned down. And although a strong, experienced director could still draw a nuanced performance out of him, if he was being honest with himself, performing was no longer giving him the satisfaction it once had. He had directed several small-scale productions at college and for youth clubs and always found it very rewarding. Perhaps that was the area he should now concentrate on.

He'd recently submitted his CV to several local dramatic societies whose work he admired. He was aware some of the larger non-professional companies paid for the services of skilled directors to help them raise their game, although the most challenging work was often in the voluntary sector, where kudos, good reviews and considerable artistic satisfaction could be gained from working with well-regarded organisations. Besides, by now he wasn't desperate for extra income so much as experience in front of a company rather than as one of its performers.

As happens when Lady Luck condescends to call, it was the one at the top of his list which enthusiastically responded. Lottie Gilchrist of the *Palantine Players* invited him to meet up and discuss possible projects.

They'd clicked immediately. A glamorous woman in her early fifties, as committed and knowledgeable as Sam was about theatre, Lottie had originally trained as an actress but, since marriage, concentrated on raising a family. When invited, she played leads with the *PPs* and currently ran the planning committee.

A Pinter he suggested she felt was slightly too niche for their middle-brow audiences, while a frothy Whitehall farce she ran by him Sam considered too ambitious. Farces might appear insubstantial fun to watch, but, having played an indignant bishop in one recently, he knew how complex they were to choreograph and perform.

Their discussion led to suitably intelligent, entertaining, but not over-exploited, plays. On a recent trip to London, some members of the committee had returned after seeing Ingrid Bergman in the title role of Somerset Maugham's stylish but intelligent 1927 comedy of manners, *The Constant Wife*, recommending it for presentation when a director with the right period flair came along.

Sam's eyes lit up. Now, he assured her, one had.

The play required a smart 'twenties set and costumes. He'd soon got to work researching the era, sketching ideas for the way the production should look and, with Lottie's help, assembling a strong cast and crew. By now everyone was collaborating well. Only the approval of the audience was required to endorse his faith in himself as a director.

Nonetheless, the off-stage drama in his private life had somewhat upset his itinerary. He'd already been required to juggle a few dates to be able to spend the long weekend in Vienna. With his day job and final rehearsals, the final two weeks flew by in an atmosphere of some panic, during which he struggled to keep all the balls in the air. Yet every so often he was conscious of a sinking feeling in his stomach when, during his lunch break or on a bus, something triggered a reminder of his commitment to Jennie. On these occasions, the Jekyll in him tried to allay his fears, pointing out the domestic benefits marriage could bring, then Hyde shot up through a trapdoor in his brain, taunting him with how much he'd miss his gay friends and related activities.

On the Wednesday evening after the second dress rehearsal, Sam handed the play over to his stage manager and cast. He could do little more now to help them. Walking home from the bus, cooling his head in the November evening air, he found himself waving across the road to a good-looking, married acquaintance, prompting him to analyse the lives of men he knew who seemed to have it, sexually speaking, both ways. Some of the married ones appeared fundamentally happy and devoted to their families, regarding their need for men as if it was an aberration, a recreational drug they'd become too dependent on. Others admitted that if they had their time over again, they wouldn't have got married but now cared too much for their wife and children to risk the devastation of a break-up. Then there were the health risks for anyone who was even slightly promiscuous. Sam, who regularly got himself checked out at a leading hospital, knew that wasn't really the point. Was there any excuse to even very occasionally sleep around and then go home to someone who totally believed in your commitment to them?

He thought of other cultures. Men had kept mistresses since time immemorial. It was once *de rigueur* in France, while some religions not only encouraged but expected polygamy. How different was that to having an extra-marital relationship of any kind? He'd surely be able to control his, by now, restless libido and make a success of his marriage, wouldn't he? Or would he dwindle into a cardiganed spouse, occasionally tempted to stray – but only to the *aberration* level? Little more than flirt, in fact. And never let it get out of hand. As if. Yet, if he really respected Jennie, would he even be thinking along these lines so early on in their engagement?

As he forced his mind to move on and consider the pep talk he should give his cast and technicians before curtain-up the next evening, he couldn't help recalling a remark Jennie had dropped into her chatter at the weekend: 'You should make the most of all this while you still can.' An awful thought struck him.

Presumably, *this* referred to his theatre work?

Did he really want that kind of stability in his life? Settling down and watching his kids grow up, concentrating on being a dad with only the odd outside theatrical project to work on now and again for diversion? Jennie, a good actor herself, seemed to have lost much of her old enthusiasm for acting since her illness and no longer found it a compelling hobby. Would she be happy to let him come home in the evening and, as soon as he'd bolted her lovingly-prepared supper, go straight out again? Would that be fair? If, on the other hand, she returned to amdrams, would they end up fighting over whose turn it was to participate in the next production, as some theatrical couples did? He needed the motivation of a script to work on as a beaver requires wood for his next dam.

The bottom line was his hunger for more from life than simply an acceptable job and a family. Selfish, maybe, but there it was. It would probably take a very special – or similarly minded – person to live with him at all. At one point, he'd thought Jennie might be that person, but, after the surreal events of the past couple of weeks, he wasn't so sure.

Much of his thirty-one years had been spent in compromise. Thanks to Joss and a more permissive society, certain constrained aspects of his character, masked for so long beneath the veneer of middle-class respectability inherited from his parents, had been belatedly unshackled. His erratic behaviour ever since might be put down to a desperate attempt to make up for lost time, but, with the prospect of more domestic responsibility and a devoted spouse, could he reverse the trajectory and settle down? More importantly, in his heart of hearts, did he want to? He'd always been an outsider. In the minority. There was something in him that enjoyed his membership of the subculture however unsatisfactory it could sometimes be. Imagine no more trips to Islington? The heavy words *settling down* needed more thought.

Soon.

* * *

On the Saturday morning before the last performance of the play, Jennie helped Sam scour Kendal Milne's for small but appropriate gifts to give leading members of *The Constant Wife*'s backstage team at the traditional after-show party: tokens of gratitude for their unseen efforts, the anticipated, enthusiastic curtain calls being considered sufficient reward for the cast. It was traditional for directors to be thanked at the party in a speech from one of his leading actors, along with a card signed by everyone and comments such as *Had a ball, mate!* and a book token to which they'd all have contributed.

A form had been put up backstage the night before, encouraging people to list the goodies they planned bringing to the jollities. A bottle of wine, plate of sausage rolls, quiche or homemade sponge to soak up the booze usually sufficed. For this production, Lottie, playing the eponymous wife, was hosting the party at her spacious home in Wythenshawe. Sam looked forward to relaxing after a tense and exciting week and, hopefully, seeing the proud look on Jennie's face as fiancée of the society's latest, gifted director. Such recognition might just calm his current anxieties and convince him they were compatible.

Maybe.

The temporary bar in the foyer of the hall in Northenden was packed with people. Some of Sam's best friends, colleagues and senior members of the society were amongst the throng, ordering drinks for the interval, purchasing programmes and chatting merrily in anticipation of what, the grapevine had advised them, was a good production.

As on previous evenings, the play was well-received with five curtain calls. Filing out of the hall, members of the audience paused to congratulate Sam, those he knew with knowing smiles and 'So, this the future Mrs Owen?' to Jennie, while others who would be going on to the party winked and muttered, 'Catch up later.'

It was planned that Jennie would drive them to Lottie's place and later, in the early hours of the morning, back to Rusholme. By now, Lottie would have changed out of her 'twenties *haute couture* and dashed ahead to warm up the vol-au-vents, leaving the rest of the cast and crew to pack up. They had roughly three-quarters of an hour to kill.

In the car park, Sam sensed that everything was not well but, as he squeezed himself into the passenger seat of Jennie's car, pressed on with, 'How would you feel about us popping into the pub down the road before making our way to Lottie's?'

A small sigh.

'Is everything ok, Jen?'

'Yes, but…'

'But what?'

'Would you be terribly disappointed if I didn't go? During that last scene, I suddenly felt very light-headed. I'm well enough to drive now but… I know this is awful of me, but I don't think I could cope with all those people I don't know tonight.'

'Jennie, this is important to me. I badly want to show you off to everyone. There'll be speeches and everything.'

'Of course. And *you* must go, but I really think it would be better if I went back to my parents for the night. I'll be fine tomorrow. I'll drop you off. I know you'll be early, but Lottie could no doubt use some help setting things out and so on.'

'There's no way…'

'I insist. Later, you can cadge a lift back into town with Bob and Greta or someone else who lives in your direction.'

'I can't possibly go to the party without you!'

'I'm so sorry, I really believed I was over all this now. Then, out of the blue… Honestly, I'd only be a party-pooper.'

Remembering what Mona had said about Jennie's health, Sam knew the evening was kaput. If he didn't accompany her home to make sure she was safe, both her parents and the company would find out and think the less of him – as, of course, he would of himself.

It was at times like this he wished he could drive. Hugh had once attempted to teach him but became irritable every time he stalled and totally undermined his confidence. Not in a position to afford a car and anyway, having always been accustomed to travelling everywhere by public transport, being a non-driver had long ceased to be a problem.

It was only at that moment he recalled how, at one point on the journey to Northenden earlier that evening, Jennie had come out with another of her unsettling remarks. 'Of course, now we're engaged, I can… well, you know, let you….' here she gave one of her playful coughs, 'go all the way.'

At the time, Sam was too busy thinking of the evening ahead to be more than mildly annoyed by the comment, the delayed reaction giving it greater sting from having simmered for best effect at the optimum moment. Now he saw she'd never had any intention of going to the party and planned to ride off to Bramhall with him all along. Mona was probably warming up their Horlicks this very moment. Even if she was too tired tonight, presumably Jennie was hell-bent on his ravishing her the following morning. She was always moaning about their own single divans not being up to the standard of the comfortable king-size in her parents' spare room where, when he stayed over and everyone else in the house was settled for the night, she'd discreetly join him.

The little madam, he thought. The hypocrisy! Playing the Victorian damsel until the ring was safely on her finger, and now she'd got it, flinging her chastity belt out of the window.

'I can't let everyone down,' he said. 'It would look really odd...'

'I've just said...'

'How about we just stay for the presentations and then make our excuses?'

'I really don't think...'

'I see.' At least, he was trying to.

Lottie had mentioned the Chairman might take him aside and invite him to write and direct the Spring show. An entertainment on a larger and far more lavish scale than *The Constant Wife*. The committee wanted to show off more of the company and, if possible, use some of the gifted children whose parents were members. 'Something historical maybe... relating to Manchester.'

Now, that would have to wait. Possibly even be forgotten.

While Sam appreciated the reasons for Jennie's exhaustion, would it have been unreasonable, he wondered, for contingency plans to have been discussed earlier so he could have made his excuses to Lottie? Maybe he should have thought it through better himself. It was strange how Jennie always appeared perfectly fit whenever she was doing what *she* wanted. Along with the high-handed way everything else connected with her had occurred over the past couple of weeks, it rankled.

Trying to calm down and once more chastising himself for only thinking of himself, he comforted himself with the knowledge that, if he didn't show up at the party, at least everyone would be too busy enjoying themselves to worry about him. Especially as they must have heard of his engagement. He could hear the comments – 'Expect he has better things to do, tonight!' followed by ribald laughter – and shuddered.

As it happened, the car belonging to Bob, the unfaithful husband in the play, was parked next to them, and at that moment he was walking up with his bags. Sam rolled down his window and quickly explained the situation. Bob sounded disappointed but hoped Sam would join everyone for the strike the next morning. Not waiting to engage in further chat, he turned to Jennie. 'Right. Now let's get to Bramhall while you're still up to driving. Unless you'd like me to call for a cab at that phone box on the corner?'

'No,' Jennie said, starting the car up. 'I think I should just about make it. Can't wait to get home to bed.'

Sam said nothing.

As he'd anticipated, on arriving at Silvan View, Stan and Mona didn't seem surprised to see them. Jennie would no doubt have run past them the likely chance of her needing to come home early. One of them would have probably said, 'Much better for you both to make your excuses and come here and get a good night's rest.' It annoyed him the way they took every opportunity to wrap their daughter in yet another layer of cotton wool. Presumably to remind him that, from now on, care of Jennie's fragility would largely be his responsibility.

One of Sam's failings was his intolerance of people who succumbed too easily to weaknesses. He never forgot how, on his eighth birthday, Bessie, despite being in great discomfort, had forced herself to supervise a party for him; not to mention the many other times she'd put on a brave face in difficult circumstances when she didn't want to let him down. And now, the woman who expected to be his wife and must have some idea how much the evening meant to him couldn't pull herself together for long enough to allow him his ten minutes of glory.

With Jennie packed off to bed, Stan and Mona courteously asked him how the play had gone before quickly turning to the subject of flat-hunting.

It appeared Jennie had arranged a couple of viewings for early one evening the following week, which he didn't know about, providing Sam with an excuse to raise his concern. 'If we go ahead and buy one of the flats before the wedding, with all our other commitments, getting it ready to move into will take up a lot of spare time and energy. We'd originally planned to give ourselves six months before…' he struggled to find the most tactful phrase, '…formalising things.' Wrong. He could see Stan already bristling but ploughed on. 'Personally, I think we' – he meant *you* but wanted to make the point that he was involved in this exercise too – 'may have booked the wedding too soon.' At least he'd accepted part responsibility for their decision. 'Would you mind very much if we went back to Plan A, even if it means having to find another church?'

If, at that point, Sam had been directing Stan in a comedy by Priestly or Galsworthy, he couldn't have asked for a better performance from his future father-in-law. Mr Bancroft drew himself up, looked down his nose and said sternly, 'Nay, lad, we can't allow that.'

'How about putting your thumbs in your waistcoat pockets before starting that speech?' he'd have advised the actor.

Stan went on, 'The sooner we get our Jennie settled properly the better. Sorry, but this wedding's going to involve us heavily, too. Mona and I are planning on a long trip to visit relatives in Johannesburg next year. We need the whole thing done and dusted well before then.'

'I see,' Sam said but thinking *so, I'm right, this isn't about us, it's all about organising things for your convenience.* And it was strange how the possibility of him and Jennie living in sin before the wedding didn't appear to be an issue for them. Although, he thought cynically, should an *accident* occur, six months would be just long enough for him to make an honest woman of her and she'd safely be Mrs Owen before any happy event occurred.

'But it's *our* wedding,' he protested.

'And she's *our* daughter,' Stan said as if Jennie was a naïve teenager and not an independent, professional woman in her mid-twenties. 'I'm sure you appreciate we've gone to a great deal of trouble to organise this for you. May 22nd it must be.'

And that was that.

Sam was too tired to argue. Besides, his own confused thoughts held him back from creating an awkward atmosphere. Stan didn't seem perturbed by his protestation, and Mona, used to her husband being in charge and brooking no interference with his decisions, threw him a Daddy-knows-best smile and proffered another gypsy cream. Maybe they understood more than he gave them credit for. Perhaps this was their way of getting the matter sorted out once and for all. Possibly Stan had sussed him long ago, with his nancy-boy voice and colour co-ordinated shirts and ties, and decided it was better for Jennie's heart to be broken sooner rather than later.

Twenty minutes on, Sam flopped shattered between the sheets of the spare room bed, remaining unconscious all night and leaving Jennie's honour uncompromised. Awaking at eight the next morning, he slipped in to give her a cuddle and explain he must catch the train back for the strike. It would give him a chance to make amends for his absence the evening before. He might even catch the Chairman, whose speciality was stage lighting and who always dismantled the portable dimmer boards.

Downstairs in the morning room, Stan and Mona invited him to join them. After fortifying himself with a cup of tea, toast and marmalade and reiterating his excuses, he tore off to Bramhall station.

* * *

The following Tuesday after work, Jennie and Sam met the estate agent outside an Edwardian house between Didsbury and Chorlton which had been newly converted into small apartments. They contemplated making an offer on one of the downstairs flats, but Sam, somewhat listless and summoning the strength to have a make-or-break talk with his fiancée when he could get her alone, demurred.

Back in Old Trafford, they found the flat empty. Sue was out for the evening. Jennie made them mugs of tea and sat beside him in the living room. 'What's the matter?' she said when they were settled. 'You've been very quiet all evening. Not having second thoughts, are you?'

'I like the flat,' Sam said, 'I think you should make them an offer.'

'Me? It'll be *our* flat.'

'Yes, but …'

'But?'

'Look, Jennie, there's no easy way of saying this…'

'What?' Jennie looked worried.

'Can't we be engaged for a while, living together, see how we get along every day and enjoy having a place of our own, without spending half our time arguing over wedding plans?'

She groaned and looked away. 'Daddy said you wanted to delay things.'

'You never told me.'

'I assumed you had seen where he was coming from and both cleared the matter up.'

'*He'd* cleared it up, you mean.'

'Now we're getting to it,' Jennie said angrily.

'You don't agree with me, then?'

'I think you're being unreasonable. They've been so supportive and gone to such a lot of trouble for us.'

'I don't think it was supportive of them, after we agreed to allow ourselves six months before getting engaged, to make a public announcement without even giving me the chance to tell my parents first.'

Jennie went quiet. Dropping her voice, she said. 'Actually…'

'Yes?'

'That was my fault.'

'In what way?'

'I… I asked him to.'

'I see. You wanted to make sure of tying me down?'

'No! I…'

'What then?'

'Ok. I suppose… yes. I… I love you so much and…'

'Right, I get it. But isn't it a pretty possessive sort of love that resorts to a trick like that?'

'If we were truly simpatico, you wouldn't think of it like that. Would you?'

True enough, he thought. 'Though loving couples usually discuss everything and reach a decision together. We agreed to become flatmates first and then decide whether we wanted to commit, later.'

Sam could see her starting to crumble. There was a long pause, during which she rallied, rose and moved to the window.

'The thing is, you don't really love *me*,' she said looking down at the street as if unable to face him.

Truth sometimes hurts, and her saying it out loud struck him like a fist in his gut. He froze. He didn't want to hurt her any more than he already had but needed to summon the courage to be completely honest. 'I... I'm *very* fond of you.'

Quietly she said, 'Yes, I believe you are. And I think I've known all along you weren't as fond of me as I am of you. Even so...' Then the final, desperate long shot. 'I'd so hoped in time...'

Feeling her turning to him, Sam knew he mustn't move or say anything. *'I suggest a count of five'* as he might have advised Lottie Gilchrist during a tense moment in Act Three. How was it that, even at such a poignant moment, he could separate himself from the scene and turn even the most sensitive moments in his life into drama?

When she received no response, Jennie sniffed. 'On Saturday night, your insensitive reaction to my wobble made it clear, but I couldn't come to terms with it – then. You don't really want to marry me, either. Do you?'

Sam swallowed.

'Do you?'

A terrible silence. He could hear the *Coronation Street* theme straining through the wall shared with the flat next door. This is the point at which life becomes not so much Somerset Maugham as commonplace Northern soap, he thought.

'I'm not absolutely sure,' he said. 'I'm so sorry, Jennie, but that's the truth. And why I wanted to give us time to find out one way or another.'

Her sniffs dissolved into tears. He desperately wanted to put his arm around her but knew that would be a serious mistake. They were both aware this was the end. However much he might find fault with the way she'd handled this pitiful episode, he had to accept the greater share of responsibility. He'd used her in a last desperate attempt to be an everyday guy and hadn't come out of it well.

How could he contrive a quick curtain?

She made it easy for him. Brushing away the tears from her red cheeks and looking at him hopelessly, she whispered, 'I think you'd better go.'

He picked up his things and left.

* * *

The next day at work, Sam received a call from the reception desk. 'There's a gentleman just left a package for you when you have a moment to pop down.' He guessed immediately what it was. As soon as he'd completed the report he was drafting, he slipped downstairs to the small office off the main corridor leading from the front of the building and pocketed the lumpy sealed envelope awaiting him.

What could he do with an unwanted engagement ring? Perhaps he should go back to the jewellers one lunch hour and exchange it for a brooch for Bessie. It was the least he could do to show his contrition for being such a disappointment as a son.

That evening as he was watching the Six O'clock News, the phone rang.

'Doing anything this Saturday evening?' Joss said.

'Not now, no.'

'You've had a cancellation too?'

'You could say.'

'I won't ask.'

'Tell you when we next meet. It's the plot for a play or film should Jane Fonda and Robert Redford happen to be available. Only no happy ending.'

'It's films I wanted to talk about, as it happens,' Joss said. 'A mate has had a better offer and left us with a spare ticket for this Saturday's All-Night Busby Berkeley screening at the National Film Theatre. Philip Jenkinson's presenting four glorious films. Think: eight hours of Ruby, Dick, Joan, Bebe, Ginger… everyone! Can you help us out? Long lie-in and brunch on Sunday included.'

'Can I help you out… *Yes!*'

They were all devouring buttered crumpets topped with toasted cheese in the cosy Islington flat prior to making the journey to the South Bank. Joss and Bren's LP of *A Chorus Line*, Broadway's current hit musical, was on the turntable. The stresses and strains of recent weeks drained away.

Here he could be himself.

Here he felt understood.

In amongst the many pictures, posters and theatre photographs that crowded the walls, he spotted the framed tapestry worked by Bren's grandmother as a schoolgirl.

In quaint lettering, he read:

To Thine Own Self Be True

Duly noted.

18

A Shrinking World

1974 – 1981
Bessie

Hugh never fully recovered from the gassing.

They sued the Gas Board but, as they'd been warned by their solicitor, soon found it was virtually impossible to take on a nationalised industry and win. They recovered their legal costs although, as Hugh said, 'with not a penny more towards a holiday' which might have helped them recover their health more quickly.

Bessie had wondered how Hugh would get through the remaining eighteen months before his retirement date. Both were conscious of the extent to which the accident had depleted their energy, but while, not being in the direct path of the gas, she had bounced back quickly, his old ebullience returned only spasmodically and for shorter periods. As soon as he could, he insisted on going back to work, coming home tired, edgy and, to her dismay, relying on his nightly tots of whisky to keep him going – on top of whatever fuel he'd had at lunchtime.

Years later, his secretary, who remained a good friend of them both, intimated to Bessie how younger colleagues had carried Hugh through his remaining time at work.

It was the worst time for anyone retiring. Whenever Bessie turned on her trusty transistor, she was assailed with news of how inflation continued to skyrocket, a situation precipitated by the previous year's international oil crisis and the subsequent demands of the coal mining unions. How would they manage if, as seemed likely, this continued indefinitely?

By Easter, the country had just recovered from a period of national depression exacerbated by measures to conserve heat and light. For several months that harsh winter, as daylight faded, people would peer out from the flickering internal twilight of their rooms to see neighbours similarly illuminated by paraffin lamps and candles. The early shutting-down of television broadcasting each evening had only added to the gloom of the long winter days, although, so Sam told them, the better-equipped theatres managed to keep audiences entertained by means of in-house generators which drenched the stage with a cold, bright light. Going to the theatre would, however, soon be a luxury they'd rarely be able to afford.

Hugh was due to retire in May. Even when blackouts became a bad memory, the continuing devaluation of the pound dragged on, demoralising everyone on fixed incomes – as they'd soon be themselves. It brought back bitter memories of the economies endured during two World Wars long consigned to the past. Belt-tightening was becoming the way things were as, every few months, the price of everything from newspapers to property rose yet again: five pence added to a loaf of bread and five hundred pounds on the price of a house. The Owens' projected income, carefully calculated for their future life in more optimistic times, was disquietingly dwindling.

When his sixty-fifth birthday actually arrived, Hugh felt sure he'd be offered a consultancy post, a time-honoured way of topping up respected ex-colleagues' pensions while tapping into their experience when necessary. It hit him particularly badly to learn this perk had been withdrawn. In the past, he'd have been allowed to keep his car, too, but instead was obliged to spend a substantial portion of his precious lump sum to buy it from his company. For a few more years, he managed to drive it until the expense of running it, along with his deteriorating confidence, forced him off the streets.

His firm at least stuck to their long-term agreement and he was able to buy the house they'd once purchased on his behalf at a generous discount, using money he'd conscientiously saved over the years in a special insurance policy. The only snag was the capital gains tax, obliging them to stay put for at least two years – or be caught by a hefty bill.

For the time being, they were trapped.

Work had always been the main motivation of Hugh's life. Not only his job but his hobby. While he was usually pleasant with neighbours and other friends, apart from Bessie, Sam, Gibby and a few special people he'd known since time immemorial, the people who mattered most to him were the members of his office team and special clients. Now he was no longer in circulation, most seemed to have relegated him to a *'remembering happy times'* note on their annual Christmas card.

Bessie always said, 'They'll carry me out of this house in a box.' But, as the third summer arrived, with no other savings to fall back on to meet the expense of the maintenance work the house now required, things were looking desperate. Finally accepting defeat, they began looking for somewhere cheaper to live.

Like many couples at the onset of old age, there were other good reasons for such a move. With Hugh no longer able to help much in the house and garden and Bessie, still with plenty of spirit but finding her mobility increasingly undermined by the rheumatoid arthritis inherited from her mother, a place that would be easier to run was becoming essential.

But where? The thought of losing face and relocating to a downmarket local property was disheartening. Unfortunately, house prices in the London suburbs were still the highest in the country. Almost anywhere else would offer better value for their money. Edinburgh, where they'd been so happy in years gone by was a possibility, but many of their friends there had moved or died. A bungalow on the South Coast was mooted, but after several trips, nothing in their price range really appealed.

And, although they were loath to admit it, perhaps their hearts weren't fully engaged in the project. When an enthusiastic young couple finally made them an acceptable offer, they ran out of excuses and tore off this time to the South West coast where two of Hugh's friendly clients had happily relocated. Yet again, none of the houses in streets that only came alive in summer, remaining empty and ghost-like during the winter months, felt quite right for them.

The stress of all their frantic travelling around brought on emotional exhaustion.

Then, one Saturday in October and by now feeling brighter, Bessie was flicking thoughtfully through the supplement of a South Manchester newspaper that had arrived in the post from Connie, encouraging them to consider moving back up North.

Did they want to put the clock back?

Apart from visits over the years to visit her sister-in-law and, more recently Sam, they hadn't spent a lot of time in the area since leaving as newly-weds thirty-seven years earlier. Connie and Hannah would be nearby, of course, but many of their old friends were no longer living. And how would she feel about moving so close to Roy and Flo? Sam had maintained contact with his aunt and godfather, and reported back on his occasional phone calls and visits to see them, but was of the opinion they largely kept themselves to themselves. An old neighbour Bessie kept in touch with at Christmas had even gone as far as to suggest that, apart from his commute into Manchester each day where he now had an office job – the Taylors' own business having long folded – both Roy and Flo lived a fairly reclusive life. Perhaps they could get away with an occasional courtesy visit to maintain contact but otherwise get on with their lives without troubling each other too much?

As she was mulling this over, she turned another page. Her eye was immediately drawn to photos of a smart Edwardian house conversion a few miles from Connie and Hannah. It set her thinking. She knew the area quite well. It was handy for buses and only two or three miles from Sam.

Wouldn't something like that be the answer?

The more she read the small print, the more appealing the idea became. When Hugh appeared with a mid-morning cup of coffee on a tray, she invited him to sit down on the edge of the bed, look at the pictures and specifications and listen to what she had to say.

By then, he'd reached the point where he'd have moved into a Nissen hut if Bessie thought she could turn it into a home. As he studied the advertisement, he could see, on paper, the place looked a distinct possibility.

Originally a large, red brick, early-twentieth-century family house, Worsley Court near Cheadle had long been converted into two double and two single-bedroomed flats: one each on the ground and first floor and, latterly, a smart loft extension on the second. The block was the right size for creating a small community. There were also well-kept surrounding grounds of lawn bordered by beds packed with shrubs, to which they'd have access. For many years rented out, since his death a couple of years ago, the owner's family had upgraded the building and were marketing the re-configured flats with long-term leases.

Was it possible to make travelling arrangements and summon the energy to view the place before the flats were all snapped up? She rang the estate agent. There was considerable interest in them, though so far, they'd received no firm offers. Next, Bessie dialled Sam's number to investigate the possibility of his looking them over for them as soon as possible and reporting back.

Having the afternoon free, he went one better and contacted Connie and Hannah in the hopes they were free to accompany him, which by chance, they were. That evening he conveyed their unanimous agreement: the first floor flat at the back of the building, with its view across the garden to playing fields beyond, would be ideal for them. Also, Connie and Hannah were only too happy to put them up should they decide to see for themselves.

Encouraged, they rang the estate agent back and arranged to visit the following day. After catching the train from Euston, a late lunch with 'the girls' and an agreeable reconnoitre of the exterior of Worsley Court and surrounding district on the Sunday afternoon, they returned the next morning to explore the flats with the agent.

Arriving back in South London that evening tired but happier than they'd felt for several months, Hugh and Bessie struggled to come to terms with the fact that they were now the provisional owners of a new home.

The following weeks were traumatic. Packing up twenty-five years' worth of possessions and memories, not to mention their mixed feelings about moving back to the area they'd last known almost forty years before in a very different era, was intimidating. There were dodgy moments too, when one or the other of them almost lost their nerve, as well as several taxing phone calls with the solicitor over the surveyor's report and other vexatious red tape.

Finally, everything was signed and sealed, and another life-changing patch in their lives drew to a climax.

* * *

Although Bessie was sad to leave Elspeth behind and give up her membership of the Forum, by the end of all the weeks of upheaval, she began to come to terms with the move. Sam wasn't always as visible a presence as she'd have liked, but at least it was comforting to know he was only a phone call and, in emergencies, a cab ride, away if they ever seriously needed him. Counting her blessings, she threw herself into the task of creating a new home for them, revitalised by the effort of getting to know new people and settling into a new world.

Hugh, on the other hand, seemed to have lost his zest for life since his retirement and was shrinking into someone older than his sixty-seven years. After a year or two at Worsley Court, he declined still further. His continued malaise puzzled their new GP. Eventually, Parkinson's Disease was diagnosed. Something else seemed to be going on as well. Bessie told Sam the all-wise *they* thought his daily intake of whisky was reacting badly with some new pills he'd been given. He tried denying himself his favourite tipple, but there was still no improvement.

The relationship changed from wife-and-husband into nurse-and-child. Hugh began falling out of bed in the night when he was an impossible weight for her to manage. Increasingly unable to cope with him at home any longer, the doctor negotiated a space for him in a new wing of the local hospital reserved for long-term, usually elderly, patients who required monitoring. All mod cons with a large, bright lounge and a view of the golf course. The inmates spent their days dozing, waking only to ask a passing orderly to reposition the cushions on their unforgiving faux-leather chairs and dunk Rich Tea biscuits into mugs of tepid Typhoo. Sadly, most were long past caring about either golf or the view.

He was put on a course of new drugs which reacted more bizarrely than the alcohol. The nurses told Bessie that Hugh was experiencing strange sexual fantasies and taking delight in recounting them to fellow detainees at inappropriate moments. That wasn't like Hugh at all. An Edwardian, like herself, he'd always had an innate sense of propriety.

Life played strange tricks, she thought. She visited him almost every day and could see he was always glad to see her, although he looked at her a little distantly. Sometimes he was quite clear-headed and cheerful and joked about his carers and fellow inmates. They tried reminiscing too, though more often than not, there wasn't much to discuss. When he was bored with his own poor health and losing interest in the world he'd left behind, they'd simply sit quietly and, she hoped, enjoy each other's company.

With only herself to look after, she now had time on her hands. After the wearing years taking care of Hugh, constantly on call with even a trip to the shops or hairdresser requiring careful organisation, her life was eerily empty. By degrees, she managed to create a new life for herself. A life of sorts. It would have been far nicer shared with her helpmate, but Hugh was out of reach. The complete Hugh, anyway.

She began re-focussing on her son but, after the many years during which they'd lived separate lives, was finding it difficult fully engaging with him again. It wasn't that they weren't in regular contact – he telephoned at least every other day and visited every fortnight to drop in on Hugh as well as herself – but she could have done with more support from him. More and more, he appeared wrapped up in his own activities and, she suspected, work and possibly emotional problems. What these were he rarely opened up about, and then only superficially. When he'd visited them in London or rung in the past, he'd always made much more of an effort to be sociable. On top of everything, he'd moved. Further away.

He was becoming something of a mystery to her.

213

19

On Reflection

1981
Hugh

The nurse placed a tray on his invalid table. Several lumps of something white in a white-ish sauce and a splodge of white mashed potato looked up challengingly from a white plate. Only a spoonful of paint-box green peas provided contrast.

Hugh's appetite, tentative at the best of times, reversed like a car in a cul-de-sac. After warily forking then chewing a mouthful with distaste, he put down his knife and fork and sat back. At moments like this, either his mother's voice haunted him with 'it's either that or nothing, so get it down you and stop complaining' in the first war, or Bessie's apologetic 'sorry love, but it's the best I could do with what was on offer' in the second.

He'd learnt to ignore the critical remarks of the less amicable orderlies as they stooped to pick up his unfinished meals. On spotting one meandering towards him with the clearing trolley, he'd pretend to be asleep as it was whisked away with a disapproving tut to be replaced by a mug of tepid tea. He'd repeatedly said he didn't take sugar – but had anyone listened?

Except Sofia.

Occasionally, he felt guilty when he remembered how he'd once made Sam eat things he didn't like. But the boy, though generally well-behaved, had sometimes been unexpectedly wilful. Kids knew all the buttons to press. It was good that they got on better these days. Not close mates, exactly, but with mutual respect.

Like that afternoon.

A busy afternoon, too. Now as replete as he'd ever be, his eyes were beginning to droop when Sofia caught him. 'I know what you are up, my lad,' she'd said, as if they were playing a game of chess.

He rather liked her cheek. No one had called him a *lad* since he was a boy – apart from Bessie who'd always referred to Sam and himself collectively as *the lads*. But she'd used the same endearing expression when discussing his junior colleagues and the kids next door, which somewhat devalued its currency. It sounded more genuine coming from Sofia, in her attractive Latin accent spiced with the odd, unexpected colloquialism she'd picked up working in Manchester. 'I will make a bargain with you,' she said. 'A few more mouthfuls and you get a chocolate digestive with your coffee, ok?' Hugh opened an eyelid and grudgingly swallowed another flavourless mouthful.

He'd grown fond of Sofia.

The day may have been busy, but it was also a good one. Hugh could tell the difference between the good and the bad. On bad days, his head became a stew of memories, snatches of sounds and conversations from the past mixed with foggy patches in which he struggled to find the right name or word. Worse were the occasional *very* bad days when he awoke to find himself in a twilight world with a heaviness in his head, the after-effect of an unpleasant dream: the repetitive sort, where it's always night and you're desperately trying to reach somewhere, never arriving and dying for a pee. He'd sense a malign disembodied voice hovering over him and, with a silent strangulated scream, come round to find Sofia gently sorting him out before he returned to the strange, dark land of his mind.

Today, though, he was clear-headed. He tried to make the most of such lucid times and even skimmed the *Daily Mail* in an attempt to make some sense of the world he'd virtually abandoned. Or had it abandoned him? His previous existence was now a van of memorabilia parked somewhere outside, with *Offers Welcomed* on the windscreen.

Today, though, he had enjoyed seeing his well-meaning if unfathomable son.

Struggling to do some simple arithmetic, he realised with a jolt that Sam must be getting on for forty. Whenever he saw him these days, Hugh felt rather sorry for him. What do you say to someone with very little conversation? They always tried kicking off with 'seen anything good on telly?' but he hated admitting to people that with the never-ending clatter and chatter of staff and visitors, the sound coming out of the set at the end of the room was never loud enough for him to catch – except for headlines, which tended to be blared out. Apparently, we were still fighting that ridiculous war in the Falklands against Argentina.

Mention of Argentina always reminded him of Rita Hayworth, the famous redhead. He'd read that she'd been born with black hair, her image, as was the case with many film stars, being the product of the studio system. But then so many things one enjoyed were illusions. How would they ever have got by during hard times without some escapism? It was a pity the recurring footage of British soldiers tearing across the archipelago's dreary rural landscape with guns in their hands wasn't *pretend* too. He'd overheard Sofia – who'd been born in Buenos Aires – arguing with another nurse about the rights and wrongs of Thatcher's decision to blow up a warship with the loss of many lives. Had such an atrocity really been necessary?

These days, he relied on his family and Sofia filling him in on things he hadn't picked up himself, not helped by his tendency to keep falling asleep. One day soon, he'd drift off and never return. That would be the best way to go. The thought of ceasing to exist no longer scared him. He knew Bessie, Connie and Sam cared about him in their different ways. His passing would, nevertheless, relieve them of any guilt related to the inevitable resentment they must feel at helplessly watching someone who'd once been essential to their life become unrecognisable.

It wasn't self-pity. It was the way things were.

That afternoon, a group of girls had given a concert comprising the sort of songs young adults – in this case, guide leaders – guessed people resembling their grandparents enjoyed. Sam, probably pleased to be momentarily let off the hook from having to chat, had gamely helped the staff turn the inmates' chairs towards the impromptu platform set up at the end of the room.

For once there'd been something they could share, if only negative criticism. It felt incongruous listening to the well-meaning youngsters' contrived enthusiasm for the music hall ditties and hackneyed torch songs they'd been tasked to perform. It gave nostalgia a bad name. Some perky pop songs of their own generation might have kept the audience awake. At one point, when a gawky teenager in a blonde ponytail broke unconvincingly into a tortured rendition of Dancing with Tears in my Eyes, he'd turned to Sam and said softly, 'This must be very embarrassing for you.'

Sam's knowing but warm look by way of response had been a rare moment of mutual understanding.

Hugh recalled the last show of Sam's he'd seen, which he'd written and directed. It had impressed him. Perhaps they'd been wrong all those years ago, believing it was the right thing to discourage him from pursuing a precarious life in the professional theatre.

There had been stretches in their relationship when they weren't on the same wavelength. Now he wondered whether they had more in common than they'd ever suspected. It continually surprised him how focussed Sam could be when he wanted. The setbacks he'd suffered might have discouraged a weaker personality, but whatever knocks he received, he usually recovered and moved on. Maybe those seven months in a hospital as a small child turned him into a fighter. Not with his fists – or his life might have been easier – but he'd always had the courage of his convictions.

Bessie complained Sam didn't visit them enough. Hugh, on the other hand, was glad his life was gainfully occupied and he was getting on with it – as he had done at his age. Sam didn't have a sympathetic ear to come home to in the evenings and give him encouragement when things were not going well, as he'd had.

Or so he assumed.

* * *

Sometimes, Hugh wondered whether Bessie's well-meaning but occasionally intrusive control of their lives contributed to his uneven relationship with his son. She always said she understood him best. The maddening thing was that she appeared to – although how could anyone ever know what went on in another person's mind? He knew he must accept responsibility for not making himself more emotionally available to Sam. He couldn't help it. While he cared about other people, he never felt comfortable encroaching on their private world.

Recently, there were a few months when an ingredient in the tablets the doctors were trying out on him had reacted badly, releasing thoughts and feelings in him that he'd never had before. He'd heard himself swearing and experiencing lewd visions. Later he'd felt mortified and caught the Sister telling the nurse how something in his subconscious must have been disturbed. 'It's the body's way of purging the system,' she'd told her. The nurse, who was probably dealing with the shocked response of nearby patients, had simply responded with a weary smile.

Once his mind settled down again, the experience got him thinking about things he'd never really come to terms with. Hugh always concealed more of his thoughts than he revealed, expressing his views largely on a need-to-know basis and leaving it to his wife – who had her own clear opinions of most things – to let off steam at the latest political furore or scandal.

Aware of how relaxed society had become over the years, he'd watched, sometimes with discomfort – or was it partly envy? – how Sam and his friends unselfconsciously discussed controversial topics. His age group tended to favour reticence; nevertheless, he sometimes wondered whether he'd been overly discreet, often opting out of a delicate or contentious conversation by brushing it aside with a flippant remark.

It was probably a good thing young people were more candid and open with each other these days, but that hadn't been his style. Perhaps he was guilty of having taken too much at face value and rarely digging into a contentious topic for fear of releasing a disagreeable odour.

When had he privately begun to assume Sam was probably *not the marrying kind*? A quaint phrase but one he preferred to the alternatives. He'd started off with the usual expectations which, as the years went by, and especially after the fiasco of the boy's fleeting engagement, faded to the point where he now wondered whether his son had any love-life at all.

Sam had always been unlike other boys. Maybe Bessie and he had tried too hard to encourage him to conform and only conflicted him. If they had, it was only for his own good. Unfortunately, what one person saw as good for you wasn't necessarily what you wanted – or needed. Not that he ever seemed too bothered. He'd always admired his son for being his own person, even when he'd incidentally courted trouble.

Besides, Sam never rubbed their noses into whatever he got up to in his free time, though, as the years passed, tell-tale signals accumulated into awkward questions. Friends and business associates would ask after him and his marital status, and when, in response to 'We're still waiting for him to meet the right girl,' they said, 'Well, as long as it's someone nice and he settles down eventually,' he'd read into their reply traces of sympathy mixed with tolerance: the ambiguous *someone*, their sex and marital status having tactfully been left blank. Had they assumed something he couldn't put into words, even to himself?

Hugh was the first to admit how much he enjoyed the saucy patter of outrageous comic actors such as Kenneth Williams and John Inman. But then, it was their job to be larger than life. Comedy had long provided a safe haven for off-colour humour and *double entendres* provided they were clever – or, he was reliably informed, subversive enough for only the initiated to appreciate. But it was one thing to laugh at entertainers who set themselves up to be mocked and another to recognise a connection between their humour and the personality of someone you cared about.

The world today was so different in that regard from when he was young. Oscar Wilde had been sentenced with hard labour for *gross indecency* only fourteen years before he'd been born. The word *indecency*, long a word associated with improper behaviour, now sounded horribly dated. For many years, nothing he'd read or learnt about sex between people of the same gender had ever encouraged him to consider it as anything but distasteful, yet, more recently, he'd begun to wonder if by *distasteful* he really meant *unconventional?*

He appreciated how, stuck away from home without the company of women, some men might be driven to improvise, but, never having been in the forces or gone to prison himself, had always presumed that, once back in the arms of their wives and girlfriends, they picked up where they'd left off – consigning those moments when they'd helped each other out to a hush-hush world where different rules had temporarily applied.

It was some of his contemporaries who'd opened his eyes as to how daring some other men were in their parallel lives. One, whom he'd taken to *Murray's Club* in Soho, during a short break in the floor show, had turned to Hugh and asked, 'Ever had a threesome, Hugh?' When he'd turned red and, trying to hide his shock, spluttered, 'N…no,' his guest had winked and added, 'I sometimes drop in on these gals in West Wittering. Phwoar! You should try it. Sometimes their brother joins in!' He'd then groaned with delight as a sextet of scantily dressed beauties sashayed onto the stage, leaving Hugh taken aback and wondering whether he'd missed out on something.

Like many older married people, Hugh experienced moments of physical yearning rarely satisfied at home. He was devoted to Bessie, but after the premature loss of their second child, that aspect of their marriage had diminished. Bessie's prolonged illness finally limited love-making to little more than affectionate nestling on a cold night. On the rare occasions she let him go further, he'd sensed he gained far more pleasure from it than she did. It had probably been the same for a lot of men, but he suspected they found other ways of dealing with their frustrations.

Once or twice, after several pints, he recalled one indiscreet acquaintance hinting at dalliances when he was away on business. It only occurred to him now that his friend Harry's references to a certain 'gorgeous – nudge-nudge-wink-wink – Mikaela' could be a cover for Mick, a mechanic in Mitcham. Though come to think of it, Harry's pink-striped shirts and flamboyant ties had been an exception to the rule in Engineering. Alas, his own uptight conscience never permitted him to go any further than an exchange of flirtatious smiles with the pretty barmaid he saw regularly at The Albert, and the odd risqué joke with his chatty barber.

Although, if he delved deep into his psyche, he was forced to admit to the odd occasion, suppressed at the time, when a conversation with a good-looking stranger or work contact had aroused more than just his curiosity. Was it so very unnatural to admire another man? Watching a particularly charismatic sportsman or a dancer occasionally led to a disquieting *what if* moment too, which he'd translated simply as *mustn't it be great to look like you*. When did the lines between *admire* and *want* begin to blur?

And women who were attracted to other women? He'd always been impressed by Connie and Hannah's devotion to each other. Why was it more acceptable for two women to be more touchy-feely than two men? Hannah had first come to stay with them after the war when Sam was in hospital, and they'd been glad of a distraction. She'd been introduced to them by Connie as *my good friend* and fitted in so well with them all, her cheerfulness helping ease their ongoing pain at that time. Had Bessie and he ever considered precisely *how* good a friend she was? Their attitude was always 'it's none of our business.' And quite right too, although they had enjoyed a social tolerance that still wasn't fully accorded to his gender. What opportunities had he missed to fully explore the buffet of carnality – and why had he always let the Edwardian gentleman within him squash any challenging thoughts as quickly as possible?

Damn those pills he'd been given which had unsettled him and messed with his head. Such thoughts were redundant now. Far too late to continue speculating what might have occurred if he'd been less of a goody-two-brogues.

Nonetheless, it helped him understand his son a little better and even wish he had parts of his life to live over again.

* * *

Sofia was now standing over him with his coffee and the couple of chocolate digestives she'd promised on a tray.

'Did you enjoy the concert this afternoon?'

'They tried hard,' he said.

'At least you stayed awake. I see your son was here with you.'

'Sam. Yes'

'I can see the resemblance.'

'That's strange. My wife can't.'

'He is very polite, isn't he?'

'Probably too much so for his own good. He directs plays and shows.'

'Really?'

'He's a clever boy. Given half a chance, he'd have put on an excellent cabaret today.'

20

The Frog and the Hawk

1981-82
Sam

His office phone rang.

It was a couple of minutes before eight-thirty. He hadn't yet taken off his coat. Damn the man!

'Hello.'

'Sam.'

'Frank.'

'About your minutes that have landed on my desk.'

'Yes?'

'I'm looking at minute five point two, Roman numeral three.'

'Hold on while I find my copy.'

'Ah.' The tone of the exclamation suggested it should have been sitting ready on his blotter.

Sam reached for a folder in his desk tray.

A new broom on a mission, tall, slim-ish, balding and forty-ish, Frank Taverner had previously been responsible for the College's increasingly important IT team. His attention to detail was known to be almost pathological. A married, family man, that never stopped him from flirting with any pretty female within his orbit – and a number outside it. As had been commented by several male colleagues, he was never as exacting with women's work as he was with that of other men. Women played up to him. Men, except for other obsessive computer boffs, were wary.

Frank's brief, it was rumoured, was to tighten up the department: both the size of the team and the space to accommodate them. Thus, from the moment Sam was introduced to him, with the instinct of a frog conscious of the hawk's shadow hovering over the pond, he'd sensed danger.

This conversation wasn't their first tense telephone call in recent months. Frank almost always chose to tackle him at the start of the working day. It was as if he was deliberately trying to catch him out. Once, a missed call, five minutes before Sam was due in the office at eight-thirty, had warranted a reproachful 'but *I'm* always here by *eight*.' The immediacy of a phone call was more unsettling than a prearranged meeting. Phones could also be slammed down before you had a chance to properly defend yourself.

'Got it,' Sam said, trying to sound bright and positive, the receiver in one hand as he fished out the offending document from his desk-tray with the other.

'There's a comma missing in the second sentence.'

'I didn't think …'

'Obviously not. And...' he continued in his silky, low-key voice tinged with irritation, 'in minute twelve point five under Any Other Business, two lines down and three words in, the word *achieve* has been typed with the *i* and *e* transposed.'

'Whoops!'

'No, not whoops. Careless. Very careless.'

'The draft was ok when it was passed by the Chairman. The errors must have slipped in when it was retyped to incorporate his amendments.'

'That's no excuse. You're the secretary. Besides, they were only his *suggested* amendments. It's for you to accept them. Why didn't you double-check it?'

'I felt sure I had.'

Preparing the minutes was only one of many tasks, and Sam knew his proofreading skills depended on how much sleep he'd had the previous night. The continual pressure of intimidating phone calls like this after a frantic dash for buses to work and coping with the early morning rush hour crowds didn't help. Then there were other problems. A particularly inefficient part-time typist, for one, on top of battling to keep up with a plethora of time-sensitive work and other commitments. The worry of his father's worsening condition and Bessie's demands on him didn't ease matters and nagged his conscience.

Though always conscientious, nothing he ever did seemed enough for either his current boss or, these days, his mother. At least his studies towards an Open University degree, which he'd embarked on a couple of years before, were going well. That and his theatre work both came easily and spontaneously to him and provided some escape from the pressure he was increasingly experiencing at the office. He needed reassurance not every aspect of his life was sliding out of control.

'Apart from those errors,' Frank went on, 'of even more significance is the way you've reported the funding issue in minute seven.'

'I identified the key points of a long and somewhat acrimonious debate,' Sam said.

'That may be, but the way it's been presented suggests we'll accept their proposal. You know perfectly well it's not something we could ever consent to. We're in charge of policy, not the Chairman or committee members. Their job is to give us advice and recommendations, not make decisions. Your job is to help edge them, tactfully but firmly, to that end. Imagine the budgetary implications!'

'I fully understand, but ...'

'Then why,' he hammered on, 'have you written *the Secretariat noted members' concern and AGREED to investigate the matter further and report back at the next meeting?*'

'Correct. It gives us time to come up with a nuanced response.'

'No, you should have stamped on it right away.'

'Sir George can be very pushy.'

'And you're paid to be pushier. Now we will have to make sure the investigation bears no fruit and we will look foolish. This isn't the first time we've spoken about your handling of that committee. I trust I can rely on you to guarantee we won't be having such a conversation again.'

And he hung up.

* * *

Sam had started working at the College three years earlier after leaving the Council's Adult Education sector in search of more responsibility – and a better salary to help him get a foot on the property ladder.

His work on the administrative team was varied, involving not only general administrative duties but acting as minuting secretary for the College policy committee and related working parties dealing with finance, governance, research and the ongoing maintenance of both the building and academic standards. The thorns in his flesh were a handful of specialists from other educational institutions and high-ranking representatives of local organisations who, co-opted for diplomatic reasons, often pushed the limits of their remit to protect or further their own interests. Funding was a particular case in point. Local councillors, especially, could be tiresome. If Sam crossed any of them, they would then complain about him, after which he'd be reprimanded for offending someone the College wished to keep on side. If he so much as courteously acknowledged their unsought proposals, he could be accused of going native.

He'd developed good relationships with most of his Chairmen, especially Sir George, who was witty, gregarious and an expert on the history of jazz. Sam was fairly sure he could count on him to help him reword the minute to everyone's satisfaction. He also suspected there was no love lost between the knight and Frank, whom he met at governors' shindigs.

Sam had enjoyed a better relationship and mutual respect with his previous boss, who had recently moved to another job. Under his leadership, despite being aware everyone at his level was better qualified than himself and the work ethos being more exacting than at the more laid-back Council office, he'd so far chugged along reasonably well. He pinned his hopes on a BA giving him more credibility.

In the meantime, Fate had other plans.

The frostiness between the two men began the day members of *the gang* – as Frank liked to call them – were individually summoned to meet him and discuss their role in it. At least, that was how it had been presented to them. The discussion turned out to be a progress review gleaned, in Sam's case, from notes Frank must have inherited from members of staff Sam rarely had dealings with. Either that, or they'd been selectively edited to provide non-committal feedback he could twist out of shape.

On being asked to sit down, Sam noted for the first time that, as well as piercing eyes, the man had a hawk nose.

He'd even been designed for the job.

The conversation began pleasantly enough. Frank briefed him on his plans to shake up the department and what would be expected of him. Nothing would happen right away, and the changes would be implemented gradually. It was only when he looked at his watch and sensed the meeting would soon be over that the *coup de grâce* arrived.

'I can tell from people I've spoken to that you are generally pleasant and helpful.' Sam winced. 'But we need people in the gang who are demanding of both themselves and others. Focussed and accurate. There's no room for arty-fartiness.'

Sam remembered reading how hawks swallowed every particle of their prey.

'I feel it's my duty to warn you, however, from other comments I've received…' His skin began to creep as he watched the beak swooping lower. '…how can I delicately put it …' Pounce. '…your *backstage darling* manner may entertain the groundlings but doesn't go down well with everyone upstairs.' Snap! 'A word to the wise. You're a college administrator, not a redcoat."

Sam gulped and felt sick.

The administrative offices were housed in a couple of corridors off the main foyer. The ground floor contained staff responsible for the Facilities & Maintenance, Student Accommodation, Finance, External Relations, Communications and Marketing functions shared across several campuses. The roles of Administrative staff, such as Sam, usually included a couple of related areas supported by a team of secretaries and clerks. The offices of the Principal, his Deputy, Frank and their secretarial backup were housed on the floor above.

Harriet Jones, the Vice Principal, was an ardent theatregoer and often joined him for lunch in the canteen. Not only had she supported his last two productions and recently lent him one of her Sondheim LPs; more importantly, Harriet was once a student on the campus where Connie had worked until her retirement, and she remembered her with affection. He wondered whether someone had passed some snide comments about this relationship which, up until now, he'd been careful not to trade on. He didn't know the Principal so well, but they always gave one another amicable smiles when they passed each other around the campus. Unless he had unknowingly aggrieved the man in some way, Frank was either deliberately blowing up a few asides out of all proportion for his own ends, or lying.

Without waiting for a reaction, Frank gave him a dismissive nod and closed the file. 'Thank you for your time. Oh, and on your way back, could you very kindly let Tina Cotterill know I'm running a bit late and won't now be able to see her until twelve-fifteen?'

Trembling with fury, Sam made his way back to his office, pausing only to put his head around Tina's door and deliver Frank's message.

'That's my trip to Lewis's at lunchtime gone bang,' she sighed.

He shot her a sympathetic look.

* * *

Over the next day or so, Sam struggled to guess where any criticism of his behaviour had come from and who he could possibly have offended.

Admittedly, ever since his broken engagement, after which he'd begun being more open about himself with a discreet number of close friends and workmates, he may occasionally have let slip his guard. It would have been unsurprising, given his extrovert personality, if, when he felt comfortable with people, he didn't sometimes betray himself. If his sexuality was an open secret at work, up until now he'd never known it do him any harm. On duty, he presented himself discreetly and liked to think he edited the showier side of his personality. Seemingly he'd failed to with some of the people who mattered.

That autumn he'd been asked to liaise with a smart, central hotel and help plan a high-level conference on the launch of a new raft of qualifications, with an opening speech by a member of the Royal Family. As well as having responsibility for liaising with Buckingham Palace and arranging the invitations, accommodation and catering, he'd also successfully ensured continuity of the timetable on the day. It had all gone according to plan. He hoped he'd scored brownie points. Yet, apart from an appreciative smile and high five from Harriet after the concluding speech, that hadn't happened. Was it a co-incidence Frank had started his job just a week before the event and quickly made known his disgust at the over-expenditure on the floral décor?

Manchester was slowly relaxing its attitude towards minority groups. Tender but green shoots were peeking through the grim northern earth, though pockets of reactionary behaviour remained. While Sam believed he knew how and when to behave himself, he sometimes miscalculated.

Like most academic institutions, the College considered itself to be a liberal, open-minded place embracing people of different religions, ethnic groups and sexual orientation – particularly those with a useful contribution to make. Indeed, until Frank appeared in his life, Sam had never experienced coercive behaviour at work. The rare hint of homophobia might be delivered as a tasteless joke rather than with malice. There were, of course, other gay people on the staff, but that didn't mean they shared anything else in common or fraternised. Once he'd spotted a lecturer chatting up a guy in The Rembrandt. They'd exchanged knowing glances but that was all.

Some weeks went by without further harassment until one evening when he was working late.

Sam was standing at a photocopier in a cramped ante-room close to his office. As he began running off a large number of reports required for distribution the following morning, he heard a door slam at the end of the corridor followed by determined feet pacing towards him.

The door opened. Frank bustled in somewhat out of breath with a sheaf of papers in his hand. 'Can you put your work on hold? I'm in a rush. My copier's run out of ink and these must catch the last post.'

'I'm sorry,' Sam said, 'I've no way of stopping the programme. The documents are set to be collated.'

'Let me try,' Frank said, pushing past him and peering at the panel of buttons before pressing each one in turn. The machine soon protested with a whine, then shuddered and stopped. He frantically pressed again. Again, nothing happened.

After a minute or so, he gave up. 'Bugger!' Turning and glaring at him, he said, 'Trust it to be you,' then angrily bore down on Sam, forcing him backwards into a corner by the side of the machine, pinning him half against the wall and half into the hard metallic edge of the machine which bit painfully into his side. Placing his left hand up against the wall to trap him and clenching the right, he drummed his fist threateningly in front of him. Sam found the strange gleam in his eyes disturbing. His face still too close to his own for comfort, Frank let his aggressive hand drop by his side and his face changed. As if he'd had a better idea.

Was he about to be assaulted? Everyone had gone home. No one would know.

For all the stupid risks he'd taken in his private life, to date Sam had only once found himself obliged to submit to another man's desires against his will. The physical discomfort was nothing to his feelings of worthlessness afterwards. Not to mention the humiliating trip to the GUM clinic and the course of antibiotics he'd been prescribed some days later.

Those feelings returned now. He told himself not to be so idiotic. Bosses didn't rape members of their staff – did they? All he had to do was knee Frank in the groin or, using all his strength, knock him backwards and make a dash for it.

Except no one would believe his story. One person's word, etcetera. He had no union to turn to. Bosses were protected by their status and the Old

Boys' network. There could be serious consequences if he made the fatal mistake of submitting a formal complaint. After all, nothing had occurred yet but this strange impasse with Frank towering unnervingly over him, his malevolent expression still tinged with something close to lasciviousness.

All at once the man relaxed, his expression changing to disdain as if saying, 'You're not worth it.' Stepping back, he picked up his papers and stormed off, leaving Sam sweating and clinging to the photocopier for support.

What had that been all about?

At school, he'd been persecuted by other boys who were bored and thoughtless. An easy target for their surplus energy. Often, though, they'd soon lost interest and an hour later would be chatting to him about homework as if nothing had happened. He learnt to shrug off such moments, belittled and powerless though he always felt. There it was all a game, if at his expense. He learnt not to bear grudges, if only for his own sanity. This year's aggressor became next year's study mate, by which time everyone would have moved on and the rules and victims had changed.

He'd never felt anything before like the highly charged atmosphere during the incident at the photocopier. That hadn't been sport but something else he didn't understand. He recalled Bessie's words. 'It's not always about you. Sometimes it's about them. To do with their own problems – only they take it out on other people.'

* * *

The months went by. With the departmental restructuring temporarily on hold, Sam concentrated on revising for his exams. Then there would be a pantomime to get off the ground and his mother to keep an eye on as Hugh's health declined still further.

He was aware of Bessie's anxiety, but her conscientious GP, Connie, Hannah and good neighbours were keeping an eye on her, especially her new friend Miriam who ferried her hither and thither. There wasn't much he could do but stay over on a Friday evening, do odd jobs for her the next morning and call on Hugh. With the tide going out, it was at least heartening there was peace between father and son.

December arrived and with it the annual staff appraisals, which always clouded any anticipation of seasonal jollities. This year, a new profiling system was being trialled. Every member of staff was awarded one to five points in each of five categories: Communication, Administration, Motivation, Tactical and Personal Skills, each broken down into subsets. On what basis the assessment was made and who contributed to it was never explained.

When his slot arrived, Sam entered Frank's office with more trepidation than usual. The interview was brief. The man remained icily remote.

'You've been allotted two or three points in each category. Twelve out of a possible twenty-five. Not very good, I'm afraid.'

Sam was beyond furious.

'You can appeal, of course. But I think if you consider the assessment carefully, you'll find it isn't far short of the mark. Bear in mind your lack of judgement, attention to detail and often inappropriate behaviour. I suggest you consider whether you're really suited to the job.'

Statements supported more by subjective criticism than facts. While Sam had every right to challenge them, he didn't care to respond, his experience at the photocopier having reinforced his loathing of the man. Seeing him on the brink of losing his self-control only confirmed how thoroughly obnoxious he was. He felt nothing but disgust. Unwilling to give Frank the satisfaction of attempting to humiliate him further, he stood up, mumbled a curt *thank you* and walked out.

Back at his desk, he made an appointment to see Harriet Jones. With overall charge of college administration, she was technically Frank's boss, although he enjoyed considerable delegated autonomy for his own patch. Sam guessed there wasn't much she could do to help him, but she might at least make him feel easier.

She did.

They met two days later. Sam's file was open on her desk. Together they went through the contentious document. Sam described the major projects he'd dealt with over the year, a number of which she'd observed herself. In as measured a way as possible, he gave his own assessment of his success and failings in each set of skills.

'What score do you think would be fairer, then?' she asked.

'I think I'm an excellent communicator and my administrative and personal skills are good, bar the odd proofreading slip,' he said with a self-deprecating grin, 'so those are all worth scores of four. Maybe my motivation and tactical skills are only average, but I'd be the first to admit I have things to learn.'

'Agreed. From what I know of your work, even then you're underselling yourself. Still...' Authoritatively wielding her Parker 51, Harriet superimposed the new ratings over the original figures. I make that three fours and two threes. Eighteen. Not so bad, and pragmatically leaving room for development? I wish I could do more for you, but Him Next Door has the final say on appeals and it gives us a little room for manoeuvre...' The look in her eye indicated further positive rather than negative adjustment.

'Thank you very much.'

They briefly discussed issues relating to upcoming social events at College. Harriet put her pen back in the glass tray on her desk to indicate the appeal was over. Sam thanked her again. 'You're very welcome. I'm glad you came to see me.'

'Have a good Christmas.'

'You too. Good luck with the panto; I'm looking forward to it!'

* * *

On the second of January, an envelope arrived franked with the OU's logo. To his delight, he'd successfully graduated.

He mentioned his BA status to only a few people, yet word mysteriously spread. Letters of congratulation flooded in from colleagues and even Sir George. His sense of achievement cheered him up. There was the excitement of the pantomime, now in its final stages of production, to look forward to and help him rise above his work problems. Then, some days later, came another summons from his nemesis. Emboldened by his academic success, he entered Frank's office.

If he'd dared to hope his achievement had changed anything, he was quickly disabused.

'Sit down. This won't take long. I've duly noted the amended profile. Harriet, of course, has a soft side she can afford. I can't. I'm bitterly disappointed at your lack of loyalty. So, zilch for team spirit. As you know, I'm ultimately responsible for organising my own department and placing people where their skills are best suited. One of my targets, as you are aware, is rationalisation. Part of your current job will soon be redundant as we grow more reliant on Archimedes.' This was a reference to the all-powerful computer the College had recently purchased partly, he assumed, with funds advanced from savings from his own and other workmates' salaries. 'Archie', as it was colloquially known, was Frank's best mate. 'I'm afraid however high your assessment score, it can't alter the staffing decisions I've authorised.'

The bastard!

'As from the end of March, what's left of your current remit will be merged with Sue Holford's clerical role in PR under Judy McKinnon. Sue's been promoted to a post in Facilities. You get on with Judy, don't you?'

A lively young woman currently on a similar grade to himself, Judy wasn't the easiest of people to work with but was at least bright and amusing. It was effectively demotion but, for the time being, a job of sorts.

'I see.'

'You'll continue to receive your current salary until the grades are revised in the autumn, by which time the current incremental system will have been overhauled.' His steely look said he'd ensure this was to his detriment.

Sam didn't react.

'It gives you a few months grace to look around for a position elsewhere should you wish. I can't do fairer than that, can I?'

Frank wouldn't rest until he'd finally hounded him out of the building. For as long as he stayed at that College his life would be miserable and he'd be forever watching his back. He was about to get up and leave when, without even looking at him, the man surprisingly segued into a tirade about how difficult his own job was and how much time he spent fighting with the powers that be on behalf of the department which he believed to be looked down upon by the professors. It was odd watching Frank play victim. Alas, he could summon no empathy for his predicament. How sadistic, after doing everything in his power to shatter every ounce of his confidence, to now hold him captive and regale him with his own problems.

When he finally paused for a decent breath, Sam glanced at his watch, frowned, got up, put up his hand, said, 'Excuse me. I've an important call scheduled in five minutes,' and left the room.

Sam was now living in a studio flat not far from Victoria station at the end of Deansgate. It was slightly bigger than his old one, but it had enabled him to get his first mortgage. Ten per cent was his, and he had decorated and tastefully furnished it with refurbished second-hand items and a few clean-cut pieces from *Habitat*. Maybe he wouldn't be able to retain it. The thought of being virtually forced out of his current job to slave for Judy McKinnon, having to sell up and, with a depreciating salary, maybe having to downsize again or – worse – move in with Bessie, was unbearable. On top of everything, when his father died, he would probably need to help his mother with some of her recurring bills.

The outlook was bleak.

* * *

The week after the pantomime, Sam met Tony for a spaghetti bolognaise and carafe of Valpolicella in a small Italian restaurant they'd long patronised in Market Street. Tony was now in a similar but more senior job in a sister college up the road.

With no theatrical commitments scheduled for a while, he was suffering from withdrawal symptoms from the buoyancy he'd experienced during the ten days of what had turned out to be a successful show, and he was conscious of not being at his best. Coincidentally, when they first greeted each other, his friend was also downbeat. His current extra-marital girlfriend had dumped him, and he seemed even more despondent than Sam.

A couple of glasses in, comforted also by the hot, tasty pasta, they were beginning to unwind.

'I hope Fiendish Frank is behaving himself better?'

'He's given me my cards.'

'*What!*'

'That's a bit melodramatic. I've actually only been down-graded. A victim of rationalisation and new technology, apparently. But he's virtually told me to get another job. The sooner I can move on, the better.'

Tony paused to drown the remaining drop of wine from his glass and looked keenly at Sam. 'It's funny you should say that.'

'Really?'

'Because…' Tony seemed to be turning something over in his mind as if wanting it to come out right. 'I'll cut to the chase. How would you feel about coming to work for me?'

Sam brightened. 'Could you cope with me?'

'Could you cope with *me*?'

One of the reasons they were friends was because they complemented each other well. As well as being affable, Tony was well-balanced and tried not to take life too seriously. More importantly, Tony possessed a sympathetic nature, was broad-minded and was often entertained by Sam's hyper moments.

'It might be… interesting,' Sam said cagily. 'You're genuinely looking for someone?'

'Of course. I'm responsible for a team consisting of three officers and four support staff. We're a jolly little bunch, but Maisie's gone on indefinite leave due to family problems and, if and when she comes back, she's asked to be transferred to a far less onerous job, possibly on Reception. It's left a big black hole. I don't know anyone going spare who could hit the ground running with her work. It's very much what you're doing now from what you tell me but not so high-level and with some interesting new projects you'd have just the right touch for, such as an in-house magazine I've had in mind for a while. Designed to keep both colleagues and the outside world up to date with current developments. Regular features on, say, the roles different people play and so on.'

Sam's imagination was moving into gear. 'Go on.'

'Probably wouldn't make a great deal of difference pay-wise. Maybe a couple of thousand?'

His spirits rose even faster. 'If you really think I'm up to it?'

'I know your strengths. The poor girl hasn't had her mind on the job for a while, and some of the people she deals with are badly in need of your sort of TLC.'

'When could I start?'

'Now. You'd probably have to give at least a month's notice, but with our colleges being practically twinned, that shouldn't be much of a problem. Maybe I could ask for you to be transferred one day a week to begin with and allow you to integrate with us as soon they'll let you.'

'Tough if they don't. My resignation will be on Frank's desk first thing on Monday. And I think I'll have Harriet on my side.'

'Great. Now, there's half a glass left in this carafe. This is on me. If it comes off, you'll have done me a favour.' He raised his glass. 'Here's to a much happier 1983!'

21

Taking Stock

1985
Bessie

Bessie had grown to like her single bed.

Bed brought you face to face with yourself. It was here the important things in life happened: emerging into the world, sleeping, recovering from sickness. Beneath a protective duvet, one grappled with decisions, rested, made love and, with luck, expired. Many people went on long walks to clear their heads or come to terms with problems and the important issues, but, for Bessie, bed was her place for pondering.

She often imagined her own ghosts of Past and Present clustering around her pillows as in an illustration by Phiz. Sometimes they remonstrated, advised restraint – or persuaded her to look at an issue from another person's point of view. She thought of St Joan's voices confronting her as she struggled for some shut-eye on her straw pallet. The poor lass had gone to the stake for listening to her conscience. Was that what they really were, voices, ghosts, whatever – a reminder of your responsibilities? Most women had their share of them. If not always saintly ones.

When love-making, her pondering had always occurred once the hurly-burly was out of the way – though she recalled one disastrous coupling when, with Hugh moments from climaxing, she'd suddenly remembered Aunt

Amy's birthday card still sitting on the hall table to be posted, wrecking the moment by wriggling away apologetically to scribble herself a reminder.

How strange, she thought, lying back on her pillows, the amount of time one spent in bed. Factoring in periods of sickness and convalescence, it came to… gracious, more than a third of her life. A varied life, too, made up of long stretches in London and Edinburgh, as well as in the North. Three contrasting cities miles apart. There were always new things to come to terms with. Never a dull moment. So many more places she'd liked to have seen. People she wished she'd met. Things she would never now do – and some she'd have handled differently.

Intimate, horizontally-placed, usually one-sided conversations with a sleepy Hugh and her alter ego had often punctuated the hours late at night. Now there was only her alter ego to debate with. She recalled lying in the Edinburgh nursing home prior to Sam's birth, terrified they'd forgotten about her. And all those months later, when she feared she might never see him again.

And now…

When Hugh first went into hospital, it was strange sleeping on only one side of the bed with, in winter, an arctic stretch of under-sheet on the other. When she'd tentatively explored the undiscovered terrain, it hadn't felt quite right somehow, wallowing in all that space, as if saying 'see what I can do now!'

Not long after the funeral, she'd turned the marital bedroom into the spare room, moved the double bed out and exchanged it for two singles: useful when Connie and Hannah stayed over, saving them the trouble of driving back to Wilmslow after an evening of rich food and libation – or when Sam brought his latest best buddy for Christmas. They always said, 'We can easily share the double; we're quite used to it,' but that wasn't Bessie's style. What they did in their own homes was their own affair. In hers, the *separate bed rule* applied. She wasn't a prude but prided herself on her social fastidiousness.

What had happened to 'Roger' who Sam was very pally with for a while? A wizard at Scrabble but rarely mentioned now. She wondered why.

The close proximity of *the girls*, as Connie and Hannah were always referred to, had been a further inducement for coming back. All the same, she was beginning to wonder whether it had been a mistake. Apart from the family losses, the Cheshire fields she'd meandered through to school during the First World War were now part of Greater Manchester's sprawling conurbation, the world having transformed in her lifetime.

So many people she had known were now gone.

A way of life extinct.

Bessie once said to Hugh, 'Life's too short.'

His reply, 'It's quite long enough,' had given her pause for thought.

Maybe that was the difference between them. Not that he'd been exactly depressive but, she admitted to herself, inclined to resign himself to things he couldn't do much about.

Unlike herself. She was a fighter.

Even so, early on in her marriage, Bessie had relinquished any lingering hope of a remunerative occupation for herself in order to support Hugh's career. Not that she hadn't stuck up for herself. She'd been fitter in her fifties than at any time since her illness and once Sam was away at boarding school had longed for a little job of her own: a couple of days a week maybe, in a lively place with interesting people. It would have put a little jam on the bread, too. Her own jam. But Hugh wasn't keen. Unusually for them, there had been arguments. It had been like a replay of her tussles with her father. On one level, she knew he'd cared about her deeply but, like most married men, assumed she'd always put his needs ahead of her own. That was the bargain women made in the days when men were usually the breadwinners. It was tacitly understood marriage comprised an unbalanced coupling, each person with their preordained role. If hers was the submissive one – technically speaking as it wasn't a word she'd ever use about herself – hadn't she only been like many middle-class wives of her generation? Few women had worked until comparatively recently, certainly not full time unless, like Connie and Hannah, they were single and obliged to fend for themselves

So, she'd lost that battle. Not that she'd ever complained. Everything considered, she knew marrying Hugh had been her best decision. A decent, undervalued man, Bessie trusted he was finally being appreciated in the vast management structure above. Not literally above, she wasn't that naïve, but wherever his spirit had landed: on some exotic shore she'd be exploring herself soon enough.

Would dying really be an exciting adventure? The conventional concept of heaven assumed you'd be reunited with friends and relatives. She sometimes asked herself, did she really want to see him again? The good-looking man with the twinkle in his eye she'd married, possibly. But the one he'd become? More important, would he be pleased to see her? They signed up to share this life – not necessarily the next.

On the surface, Hugh was assertive and good-humoured, but underneath lay deep pockets of insecurity. She'd spent much of their married life bolstering his ego. Professional recognition had mattered more than anything else. More than herself? A tricky one, that.

For a long time, she missed Elspeth and her stimulating afternoons with the Forum as a *political activist*. She smiled at her own little joke. No, she'd never brandished a placard outside the Houses of Parliament or lain down in Trafalgar Square, though it might have been fun. She smiled to herself. A blue-rinsed housewife carted off by a burly cop – hopefully in one of her best hats!

Thinking of that other fallow period and how Elspeth had saved her from herself had helped her this time. Now a member of the local Women's Institute, she also attended regular coffee mornings and lunch buffets at the church hall – and was cultivating more friendships.

As well as the people she met outside, there was faithful Miriam and the elderly Mr Hargreaves both downstairs – and Mrs Parkinson, with the jolly family which visited her regularly, across the landing. Connie came over once a fortnight, often with Hannah, when they'd drive into Cheshire and Derbyshire for little jaunts and try out new pubs for lunch. Yet, as time went on, she was noticing more the effects of her chronic arthritis. It wasn't crippling yet. She could still take the bus for short shopping trips and cajole someone with a car to take her further afield. But in another five… ten years… if she lasted that long?

Time was hurrying by like an intercity train on the last lap of its journey, anxious to reach the terminus on schedule. It made her all the more determined to make good use of it before she became further incapacitated. She wanted to see more of the people who mattered to her and was sad when some seemed not to want to indulge her.

Some*one* in particular.

When they first returned to Manchester, things had been quite amicable, but her relationship with Sam was growing more tense. They were finding, as Elspeth might have put it, their agendas clashed. And clashing with greater frequency. Why?

She needed his company and support more than ever. What were the things going on in his life he was so unwilling to share with her? Was it the people he spent so much time with? He'd tried explaining, but she couldn't get her head around it and never lost hope he might yet turn up with another pretty girl in tow. None of his friends seemed to lead what she would consider stable lives. Sam was now at an age when it might soon be too late for him to settle down.

Bessie sighed.

She spent a lot of her time worrying about how she might manipulate their relationship back to where she would like it to be. After all, he was her only child and she was his mother. He had responsibilities. He owed it to her to be more attentive. Whose fault was it their relationship had become strained? If she was being honest with herself, they were probably both to blame. Normally confident in her judgement of situations, she couldn't get to grips with this latest stand-off at all. Hard as she tried to relegate her concerns to a drawer in her mind, they screamed to be let out. It was no use continually moaning at him; he could be so touchy. Volatile even. Rows didn't do her health any good, and alienation would damage them both.

Stretching her arm out to the bedside table, she switched on her *Roberts* transistor.

She preferred the talks on the radio to music. Chirpy tunes following her around the clock and yard after yard of Classic FM were not for her. She loathed muzak in the High Street, too: rocked-up versions of old faithfuls churning out as you desperately searched for pilchards in the wrong aisle of Sainsbury's. Especially irritating from Halloween until Christmas was the assault on your ears from jazzed-up seasonal favourites as you tried to make yourself heard at the check-out. Sales staff must be driven crazy from the overkill. Or did they become aurally anaesthetised?

She remembered gentler times in her youth when music was largely reserved for church services and dedicated places of entertainment. In her head, she still heard the majestic tones of the organ at the Paramount, Oxford Road, Souza marches around the bandstand on Saturday afternoons in the park and the tinkly tunes of Pierrot shows at Blackpool.

The pips advised her it was now nine o'clock. Patrick Magee had finally been found guilty of bombing the Grand Hotel, Brighton, during the Tory Conference and sentenced to life imprisonment. If Bessie sometimes quarrelled with the dogmatism of her heroine, Mrs Thatcher, her heart had gone out to her and more especially the Home Secretary's wife, Margaret Tebbit, after being paralysed in the IRA attack. She admired people with courage.

Thinking of the redoubtable Mrs T reminded her that her home help, Mrs Bingley, another force to be reckoned with, would be arriving to give the place a going-over at ten. Then there was her fortnightly trim-and-set with Tanya around the corner at eleven-thirty. Better get a move on.

Throwing back the duvet, she gingerly swung her legs over the mattress, catching sight of herself in the long wall mirror. Post-sleep dishevelment aside, she didn't look too bad for a woman of nearly eighty, despite some natural sagginess and the inevitable crows' feet. She'd always taken a pride in her well-maintained hair, too. Formerly plump-ish, age and a smaller appetite had trimmed her former excess flesh. With her bandy arthritic knees, her figure no longer suggested the athletic tennis player of yesteryear, but, on a good day, she could still hold her head high.

A busy morning ahead, she thought, moving into the bathroom and turning on a tap. Then there was the afternoon to look forward to. Giles was due to pop in for a cup of tea.

After that, maybe an hour with the latest *Woman's Weekly*, *The Archers* and a routine glass of Bristol Cream followed by something on a tray; a *Miss Marple* and then bedtime.

A full day.

22

The Best China

1985
Bessie

'Come in and sit down.'

Bessie gave Miriam a brief peck near the top of her cheekbone. She believed in demonstrating warmth but discouraged tactility. The coffee table gleamed with her plated silver tea service and best china, seconds from a Marshall & Snelgrove sale years ago. The remnants of a small feast nestled on crisp white doilies: plates of triangular egg and cress sandwiches, crusts tidily trimmed; sultana-packed scones smiling with butter, and the mandatory slices of Bessie's date-and-walnut loaf which had graced many a parish fair.

She always made a point of saying how, as a northerner, she kept open house, though neither of them would have dreamt of barging into the other's flat except in a dire emergency or, as happened today, to briefly confirm a social arrangement. Normally they only visited each other for a tannin fix after an outing together or when a Worsley Court-related issue required discussion, after which there might even be a glass of left-over Blue Nun.

Tomorrow was their regular shopping day in the village, but Miriam wished to visit a shoe boutique near Poynton. Did Bessie have time for a little adventure? If so, it might mean adjusting their timings.

'That would be lovely,' Bessie agreed, delighted at the thought of a jaunt. 'With winter approaching, I should look at some sturdier shoes myself. Not that they'll get much wear.' She could see Miriam taking in the soiled plate with its scrunched paper napkin, the half-drunk cup of tea sitting awkwardly on the sofa side of the table and tell-tale dents in the floral cushions. No doubt she was wondering who they belonged to. 'Sorry about the mess; we've not long finished tea.'

Having for a long time rented a room in the house of a nearby family, the death of an aunt not long before her retirement had provided Miriam with a windfall. At sixty, she'd finally become a proud homeowner and the first person to move into the upgraded flats. She'd lived alone in the empty building for several months until the Owens snapped up the more palatial two-bedroomed apartment above her.

That was almost nine years ago.

Knowing Miriam existed largely on a modest pension from the clerical post she'd held with an insurance company for many years, Bessie, initially aware Miriam might feel the poor relation in their relationship, always tried to put her at her ease. Since Hugh's death and the considerable diminution of her own revenue, things had evened out. Her continued need to keep up appearances while surreptitiously cutting corners was more to do with northern pride than overt snobbery.

She remembered the morning they moved in. Miriam catching Hugh struggling upstairs with their bags and cases and, after offering them coffee, helping kill the restless hour before the van arrived. What a difference eight years made. Stairs were no problem then. Now she regretted they hadn't chosen the flat on the ground floor, despite its closer proximity to daytime noise outside.

It had only taken the few hours after Miriam had welcomed them so warmly for them to feel comfortable with each other. Despite the hefty age gap, they'd soon found themselves laughing at the same things and discovering they shared a no-nonsense approach to life.

Approach. Not necessarily views.

Bessie was aware Miriam, who admitted to being a socialist, would never be reconciled to her own admiration for the current occupant of Number 10, even if she was a woman. Yet both quickly learned to respect each other's space: actual and political. They agreed they both preferred Dynasty to Dallas and enjoyed guessing how various plot threads might develop.

Now, with Sam living further away and always so busy, Bessie was increasingly dependent on Miriam's company – especially on her friend's chauffeuring facility. During those last eighteen months, Miriam's lifts to visit Hugh in hospital had been an enormous help. To give Bessie her due, she always gave Miriam money for petrol and demonstrated her gratitude in many neighbourly little ways but singularly failed to notice she was starting to take her newest friend's generosity for granted.

Miriam looked over the top of her spectacles at the spread before her. 'Obviously someone very high-ranking... your visitor?' she said pointedly with an affected sniff. Normally, when they invited one another into their homes, they made do with mugs, a shared tea bag and a couple of Jammie Dodgers.

'It's fortunate you've dropped by to help me eat it up,' Bessie said. 'It'd be a shame for all these sandwiches to go to waste. Or I could wrap some up for you to take away with you?'

'That's sweet of you. Actually, I'm famished. I got carried away listening to a programme about Lillian Hellman and forgot all about lunch.' Miriam settled herself into her armchair and helped herself as Bessie topped up the teapot.

'Funny sort of day,' Bessie said, returning and filling Miriam's cup. 'Can't make up its mind. My gammy knees don't take kindly to the damp.'

'That's October for you. Unsettling. Like March.'

'The in-between months.'

'Yes,' Bessie murmured thoughtfully as she poured a cup of tea and handed it to her. 'I've been entertaining. Giles, as it happens. You've just missed him. Had to dash off to pick up a lowboy in Davenport.'

She could see the cogs going around ah, so, it was Giles and tried not to notice the almost undetectable frisson of embarrassment mention of his name caused.

'Nice man,' was all Miriam said, 'but then, we're so lucky with our neighbours.'

Was she aware they were both in double-bluff territory here? Bessie always assumed Miriam knew she knew about her friend's aborted tendresse with the local choirmaster. Conscious of this, she'd always regarded it to be a tacitly understood and respected no-go area, hence her reason for tactfully not revealing the name of her previous guest until she was comfortably settled with a plate on her lap.

Naturally discreet, over the first couple of years of their friendship, Miriam occasionally let slip sufficient snippets from her past to enable Bessie to build up the basic facts of her backstory. How her father, working alongside other Jewish intellectuals in Heidelberg in the early thirties, was one of the first people to foresee the conflagration ahead and seek refuge in Switzerland. And how, when the situation became untenable there, too, Professor Jachmann and his family – the Jackmans as they later became – smuggled themselves, not a day too soon, across the rest of Europe to the English Channel. Initially staying with relations in South Manchester, the family had then established itself in the area, assisting with the local war effort and becoming respected members of the community.

Family history was one thing. Miriam chose to reveal only the barest details of her private life. So, one day when she was in one of her rare revelatory moods and Bessie cautiously raised the issue of erstwhile admirers, she'd simply admitted to her failure in that department and smartly dropped the matter. Sometime later, in a wistful moment, she'd also referred to a gifted trombonist who had been important to her in her youth and the termination of the relationship due to a climbing accident. Piecing the bits of the jigsaw together, Bessie then concluded the tragedy must have been the reason for Miriam's subsequent nervous breakdown and why she'd abandoned both a promising career as a concert singer and any further interest in men.

That was true only as far as it went.

Vera Eckersley, a WI acquaintance Bessie often met in Tanya's Salon along the road, once later volunteered how, on joining the local choral society, everyone noticed the way Giles and Miriam had quickly gelled. It was 'hardly surprising,' she'd said, 'given their mutual love and knowledge of music.' Although, much as people speculated, there were never any grounds to assume the relationship ever developed into something serious. In any case, it would have been inappropriate given the presence of Giles's saintly, invalided wife, Doreen. Nevertheless, when she was in hospital for a spell, they'd been regularly seen socialising. As soon as Doreen was strong enough to return home, Miriam reverted to being just another friendly face among the contraltos. Not long after, Doreen suffered an unexpected but fatal heart attack.

'At the post-funeral buffet, I saw Miriam go up to him and gently touch his arm to express her condolences...' Here, Vera lowered her voice significantly. 'Giles glanced at her gratefully but distantly. And... oh, the way she turned away distraught and half-staggered out of the village hall was heart-breaking. I'll never forget it. Maybe it was grief fuelled by guilt that sent Giles into retreat, but the Winter Festival miscellany came and went, then the Cantata Academica in the spring and events in the years that followed. They've continued to behave pleasantly enough with each other at choir practice, but, as far as curious eyes can tell, the old intimacy never returned.'

Even allowing for Vera's Woman's Own take on the story, it struck Bessie as odd that Miriam continued not only living in the area but taking a leading role in choral life. Maybe her itinerant existence as a youngster had disinclined her to settle elsewhere, whatever the cost to her pride.

Following Vera's story, Bessie always thought she'd observed – or maybe imagined – some gaucheness in Miriam's demeanour around Giles at local gatherings. She certainly deserved to meet someone suitable with whom to share her life. With her clear skin, dainty physique and dark hair – albeit now subtly tinted by the gifted Tanya – she was still an attractive woman and looked considerably younger than her years.

To the best of her knowledge, the Miriam-Giles whatever-it-was occurred before Bessie moved into the area and also befriended him. They'd hit it off one day when she'd visited his shop for advice on a reliable French polisher for her gateleg table. Commenting on a good copy of a Stubbs in the shop, they discovered a shared interest in horses and, ever since, had phoned each other for hot tips – or commiseration if, later, the beast let them down.

Initially trained at the Royal Northern Academy of Music and, for a while, a cellist in The Hallé, Giles had inherited his father's successful antique shop near Worsley Court, and the flat above it, and swapped his itinerant musical life for that of niche shop owner with choral work on the side.

It was he who now facilitated Bessie's flutters on the horses. With her love of all things equestrian, some of the remaining delights in her life were the horse racing and show jumping transmissions on Saturday afternoons. Unlike her father, she had enough self-control to sensibly manage her limited income and spend only a careful sum each month on her hobby, as she called it, never betting more than she could easily afford. It was the thrill of the race that mattered. That intensified when a horse she'd gambled on won, but it wasn't the end of the world if it didn't. Generally speaking, having good intuition herself and with sound advice from Giles, her wins marginally exceeded her losses. Most weeks, she was left with enough interest from her wee bit of fun to fund her newspaper bill and a box of chocolate gingers. Occasionally she might even treat Miriam to a cream tea.

'Yes, a good sort, Giles,' Bessie said. 'Wonderful head of hair.'

'Indeed.'

'He keeps his ear closer to the racetrack than me. I invited him over to catch up on the gossip. You can tell him things and… well, know they won't go any further, can't you?'

Miriam simply smiled in her guileless way.

'I was saying to him, with my knees, I'll probably have to sell up myself sooner or later. What did he think I'd get for this flat? "Wait till the market picks up," he advised, "or you could consider remortgaging." Yes, I said, there's one thing about having property: you can always use it as cholesterol.'

Miriam's smile widened. 'I don't think that's quite right,' she said tentatively, as if terrified of risking Bessie's irritability but doing so all the same. It didn't do to correct her, even when she was wrong. The malapropism was glossed over with a 'well, you know what I mean,' as she bit into her neglected slice of date-and-walnut.

There was a moment's thoughtful silence before Bessie's face tensed and she looked confidingly at her friend. 'Actually, if you're not in a hurry, I'd quite like your advice.'

'I've nothing planned. How can I help?'

'It's about Sam,' Bessie said with a slight sigh. 'He's coming for his supper tomorrow, but I'll expect him when I see him. Goodness knows what he does with his time.'

'Ah,' Miriam said. 'Young people. Always busy.'

'Indeed. I'm lucky to be granted an evening at all.' Bessie had related Sam's unhappy teaching experiences and their consequences, guessing, correctly, that having both experienced major crises in their lives, they might understand each other and get along, which they did. Certainly, Boxing Days were enlivened when Miriam came up to join them for cold turkey salad and the mandatory board game. Nevertheless, that was no reason she shouldn't have the occasional moan about him. In fact, it helped to have the viewpoint of someone in between their ages who knew him quite well.

'He could have got himself a better job by now,' I told him, 'if he'd played his cards right. "Well, as long as he's independent," Giles said, "and no worry to you."' She paused and glanced out of the window. 'I do hope he'll be punctual. Not like that other time.'

Miriam almost missed her cue. Catching the you-haven't-been-listening glint in Bessie's eye with barely a blink to spare, she blurted out, '*Other* time?' as she reached for the last sandwich.

'I'd planned a lovely bit of fillet. Potatoes all sliced and ready to be sautéed the way he likes them. Oddly enough, Giles was asking after him earlier. When I mentioned his extra-curricular activities, he raised an eyebrow, which took me back a bit.'

Miriam maintained a straight face and said nothing.

'Anyway, that night, when he finally showed up,' she went on, 'he barely stayed three hours! And his face, well… I've never known him look so pale and drained. I thought he'd lost some weight, too. "You don't look your usual self," I said. "I hope you're looking after yourself properly?" Big scene. "There's nothing wrong with me," he said. Anyway, it was a tense meal, and he'd barely finished his crumble when he grabbed that dreadful zip-up thing he calls a jacket and headed for the door. Only then did I realise he wasn't planning on staying the night as he'd promised, and I found myself having one of my little turns. "I'm not feeling so good," I said. "It's my angina." "Stop putting it on," he said. "Do you think I enjoy all this?" I begged him to stay. I'd been relying on it. I really enjoy a bit of company at the weekends. But he always has something on that's more important than me. It's either a first big run-through or what he calls a "well-earned evening off" with Tom, Dick or Harriet no doubt. That night, he hadn't any real excuse that I could see, and…'

'I'm so sorry,' Miriam said.

Bessie absent-mindedly forked her last piece of cake into her mouth and chewed thoughtfully, before going on: 'I hate to think of him leaving and there being bad blood. Supposing something had happened to me? He'd never forgive himself. "If you do stay," I said, "tomorrow morning I'll do your favourite: chopped egg and soldiers. Then, if you could get me some bits and bobs from along the road, that big bed at the front needs raking. Mrs Overton's away too, so I was hoping you'd sort her post for her… She'd be so grateful." But oh, no. "Must catch that five-past-nine bus," he said. "Have to be up in town early tomorrow. People to see. You know how it is." I didn't.'

'Packs a lot into his life, doesn't he?' Miriam said. 'What is it he does again?'

'God knows. Running committees and things. Not my idea of a proper job. Though he's never been a worry work-wise, I'll give him that. Always sorts himself out somehow. He may not be a budding Richard Branston, but…'

'Branson,' Miriam gently corrected. 'Branston's the pickles.' Another withering look, which Miriam ignored, her face having grown thoughtful. 'You must have been concerned he wasn't looking his usual self, though?'

'I was. He's not been a good colour for some time.'

Miriam paused and frowned, before saying guardedly, 'It must be a worry for you. With everything that's going on…'

'What d'you mean?'

Miriam looked as if she wished she could retract her previous remark but battled on. 'All the terrible things you read about in the papers.'

Bessie narrowed her eyes. 'Things?'

'Affecting… single men. Mainly.'

'I'm not sure what you mean.'

'It was so sad about Rock Hudson, wasn't it? Those delightful, frothy comedies with Doris Day. They don't make them like that anymore.'

Bessie's eyes widened as the penny dropped. 'You mean the terrible disease that's always in the News?'

'Yes, AIDS,' Miriam said.

Another pause as the subtext sank in.

'Why should Sam…?'

'I didn't mean… Oh, I'm sure you've absolutely no reason to worry.'

But Bessie's stomach was churning over. Although a curious person, there were limits to the information she could handle on aspects of life she found difficult to comprehend. In her darkest hours, whenever she considered Sam's friends, some of whom she'd met – nice lads, most of them, if rather precious – she avoided dwelling on any suggestion that Sam's dealings with them might involve more than mere companionship. Apart from Constance and Hannah, whom she regarded as family and who didn't count and, anyway, had never been caught giving each other anything more than a warm hug – her experience of single-sex bonding was limited to what she'd picked up from the media.

Except, she realised with a jolt, they did count. In the dim recesses of her memory lurked the memory of Roy's deep friendship with Billy. Only recently had she found herself considering how strange it was that, around that time, she and Roy began drifting apart.

Was that happening to her and Sam? Was it because she had been in denial for so long about the full nature of the one person, after Hugh, she'd been closest to? Had she in some way alienated him?

257

'I'm so sorry,' Miriam rattled on, 'I really didn't mean to upset you. These things can happen to anyone. It only takes one…'

'Are you implying that Sam…?'

'I'm only trying to say…'

'You have your suspicions?'

'Would that be such a big problem for you, if he… Well, if he's…?'

'What?'

'Gay.'

'Yes. I mean, I'm not sure.'

'I had gay friends when I was at college. Good ones. Of both sexes. And I count Sam as one. Two of my fellow students flat-shared – which was sometimes used as a euphemism for more than merely cohabiting,' Miriam said. 'It wasn't easy for them – then. But it's accepted today.'

Bessie thought for a moment as the implications of what was being discussed accumulated in her brain. If Miriam had made these assumptions about Sam, then other people would probably have too. 'Yes. I fear I've been kidding myself for a long time. I think, from remarks he made, his father had some idea. And Elspeth too. But she's very worldly and can be larger than life herself.'

'Did you sense your husband was all right with it?'

'We never fully discussed it. Whenever Sam's social life came up, he either frowned and changed the subject or came out with something like, "I'll never understand that boy."'

'With regard to this appalling virus, at least this is Manchester and not London, which has the largest number of cases – if that makes you feel any better. Being a Jew, I understand what it's like to be looked upon as different from everyone else. I've always been an outsider. Many gay men feel the same. Although Sam has always appeared totally comfortable in his own skin to me.'

'So, you… knew. All along?'

'An intelligent guess. It wasn't my place to say anything. That was, until I saw you looking concerned just now and I thought it might help for you to have someone to talk to.'

'Yes,' Bessie admitted ruefully, 'it has.'

Miriam finished her tea. 'Anyway, I'm sorry if I've put any horrid thoughts into your head. I'm sure he'll turn up as right as rain tomorrow as he always does.'

But Bessie had been given a nasty fright. Not only did other people seem to know Sam was like that but how, despite all the current fuss about AIDS, had she not made the possible connection between him and the disease. The possibility he might die from it, even if hopefully remote, was terrifying.

'Don't fret about it,' Miriam said, getting up to leave.

How could she not?

'Give me a bell when you're ready, tomorrow.'

'Lovely,' Bessie said absently.

Perhaps, to be on the safe side, she should contact her solicitor about amending her will.

23

Emerging Pride

1985 – 1989
Sam

The *gay plague*, as it was referred to by right-wing bigots, was very much in the minds of Sam and Joss the following weekend as they chatted in the New Union pub on Canal Street early on the Saturday evening. Joss had come up for a play at the Royal Exchange. They'd just enjoyed a meal at a restaurant in nearby Piccadilly and were killing time over glasses of wine.

'Then these deep red marks appeared on Mark's legs and wouldn't go away,' Sam said.

'I scrutinise every inch of my body every night when I wash.'

'Me too. Not that I think I've anything to worry about. Although I think that, then suddenly remember an error of judgement in The Coleherne a couple of years ago and begin shivering with anxiety.'

'Poor man. D'you know how long he may have?'

'It varies from person to person, apparently,' Sam continued. 'At the moment he's still well enough to carry on more or less as normal, but the prognosis isn't good.'

'Does he know how he caught it?'

'He told me he went to New York in 1982 and behaved outrageously in the clubs and bathhouses. No one had any idea what was happening then. Now, of course, it's everywhere.'

'It's terrifying,' Joss said. 'We've a friend who's tragically got it too and can't even visit him in hospital. And we dread going into our local, The Kings Head, for fear of hearing more bad news. You don't know which of your drinking mates may have tested positive this week. I'm terrified of asking anyone I know who's lost weight how they are, too.'

'It's not quite as bad up here,' Sam said, 'but all the same, everyone on the scene is petrified. Later on, when it gets busier in here, there's a hyper atmosphere as if everyone's trying to mask what they're thinking and pretending things are normal.'

'Makes you wish you had shares in Durex, doesn't it?' Joss added with a cynical smile.

'Ugh! Behave yourself, you're in Manchester now. Your Southern black humour won't go down well here!' It was said with a grin, but both men knew it wasn't a laughing matter.

'According to *Gay Times*, things are warming up in the North,' Joss said. 'Politically as well as medically.'

'Yes. We had our first Pride-type event in the summer, partly funded by the Council. And Manchester's new AIDSline is only the second in the country. At least it's a *V-sign* to that bastard Anderton and his homophobic henchmen. The police are still regularly raiding our pubs. There are, however, signs the tide's beginning to turn. Many of the raids are becoming increasingly token. Some of the officers are almost sympathetic.

'Especially the queer ones!'

'The law of averages and all that. Gives the term *bent copper* a new slant, doesn't it?'

'Who's being facetious now? Actually, I've always wanted to score with a policeman.'

'In uniform, of course.'

'Of course! Seriously though, the only good thing that can be said about the whole ghastly situation is, it's helping to raise awareness of the stigma of being gay. It's sad that it takes a pandemic to mobilise the community. What's so shocking is how the bad press we're getting is affecting audience attendances for marvellous gay-themed shows such as *La Cage Aux Folles* at The Palladium. There are rumours it may fold soon. It's all due to ignorance and bigotry.'

'I hope you're being very careful when you're on the pull?'

'Anyone who invites me back for a coffee, or vice versa, gets a thorough grilling. That is, if they don't start asking questions first. Frankly, *pulling* boils down to little more than a quick cuddle these days. People are that scared – unless you know the person very well, and then, even after you've taken all the necessary precautions, you feel guilty.'

'Tell me about it. Have you and Bren been tested yet?'

'No. I suppose we ought to, though neither of us has much time or inclination for playing the field. We wouldn't want to run the risk of putting the other in danger, anyway.'

As Sam took another swig of his wine, Joss looked around the pub to indicate he was ready to change the subject. 'It's still very tatty around here, isn't it? Not very welcoming,' he said, peering through the bar's tiny mottled window panes into the street outside, 'and not helped by the dismal street lighting and badly maintained properties.'

'Ee, it were all cotton mills along the canal, when I were a lad,' Sam said. Returning to his normal voice, he added, 'And when they all closed down, these streets began doubling up as a red-light district and trolling ground. Apparently, the gays and girls provided cover for each other. You'd be wandering about looking for trade when the word went around, 'Cops!' The men grabbed the hand of the nearest tart, pulled her into a clinch and pretended to be courting. 'Me and Irene here are on our way for a pint at The Rembrandt before home time, officer. No law against that, is there?'

'By the way, how did you get on with your mother last week?'

'Funny you should bring that up. I think someone must have been talking to her. She seemed terribly genned up about everything all of a sudden.'

'You mean she's no longer in denial about you?'

'I think she's got the message but is confused. She'd tried educating herself by listening to radio programmes about it, consoling herself with the fact that in Africa women catch it too.'

'She found that *consoling*?'

'Said she'd decided to change her will and would select someone else to inherit her precious furniture and whatever she's still got in her piggy bank in the event I die before her. Practical to the end, our Bessie.'

'At least she's making progress. You have to give her marks for trying.'

'I think we're getting there gradually. But she refuses to give up completely. When we sat down to our meal recently, she actually came out with the perennial: "You know, I still think there's nothing much wrong with you the right woman couldn't fix."'

Joss laughed. 'And you replied…'

'You remember all those musicals you took me to on my afternoons off from school? It wasn't Marge Champion I fancied. It was Gower. "More potatoes?" she asked and quickly changed the subject.'

Joss roared.

Sam was painfully aware that in recent years he hadn't been the son his mother would have liked. When he was growing up, they had been strong allies, and there was still a special bond between them. It was odd that just as when her own parents had really needed her, she'd let them down by getting married and moving away from home, he, after leaving college, had decided to stay in the North and continue to build a life for himself there. It hadn't been a deliberate decision to avoid returning to London, to rotate again within the orbit of her magnetic force. He'd applied and been provisionally accepted for teaching jobs both in South London and in Manchester, but the first position was only a nominal place in a school to be decided nearer the time, whereas he'd been recruited specifically for the school at Withington, visited it and been drawn to its ambience and friendly staff.

It was only as Hugh's health began seriously to deteriorate that Sam found, whenever he returned home, how potentially suffocating his mother's need of him could be. No longer able to confide in the way she always had with Hugh, she turned to him increasingly as a sounding board. If he'd been working and living at home, he knew it would have become stifling. Within weeks of moving back to Manchester, he'd realised how wise he'd been to create space between the two of them. If he had been too easily 'on call', he'd never have been able to have done all the things which made him a fully-rounded person.

Not that he didn't recognise his responsibility to Bessie and tried hard to make time for her and keep in regular contact. But it was never enough and never would be. Until the day she died, he would juggle his professional, personal and filial commitments as best he could, the cricket on his shoulder forever glancing at him beadily to remind him of his duties There always seemed to be times when he was short-changing one or the other. Unfortunately, Bessie seemed to have the cricket under a spell.

Sam spent a lot of time arguing with it.

Finally, Bessie's having to face up to Sam's being gay had recently added additional tension to their relationship whilst she came to terms with the ramifications of the fact.

'D'you think your father ever guessed?' Joss asked.

'Probably. Nothing was ever said. I wondered about *him* occasionally.'

'Really?'

'He'd be watching the television and come out with remarks like *he's a handsome man*. My mother, taking the remark on its face value, would probably have agreed.'

'My Dad says things like that too but puts it like, "I think I must be turning, Alison. That guy's very good looking." But then, she'd probably snort and add, "And far too young for you!"'

'Once, my father complimented the husband of a friend of mine on his good looks, which was mortifying. I'm sure he said it in all innocence, but what was going on in his subconscious?'

'We're all on a spectrum anyway, aren't we? Whether we realise it or not. Even you got engaged.'

'Don't remind me! I can't forgive myself for mishandling the episode so badly.'

Joss gave Sam's hand a squeeze. 'It was something you had to discover the hard way,' he said. 'Things worked out for the best in the end. For both of you. It would have been far more traumatic if you'd split further down the line. By which time there might have been young children involved.'

Sam looked at his watch. 'It's nearly seven; we should be making our way. I want to order drinks for the interval.'

The next afternoon, strolling home from seeing Joss off at the station, Sam once again thought how nice it was having someone to talk to who spoke the same language as he did. So many languages, in fact. How lucky Joss and Bren were to have each other to discuss what was going on in their lives and support each other. He could never settle for a partner who had different interests to his own. The husband of one of the girls he knew spent most of his spare time glued to sports events on TV, or so she said. Sam suggested she bought him his own set to watch in another room. But that was hardly the point, was it? Living with someone else was about doing things together. On the other hand, having too much in common could be boring.

* * *

Sam's friend Mark reviewed plays for a tourist magazine. When he had a spare ticket, he'd always invited Sam to tag along. When he fell ill, he largely dropped out of the social scene. Nonetheless, not long after Joss' visit, Sam bumped into him at a concert at the Bridgewater Hall. Three months later, Mark's flatmate rang to tell him he'd died on Boxing Day, at home surrounded by friends.

He felt Mark's loss keenly. They were the same age and had a lot in common. Fortunately, they hadn't connected romantically since before Mark's fatal trip to the Big Apple. At least, unlike many victims of HIV, he'd not spent his final days in an isolation ward, treated at arms' length by the medics, never to see the people he loved again.

Not long afterwards, Sam met and teamed up with Tom, a music teacher and opera lover who, for the next two years, became a weekend companion and low-key lover and would remain a good friend. The rest of the decade, despite the constant health fears, was a stable and generally rewarding time.

As anticipated, thanks to Tony's support, he was now in a job with greater responsibility and a considerable leap in salary which didn't overtax him, allowing him to continue directing, and sometimes appearing in, non-commercial stage productions.

Bessie could be a thorn in the flesh, but for a while their relationship was more or less on an even keel. He got on well with her neighbours, especially Miriam, whom he could turn to for a mutual grouse when his mother became too demanding.

When the liaison with Tom ran out of steam, he was left reflecting on the extent to which it had been nice to have someone to link up with on a regular basis, but he was aware that for a permanent relationship he needed something more than Tom was able to give. It was reassuring it applied the other way round, too. This time there was no guilt involved.

Now in his mid-forties, he could look back on a period of consolidation. He'd added Honours to his BA, was enjoying his work and had built up a varied CV of dramatic work. All he needed now was to exchange his cosy flat for a small house with a garden where he could spread himself more.

Connie's health had been failing for some time and, over the past year, she had become so unsteady on her feet it had been necessary for Hannah to convert the sitting room into a bedroom for her. When she went into hospital with a respiratory infection, everyone feared the worst. She appeared to be improving and was transferred to a convalescent home. On the journey, her breathing worsened. Two days later, he received a sad call from Hannah.

With Hannah having more than enough money of her own, Sam, as Connie's only nephew and godson, and Bessie, her oldest friend, each inherited half of her savings and investments. Bessie now had a little more financial room to manoeuvre if she needed work doing to the flat or to get him to take her to Lytham for the weekend, whilst he had sufficient capital to extend his mortgage and move to a more permanent location.

If, God willing, his health survived the current crisis, he could, hopefully, begin to settle down.

24

Slippery Surface

1989
Bessie

Putting her wallet back in her handbag, Bessie failed to spot the temporary *Slippery Floor!* sign between the checkout bays and exit doors.

'Are you ok?'

'I'm not sure. If you could just let me be for a minute or so…'

Five minutes went by, during which various store officials fussed over her as she lay surrounded by the contents of her upturned trolley basket on the still-wet floor and attempted to make her comfortable. While she silently screamed for Miriam to stop wittering on about how she was to blame for not warning her and being as much use as a rubber screwdriver, it was left to another shopper, a pleasant woman in a rather loud duster coat, to come to her aid. Bessie tried to haul herself up, but her legs gave way. She sank back helplessly again onto the floor, her head supported by a wad of plastic carrier bags the lady had found.

A spasm in Bessie' abdomen warned she needed to relieve herself. Oh, the indignity of it all, she thought, as a shadow fell across her recumbent body and an imperious figure in a structured suit gazed down at her, the glassy smile failing to hide her irritability at being dragged away from her coffee break. 'Now, young lady, we'd better get you sorted.' Patronage to add to her humiliation.

The ambulance arrived. Her mind flashed back to the day of the gassing. Life had never been quite the same after that. Her old age was becoming marked by calamitous events. Would this be yet another dismal milestone?

Once at the hospital, she was soon whisked into the X-ray suite, then left to stew on a gurney. After a while, she felt peckish. Miriam brought her a bag of crisps, something chemically pink and fizzy in a bottle and a bar of fruit-and-nut from the Friends' shop. Cadbury's chocolate always reminded her of the impromptu midnight feasts she and Roy secretly enjoyed on hot summer nights when their parents were out with friends and Flo, supposedly keeping an eye on them, vanished into the nearby park with her latest inamorato. It might just see her through until…

Until…?

Miriam stayed for an hour or so, then went home with contrived reluctance to put Bessie's shopping away. She promised to keep in touch with the hospital about what would happen to her. It was fortunate she'd been with her. Today was an exception. She'd bribed Giles to close the shop for a long lunch hour with the promise of chicken-in-the-basket in the Whale & Anchor. At the last minute, he'd been obliged to dash off to see a man about a torchere plant stand in Newton-le-Willows, and she'd resorted to begging Miriam to help her ensure she had enough food in for the weekend.

Miriam was becoming harder to track down these days. Several times recently, when Bessie suggested a day out, maybe to Lyme Hall or Tatton Park, it was always the same. 'I'm terribly busy.' She'd never been terribly busy in the old days. What had happened to their weekly sprees, once sacrosanct? Only a year ago, she'd thought they were getting really close and started to think of Miriam almost as a younger sister. How long ago was it since their last trip to that shoe shop in Poynton where she'd picked up those nice slippers in the sale? A new pair wouldn't go amiss right now, especially if she was to be confined to barracks for a while.

Following the AIDS scare, Miriam was the person she'd first thought of as a fallback in her will. But Miriam was becoming unreliable. A great disappointment, in fact. Another call to Mr Jessup to revise that codicil might be on the cards. Admittedly she'd come up trumps today. But then, it was an emergency. Let's see if it led to a general improvement.

After another couple of hours, she was wheeled into a small ward of four beds, whose other occupants seemed either unconscious or unwilling to give her more than a sad, watery smile – of what, welcome? Disappointed, perhaps, that she wasn't bright, young and bubbly? Those were the days.

Once transferred to an empty bed in the corner by the window, she settled down and glanced out at what had faded into a dreary late afternoon with dark clouds gathering. In due course, a student doctor arrived to tell her the X-rays revealed a broken wrist and a bruised spine.

'Am I to be kept in?'

'Afraid so.'

'Until?'

'You're able to go home and look after yourself. We'll need to take it a day at a time. I'll know more after the doctors' conference tomorrow morning.'

It was at that moment she began fretting. Had she remembered to adjust the central heating before leaving that morning? Or watered the expensive begonia Sam brought on his last visit? She'd never forgive herself if the heat had been left too high and the plant wilted and died. What had been the sell-by date on that duck à l'orange, and who would cancel her chiropodist appointment tomorrow and shampoo-and-set with Tanya on Monday if she wasn't released?

Above all, could someone ring Miriam and ask her to let Sam know?

She had already asked for a phone and tried ringing him at the office, but, as expected, there wasn't a reply. Typical. You could never rely on his being there when you wanted him. He made a rubber screwdriver seem quite serviceable. Not only did he live too far away to be any use when she needed him in a hurry, but his new house, cosy and tastefully decorated as it was, wouldn't be suitable for her to convalesce in – should it come to that. There was hardly enough room to swing a cat in that spare room. And as for the dodgy bannisters on those steep stairs…

She'd tried getting up to go to the loo but was unable to walk, causing a frenzy when a passing nurse spotted her, summoned a commode and pulled the screens around her bed. How long could they keep her here? If the worst came to the worst, she might have to spend some of Connie's money on a respite at that nice-looking convalescent home on the corner of Eskdale Drive. Or explore what social services had to offer. No. The idea of someone turning up twice a day to help shower and dress her and ensure she ate something was out of the question. Very demeaning. One day it might be necessary, of course, but she intended to put it off for as long as she possibly could.

As usual, she was getting ahead of herself. As long as she had her marbles, she'd find a way of looking after herself.

Her tombstone would read: *She managed well.*

She thought of Flo. How was she coping these days? The seven miles that separated them could have been seven hundred. Especially since she'd been plagued by her own mobility concerns, there had been little contact between them. Cards at Christmas and the odd bit of gossip about them if she bumped into old mutual friends. But she rarely had the chance to do that these days. It had been a matter of 'who would make the first move'. Always believing in her own moral authority, she'd never seen any reason for taking the initiative, only to find them scratching at old wounds. Best to leave well alone and initiate a dialogue only when strictly necessary.

It had come as a shock when, after making the effort to ensure her sister was one of the first people to be telephoned the morning Hugh died, she was told, 'Oh, I meant to let you know, Roy passed in January. He'd been having circulatory problems for some time but didn't want anyone to know.'

Bessie had been stunned. 'I didn't see it in *The Telegraph*,' she'd said indignantly, fighting back tears. 'You should have let me know.'

'A private funeral,' Flo said. 'No fuss, he always said.'

A wise friend once told her, 'When people treat you badly, they never forgive you.' She was reminded of that now. Despite everything, Bessie wished she and Roy could have patched things up.

Possibly out of feelings of discomfort on both sides and a sense of time running out, with neither of them wishing to end their days incommunicado, for a brief period after Hugh and Roy's deaths, maybe in an attempt at solidarity after two major losses, they'd made the effort to occasionally chat on the phone and swap clumsily-phrased notecards. Flo once even sent her a cardigan she'd knitted, intended for herself which 'hadn't suited her', or so she said. Why? Residual guilt, loneliness – both? Bessie reciprocated with some perfume sent for her birthday that hadn't suited her, either. After which the tentative rapprochement faltered.

Too little, too late.

Sam was visiting his aunt in Chorlton one weekend when he spotted a *For Sale* sign by the front gate. Without telling anyone, Flo had made arrangements to sell up and put her affairs in the hands of a greedy bank. She was now bleeding to death, financially speaking, in a care home in Whalley Range.

Bessie hoped to be spared a similar fate. Except as a very temporary measure, that would really be giving in.

The knowledge that the family house had gone, and probably any hope of even a token inheritance for herself or Sam, was something she'd long come to terms with. She'd been grateful to Sam for maintaining the contact. She still encouraged him to drop by and see Flo, especially if she was ill, and ensured he remembered her birthday, too. The pair had always got on quite well, although he said he was slightly wary of her.

The following morning, the doctor was more upbeat: 'Nothing that a month's bed rest and physio won't cure. Long term, you'll have to watch that knee of yours. It's already been weakened by the arthritis, and the fall today will have hastened further problems. I'm going to try you out on hydromassage to wake up your back, too.'

'A month?' she said, horrified.

'We can't risk you going home on your own until you walk again.'

Bessie watched the rain drops chasing each other down the window as if the day was shedding tears on her behalf. Straining to reach for an old *Daily Mail* left by her predecessor on the bedside cabinet, which someone had forgotten to bin, the tenderest places of her body yelped in unison. Gritting her teeth, she put on her glasses and scanned the TV shows she'd missed.

Now she'd never find out who killed that poor hitchhiker. More importantly, what about the drama of her own life?

She thought again. Why were so many of her newer but erstwhile reliable friends deserting her and no longer wanting to spend time with her? She always paid her way. Once upon a time, folk had queued up to play tennis with her. Now it was hard to get anyone interested in a game of whist.

Here she was once again. Another bed. More pondering.

Reproaching herself, she thought of one of her mantras. 'No one likes a moaning Minnie,' she told herself. 'I must face up to being eighty-four.' Given the increasing unreliability of her skeleton, she had to accept what might be in store for her further down the line.

How much longer she would be able to stay at Worsley Court? Her arthritis, not helped by death traps in supermarkets, was encroaching like coastal erosion. Her days of freedom might be numbered. It was the flight of stairs up from the ground floor that was always the killer. She was already losing her autonomy and becoming dependent on the kindness of other people to do her serious shopping.

'What you need is one of those stairlifts,' Sam kept telling her. 'Then you could still pop round the corner to the nearby shops.'

'And you think I'm likely to persuade the people who manage the flats, not to mention my neighbours, to agree to that, even if I paid for it myself?' Though she had to admit it would make a lot of difference. The nurse told her he'd rung last night and would be visiting her later today. Squeezing her in between engagements, she thought. All the same, it would be nice to see him, as long as he didn't sit sullenly and keep looking at his watch.

Later, Miriam brought her clean nighties and other necessary items from home and took away her dirty clothes to wash. Then came her first big adventure: a trip to the hydromassage therapy bath. Basically a jacuzzi, it not only helped revitalise her sore discs but proved relaxing and enjoyable. She finally had something to look forward to each day.

Slowly, life seeped back into her damaged limbs.

* * *

By the third week, she was champing at the bit, and in the middle of the fourth, rest and therapy having worked their magic, Bessie was discharged.

While it was nice to be home again in her old surroundings, she was surprised to find herself missing the camaraderie of life on the little ward.

Elspeth, on a visit to her cousin in Southport, rang to invite herself over, arriving thoughtfully, as always, with a packed lunch. Amongst all her other news, she brought her up to date with what was happening in Kent. Hard to believe fifteen years had passed since all those challenging but friendly debates. It was poignant to hear how many of her Forum contemporaries were falling by the wayside due to natural causes. The sisterhood remained only in spirit. Even Elspeth, five years younger than herself, was taking more of a back seat, though her voice retained much of its old vivacity. As soon as the pair began discussing politics, the years melted away and she was once again stimulated by their lively exchange of views. When the time came for her friend to drive back to Merseyside, Bessie had regained that sense of well-being lively company always gave her.

Giles's Saturday visits to arrange her bets and enjoy a drink with her were reinstated, although Miriam, having established that she had everything she needed, became even less of a presence. She tried raising the matter with Giles, but he always deflected any conversation involving her by reminding her that Miriam now had a part-time job at a picture framer's in Heaton Mersey.

She extended Mrs Bingley's hours and also arranged for her to do essential weekly shopping, but it wasn't the same as carefully planning the requirements of a week's menus with someone who really understood what she liked, over a chatty cuppa. Above all, she missed having Miriam on call with her car whenever she needed to go anywhere.

After a few weeks, if it was a nice day and there was someone with her, she found she could still summon sufficient strength and mobility to stagger along with a stick to Tanya's or pick up an evening paper and a few odds and ends from the corner shop, but there was always the problem of getting both her purchases and herself back home.

Sam bought her a fold-up wheelchair, which she loathed and would use only when it when absolutely necessary.

The walls were closing in, but she was determined to battle on.

25

The Man in the Gardens

1992 – 1994
Sam

Things were changing along Canal Street.

A new state-of-the-art bar, Manto, had opened, its rows of clear windows looking outwards rather than hiding from the world as did many gay pubs. The locality's furtive and down-at-heel atmosphere was finally dispersing. Thanks to growing support from the local council, it was becoming increasingly acceptable to be out and proud in the city.

Although the bar would soon be buzzing, at five-thirty on a Tuesday evening the place was still quiet, with only a few people dotted around refreshing themselves before going home after work. Sam, a glass of bitter in his hand, gossiped with the friendly barman. Wednesday was currently his free night from his theatrical responsibilities and he was still deciding how best to use it. Domestic chores awaited at home, but the late July sun emerging from behind a cloud was streaming in through the windows. It beckoned him back outside and to, at the very least, idle away some time in the sun and see who might also be out and about.

Finishing his drink, he gave a salutary wink to the barman and wandered along to Piccadilly Gardens. An empty bench he espied on a corner overlooking the tidily organised beds of multi-coloured dahlias would do nicely. Taking his Jilly Cooper out of his briefcase, he sat down, crossed his legs and picked up from where he'd last stopped reading.

A quarter of an hour passed. Chuckling at yet another risqué pun, he glanced up to see a man, about his own age, sitting at an adjacent bench, looking at him and smiling.

He nodded affably back.

'One of her best,' the man said.

'I'm certainly learning about what goes on behind the scenes in commercial TV,' he replied.

'Jilly's my guilty pleasure. My wife prefers Stephen King, but I get enough suspense at work.'

'Nice to read something light and humorous once in a while.'

Sam kept wondering where he'd seen the man before. Not so long ago, either. A likeable face, too. You might describe it as lived-in-good-looking with its well-kept beard and moustache, neatly topped with well-cut silvering hair. He was also dressed quite smartly in a pale blue shirt and silk tie, the grey jacket of his summer suit sitting beside him with his leather attaché case. Those and comfortable but expensive-looking shoes shouted *executive*.

'Turning into a pleasant evening.'

'Indeed,' Sam replied, wondering if that was the best follow-on he could do.

'Anything planned for it: a little light gardening, a nice meal or…?'

'Nothing planned, no,' Sam said, swallowing the temptation to be overly flirtatious by adding 'not even *or*' as he slipped a postcard Connie had sent him, of Renoir's *Les Parapluies*, between the pages of *Rivals* and closing it, his curiosity pressing him to see where the conversation might lead.

As if emboldened by Sam's response, the man flashed another smile. 'A pity. Me neither.'

Was that a come-on or simply a pleasantry? If the latter, the reference to a wife was discouraging. Not that Sam was averse to being chatted up by attractive married men. At forty-seven — even though people told him he could pass for thirty-eight — he couldn't afford to be too picky. Nonetheless, he was only too aware such liaisons turned out to be short-lived and unsatisfactory. He settled on pleasantry. 'I decided I deserved some *me* time in the sunshine before going home. You?'

'The same. I don't get away from work until later, but had to pop into Waterstones for a book I promised my daughter for her birthday.'

Sam took the plunge. 'D'you work near here then?'

'At the Infirmary.'

Of course, that was how he knew him. So, his first guess had been wrong. Not Business but Medicine. 'Gastroenterology?'

'Cardiology, actually.'

'Oh. Only, a couple of months ago I had a barium meal test there. Not that I want to bore you with my health issues when you've escaped from that for the evening, but I was sure I recognised you from somewhere.'

'I'd have been more likely to have seen you if you'd come for a heart scan.'

'Anyway, I'm sure I saw you floating around.'

'Quite possibly. Though dashing between floors more likely than floating. I was moved to an office in the same block around then while mine was being redecorated. Look...' he indicated the spare place on his bench and put his case down on the pathway, 'it's tiring shouting at each other. Why not join me?'

Now really intrigued, Sam moved across to sit between the back and the arm of the other bench.

'I'm Robert, by the way, Robert Harvey at work but Robbie to friends.'

Sam shook it. 'Sam Owen.'

'So, what do you do, Sam?'

'I'm an administrative dogsbody at the college down the road.'

'Not far away. Then you might have seen me almost anywhere around here.'

No, Sam thought, it was definitely in the hospital but maybe it was politic to keep the matter open.

'If you don't mind me asking, you don't sound like a native of Manchester.'

'I spent my early life in Edinburgh and London, with four years at school in Suffolk,' Sam explained.

'Ah, a cosmopolitan.'

'Sort of. Paris and New York might have been even more… broadening though.' The gleam in the man's eye confirmed he'd picked up on the subtext.

They continued chatting for some minutes in this half-jokey, half-evasive vein, during which Sam found himself increasingly warming to the man and visualising his firm but gentle bedside manner.

Eventually, Robbie said, 'I'm feeling parched. I don't suppose you'd care to continue this conversation over a quick drink up the road?'

'Why not.'

'I can't be too long as I'm expected back for a late supper, but we can't just leave things as they are, can we?'

Did he detect another playful look?

As well as his favourable first impression of Robbie, Sam saw the wisdom of gaining a friend at court – or rather, hospital. Not wishing to mix pleasure with… pleasure, he hoped they were heading in the opposite direction to Canal Street.

'I sometimes go to the hotel over there,' he said, turning and pointing vaguely in the direction of the massive bronze statue of Queen Victoria. Sam sighed inwardly with relief. 'It's quiet and discreet.'

Getting up, Sam noted that Robbie was taller than himself and, as he strode confidently across the road with his jacket slung casually over one shoulder, how his cotton shirt clung nicely to a compact chest and stomach.

Once in the hotel bar, Robbie insisted on buying the drinks. 'I invited you, remember?' Sam sat down at a table in the corner while Robbie ordered two spritzers. One learnt a lot about people from watching them at a distance: the way they speak to other people and handle themselves. From his observation of him so far, he'd mentally ticked all the right boxes.

'I imagine you don't have much spare time for any interests outside work?' he said as Robbie put the glasses down on the table and sat down opposite him.

'As you gather, I enjoy reading. Also swimming and walking. Going to films and the theatre – gardening too.'

'Really?' Sam said, trying not to sound too enthusiastic.

'You?'

'I'm into those things as well. Gardening, though, is new. I've not long moved into a recently-built starter home Oldham way. There's a bit of ground at the back I'm having fun cultivating. And theatre,' here he gulped, terrified of putting the guy off, 'is my greatest passion.'

Far from stopping the conversation in its tracks, it naturally segued into a lively discussion on what they'd recently seen and enjoyed.

'My eldest daughter, Laura, almost eighteen, is a promising dancer,' Robbie said. 'Tap, ballroom and some ballet, although she's grown a fraction too tall for that and is concentrating more on Latin-American. She sings nicely and has acted a bit at school too. Carrie, who's a couple of years younger, is approaching her GCSEs.

'And your wife?' Sam asked. 'What does she do?'

'She's a librarian. Sorry, *Chief* Librarian,' he added with a hint of ridicule in his voice.

They discussed local amenities in the areas they lived. Only two or three miles apart, it turned out, but on different bus routes.

The time passed easily and pleasantly. It wasn't until they were in the middle of a good moan about the inefficiency of local refuse collections that Sam saw Robbie catch sight of the time on the clock above the bar. 'I'm so sorry, I'll have to wind this up very soon, or Vee will kill me.'

'Oh, but we haven't discussed my heart problem, yet,' Sam said, half-jokingly.

'I'm sorry. That'll have to wait till next time.'

'Next time?'

'If you'd like to meet again?'

'You're allowed to fraternise with patients, then?'

'There are pages of official guidance on the boundaries between doctors and their patients, but… well, you're not my patient, are you. Anyway, you only *think* you saw me?'

281

He was right. Whether or not something was going on here, the man appeared to be playing things cautiously.

'When are you free then?'

Robbie rummaged in the bag to check his diary. 'I never know how long I'm going to be most evenings, but I attend a weekly team meeting on Wednesday afternoons which is always over by six, if that's any use?'

'I owe you a drink so… as you don't live far away, why not come and have a bite with it at my place?'

'I'd like that. Thanks. It's also my wife's night out with the girls. I'm often left to sort myself out food-wise those days and won't be missed.'

Why would that matter? Already, they were concocting little ruses, Sam thought. What was going on here? Why hadn't he stopped himself before diving in with an invitation to his home? And for a meal, too. Robbie might have been making all the moves, but he had responded to each with indecent haste. Why couldn't he have simply arranged to meet him in the same bar again, and taken things at a gentler pace to discover more about him? At least he should have tried putting on the brake to prevent himself falling for yet another man who was well and truly spoken for. Hadn't he learnt his lesson by now? Wilfully ignoring his better judgement, Sam produced a card from his wallet with his professional details on and handed it to him. 'Shall we say six forty-five-ish?'

'Great! I'll phone you if I'm held up. Coming my way?'

They reached Robbie's stop first at the bus station. He turned to Sam, took his hand and squeezed it, looking at him intently a second longer than was strictly necessary.

Sitting on his own bus as it pulled away, Sam pondered on why Robbie was so eager to keep in touch. He might have read him all wrong and could end up with egg on his face. Every, what he'd imagined, *significant* look since they'd met might only have been his imagination playing games – the desperation of a degenerate, single male. It sounded as if Robbie was a devoted father and probably a contented husband, too.

Or… was he?

* * *

What do you give someone you don't know to eat? He might be a vegetarian, a vegan or even a pescatarian for all Sam knew. Although he'd given Robbie his number, the only way he could contact him in an emergency would be through the hospital switchboard – and that would have to be a very last resort. Sam pictured himself talking to an overworked secretary. A line like 'if you could ask him to get back to me with any food fads – he'll know what it means' would definitely test doctor-patient protocol.

On Tuesday evening, an enthusiastic voice message confirmed Robbie's visit. He finally opted for moussaka topped with plenty of crispy cheese and sliced tomatoes with a mixed salad. There was a decent Burgundy in the rack a previous visitor had brought. And he'd never gone wrong yet with sliced mango, strawberries and ice cream for afters. Easy.

Twenty-four hours later, an appetising aroma of about-to-burn cheese topping emanated from the stove in Sam's small galley kitchen and out into the hallway. He turned the temperature control down and admired the neatly arranged tossed salad which sat in one bowl on the worktop and the red and yellow fruits in another. In the other room, his gate-legged table was tastefully set for two, with his smart Prints of Old Manchester table mats, colour-coordinated linen napkins, John Lewis wine glasses and cutlery.

Sam loved his new house. The middle one in a terrace of three red brick starter homes built in the late eighties, he'd been fortunate in buying it in excellent decorative order from another single guy. The hallway led to an all-purpose living room, at the end of which were French windows leading out onto a small patio. Beyond the house, what had been a boring sward of grass was slowly being converted into a charming garden with young flowering shrubs and small bushes upon which he gazed proudly every morning from his bedroom window. Upstairs were a bathroom and a spare room which doubled as his office.

At the agreed time, the doorbell rang.

Robbie was standing on the doorstep clutching a bottle of Lambrusco and a box of Belgian truffles. His fresh appearance and slightly damp hair suggested he'd enjoyed a shower before leaving the hospital. He was even better-looking than Sam remembered.

'Come in. You shouldn't have brought anything,' Sam said as he led his visitor past the tiny kitchen and into the living room.

It was the moment he had dreaded. Having spent only two hours with Robbie a week ago, they needed to re-discover the delicate connection they'd made. A voice inside him told him to look on it as a purely social visit, but he knew he'd be deeply frustrated if something tactile wasn't involved. Why else had the man jumped at his invitation?

He started to panic. 'I was planning on eating out on the patio but it's threatening rain so I've laid the table indoors. I hope that's all right?'

'Perfect!'

'The Lambrusco would be great, but I'm afraid I've already opened a bottle of this…' He picked up the Burgundy. 'If that's…'

'*Pas de problème!*' Robbie put up a hand. 'Mine would need chilling, anyway. Relax, it's all going to be fine. Besides, I'll try anything once,' he said with a twinkle.

That did it. Something gave way.

'Which reminds me, I haven't said hello to you properly yet.' And before Sam's equilibrium could re-tune to the way things were heading, he found himself swept up in Robbie's firm embrace.

'I told you, relax!'

He did.

'I've been wanting to do that ever since I first saw you laughing on that bench,' Robbie said gently letting him go.

'I've been wanting you to, too.'

'Thank God I've not made a fool of myself, then.'

'No way. But you kept going on about your family and …'

'You think the two things are mutually exclusive?'

'Aren't they?'

'Long story. Better loosen my tongue with that wine.'

Over supper, the two men opened up to each other more. Wishing to concentrate on his new friend's predicament, Sam quickly summarised his own emotional journey. '...So, you see, it's all been rather erratic and unsatisfying,' he said at length. 'But you. You seem happy enough?'

'I am, in many ways. Correction: should be. We married before I'd completed my training, and I've thought for a while now that I was maybe too young.'

'Before you realised you wanted... other things?'

Robbie nodded.

'Sorry, that was presumptuous.'

'Not at all. We both wanted to have children as soon as we could afford to – which was... is... the best part. Neither have I ever had any problems fulfilling my marital obligations. But increasingly, I've grown to accept that I'm really attracted to men. Unfortunately, we grew up in a world where we were either straight or queer – and to be the latter was very tough. There was no way of compromising.'

'Absolutely.'

'The truth is, apart from the girls, nowadays Vee and I no longer have much in common. Over the twenty-odd years during which we should have grown closer, we've actually moved further apart. She married a student and, for a while, times were financially taxing but happy. Thanks to the generosity of our families, we managed to get a pleasant home together and create the kind of life we thought we both wanted. Somewhere along the line, though, we got bored with each other.'

Robbie paused as if to consider how best to amplify this. 'When we were young, we laughed a lot and enjoyed being a family and doing things together. But Laura and Carrie are almost adults now and, each year, becoming more independent, while Vee is caught up in her interests: yoga, dancing, Cats Protection and so on. Not that I don't like cats, I hasten to add; I do. But the constant chatter about what I can best describe as feline politics, along with her other obsessions, however worthy, can be wearing.' Here, he gave a helpless gesture. 'And I sense it cuts both ways.'

'I've had similar problems with potential partners on both sides of the divide,' Sam said. 'In some cases, they enjoyed living parallel lives. Opposites attract and all that. But I need close friends with whom I can share my own interests and intellectually engage with.'

'That's what I always wanted too. But nowadays we always seem to be arguing about cultural things instead of celebrating them. I have to keep my Jilly Coopers well hidden. She considers them very naff.'

'Have the girls any idea yet what they might want to do?'

'Laura's already considering a Performing Arts degree, while Carrie's still mad about horses and busy at the equestrian centre every weekend. Laura definitely has talent both as a dancer and an actress, but I wouldn't be surprised if Carrie swaps horses for some sort of therapeutic or care work. She's a very hands-on person, intuitive and good with people, always wanting what's best for them. Quite mature for her age, really.'

'They sound delightful,' Sam said.

'Yes. But soon will be, if not entirely off our hands, even less at home. Then we'll each have only the other to face across the supper table. As it is, I arrive home full of the latest clinical trials and watch Vee's eyes glaze over. Apart from *Morse*, we don't even enjoy the same TV programmes anymore. Our home life has always revolved around the girls, but already there are many days when the carousel's going round with only two fractious riders on it. To be totally honest, Vee and I don't really need each other any longer, either.' He emphasised *need* so Sam would know exactly what he meant.

'That's... sad.'

'I shall always like and respect her, and nothing can erase the memory of those early years, but the thought of the two of us moving on into old age together isn't something I relish. Nor do I imagine, deep down inside, does she. It was our silver wedding earlier this year. We celebrated in Italy with the girls. The days were the best part and we really enjoyed them, but the nights...'

Sam raised his eyebrows. 'The old spark had fizzled out?'

'I think we'd both seen the holiday as a chance to re-connect. Don't misunderstand, it was a pleasant holiday, but...' he shrugged. 'Also, I've had a feeling for some while that she's involved with her assistant librarian. I don't know for sure whether anything physical is going on, but it's *Alex this* and

Alex that all the time, almost as if she's trying to rile me into confronting her. The only reason I haven't is that I kid myself her perfidy gives me an excuse for mine.'

'Alex*ander* or '*andra?*'

'*Dra.*'

'Interesting.'

'I'm suspicious about the woman's motives, and, while I doubt it's a girl-on-girl thing, they've known each other for a while now and are very close. You come between a woman and her best girl friend at your peril. Whether they're sleeping together or not is immaterial, but both are very hot on women's rights.'

'Good on them.'

'I totally agree – in theory. But it makes them defensive and fiercely protective of each other. That can be alienating, especially in a fragile marriage. And it sometimes feels like Alex is a rival.'

Sam wanted to get the conversation back to themselves. 'So, d'you pick up a lot of trade in Piccadilly?'

'No way. I'm a very occasional *Gay Times* Personals man. Even then, I have to keep the paper well hidden. I tear out the relevant ads and dive into an empty office to make phone calls before going home. Once I accidentally left a copy on my desk after lunch and had to tell the nurse assisting me that I'd seen it on a chair in the waiting area and picked it up to safely dispose of. He gave me a very strange look.'

'He, eh? I'll bet!'

'Yes, I'm fairly certain he'd be sympathetic: he's as camp as a chorus boys' picnic. As you can tell, I have this...' here he grinned with mock self-deprecation, '...*image* to protect and need to be careful how I behave!'

Sam nodded. He liked it that Robbie didn't seem to take himself *too* seriously and wished to know more about other people he'd met, however casually.

'Most of the men I've met have been decent guys. But it can never lead anywhere, however much a discreet, regular date would be nice. And... it solves a temporary problem.

That was him put in context, Sam thought.

'I very rarely do the bars. I'm less worried about getting caught by colleagues – after all, they'd have some explaining to do themselves – it's meeting one of my patients I worry about. Manchester can be gossipy.'

'Indeed,' Sam said with feeling. 'Especially *the scene*.'

Not that I get much chance to go out on my own, or you and I might have bumped into each other before.'

'How long…?'

'Is a piece of string?'

'I meant, for how long have you… well, don't we all reach a point when we finally admit to a need to explore that side of ourselves?'

'I was in denial for a long time. For as long as sex with Vee was good, I could put all my extra energy into work and suppress my curiosity whenever a nice-looking man came into sight. It's only the past few years I've tentatively explored more of what you call *that side* of myself. I'd like to continue doing so, too, before I grow too old and unattractive, without guilt for a relationship that's run its course.' Here he paused to stretch his arm across the table to take Sam's hand.

Sam, already moved by Robbie' story, was now aroused by this further development.

Robbie pressed on. 'I just don't want you to…'

Sam looked up. 'What?'

'…feel I might be using you.'

Like that could happen. 'It takes two to tango,' he said feeling the ground begin to give way beneath him.

'Or mango,' Robbie said, withdrawing his hand and taking a final spoonful of fruit salad. 'That was delicious.'

'Thanks. But…'

'What?'

'Nothing.'

'Go on. Say it.'

'Use me.'

Keeping his eyes fixed on Sam's, Robbie got up, moved around the table and pulled Sam to his feet for a long ice-creamy kiss.

'Ready to go upstairs?' Sam whispered at length.

'Thought you'd never ask. Wish I hadn't had that second helping, though!'

'Me too!'

* * *

Afterwards, they lay contentedly propped up in each other's arms, learning more about each other's likes and dislikes, especially food, holiday destinations, culture and people.

Sam, for whom exercise straight after food was, as Robbie had pointed out, a bad idea, finally opened up about his medical issues. Recently he'd begun having what – or so the Infirmary had advised – was chronic Irritable Bowel Syndrome and probably stress-related. Well, he'd worked out for himself that a bout usually occurred when an escalation of his mother's issues, last-minute work on a big production and pressure at College coincided. The condition was currently under control, but his consultant had agreed to monitor the problem on a six-monthly basis.

'How did you get into cardiology?'

'When I was at university.'

'Which was…?'

'Cardiff.'

'I thought I detected a slight Welsh lilt in your voice?'

'I was born and went to school in Lisvane. My parents, brother and sister still live there. It was where I met Vee, who was still at college herself. Her first job was in the local library. Then, my first job opportunity was here. We moved and have been here ever since.'

He explained that Verity's night with the girls involved a yoga class followed by a long, gossipy pub meal that stretched well into the evening. Occasionally they went line-dancing or simply socialised.

'So, I'm all yours until ten o'clock,' Robbie had said.

Reflecting later, Sam thought how much it had been like the early times with Joss. Satisfying yet comfortable, as if they'd known one another a long time.

* * *

They met again the following week. And the next.

Wednesday evenings became a regular event. Robbie had got his wish for a regular date. He certainly seemed hungry for affection, which initially suited Sam – until he found himself looking forward to their time together more than he knew he should. His good intentions not to take the friendship too seriously began to fade.

Sometimes he pulled himself up short. Was the degree of guilt from entangling his life, yet again, with someone already in a long-term partnership really worth it? Sometimes he wondered if this was how mistresses felt, even if, admittedly, he wasn't a kept one.

If he must be compulsively drawn to married men, why couldn't they at least be divorced or decently separated?

In worrying about not only his own responsibility in the clandestine affair but his wish not to become an added problem for Robbie, it hadn't yet occurred to him his friend might subconsciously be preparing him to be a solution. As long as he was needed, but not making the running, it would be alright. Wouldn't it?

There couldn't be anything wrong with *being there* for someone. Could there?

The rest of the summer sped by. Then autumn. The men's emotional dependency on each other increased by the month, yet Sam was determined not to expect more from Robbie than he was in a position to give. For his part, Robbie explained that, although Sam was becoming very important to him, he wished to stay with Verity until Carrie left school.

By Christmas they'd become an essential part of each other's lives. Often, they would now meet up each week at a friendly but inobtrusive café for a quick meal before catching the bus to Sam's.

The die was cast.

As far as fidelity was concerned, while recognising they were now in some sort of untidy arrangement, they also agreed to play very safely. After all, Robbie was still required to occasionally honour his marital obligations, and Sam needed to keep himself occupied at weekends. That might involve cultural activities and seeing his mother or, more sensitively, Joss, or another of his good friends. Despite this conditional freedom, Sam always ached for Wednesday evenings and, if he ever wandered into town on a pleasant Saturday evening to visit his old haunts, was happy simply to socialise with whomever of his acquaintances he bumped into.

* * *

It wasn't until about a year later that, quite unexpectedly, something threatened the relationship which, until then, had been kept secret apart from a couple of their close friends who'd been advised in strictest confidence.

Sam was in the throes of planning a production of *West Side Story* with a company he hadn't worked with before. They rehearsed not far from where he now lived. Scheduled for late April, after preliminary chorus rehearsals to familiarise everyone with the score, principals' auditions were scheduled on the last Sunday of the month.

Getting to know and agree *modus operandi* with a new musical director and choreographer could be challenging. The three of them had been appointed by the company's committee and, as the person nominally in charge, it was important Sam collaborated satisfactorily with them. Fortunately, he usually had a clear idea of what he wanted to achieve, which normally inspired confidence and allowed him to carry the rest of the creative team along with his vision. Making it work, though, depended on satisfactory casting. This was when the three of them might find they had diverging agendas. Some musical directors always went for the best singing voices irrespective of the performer's acting capabilities and looks, while choreographers tended to give preference to people who moved well even when they weren't required to dance much.

Additional problems could arise when the auditioning panel was augmented by committee members whose appreciation of the finer artistic issues involved were variable. Sam's heart would sink when it was said of a weaker auditionee: 'she (or he) always auditions but never gets a part' which, interpreted, meant 'this time they should be given a chance.' Likewise, the dreaded phrase 'we've got to find something for her, she's the ticket secretary.' The selection of a final cast list was usually a compromise. He always prayed his firm direction would finally even things out.

Assembled in a church hall on a chilly winter afternoon, the five members of the panel sat halfway down the hall facing the stage. For *West Side Story*, two young women were required who could both pass as Puerto Rican: an ingenue for the leading role of Maria, who falls in love with Tony, formerly a member of the Jets gang, and another to play Anita, the fiery partner of Maria's brother Bernardo, leader of the Sharks.

Maria, despite being the leading role, was easy to cast. There were several attractive and experienced performers in the company who could handle a straight singing and acting role and get away with playing younger than they were. Anita, although a smaller role with fewer numbers, needed to also be an outstanding dancer with plenty of fire.

The application list remained on the notice board until the ordeal was about to start, leaving the panel little time to note the names of the people to shortly appear before them. Now, with the two older women's roles out of the way, Sam, the musical director – or MD – and the choreographer were informed by the Chairman how, at the last moment, a fifth applicant's name had been added.

With the Marias out of the way, one by one, the Anita hopefuls were put through their paces, each being required to sing the verse and chorus of the energetic *America* number and perform some improvised movement for a section of the important dance break. They were then asked to read a page or two of dialogue with some of the auditionees who might play opposite them, in this case, the scene where Anita tries to get a message to Tony but is intimidated by the Jets.

The first girl possessed a nice voice but was too fat, with limited dancing skills. The second, dark-haired and talented but, at thirty-eight, with the best will and make-up in the world couldn't have passed for a late teenager. The third sang, danced and acted convincingly but looked far too young. The fourth was the girl who'd already auditioned for Maria and, although no final decision had been made, knowing smiles and nods between the three key members of the panel suggested she was the strongest contender for that role so must be discounted as a potential Anita.

When they'd all been seen and thanked and 'Next please' called, the casting team looked at each other in desperation. Janie, the choreographer sighed the loudest. 'This last one better be good.'

Onto the floor walked a pretty, assured girl wearing what later turned out to be a convincing dark wig. She could have been anything between seventeen and twenty-three. As she segued from song to dance to dialogue with an acceptable Latin accent, it was clear she had the skills and personality for the role.

The verdict was unanimous. Even the Secretary's protestation that, being new to the company, by rights, she should serve in the chorus for a show before taking on a principal role, refused to sway them.

'That's the one we want,' the MD insisted. 'She coped with that tricky tempo like a trouper.'

'Obviously a trained dancer,' was the choreographer's contribution.

'I warmed to her as soon as she entered the room,' Sam agreed. 'What was her name again?'

The secretary checked her notes.

'Laura Harvey.'

26

Trouble Ahead

1994
Sam

'Why does this always have to happen to me?' Sam demanded. They were sitting on the sofa enjoying a glass of wine.

'Is that a rhetorical question?' Robbie said.

'How is it I always seem to land myself in impossible relationships? Why can't I be contentedly promiscuous like other men I know?'

'If you mean, why are people like me attracted to you, perhaps it's because you're not afraid to take emotional risks at whatever cost. And you're possibly too nice.'

'*Nice!* Apple sauce and dormice are *nice*. What you mean is, I'm inoffensive.'

'I'll ignore that.' Robbie helped himself to another handful of crisps and took a large sip of Merlot. 'Only sad, insecure people angle for compliments.'

'I can cope with sad and insecure.'

'Dearie me, it's one of those days, is it? What I'm trying to say in my obscure way is, you're a born homemaker and almost fussily welcoming. Caring too. I never knew anyone who worries as much about their friends as you. Perhaps you attract people who are used to agreeable domestic surroundings, stability and consideration. Just as some are drawn to people who resemble their mothers or fathers. Maybe we, that is my category of needy, failed heterosexuals, subconsciously search for something similar again.'

'Am I like your mother or father then?'

'A bit like my mother, actually. She liked a pleasing, orderly space in which to live and work. Other single men I've met, albeit a short list to date, either live in chaos or piss-elegant grandeur.'

'Sam patted his favourite embroidered cushion in mock indignation. 'I'm not piss-elegant?

'No. Nor chaotic.'

Sam struck a Dying Swan pose.

'As soon as I stepped in here, I felt at home. I just wish you didn't feel you had to try so hard to be liked. Stop worrying about how people perceive you. I'm sure most of them accept you as you are, warts and all, and expect you to do the same with them. Who cares about the odd character blemish? You can't be loved by everyone. Just be yourself. Sorry. Unless all this is a roundabout way of saying you're not happy with whatever-it-is we have.'

There was an uneasy silence, heavy with the implications of what that could mean, before Sam said, quietly, 'No, it's me who should be sorry.'

'There you go again. You're the only person I know who can turn self-pity into a virtue. It's Not Always About Sam. Well, this conversation is. But try and stand back and...'

'Contextualize?'

'Yes. Start putting yourself in other people's shoes and look at where they're coming from. Imagine how you might fit into their world at any given point in time. Listen for remarks that may suggest they're either going through a rough patch or are very happy. Accept they're not always in a position to elaborate on what is happening to them, that their minds are maybe elsewhere – and try to see things from their perspective.'

'To re-write Wilde, I suppose our insecurities are the baggage we all carry around with us.'

'My bag's probably even heavier than yours, but I don't worry about it so much.'

'Or bore people with the contents.'

'I'm a doctor. People come to me for help. Not the other way around.'

'A medical doctor though, not a psychiatrist.'

'Anyone who serves the public needs some psychology in their armoury.'

'And are we... good then?'

Robbie put his finger over Sam's mouth, then said, 'Anyway...'

'What?' Sam looked at him with curiosity.

Robbie took his hand. 'I'm sorry I've caused you so many problems, but we knew this...'

'Affair, romance... whole damn thing?'

'... whatever, wasn't going to be easy. I only know that I can't imagine what my life would be like without you now.'

'Nor me without you. All the same...'

'What?'

'I wish you'd warned me Laura was likely to show up at my auditions.'

'I honestly didn't know. It seems one of her friends heard they were doing the show and said she'd make a great Anita. A last-minute decision. Teenagers are secretive creatures. They do things and tell their parents afterwards. She's old enough to vote, have a baby, star in a big show – and edit what she wants us to know. How's she doing, by the way?'

'Accused me of not telling her exactly that.'

'She's that bad?'

'No! That she's going to be fantastic. I can hardly fault her. My work's cut out with the leading lady, Manchester's very own Bonnie Langford as she sees herself. She's very capable, but indulgent directors have allowed her to develop facial tics and gestures she considers essential to her own brand of stage magic. "Try to be less knowing," I told her. Laura, mercifully, hasn't had time to discover quite how good she is and acquire bad habits. She follows my direction to the letter and then adds her own sparkle.'

'What did you say to her, then?'

'Apologised profusely and assured her I was delighted with what she's giving me.'

'That's what she told us.'

'You mean she's been talking about me at home? I thought you said she was secretive.'

'Not when she wants to impress us. If there was a huge poster of you, it would be up on her bedroom wall.'

'Like father like daughter.'

Robbie threw a cushion at him.

* * *

All might still have continued uneventfully if, some weeks later, when the curtain fell on the First Night performance, Verity hadn't arrived backstage to give Laura a lift home and insisted on meeting Sam. A slight, pert, pretty woman in her mid-forties with a mass of red curls and green eyes, wearing a smart navy jumpsuit and quilted jacket, she matched Robbie's description of her, although he was unprepared for the husky, commanding voice.

After congratulating him on 'a promising production', she added, again as if encouraging a junior member of staff, 'I can see it needs a little more polish, but another four nights in front of good audiences will no doubt make all the difference. I'll be along again on Saturday with my husband and let you know what I think then.'

Patronising cow, Sam thought. In his darkest hours, he'd anticipated coming face-to-face with his lover's wife and mentally prepared himself for the acute discomfort such an eventuality might release. Instead, he squirmed indignantly under a big false smile.

More embarrassment was to come when members of the company, their families and friends gathered on the Saturday night after the final performance for drinks and mutual admiration in the theatre foyer and bar area. From the doorway, he spotted Robbie's party. Standing next to Verity was an attractive redheaded teenager, who had to be Carrie, chatting to her sister. With her, however, was a pink-faced guy with very dark hair in a floral shirt. He knew Damian from misspent evenings in The Haçienda club. He was often with an older woman in her mid-thirties, rather butch with short blond hair, who always seemed uncomfortable on the disco floor. Tonight, however, he was alone.

Catching Robbie's eye, Sam braced himself and swanned over. After saying hello and introducing himself to everyone, Verity gave him the thumbs-up, which at least made him marginally better disposed towards her. When the moment came to shake the hand of the last member of the party, to his horror, Damian winked and coyly said, 'Well, just fancy!'

Picking up the salutation, Verity asked, 'You two know each other, then?'

'Ships that pass…' the man said, with a dismissive smile. 'Occasional drinking buddies, aren't we, Sam?'

'Indeed,' Sam replied, hoping the subtle lighting was helping disguise the flush of embarrassment and annoyance invading his cheeks. 'What are you up to, these days? I haven't seen you for a while.' Given the twenty-plus-year gap in their ages, it crossed his mind the Harveys might possibly be surprised the two men were acquainted. Not that they'd ever done more than chat at the bar and occasionally join each other on the disco floor when there wasn't anyone more interesting around. Good company though Damian was, young men weren't really his thing. Tonight, he'd have preferred him not to have been there, though he was curious as to why he was. 'And how do you know…?'

'…Laura?' Damian prompted. 'I'm her singing coach.'

Of course he was.

'After landing the part, a colleague of Verity's suggested she came to see me for some extra tuition. I think you'll agree she's done pretty well?'

'She certainly has,' Sam said, turning to the girl whose eyes were still sparkling from the excitement of the past week. 'I predict a great future for her if she decides to take up Drama professionally.'

Now where had he heard something similar said long ago? And here he was, thirty-odd years on, a possible mentor of someone else with talent. At least in today's world, should Laura decide to pursue such a career, her parents were unlikely to dissuade her.

Telepathic as always, Robbie said, 'Her mother and I will wholeheartedly support any decision she makes. After all, you initially trained as a drama teacher, didn't you, Sam?' At which his heart leapt into his mouth, terrified he'd accidentally betrayed they already knew each other. In the nick of time, he must have realised his gaffe. 'Though I… er… believe Laura mentioned you'd opted for teaching rather than acting itself, didn't you, dear?'

'Did I, Daddy?' Laura returned, slightly perplexed.

'Or maybe I read that in the programme?' he added hastily.

Sam sighed with relief. It was true he sometimes chatted to her during comfort breaks at rehearsals, but only to give her notes. He'd assiduously avoided any reference to their personal histories.

* * *

The following Wednesday, Robbie and Sam attempted to make light of the events of the evening and downplay their growing fear of danger ahead.

'At least I've met your family and know who you're talking about now,' Sam said.

'Yes. And were such a hit you've been invited for tea next Sunday.'

'Really?' Sam suddenly felt uncomfortable. 'Is that wise?'

'No, but Vee wants to discuss the opportunities open to Laura. Also, I…'

'Yes?'

'Hope you won't be cross, but I confessed to her I'd bumped into you at the Infirmary as a patient.'

'But we…'

'I know we haven't properly, but it seemed the best way of saving any future embarrassment. Actually, I may have embellished the extent of my professional involvement with you. Vee can spot an anomaly a mile off, so I thought it best to come clean in case anything else slipped out during your visit.'

'Black mark for you. On-your-guard note for me,' he thought.

After that, Sam sensed he was being slowly sucked into Robbie's other life. Years later, he'd argue with himself he should never have accepted the invitation. Yet, not to have done so would have been rude, and Robbie might have thought he was letting him down. Besides, repeated postponements could have raised suspicions too – and would it have changed the eventual outcome anyway?

He genuinely liked Laura, who, so focussed on the theatre, reminded him in some ways of himself at her age. He was flattered they thought he might be able to advise her, though he could do little more than recommend several colleges she might apply to and offer to supply a reference.

The Harveys lived in a smart, tastefully furnished detached house between Oldham and Middleton. In the event, it turned out to be a pleasant afternoon, although knowing how frustrated Robbie was becoming at home, Sam couldn't help wondering whether the cheerful atmosphere was a genuine attempt on everyone's part to enjoy themselves, contrived for his benefit – or possibly both. If the girls sensed something was amiss with their parent's marriage, they didn't appear unduly concerned. Maybe they'd got used to it. His first impression of Verity as a tactless bossy-boots was largely accurate, but on her home territory he saw, as well as being a good mother and an excellent cook, there was a softer side to her. She also had an entertaining, if slightly acerbic, sense of humour, which partly explained why Robbie had once fallen for her.

Over the meal, Sam got to know the effervescent, sporty Carrie, who, like her sister, was also good company. The matter of Laura's possible career options was discussed, and Sam was deluged with photos of her in various dance competitions and school shows which provided an excuse to bring out nostalgic family and holiday snaps. While he maintained an interested façade, he found viewing pictures of their once normal, happy life unnerving. It made him unhappy to think he might be a Trojan horse.

Verity added to his discomfort by raising plans for their future and a proposed cruise of the Baltic. He saw the girls' eyes light up but noticed Robbie's features tighten. When he said, 'Well, we'll have to see if Cardiology can afford to let me have all that time off,' a flicker of concern passed over Verity's face.

In an attempt to move the conversation along, Sam asked whether Laura had any intention of continuing her singing lessons, momentarily forgetting the dangers lurking in that topic. 'It depends on whether or not Dad will continue to subsidise them,' she said with a sidelong glance at Robbie.

'You know I will, if it's what you really want.'

At which point, Verity piped up. 'Funny you knowing Damian, Sam!' Side-splitting, he thought. 'Nice young man. We got him through a good friend of mine. He really helped Laura with her projection and resonance.'

'Way OTT, but a wonderful teacher,' Laura said.

'Yes,' Sam said quickly. 'He coaches several singers I know. Our paths have crossed socially before, although I wouldn't call us friends.'

Verity smiled pleasantly. 'Very village-y, Manchester, isn't it? And must be especially so on the amdram scene?'

'Indeed,' Sam said.

He found the enigmatic smile she threw him unsettling.

* * *

Once you get to know people, it's surprising how often you keep bumping into them. Thus, over the next few weeks, Sam ran into Laura in the Arndale Centre, Carrie at a bus stop and finally Robbie, Verity and Carrie at a Saturday matinee at the Royal Exchange. On that occasion, they ended up afterwards in the coffee shop, chatting for twenty minutes before going their separate ways.

Sam felt duty-bound to return their hospitality and invited them for a buffet lunch the following Sunday.

At one point after the meal, Robbie stood up and, with the straightest face he could muster, asked if he could use the loo, to which Sam, also struggling not to grin, informed him, 'At the top of the stairs.' A trivial enough exchange, but it highlighted how cautious they had to be.

They must have given something unwittingly away, for soon after Robbie warned him, 'Vee seems to have worked out we're closer than we've presented ourselves to be. "You two have obviously hit it off," she said. "Isn't fraternisation between doctors and patients frowned upon?" I think she's a tad jealous.'

'Has she any right to be? What happened to that colleague of hers... Alex?'

'I forgot to tell you. Turns out Alex is a bit of a... fruit fly – if that's the expression?

Sam nodded. 'Well, surprise, surprise!'

'She's divorced, and I've a suspicion she might be *sympathetic* herself. Apparently, she hangs out a lot with camp Damian. He's her best friend, in fact.'

Sam's heart sank. The strapping blonde was close to both Verity *and* Damian.

'For some reason, Vee's become rather intrigued by... all that.'

'All what?'

'Manchester's alternative social scene.'

Sam cursed the day he'd ever got chatting to Damian. '*Very* village-y Manchester' indeed! 'Just as long as it doesn't become all *us*. Could be dangerous. We must be far more careful. At least our Wednesdays are sacrosanct.'

'As a matter of fact...'

It was a phrase that often proceeded an awkward admission, Sam thought. 'You... you haven't... told her about them?'

'Well...'

'Robbie!'

'Not in so many words. A while back, one of her yoga crowd's Thursday evening shift was changed to Wednesdays. They've swapped nights.'

'To Thursdays when I'm nearly always rehearsing?'

'Sorry. It's meant finding another excuse for being not being at home then.'

'What sort of excuse?'

'Work. Which is partly true. Someone suggested we move on from our regular Wednesday meeting and congregate informally in the pub. Our workloads have been getting out of hand and it's a good opportunity to gossip about things that would be inappropriate in a formal meeting. I get to hear about things that affect the hospital in general. My boss is there and it would be undiplomatic to miss it. It's quickly become a regular event. There's a lot of back-scratching and commiserating – and I can still make my excuses around seven and get away in time to see you.

'So that's why you've been late recently.'

'Yes.'

'And I thought you were getting fed up with me.'

'That too, of course. Seriously, what's more problematic… I can't kid Vee the pub sessions go on too late, so have said some of us go on for a meal. And even…'

'Yes?' Sam asked, his head swimming.

'That sometimes… I meet… you.'

'Ugh!'

'Sorry.'

'At least it's out in the open now. I suppose.'

'That's not all, unfortunately.'

'Go on.'

'From the odd remarks she drops about how *nice* you are, I'm sure she guesses you and Damian are both…'

'Faggots? Although if she imagines he and I are more than just good friends, that deflects attention away from us and cements the notion you and I are simply platonic friends.'

'She's never had any reason to suspect me of having affairs with anyone of either sex.'

'Unless you make a habit of leaving copies of *Gay Times* lying around at home, too.'

'And I have to trust Damian and Alex don't discuss your… erm… dancing skills,' he retorted.

'Touché! Though, if that's a euphemism, I can assure you some tentative hip-hop steps are the only interactive moves Damian's ever got from me!'

Robbie jokily raised a querying eyebrow.

It didn't feel like a joking matter to Sam. More like a large, clammy net was closing in on them.

As the weeks passed with no further developments, Sam hoped they were worrying unnecessarily and put his fears on hold.

* * *

In July, they celebrated their second anniversary with a replay of their first meal together, this time replacing the Burgundy with Tesco's best Prosecco. As well as raising glasses to themselves, they drank to Laura. Her parents had expected her to apply to Manchester University's Drama department, but, much to Sam's relief, she surprised them by announcing she'd elected to live away from home and been accepted by the Guildhall School of Music & Drama in London. Sam patted himself on the back for putting the distinguished institution at the top of the list he'd given her.

Watching Robbie growing increasingly dejected as ten o'clock loomed each Wednesday evening, Sam became terrified it was only a matter of time before something snapped in the Harvey household.

One Sunday in early August, his mother was feeling especially harshly treated. Due to other commitments, Sam hadn't been able to visit her the previous day as originally planned and was making a special journey. Sod's law prevailing, as so often it did when he tried to do the right thing by both Bessie and his other obligations, he was let down by the timetabled half-hourly bus service. One of the drivers failed to turn up for work, keeping him waiting fifty minutes before the bus finally lumbered up.

He wondered, not for the first time, whether he should invest in a mobile phone. To date, he'd managed his own life satisfactorily without one, but at times like this, having the facility to warn her of the delay might have eased his stress level, appeased his conscience and staved off an ugly scene. Or would it? She'd only have said 'why can't you find a phone box like normal people?'

When he eventually turned the key in the door at Worsley Court, the roast was overcooked. But a carving knife couldn't have sliced through the bad odour caused by his late arrival, now mingling with the gamey smell of over-done lamb.

Bessie brushed aside his excuses with, 'You know you should always go for the bus before the one you really need,' adding with a sniff, 'especially today when you knew I'd be cooking something special. I'd rather you didn't bother coming at all if it's such an effort.'

'That's not true,' he said as kindly as possible and spent the next twenty minutes negotiating the thin ice between them with as much care as Eliza on the Ohio River – perhaps over-doing his compliments on everything from the roast potatoes to her floral centrepiece. 'A few white dianthuses always bring an arrangement to life, don't they?'

'You won't get around me that way!'

But, by the time he'd swooned over her signature honeycomb mould, his efforts to bring her round had almost become a joke, things were less tense and he felt able to risk some amusing anecdotes about his life. 'And how about you?'

Bessie finally relaxed and brought him up to date on the local gossip. 'Penny upstairs is getting married and has sold her flat. Not that she's been there long enough for us to be more than passing acquaintants, but it will mean more banging about for a while.' After that, they passed on to other village news and the time slipped by with its old ease.

He was just congratulating himself things were back on an even keel when he made the mistake of asking her how Miriam was. 'Oh, her. As you know, I haven't seen much of her since my fall – and that's a while back now,' Bessie said, pursing her lips. 'When I do, it's like speaking to a different person. She's gone all busy-busy. Always was rather secretive about some things, but now she just smiles politely and completely clams up. Shopping continues to be a problem. Mrs Bingley gets all the basic bread-and-butter stuff for me, it's… well, having someone to look for the more personal things, who appreciates my particular tastes. Mrs B, bless her, is a sweetie but couldn't tell the difference between a snapdragon and an antirrhinum.'

'There isn't any.'

'Quite.'

Best not query the absurdity of her logic, he thought. Not when he'd worked her into a better mood. 'How about Giles?'

'Still places my bets for me, but he too is preoccupied these days. Doesn't have time to carry out little jobs for me like he used to. Though, from odd remarks from other people in the flats, I've my suspicions about them... both.'

'What sort?'

'A long story. How's your current show going?'

After a good afternoon's chatter, around five and now with more of a spring in his step, he made them both a cup of tea and began winding things up.

'Don't leave it so long, next time.'

'I'll try not to.'

Before leaving the building, Sam knocked on Miriam's door.

When she saw who it was, she first looked sheepish then managed a grin. 'Good timing, come in. I was about to put the kettle on.'

'Thanks, I've only just had one with Mum, but I'd love to pop in for a few minutes if you're not busy. It seems ages since we had a good natter.'

As she led him into her living room, he noticed the sofa was already occupied. 'You know Giles, don't you?'

He'd met the man on a couple of occasions at his mother's and knew the couple's back story. Catching them informally together explained his mother's suspicions.

'I'm glad you've popped in. We've some news for you.'

'Ah.'

'Giles and I are moving in together.'

'That's *very* good news.'

'Well, we've known each other a long time,' Giles interjected, 'but only recently started seeing each other again... properly,' he added.

'It means I shall be moving out,' Miriam said. 'His flat is bigger for two people. I'll be selling up, and your mother will have yet another new neighbour to work her...' she paused as if to find the right word, '...magic on.'

'*Black* magic?'

They all tittered.

'Mum mentioned the top flat was on the market again,' he admitted.

'It went quickly. A pleasant woman has bought it. Bit younger than you. She was here yesterday measuring up and is due to pop in again today.'

'You've met her then?'

'I don't miss much here on the ground floor. We caught her for a brief chat on our way out yesterday just after she arrived. By the way, we'd be grateful if you didn't mention about Giles and myself to Bessie just yet.'

'Actually, it's Mum I wanted to see you about.'

'I expect she's been complaining I don't see her a lot these days?'

'Well...'

'Actually...' Here Miriam smiled at Giles. 'Bessie's partly responsible for my moving.'

'Really?'

'One day a few months ago, I was obliged to skip choir practice to take her to visit a friend. And collect her afterwards. I was very angry and knew it had to stop. How can I put this...' Miriam faltered, and Sam saw she was finding the discussion embarrassing but inevitable. 'You and I have always got on well, so I hope you'll understand. But...'

Again, Giles finished her sentence. '...Your mother takes over people's lives.'

'I don't think she realises it,' Miriam continued. 'She's a brave woman in so many ways and has amazing insight and wisdom. I'll always be grateful for her kindness to me when we first met...'

Sam saw a *however* hovering. And again, Giles provided it, as if conscious how difficult it was for her owning up to what had been allowed to occur. 'Miriam has been your mother's unpaid driver-cum-secretary companion for too long.'

Miriam swallowed hard. 'Having observed Bessie closely for some years, I don't think anyone fully realises the pain her arthritis causes her. It only hardens her resolve not to give in to it. Her will to survive is fierce – but it's at a cost. Mainly to her relationships with the people she relies on, being dependent on them but on her terms. I had to regain control of my life.' She gulped. 'It was getting to the stage where I needed counselling.'

Giles put his arm around her. 'Which was when she turned to me.'

Again, they looked at each other in a way that excluded him. Sam frowned. 'I can totally relate to all you're saying. I've seen this coming for a while, but she rarely takes any notice of me if I try to make her see another person's point of view. I presumed she only used the thumbscrews on me because I'm her son. I never realised she was doing it to you, too – at least, not to this extent.'

'I couldn't even take a few days off work after Easter,' Miriam went on. 'She'd already planned how *we* were going to spend them. The next time I spoke to her, my summer holiday was all mapped out as well. She's a force of nature and a powerful one. I can see how she must have energised and propped up your father when he floundered. My failing has been in allowing myself to succumb to her subtle brand of emotional blackmail. Because Giles is a friend of hers too, he understands and has helped put things in perspective.'

Sam turned to Giles. 'I don't know what she'd do without her weekly bet.'

'Don't worry, that won't change,' he said. 'I do it when I place my own. Also, I'm lucky, as Bessie has the knack of getting on particularly well with men. Not romantically, of course, but she talks our language when it comes to sports, and has a sound, if under-used, business sense. With all due respect to Miriam, who's been amazing, she knows I won't take any nonsense from her. In an odd way, she likes that.'

'Not my style, standing up for myself,' Miriam said with a wry grin.

'Bessie can be very grounded, Giles continued, 'and has a pawky sense of humour – when she's not being Hyacinth Bouquet.' Here Miriam looked sharply at Giles, as if warning him not to go too far, but he continued nonetheless. 'I've learnt to make it very clear to her when I'm available and when I'm not. And it helps I don't live on the premises. People who do are particularly vulnerable. As Miriam says, since her accident, Bessie's knees have got much worse and she's got more reliant on others. But, much as we're fond of her ...'

'We're having to take a step back.'

'Yes,' Sam said, 'I can see.'

'We understand what a very awkward position you're in, as her only child. She's never recovered from your moving to the other side of town, you know. It's put you just beyond immediate reach and it scares the wotsit out of her.'

'I wouldn't have had a life of my own if I'd stayed within striking distance.'

'Absolutely. You're entitled to it. You do so much for her, too,' Miriam said.

'And it would be equally wrong if you lived next door and were fussing round her all the time. She has to be in control and have everyone at the end of a leash,' Giles added. 'We sympathise, but at the end of the day, she's not our problem.'

Sam knew they were right. He had to find a way of subtly supporting his mother more. Unfortunately, Bessie wanted people, including himself, only *when* she wanted them. 'I'm grateful to you for explaining the situation and making your position clear.'

They moved on to briefly cover less controversial matters. Sam then made his excuses and left, slipping out of the building, frustrated and dejected once more. Whenever there were these predicaments, he remembered Bessie as she'd been when she was younger, before age and pain made her so uncompromising: always knowing what she was about and taking life in her stride. There were still times when flashes of her old spirit and integrity emerged, when she'd rise to a challenge and become Queen Bee again. It was the patches in between which were the problem.

As he opened the door of the main entrance, he was in time to see a small car pull up outside the building with a woman inside.

With a shock, he recognised the Wagnerian frame and fair hair.

He continued walking.

* * *

By the end of September, Laura was happily installed in a flat in Clerkenwell with two other young women students. Robbie reported she was already having the time of her life. Carrie, on the other hand, was juggling horse competitions with revision for her GCSEs and was either not at home or locked in her bedroom.

By the middle of October, there was a decided hint of autumn in the air. One evening as Sam settled down to watch *Lovejoy*, the doorbell rang. Through the frosted glass pane, he saw Robbie's familiar profile.

Not only was it unusual for him to visit at weekends, but he was supposed to be with Verity in Paris. After taking some of his holiday entitlement to attend a two-day symposium he'd been invited to in Macclesfield, Verity then pressurised him to find an excuse to forgo it. In the interests of family harmony, he'd done so.

It was raining. Robbie stood on the doorstep looking not only very damp but hunched and uncharacteristically dishevelled. He immediately saw something was wrong. 'Come in. I thought you'd be getting ready to attend Vespers at Notre Dame?'

'Vee's gone with Carrie instead,' Robbie said putting his arms around him and clinging on to him damply. 'Another last-minute change of plans. You... you once made the mistake of saying if I was ever in need of somewhere to chill out for a day or two, I could come here?'

'And, by the looks of you, *freak* out?'

'I've been sussed.'

'Whisky, coffee, tea?'

'Coffee would be fine, thanks.'

'Turn off the telly and relax while I go and make the coffee. I'll hear chapter and verse then.'

Sam went into the kitchen and filled the kettle. Various scenarios flashed through his mind as he thoughtfully poured boiling water onto the coffee granules, topped up the mugs with milk and took them in to join Robbie on the sofa.

'Right,' Sam said, 'what's happened?'

'As you know, things have been simmering over the past few months. Until recently, Vee's been too busy helping Laura get ready for college to think about much else. The conversation tends to revert to vague plans for the future and stalls when we can't agree on what we want to do with it. In the end, we get tetchy – or tetch*ier* – with each other. Like when I had to persuade her that we couldn't afford the Baltic cruise, have the house externally redecorated *and* subsidise Laura in London. Vee was insistent we did something special at half-term. When she saw St Petersburg wasn't going to happen, Paris became a last-minute ditch to take us out of ourselves and try to re-connect. Also, she's not been there since she was a schoolgirl and always wanted to go back to see the place with an adult's eyes.'

'Nice for Carrie now, anyway.'

'She had plans to stay with a school friend over half term but agreed to go on condition she visited *The Musée du Cheval* at Chantilly.'

'And you?'

'I'm really at the end of my tether. I can't take any more. I told her a lot of important people would be at the symposium and, although it would be something of a busman's holiday, I'd decided I couldn't afford to pull out after all.'

'How did she react?'

'Understandably livid. Put on a good front for Carrie, of course, but we didn't part on good terms. In fact, I've never known her quite so icy before. I think she must realise this is the beginning of the end.'

They sat holding hands for a few minutes.

'Over the past couple of weeks,' he continued, 'she's been asking more and more questions about you, too, and what we do when we meet. It lit the touchpaper yesterday when I told her to stop being such a busybody and that I'd never wanted to go to Paris in the first place. I'm not sure if she correlated the two issues.'

'Let's hope not.'

'Anyway, as we see too much of each other now anyway, what I really needed was a few days' peace and quiet on my own. Except...'

'Yes?'

'I don't want to be on my own.'

'No?'

'I'd rather be… here. With you. If you could put up with me?'

Sam gulped. 'I meant what I said. You're very welcome.' Although he couldn't help thinking it would officially make him an accessory to the disintegration of the Harveys' marriage if Verity found out. Nevertheless, he kept his thoughts to himself and simply asked, 'To help me plan – for how long?'

'They don't come back until Friday. I'll be in Macclesfield on Tuesday and Wednesday, although I'd like to cancel my hotel room, drive down early each day and come back late in the afternoon.'

'What if she contacts the hotel?'

'I'll ring her before I leave and explain that I'm motoring down.'

'Isn't it all rather risky though?'

'Probably. But I've got to the stage where I really don't care.'

* * *

Over the next few days, Sam disappeared into a bubble of denial as he wallowed in the novelty of sharing his life with Robbie and the chance to discover how domestically compatible they were.

He needn't have worried. Their time together showed Sam how much easier-going a man from a long-standing relationship was to live with, compared to some of the single male friends he'd put up, when there always seemed to be a race for the bathroom in the morning, followed by endless abluting and primping before anguishing over how well they liked their eggs done.

Robbie, on the other hand, was a model guest. He took everything in his stride, lacked personal vanity, ate whatever was set before him, and sensed when to quietly disappear and lounge with a magazine to let Sam get on with chores he could only do on his own. He was both delighted and surprised when, diverted by a lengthy phone call, everything in the sink was quietly washed up and put away. On one occasion when his back was turned, without prompting he'd heard chuntering in the background and looked through the window to see Robbie systematically mowing Regency stripes into his tiny lawn.

It was exciting watching someone else's socks mingling with his as they flopped round in the washing machine. It felt as if they were already a couple. Having someone to spend time with in the late evenings was a novelty: snuggling together catching up on recorded TV episodes missed due to other commitments and not having to clock-watch all the time. Above all was the pleasure of going to sleep with someone you cared about with their arm around you, and waking up with them still reassuringly close in the morning. On the nights neither was otherwise engaged, they went to the cinema or theatre. It made Sam feel young again to be furtively holding hands with a man in the dark.

When in town, while they tried to avoid places where they might see and been seen by people they didn't wish to, they knew it was pointless being too careful. After all, they were only two friends having a night out together.

As things turned out, however, they should have taken more care with their body language. Their stolen window of bliss came to a sudden end when, on the Saturday morning, Robbie returned home to face the music.

27

Meltdown

1994
Bessie

The woman timed it well.

As she took elevenses coffees on a tray into the living room, Bessie caught Alex looking intently at a family photograph on the bookcase. 'How long ago was this?'

'Let me think… It was taken the last Christmas we were all together before Hugh went into hospital. About thirteen years ago.' She set down the tray and indicated the armchair. A pleasant woman, if, on first acquaintance, a bit dour, Alex had knocked on the door to introduce herself not long after moving in some days earlier. When, about to leave, she'd said, 'Must dash now and get a few bits and bobs before the shop shuts,' Bessie had taken advantage of the situation. 'Would it be cheeky of me to ask you to pick up a pint of milk for me at the same time? I'm right out.'

'No probs.'

Alex rang her bell again the following week to see whether she needed anything, enabling her to stock up on some luxury items again. She'd called this morning, too. Bessie hoped a useful routine might be starting up.

'I discovered the photo yesterday when I was rummaging through the bureau. It fits that old frame nicely,' she said.

'It certainly does.'

Alex moved away from the bookcase and sat down as Bessie set the mug of Maxwell House on the coaster nearest to her and proffered a plate of petticoat tails. 'No biscuits for me, thanks,' she demurred. 'I've my figure to consider. But the coffee's very welcome.'

Bessie weighed up the woman's well-styled short hair and full bust shown off to good advantage by a bold red check blouse under an open denim jacket, below which buttock-hugging jeans tapered down to a pair of trim, ankle-booted legs. She wished she'd been able to appear so at ease with her own voluptuousness as a younger woman, but clothes were far less casual in those days.

Nodding to the bookcase, Alex said, 'He hasn't changed much, Sam, has he?'

Taken aback, Bessie said, 'You know him?'

'Not well, but we've been introduced… socially.'

'What a coincidence. When?'

'Some time back. We sometimes frequent the same watering places and have people in common. I recognised him immediately.'

Sam a drinker? That was news to Bessie. Certainly, he'd always rejected offers to share a beer with his father, but then he seemed to have changed in so many ways over recent years.

'I must organise a flat-warming soon, and you can meet them.'

'That would be nice.' Bessie opened her handbag. 'Now, I must settle up with you for those things you got me. The days when I could pop out for a loaf of bread have virtually gone. I can make it to Tanya's and the post-box and back, but that's about it. Unfortunately, my regular helper is moving out.'

'Number Two downstairs?'

'Yes.'

'I saw the sign up outside. It's all change here, then.'

'Nice to have some younger people around, though.'

'I have to shop for myself, so it's no trouble getting anything you need at the same time, especially with the car. Really, I'm only too glad to help. Maybe I should treat myself to one of those shopping bags on wheels for strolls to the corner shop?'

'That's very kind of you, but I trust a pantechnicon won't become necessary! There now, fifteen pounds fifty-four.' Bessie counted out the money by Alex's coaster, adding a separate pound coin.

'That's too much!'

'No, if you're going to be kind enough to help me out, you must at least let me give you a token for your trouble. It'll buy a bottle of washing-up liquid or something.'

'That's very naughty of you. It's a pleasure, honestly. I don't want us to get off on the wrong foot by arguing – but thank you,' Alex added with a smile as she put the money away in her purse. In doing so, her somewhat dour expression seemed to melt like a hot lamp on butter.

She was rather nice, Bessie thought. Kind, thoughtful and seemed to be another loner – as she had been for some years now. And fancy her knowing Sam, too! 'Have you seen my son recently?'

'Not for a while. He's only an acquaintance but knows my chum Damian and also my ex-boss's husband. I was offered promotion at the college along the road. Hence my moving here. In fact, I'm expecting Vee to visit this afternoon. She's been in Paris. I had a postcard from her this morning hoping I was settling in. She'll be back by now.'

'Small world, isn't it?' Bessie said lightly, the wheels of her curiosity turning.

'Damian was giving her daughter singing lessons.'

'That small!'

'Indeed.'

'I hope you'll be very happy here.'

'I think I will.'

'And please feel free to knock on the door if ever you need…'

'A cup of sugar?'

They laughed.

'Yes.'

Bessie felt happier than she had been for a while.

* * *

There was an insistent ringing. By now it was mid-afternoon. Bessie awoke on top of the bed, her *Woman's Weekly* article about the home life of a much-loved soap star having slipped onto the carpet. When the front doorbell rang even more persistently a second time, she patted her hair, fumbled for her stick, called, 'Just a moment,' and walked carefully to the door.

A flustered, shortish, middle-aged woman in a green cagoule stood on the mat, her red hair in need of a comb.

'Mrs Owen?'

'That's right.'

'I hope this isn't an awkward moment.'

Ignoring the question, Bessie asked her own: 'And which charity are you from?'

'I'm not from any organisation. I'm Verity Harvey – a friend of Alex's upstairs?'

The name came back to her. 'Of course, she mentioned you were visiting her today. I trust you liked her flat?' She really wanted to return to her nap, but was prepared to be pleasant for a moment or so, if unsure what to do with the woman if she insisted on lingering. Had Alex sent her, and if so, why?

When her smile wasn't returned, she noticed the serious look on the woman's face. With each second that passed, it intensified. Bessie had a sudden presentiment it might be unwise to keep her on the doorstep. Walls, especially those of flats, had ears finely attuned to anything that could be recycled as gossip. 'Will you come in?' To her surprise the woman nodded, putting her even more on her guard. As she led her into the living room, Verity went on, 'I came with a belated house-warming gift, then, as we were chatting, she mentioned your son…'

'Yes,' she said. 'I understand you know him.'

'More significantly, so does my husband.'

'Ah,' Bessie said, still wondering where this was heading.

'It's Sam I came to talk to you about. If you have a moment.'

She didn't like the way this Harvey woman said Sam's name as if biting into a lemon. 'Is he in some sort of trouble?' Verity gave a wry smile and raised her eyebrows. Bessie's heart sank. 'You'd better sit down tell me about it.'

She perched on the edge of the armchair, went quiet for a moment and then frowned, as if unsure where to start. Bessie watched her with impatient curiosity.

'I've had suspicions for a while that Robert – my husband – was up to no good, but hadn't fathomed out with whom.'

'Suspicions?'

'I mean, I'd sort of worked out that Sam was...' here she paused uncomfortably, as if unsure how to finish her sentence.

'Go on.'

'Well ...'

'What?'

'Gay.'

Bessie's heart sank. A word, once so cheerful, which now left a bad taste in her mouth. She pursed her lips before saying defensively, 'Had you?'

'Yes.'

'And?'

'I'm so sorry to have to tell you this but...' Again, Verity hesitated.

'Go on.'

'There's no easy way of putting this...'

'Try.'

'Today I discovered they've...' she swallowed and blinked uneasily, '...been sleeping together.'

Bessie's brain stalled for a few moments. Had she heard incorrectly? She began feeling slightly queasy. She saw the woman watching her intensely, lips puckered and allowing time for her bombshell to sink in. Surely Sam would have forewarned her if he'd thought there was any chance of her becoming involved in a situation like this?

'What makes you so certain it's my son?'

'We were both supposed to be going away to Paris, but, at the last minute, Robert decided he didn't want to. As soon as I got back this morning, I could tell, from the way the house looked exactly as it did before I left, he hadn't stayed there. Cushions set neatly at the same angles on the sofa the way I like them, plants drooping for lack of water, items going off in the fridge and so on. I asked him point-blank where he'd spent the week. When he dissembled with 'a chap at work invited me to stay' but wouldn't specify exactly who, something clicked. He has a way of avoiding my gaze and quickly changing the subject when he's lying. Lots of little things I'd picked up over the months gelled, and how some I'd asked him about he'd slithered away from providing an explanation for. Out of the blue, I heard myself saying, "You've been with Sam, haven't you?" At which point, he realised he'd exhausted his prepared script and everything came tumbling out. In some ways, I think it was a relief for him. But just now, when Alex told me Damian had accidentally found himself following Robbie and Sam out of a cinema last week after a film and caught them brushing hands and briefly linking fingers, I went bananas. The knowledge they were parading themselves as lovers in public was too much.'

It crossed Bessie's mind maybe her new neighbour wasn't as nice as she appeared and was simply exploiting her as a source of unpleasant gossip. 'That explains why Alex was so interested in my photograph of him,' she said, indicating the bookcase.

'Yes. But none of this is Alex's fault. Damian only rang moments before I arrived this afternoon. You mustn't blame her. It was only after I told her that we put two and two together. Until today, she'd no idea you were Sam's mother. In fact, she was reluctant to tell me what she knew but could see the state I was in and feared I'd only blame her if I discovered later she'd known all along.'

Bessie was completely out of her depth.

'She likes you a lot, by the way.'

Well, that was nice to know, Bessie thought. Although *a lot* was rather overdoing it on the basis of a couple of short meetings. 'I really wouldn't want this conversation to change anything between you,' Verity went on. 'She doesn't know I'm here. It was a heat-of-the-moment thing. And, now with brief hindsight, probably wrong of me.'

It probably was, Bessie agreed. She always believed in sleeping on a problem before involving other people.

When Verity spoke next, it was in a softer voice. 'I can see this must be a terrible shock to you…' If the remark momentarily lulled her into a false sense of security that the woman appreciated her point of view, the next pierced her like a stiletto. 'Although you may be accustomed to his behaviour – I presume this isn't the first time your son's done this sort of thing?'

How dare she come into her home and insinuate, however indirectly, that she was accustomed to or condoned, Sam's inappropriate intrigues! To give him his due, he'd always been very discreet about his private life. Now pushing fifty, this was the first time he'd ever deeply embarrassed her.

'He comes across as such a charming, well-mannered man.' Then she went on, digging herself deeper into a pit. 'Please don't think I'm being deliberately spiteful here…'

Weren't *deliberate* and *spite* phrase mates, Bessie wondered?

'…But I think you ought to know the kind of person he really is.'

'Usually a very decent one,' she responded with asperity. If she didn't understand Sam, who did? Even if she wasn't on his wavelength where contemporary attitudes about things such as pansexuality – a word she'd heard on *Woman's Hour* and hoped she'd understood correctly – were concerned, she believed her son to be fundamentally an honourable man. He'd never hurt anyone intentionally, only in complicated circumstances which had spiralled out of control.

But by now, with the emotional vortex of the past few hours taking its toll, Verity's righteous indignation was flagging. 'You really must excuse me; I'm not thinking straight at the moment,' she mumbled, searching for a tissue in her bag and dabbing her eyes.

'Look,' Bessie said, 'what you've said is shocking. But shouldn't you be tackling Sam rather than me?'

'I hoped you might have some influence over him… ask him to back off, *or…*'

Or what? Bessie wasn't good at taking instructions from strangers. Especially when they couldn't finish their sentences. Whatever Sam had done, she wasn't impressed at being used as a way of getting back at him. Verity's visit was nothing short of vindictive. Understandable, perhaps, but not the way she'd been brought up to go about things. Supposing he'd been having an affair with another woman – would the husband have turned to his mistress's mother for help? Though who knew in these strange times. The old rules had ceased to apply. She decided to ignore the abandoned *or* and simply said, 'Did you?'

'A knee-jerk reaction, perhaps. And…'

There's more? she thought, fearfully.

'Most humiliating of all…'

'Yes?'

I had to insist Robert got himself tested.'

'Tested?'

'For HIV.'

Acronyms confused Bessie. She looked blank.

'A-I-D-S' Verity said.

'Oh, of course.' A terrible fear replaced her indignant confusion. 'You mean, you think my son is…' she could hardly bring herself to say it, '… sick?'

'We'll have to wait and see about that. But put yourself in my position.'

Now she was being asked not only to help the woman but to identify with her. How could she? 'This has hit me out of the blue too,' she said. 'I could do with half a finger of brandy while I think it through. How about you?'

'Thanks, but I'm driving.'

'Tea, then… coffee?'

'Honestly, I'm fine.'

'Then if you'll excuse me just a moment.'

'Of course.'

The brandy, normally used only for sauces and medicinal purposes, was kept in a kitchen cupboard. Searching for it gave Bessie a couple of minutes away from the tense atmosphere in the other room. It was part-hidden on the shelf behind treacle and syrup tins, honey jars and bags of dried fruit. Never, Bessie thought, as she carefully poured the caramel liquid into the bottom of a tumbler, swirled it around and inhaled its heady aroma, had she ever seriously suspected her husband of having a relationship with another woman, let alone a man.

And where on earth had Sam inherited this rogue gene?

All her life, she'd avoided any attempt to envisage Connie and Hannah's activities when the lights went out. Like the intimate behaviour of one's parents, it was hard to visualise anyone you were close to involved in nocturnal gymnastics with other people. And then there were Roy and Billy. In her defence, it was only very recently she'd begun to come to terms with the idea of two men or women, not just pleasuring each other, but indulging in bizarre and unhygienic practices in lieu of a normal love life.

But that was the price she paid for having an inquisitive mind and making herself read that frightful, if un-put-downable, Jackie Collins she'd picked up in a job lot at a WI jumble sale.

Nevertheless, limited as her own carnal experiences may have been, she was far from stupid and was attempting, albeit late in life, to come to terms with the realities of the contemporary world. Years ago, and even now among her contemporaries, certain topics would have been considered *infra dig* in polite company. Bessie, who prided herself on her clear-cut views on social morality, was now adrift in choppily unchartered waters but doing her best to understand.

Then there was the suggestion Sam might have deliberately put Verity's health at risk. That was unconscionable and had given her a jolt.

With one of those tricks the brain can unexpectedly play, assisted no doubt by the effect of the brandy, she suddenly saw the problem from another angle. Verity's tactless manner was unfortunate. She hadn't taken to her, it was true – unlike Alex who appeared more engaging, vulnerable even. Yet that was no reason why she shouldn't face a harsh fact: the woman was much to be pitied.

The more she thought about it, the more she was found herself precipitated into a *volte-face*. Greater than her loyalty to her son was, surely, that to her own sex. Verity had indeed been badly served by both her husband and Sam, who, whatever his excuses, had exercised poor judgement in ever befriending the family.

A Damascene moment.

Only a child when the suffragettes first defied the status quo, Bessie had always admired their struggle against men's inhumanity to women, an ongoing struggle with which she had herself become identified during her years with the Forum. When a woman was suffering due to a man's betrayal, her conscience demanded she gave that woman her full support.

Verity's complaint wasn't straightforward. This wasn't a situation such as the one she'd fielded years before when Sam was a teenager and the neighbours had complained about him playing his LPs loudly late in the evening. Any woman discovering her husband to be seriously unfaithful deserved another's pity, but discovering it was with a man was far more devastating and demeaning. Little wonder Verity had presented her plight so baldly. She was fighting for her family life and hitting out in profound pain at the nearest target to hand.

Returning to the living room, still clutching the tumbler of brandy, Bessie became aware the short break had also given the injured party time to re-set her demeanour.

'Mrs Owen …' Verity began, in a calmer voice than previously.

'Bessie, please.'

'I'm very sorry to have dumped all that on you. I'd not given enough thought to your own feelings. This can't be easy for you, either.'

'On reflection, I can see it was brave of you to come. What I'd be interested to know, however, is …'

'Yes?'

'How long have you been aware of this situation with your husband?'

'Robert has never, to my knowledge, cheated before. It took a while for me to become alerted to what I first thought might be a case of *playing away*, and assumed it was with a female colleague. As I've indicated, our marriage is far from perfect, but I like to think I've worked hard to keep us all together for the sake of the children and would, in due course, have discussed our futures either together or separately. Nonetheless, this business changes everything.'

'How many children do you have?'

'Two girls. One just starting at uni, the other in her mid-teens.'

'At least they're at an age when they can look after themselves, though it will hit them very hard too.'

'Indeed. They adore their father. I can't imagine the damage this may do to them.'

'Quite.'

'I liked to think we've always given one another some slack. We each do our own thing one evening a week. I hadn't realised the licence Robert was taking on his nights off.'

'What first alerted you to his behaviour?'

'I was turning out the pockets of his trousers for the cleaners a couple of weeks ago and came across a small, screwed-up envelope.'

Failing to pick up the hidden meaning, Bessie looked puzzled 'A note... letter?'

Verity looked awkward but battled clumsily on. 'A plastic wrapper...' Bessie still looked blank. '...a *French* letter.'

Bessie's stomach turned over at the bald euphemism and turned her face away. 'I can't imagine how you must have felt.'

'I wept.'

Bessie looked at her earnestly. 'Of course. May I ask...'

'Please.'

'How did you and your husband meet Sam?'

Verity explained about *West Side Story* and how Sam and Robert knew each other from the Infirmary.

'So, your husband's one of Sam's doctors?'

'I'm not sure of the details but it's where they first saw each other, apparently. If he has been involved with treating him, on top of everything else, his becoming involved with Sam is extremely unprofessional. Should the hospital discover what he's been getting up to with his patients…' She paused then added sotto voce, her manner suddenly becoming menacing, 'I've half a mind to… Well…'

Bessie was alarmed. What was she considering doing, exactly? While she admired Verity's ferociousness, she sensed danger in her *woman scorned* rhetoric. It would be awful if Sam, who hadn't had an altogether easy life, was involved in a public scandal.

'Forgive me for saying this,' she said, 'but I don't think bringing the matter to the attention of the authorities would help you and your family…' Or ours, she omitted to add. But Verity only pursed her lips tighter still. 'It could rebound on you and the girls if Robert lost his job.'

'Still, with the mood I'm in…'

Bessie emptied her glass. The brandy was losing a battle with the fatigue brought on by the disagreeableness of the past hour. She needed to be alone now to finish her afternoon rest. With the help of her stick, she hauled herself decisively to her feet. 'At least the matter is now out in the open. I'll certainly have a word with Sam and strongly advise him to keep his distance from your husband from now on. You need time and space to sort things out between you. I wish you well.'

Verity took her cue and also stood up.

'The thing is,' she said as they moved into the hallway, 'I'd never remotely considered Robert was even slightly that way inclined, until very recently. Now, other things are starting to make sense. Like the time he became very upset when one of the young junior doctors he got on with very well with mysteriously left to go to another hospital. He said it was due to a disagreement with a senior consultant. Well, that was what he told me. I never understood why he took it so personally. Maybe I do now.'

Bessie held out her hand. 'Human beings are very complicated. Aren't we?'

'It seems so,' Verity said, clasping it. 'Thank you for listening.' She stepped out into the communal passageway. 'Goodbye.'

Bessie smiled wanly and shut the door behind her.

*　*　*

After Verity left, Bessie made herself a cup of tea and tried ringing Sam. There was no reply. She left a message on his answering machine, summoning him to come and see her as soon as he could.

She'd been far more affected by what she had learnt than she'd care to admit. Sam wasn't the only actor in the family. The skills she'd once summoned to play Bassanio at school could still kick in when required. If truth be told, the revelations hadn't come as a complete surprise. A voice lurking at the back of her mind had, for a long time, cautioned her that Sam's life might, at any moment, take an unexpected turn. For some while, she'd been half-preparing herself for news not to her liking, as had turned out to be the case.

Disagreeable though all this was, she doubted the relationship could threaten Sam's livelihood unless Verity was hellbent on causing trouble. Even then, it would most likely burn itself out. People gossiped unkindly about unconventional relationships, but she understood the world was far more relaxed nowadays about men living together, even in the current climate. It was to be sincerely hoped news of Robert's behaviour would be handled discreetly. Comparatively comfortable though she appeared to people, Bessie possessed only emergency savings and would be unable to help her son if he lost his job due to a scandal and could no longer pay his mortgage. Her flat, with its minuscule spare room, was hardly suitable for long-stay guests, let alone lodgers.

It was now twenty years since Sam's breakdown had forced him out of teaching. He'd sorted himself out in a relatively short space of time then and would do so now, even though the nature of the crises were different. Like herself, he was a survivor. Survival, however, was only the bottom line. Bessie wished to see him more settled before he grew much older and she was no longer around to advise him.

It said a lot for her that, despite her old-fashioned views, she'd sufficient wisdom to take out of the fiasco the notion that, if Sam was never to find a woman to provide some necessary stability in his life, a same-sex companion, as Hannah had been to Connie, was preferable to none at all. Though, ideally, not someone's husband unless the marriage was totally beyond repair.

The more she considered the matter, the more it strangely re-energised her. The Harveys' lives had been turned upside down, but having to cut Robert from his life would affect Sam badly too. However inappropriate the relationship, he invested a lot in his friendships, and this one had probably meant a lot to him. He'd feel a huge sense of desolation when the man returned to his wife as, inevitably, he must. It would take him a while to recover and would need someone to turn to.

Could this mean she might see more of him?

Bessie had a new purpose in life: to help her son face up to this disaster and come to terms with the fallout. Not having been fully sexually charged herself enabled her to be objective. Bessie didn't understand unbridled desire, but she did understand love.

Sam would require support from someone he would listen to.

28

Fallout

1994
Sam

Having given up stewing at home and hoping for news, Sam, in ignorance of the dramas being played out elsewhere, had gone for a walk across Saddleworth moor. There the fresh air helped him consider some *what if* scenarios.

Arriving home again around five o'clock, more relaxed but still uncertain as to how his relationship with Robbie would ultimately play out, he was heartened to see the red light flickering on his answer machine. There were two messages waiting. The first, from Robbie, to say everything was now out in the open and that Verity had zoomed off in the car, presumably to see Alex. The second from his mother, timed some hours later, demanding his presence ASAP. He'd immediately phoned Bessie back and, after a brief heartfelt apology for her being dragged into the crisis, told her he was on his way to Cheadle.

Never having seriously let Bessie down before and dreading coming face to face with her, Sam was surprised when their interview turned out to be more low-key than he'd dared hope. Even the bus had been punctual – a good start.

Neither voice was raised. But then, his mother often came into her own in a real crisis, playing down her flair for melodrama and becoming calm, focussed and practical. After all, she could afford to be pleasant when she believed her experience of life empowered her to interpret events correctly. They might rant and rage over imagined slights and verbally contest each other's increasingly diverging politics, but when it came to serious personal matters, their mutual respect kicked in. Of course, Sam had his own very personal view on the situation, but, in this instance, his acute remorse over how Bessie had been unfairly dragged into his love life entitled her, for the time being, to assume the upper hand – or at least imagine it did. When the chips were down, bluster and blame only distracted from cool analysis and agreement on a possible way forward.

From any angle, and however much he might kid himself Robbie's unsatisfactory marriage wasn't really his problem, given the strong bond between the two of them, he owed him his support. Yet, it was irrefutable that he'd knowingly contributed to the implosion of an entire family, the repercussions of which would affect several interconnected lives for years to come.

His realisation of how badly he came out of the debacle made him deeply unhappy. While he'd never regret meeting Robbie, Bessie reminded him – not that he needed her to – his biggest error was to have accepted the family's hospitality. At least if he had been obliged to turn down a good 'Anita', he'd still have been labelled *the enemy* by Verity, and probably Laura and Carrie, but could have remained an anonymous missile, a concept. Not a person they'd got to know and grown fond of, who'd betrayed them.

It was sobering to think how, in other cultures, Robbie and he might have been publicly hanged, shot or beheaded on two capital charges: infidelity and sexual perversion. He'd read there were Middle Eastern countries where they even dropped gay men from skyscrapers or a scaffold with piano wire around their necks.

Bessie made it clear it was Verity she felt sorry for. When, amongst her other fair-minded yet firm instructions as to how he should handle himself from now on, she told him he must completely cut all ties with Robbie and his family, he knew better than to argue with her. He saw some wisdom, however, in her advice to write – rather than phone or see his lover – and warn him he felt it was in their best interests they kept their distance from each other. Bessie had meant for ever. He intended to keep the period of time open.

* * *

The street lights were out as Sam left Worsley Court, the twilight having softened to a deep blue velvet and the vestiges of the sunset now a thin strip of purple-pink above the horizon.

Making his way to the bus stop, he spotted a figure he recognised approaching him a few hundred yards off.

His first thought was to cut Alex dead, or maybe walk past her as close to the kerb as possible with his head lowered deep in thought.

Too late, she was within his gaze. Out of the corner of his eye, he caught her giving him a baleful glance as she passed by. Then, to his surprise, her footsteps stopped.

'Sam?' she called.

He halted too and turned. 'That's me.'

'Look, this is ridiculous.'

'Alex, isn't it?'

'Yes. I just wanted to say…'

'Yes?'

'I may be Vee's friend, but I'm also your mother's new neighbour.'

'So, I gather.'

'I thought Bessie and I had hit it off and would hate this furore to make things difficult between us.'

'Right.'

'I had no idea Vee would go and see your mother,' she went on. 'Telling her how Damian spotted you that night wasn't something I enjoyed passing on. Not to have done so, though, would have made things very awkward, and, sooner or later it would have rebounded. After all, she is my best friend.'

Sam thought of Joss and wondered whether he'd have done the same if he'd discovered something he didn't like hearing about Bren. It was a moot point.

'I was taken aback when Vee went berserk and fell to pieces,' she continued. 'It wasn't as if she didn't already know what was going on. I guess the thought of the two of you sharing an intimate moment in public touched an already raw nerve. It isn't something she and Robbie have done in a very long while. The romantic connotation of the gesture would hurt her almost as much as the, er… greater issues. Also, I'm concerned about your mother.'

'I'm not sure you need be.'

'She's a honey…' Not a term of endearment Sam had ever considered in the context of his mother, but the apparent genuineness of Alex's desire for them to move on mollified him.

'The couple of times we've met, she's been most kind. Bessie's good company and has already helped made me feel at home in Worsley Court. I'm only sorry I've unintentionally aggravated a potentially awkward situation. I'd hate her to think I was a trouble-maker.'

Don't push your luck too far just yet, Sam thought. It still rankled that Alex was also friendly with Damian, but he saw where she was coming from.

Still, seeing as she was being open with him, he decided there was no harm in being honest with her. 'She can be a bit of a gorgon but also knows how to be pragmatic. Especially with anyone who might be of…' he'd nearly said *use* to her but changed it to *help*. 'I appreciate you have Verity's best interests at heart but can assure you Robbie has been unhappy for a long time. However unfortunate the circumstances and badly he and I have handled this debacle, we mean a great deal to each other.'

'I get that. And, of course, you're right. Things haven't been running smoothly in the state of Denmark for ages. Their problems go back long before you came on the scene, but Verity refused to acknowledge them. I'm sure Robbie will have told you.'

'Yes, but it's helpful to hear it from someone else.'

'At least we needn't be sworn enemies?'

If it helps my mother, Sam thought, but all he said was, 'Thanks for stopping, anyway.'

'I hope it clears the air somewhat?'

They looked awkwardly at each other for a moment, then managed to share faint smiles of... relief, mutual understanding, both? He hoped so.

The quietness of the evening was disturbed by the distant purr of a bus heading around the corner and towards them along the road. 'Look, that's mine. If I hurry, I might just catch it. Bye.'

The driver saw Sam running and waited for him.

Once on board and seated, he mulled over the conversation. Something in Alex's manner had suggested that, despite or possibly because of her friendship with Damian, even if she wasn't a fully signed-up member of the Canal Street colony, as an unconventional person herself, she could empathise with other people who were. And who knew what innocent but telling remarks about her sparring parents Laura might have let slip between arpeggios? Also, while people should support their friends in times of stress, it didn't stop them from having their own private thoughts.

* * *

Sam sat down late that evening with a heavy heart and, after several false starts, wrote Robbie as unemotional a letter as he could muster. He posted it the next morning on his way to work and was therefore surprised when, around twelve-thirty on the Tuesday, the phone rang.

'I've left home,' Robbie announced.

Sam swivelled his chair round and, not wishing prying ears to overhear, lowered his voice.

'You've what?'

'Taken the day off work. Fortunately, I had no procedures booked. And I've...'

'Yes?'

'Found a bedsit in Salford. I'm off to look at it after this call.'

'That was quick. What happened?'

'It was Vee. I've been seething ever since I heard she visited your mother. I told her she'd no right to drag a very old lady into our business. "How else could I begin to get back at both of you?" she stormed. Things got heated, she lashed out and we both said a lot of things I hope we didn't altogether mean.'

'Oh, God!' If Sam had foolishly hoped this matter could have been dealt with in a civilised, orderly way, he now knew they were all in for a long and messy period in their lives.

'Deep down,' Robbie said, 'she knows things haven't been right for ages and won't accept it might easily have been herself who'd made the first move. A woman scorned and all that. She will never accept she may, even partly, be in the wrong.'

'That's more or less what Alex said.' Checking that there was no one in earshot, he lowered his voice before summarising their conversation.

'It's good to know someone's not too judgemental.' Robbie sounded slightly relieved. 'Vee threw every bit of ammunition she could at me: the sanctity of our marital vows – despite the fact we never go to church – the need to put on a united front for the sake of the girls. Oh, and the hardy annual, if she'd always made the effort why couldn't I? Then, when she saw none of it was having any effect, she trotted out the HIV hand grenade and threatened to go to my boss or the General Medical Council if I didn't have myself tested forthwith.'

'When the professors are at it like rabbits with every other woman who tosses her tail at them!'

'Every other *woman*, maybe.'

'Even in today's world?'

'Indeed, underneath their sophisticated, liberal-minded veneer, many of them are hypocrites. If you're enjoying a bit on the side out of hours, you're regarded as something of a lad and, often, envied.'

Sam chose not to bridle at the suggestion he was a *bit on the side*, but Robbie hadn't finished. 'A person of the same gender, however, would be considered irregular and, if not exactly a capital offence, seriously frowned upon unless the relationship was very discreet and long-established. I know at least one surgeon who lives with another man, but I discovered the fact by accident. It isn't general knowledge.'

'How have the girls taken it, or don't they know yet?'

'At the height of the row the other morning, in walked Carrie from meeting a friend, and, before I could tactfully try and cover up what had been going on, Vee blurted out, "I think you should know that your father's gay and having an affair with Sam Owen."'

'How did she take it?'

'Justifiably badly. Went white as a sheet and said she hated me. I haven't seen her since but think she's oscillating between home and a school friend. I must try and ring Laura before she gets to her first. I'm dreading it.'

'You may find it easier with her. Not only is Laura older, but she moves in circles where a number of her friends are in same-sex relationships. Also, although I can see both your daughters adore you…'

'Did.'

'…and will do so again… I always got the impression you two have a special bond. She may appreciate better what has been happening.'

Here Sam could hear Robbie welling up. He waited for him to pull himself together. When he did, he confessed, 'I'm in a terrible mess. I left them comforting each other, went out and walked for hours. Last night I packed a large case with enough clothes and stuff to see me through for a while, put it in the boot of the car and slept in the spare room. I left this morning before they were up and had breakfast at Macdonald's. Frankly, I can't see any way back. Can I come round this evening?'

'Of course. I'll put together some pots and pans and things I don't need, to tide you over. I've a duvet set I rarely use, too.'

'Many thanks.'

'But I should warn you…'

'I'm almost immune to warnings by now, but go on…'

'I've posted you a letter to say I'm steering clear of you for a time.'

There was an audible gasp at the end of the line. Then a strangled 'Why?'

'I didn't want to be any more of a problem to you... all.'

'You will be if you're not there for me.'

'Then ignore it. Knowing the post, you may not get it for a few days anyway. I'll see you this evening and help you settle into your new...' he was about to say *home* but changed it to '...place.'

'Thanks. Actually, I feel the need for somewhere on my own until things settle down a bit. And, incidentally, the last thing I told Vee before I left was that I was leaving home for myself, not for you. Hence the bedsit. Although I was expecting to spend quite a lot of time with you.'

'And you will. Just be patient for a few weeks. It'll be as bad for me as for you, but you can't be seen to be shacking up with someone else too soon. She'll be building a case against you.'

'Or worse, in between sharpening her dagger, still hoping to patch things up. I can see you wish to play down your role as the scarlet gentleman in all this,' he said a little unkindly.

'Scarlet doesn't suit me. Burgundy perhaps.'

'Burgundy certainly suits you well. Especially a bottle.' They laughed. A strained laugh but one that helped ease the tension.

Sam knew his decision was hard for Robbie. They'd both miss seeing each other badly, but temporary separation felt the right thing. He must be given the chance to establish himself as an independent person, sorting himself out and not fleeing from a broken marriage into the arms of the person other people who knew would consider *the problem*.

The practicalities of the Harveys' separation, assuming there was to be one – there was always the possibility they might not go through with it after all – would need to be thrashed out. Then there was the heartache involved in breaking the bare bones of what had happened to two sets of elderly parents. Verity's mother lived some distance away in Preston, but Robbie's mother and father had a house in Sale. There would be heartache for the wider family, too.

* * *

In the event, Robbie only returned home once – to collect the remainder of his possessions. He and Carrie eventually reached a rapprochement of sorts and met each week for supper in a restaurant. As Sam had suspected, after an emotional scene, Laura pragmatically came to accept the situation.

Within six months, Verity became heavily involved with a structural engineer she met through *Seeking Company (for the over-forties)*, a dating agency, and had moved in with him. Sam and Robbie maintained their separate homes but were never far from each other for more than a few days at a time.

Bessie, who must have been aware her instructions for the pair of them to remain apart had been only temporarily adhered to, never mentioned Robbie at all.

29

Finale

1995
Sam

The next year, Sam bought a second-hand car and took driving lessons. He called her Trixie because she could be difficult to manoeuvre. Never mind that her stubborn gears might never give him the confidence to pass his Practical Test, as long as the project proved to Bessie his honourable intentions.

One evening in late May, after work when the light was lingering well into the evening, Robbie accompanied him to Worsley Court with Trixie to deliver a fold-up trolley his mother had decided she needed and which they'd tracked down in a local *Argos*.

Sam parked the car. Robbie moved onto the back seat, curling up with a cushion, a Jilly Cooper and a bottle of Diet Coke, to help while away the hour Sam expected to spend alone with Bessie.

Once the Entryphone door catch was released, he carried the trolley up the stairs and let himself into the flat. Laughter emanated from the living room. She wasn't alone. Sam sighed inwardly with relief. That was a good sign. Bessie was usually in a benevolent mood with, or after having, visitors. He found her entertaining Alex. Both women were clutching the mandatory mugs and chuckling over a local newspaper article her neighbour was reading out to her.

'Sam! I expect you've had your meal,' she said after he'd kissed her and nodded to Alex.

'Yes, thanks. I'm only here for a short while to deliver this. I hope it meets your specifications.' He opened up the trolley and gently helped her to her feet so that she could look at it properly.

'That's perfect! It'll do me nicely. Bless you, son. How much do I owe you?'

'Call it an early birthday present.'

'Really? That's very good of you. I think it deserves a coffee at the very least. And I've some little Bakewell tarts finishing off in the oven.'

'Great. But, can't I get them?'

'No trouble. I need to check on them. There's nothing worse than blistering your mouth on hot food.' As Bessie staggered into the kitchen, Alex made as if to go. 'I was only here to pick up your mother's list for tomorrow. I should leave you two alone?'

'Please don't. It's nice to see you.' He motioned her to sit down again. Which she did.

When Robbie first separated from Verity, given Alex's close friendship with his soon-to-be ex, Sam felt uncomfortable seeing her at Worsley Court.

He needn't have worried. Within months of Robbie's leaving home, Alex was complaining she rarely saw Verity these days. She made it clear that, although she was still on good terms with her ex-boss, now distanced by her new job and with Verity's re-energised love life absorbing much of her spare time, something had subtly changed in the dynamics of their relationship.

They were becoming quite relaxed with each other, in fact. Sam noted Alex's ability to manage her different loyalties with a sensitivity Verity lacked. The off-putting front Alex presented to strangers was a self-protective façade, and, while she was well-meaning, she could also be what Bessie might have termed a *tough cookie*. Unlike Sam, and until more recently Miriam, Alex won Bessie's respect by handling her – as she did difficult students in the college library – pleasantly but firmly. She permitted little negotiation on how she chose to allocate her time between work and social schedules.

After Sam and Robbie became a recognised couple, Sam rarely visited Canal Street.

Nor was Damian's name ever mentioned.

'I hope things are beginning to sort themselves out?' Alex said.

'Thanks. Divorce proceedings have been instigated, but it will take a couple of years for them to be concluded. Robbie's now got a smarter flat, which will have to do him until his money comes through. You'll appreciate that because of his job, we're being very discreet. Maybe in a few years, everyone will have got used to the idea. Then we may consider finding a place together. By the way, thanks for everything you're doing for Mum.'

'She's a wise old bird.'

'I'm afraid things between us are still a little bit... tricky.'

'She'll come round when she sees it's in her interests to do so. I'm surprised with all her health issues she hasn't already pounced on the idea of having her own pet medical consultant on tap. And another chauffeur, too... when you're fully launched, that is.'

A voice floated through to them. 'I hope you're not talking about me.' Bessie staggered in with a tray holding Sam's coffee, a plate of tarts and paper serviettes.

'As if,' Alex said.

'Good journey?' she asked as Sam helped her with the tray, took his drink and food and sat down.

'Yes, despite the rush hour traffic, I drove all the way.'

'You *drove?*'

'Look out of the window and you'll see her – Trixie that is.'

Bessie looked bewildered.

'I think that's the name of the car, Bessie,' Alex said.

'Ah.' Bessie didn't stir herself but watched Alex and Sam go to the window and look down at the elderly red mini parked outside the block.

'She's cute! Well done, you,' she said. 'You'll have a lot of fun with her.'

'Surely you're not allowed to drive on your own yet?' Bessie said.

'I have someone with me.'

'Then why didn't you say. Who?' she asked, as if she didn't know.

'Robbie,' Sam admitted.

Bessie's face fleetingly clouded over before settling into a resigned look. 'Well, you can't leave him out there on his own.'

'He's perfectly happy with *The Man Who Made Husbands Jealous*.'

'What, while we're eating and drinking in comfort up here? Go down and bring him up.'

Sam glanced at Alex who gave him a knowing wink. He looked again at Bessie to make sure he'd heard correctly.

She threw him a look. Part Sphinx, part Lady Catherine de Bourgh.

He went downstairs to fetch Robbie.

THE END

ACKNOWLEDGEMENTS

My sincere thanks to my partner, John, who has supported me magnificently throughout this 'lockdown' project, proofreading, providing insightful comments at each stage and contributing artwork for the cover.

I am also most grateful to Di Procter for her detailed examination of the first draft and many helpful suggestions; my good friend Joyce Troughton and my brother-in-law, David Oakenfull, for their constructive and encouraging feedback.

Above all, none of this would have been possible without Patrick, Sophie and everyone at *Publishing Push*. I am indebted to them for all their hard work and guiding me and my book through to publication.

Printed in Great Britain
by Amazon